# Third Debt

## INDEBTED #4

## PEPPER WINTERS

Third Debt (Indebted #4)
Copyright © 2015 Pepper Winters
Published by Pepper Winters

All rights reserved. No part of this book may be reproduced or transmitted in any form, including electronic or mechanical, without written permission from the publisher, except in the case of brief quotations embodied in critical articles or reviews.

This is a work of fiction. Names, characters, businesses, places, events, and incidents are either the products of the author's imagination or used in a fictitious manner. Any resemblance to actual persons, living or dead, or actual events is purely coincidental.

This book is licensed for your personal enjoyment only. This book may not be re-sold or given away to other people. If you would like to share this book with another person, please purchase an additional copy for each person you share it with. If you are reading this book and did not purchase it, or it was not purchased for your use only, then you should return it to the seller and purchase your own copy. Thank you for respecting the author's work.

**Published:** Pepper Winters 2015: pepperwinters@gmail.com
**Cover Design:** by Ari at Cover it! Designs:
http://salon.io/#coveritdesigns
**Proofreading by:** Jenny Sims: http://www.editing4indies.com
**Proofreading by:** Erica Russikoff: http://www.ericaedits.com/
**Images in Manuscript from** Canstock Photos:
http://www.canstockphoto.com

This story isn't suitable for those who don't enjoy dark romance, uncomfortable situations, and dubious consent. It's sexy, it's twisty, there's colour as well as darkness, but it's a rollercoaster not a carrousel.

*(As an additional warning please note, this is a cliffhanger. Answers will continue to be delivered as the storyline resolves. There are six in total.)*

Warning heeded…enter the world of debts and payments.

If you would like to read this book with like-minded readers, and be in to win advance copies of other books in the series, along with Q&A sessions with Pepper Winters, please join the Facebook group below:

**Indebted Series Group Read**

I'D GIVEN MY heart to my enemy.
I'd fallen.
Fallen.
Fallen.
*Hard.*
There was no bottom to my affection. No limit to what I would do to protect it.
Jethro was mine and it was up to me....
...up to me to end this.
I was no longer trying to save myself.
I was trying to save him.
From his nightmares.
From himself.
From them.

# Nila

HOW HAD THIS happened?
Where did it all go so wrong?
Jethro was supposed to love me. I was supposed to love him.
Yet he'd given me over to his family. He'd bound the ropes, blindfolded my eyes, and gifted me to his kin.
"Know what time it is, Nila Weaver?" Daniel breathed in my ear.
I jerked away. The restraints around my body meant I couldn't run, couldn't fight; I couldn't even see.
*Oh, God.*
*Please don't let them do this.*
I wanted to scream for Jethro to save me. I wanted him to put an end to this and claim me once and for all. Didn't our connection mean anything?
*You know it's all different now.*
Ever since I'd returned to Hawksridge Hall, things had been different—horribly, *horribly* different.
The fire crackled in the billiards room where the Hawk men had been playing poker. The air was hot and muggy and laced with cognac fumes.
Tonight, I'd had plans to end whatever changed between Jethro and me forever.

But now…those plans had changed.

Kestrel ran his fingers over my collar. "Relax, little Weaver. It will all be over soon."

Cut chuckled. "Yes, soon you can go to sleep and pretend none of this happened."

My ears strained for one other voice. The voice of the man who controlled my heart even though he'd thrown it back in my face.

But only silence greeted me.

Daniel snickered, licking my cheek. "Time to pay, Weaver."

Someone clapped and in a voice full of darkness and doom said, "It's time for the Third Debt."

*Two Months Prior...*

# Jethro

I MEANT WHAT I said before.
I meant it with every bone in my body.
*Someone has to die.*
I still stood by that conclusion. Only, I'd hoped it wouldn't be me.
Too bad wishes never come true.
I'd always wondered what it would feel like. How I would react, knowing that I'd failed. I'd lain awake so many nights trying to imagine how I would behave when my father finally had enough. I'd scared myself shitless fearing I wouldn't be strong enough, *brave* enough, to face the consequences I'd lived with all my life.
But none of that mattered now. I'd done what I swore never to do and revealed myself. My father knew there was no changing me—he would come for me.
But so fucking what?
*She's safe.*
That was all I needed to focus on.
I'd done my utmost to be the perfect son, but I'd been fighting an unwinnable battle. No matter how much I wished I could be like them—I wasn't. And it was pointless to keep fighting.
Not anymore.

*I'm done.*

I was done the moment Nila called me Kite and admitted she loved me.

*Fuck, that isn't true.*

I was done the moment I set eyes on her in Milan.

I stood looking out the window, gripping the windowsill with white fingers. The view of Hawksridge—of manicured hedges and vibrant rose bushes—was no longer in colour but black and white. Before my very eyes, the sparkle and dynamism of life left me as Nila stepped into the black sedan below.

How could the ebullience of the world suddenly disappear, leaving behind a monochromatic disaster the second she vanished?

The moment she'd left the dining room, I'd removed myself from my father's smug glare and managed to hold it together the entire three minutes it took to walk down the corridor, putting enough distance between me and the people who couldn't see me break.

I'd managed to keep walking until there was no one to see me, but then my self-control snapped. My legs had propelled into a run. I'd fucking sprinted to the bachelor wing while every step twisted my ice into daggers, making me bleed, making me care.

I hadn't stopped until I'd slammed my hands on the windowsill and looked through the wavy centuries-old glass at the procession below.

My heart lurched as a man in a suit closed the car door, barricading me from her forever. There were no flashing lights, no decals warning criminals who they were.

These policemen had come to steal what was mine with stealth. They knew they'd trespassed and broke treaties far older than their years with the force. My family had immunity, yet I'd underestimated Vaughn.

He hadn't turned to the law to help. He hadn't even enlisted mercenaries or other stupid ways that Weavers had done in the past. No, he'd been smart. Bloody bastard. He'd used social media to rally a public force. Even with our wealth and influence, we couldn't fight against the outcry of millions of people.

Fuck Vaughn.

Fuck his tampering.

My fists curled on the windowsill as the policeman tapped the side of the vehicle as if he'd fucking won. Him. Them. *The Weavers.*

They'd won.

*She's ruined me.*

Destroyed me.

I glared at the car, willing Nila to look up. But she didn't. Her silhouette, staring resolutely ahead, was obscured by tinted windows.

She'd obeyed me and left the dining room.

*She didn't look back.*

Now, I would've given anything for her to look back. To change her mind.

A terrible churning began inside.

Everything that I'd swallowed and kept deep, deep down flew to the surface. It grew and grew stronger, harder, *faster.*

My fingers dug like swords into the soft wood.

Even though I wanted to kill the police with my bare hands, I managed to stay in my wing as the engines of the three cars rumbled into gear. They pulled away from the house. The noise of their tyres on gravel didn't reach my window, but I had no trouble conjuring the sound.

It sounded like glass being crushed beneath grinding stone. It sounded exactly like what was happening inside me: every organ shattering into hell.

I held it together just long enough for the convoy to disappear over the ridge, slithering like a poisonous snake, taking what was mine.

*Come back.*

*Never come back.*

I should've known this would happen.
I was always destined to this fate.
It was inevitable.

In a way, I was grateful to Vaughn. He'd rescued her when I didn't have the fucking balls. He'd taken back his sister because he loved her enough to *fight* for her. She was better off with him, away from me and my fucked-up family.

The last of the convoy disappeared.

With a bone-deep sigh, I gave up. I let the glass inside me splinter and detonate. I permitted myself to do what I could never do. I let down my walls. My many, many walls.

I lost myself.

Bending in half, I rested my forehead on my knuckles as I suffered the worst unravelling I'd ever lived through.

*See, Nila.*

*This is what I meant when I asked you to* see *me.*

She thought she lived in an intense world? It was nothing compared to what I endured. Nothing compared to the condition I'd been cursed to bear.

Grief, terror, and guilt howled and roared with utmost ferocity.

I became hollow, empty—carved out by emotions. It was all too much. All I wanted to do was...*fade*. Fade away from biting words and gnawing consequences.

"Jethro."

*Shit.*

As easily as it'd been to drop my walls, it took a herculean effort to rebuild them. Ice brick after ice brick, I did my best to reconstruct the igloo I'd lived in all my life. But it was no use.

With a face twisted in defiance, I spun to meet my father.

He stood in the doorway, key in one hand and an implement of discipline in the other. We stared at each other. Matching eyes and Hawk blood. How could two men, bound by lineage and family, be so completely different?

"Come along. You can't run from this. Not anymore."

Clenching my jaw so hard my teeth almost turned into

diamonds, I looked one last time at the emptiness outside my window. Watching her go was absolute torture, but seeing her return would be the worst punishment of all.

*Stay away, Nila Weaver. Never come back.*

"Jethro," he snarled. "Your disguises won't work this time."

He couldn't even give me a second to say goodbye. To imprint every last detail of Nila onto my soul so I could carry her with me to the underworld. He couldn't even give me the courtesy of being myself just *once* before it was over.

Bastard.

Absolute fucking bastard.

I glared at my father. His face was as sharp as the stones we smuggled.

"What have you done with Jasmine?" My sister was in a state. I hadn't seen her so emotional in years. "She needs someone to be there with her when you tell her what you've done."

Cut sniffed. "Kestrel is with her. And he'll stay with her as long as she needs."

At least Bonnie and Daniel weren't chosen to console her. The thought of leaving my sister disembowelled me.

Balling my hands, I forced myself to find courage.

Cut moved closer, his arms steadfast by his sides. "I was fair to you, son. I gave you more chances than you deserve."

So many options flashed before my eyes. I could beg for mercy, threaten him—even commit murder to protect myself.

But Nila had been in my life for two months.

My father had been in it for twenty-nine years.

He'd done his best with me. Through his manipulations and crazy conditioning, we'd both thought I could change. It wasn't his fault he had to do this.

*It's mine.*

I dropped my eyes, keeping my mask resolutely in place. "Send me away. Disown me. Do whatever you want." I kept staring at the carpet as I pleaded for leniency. "You have my word; I won't come back."

*I'll run with her. Take her where you'll never find us.*

Cut chuckled. The sound was like a babbling brook in hell. "I have no intention of doing this half-assed, Jet. This is what has to happen. Don't prolong it." Raising his arm, he pointed the gun at my chest.

Everything went into fucking lockdown.

My eyes zeroed in on the weapon; no amount of courage could prevent me from debating the worthiness of my life. Yes, I wasn't like him. But fuck, I'd tried. Didn't that mean anything? "I'm still your son."

He pursed his lips. "Debatable after the past few months."

"I disappointed you. I proved unworthy, but for Christ's sake, just let me go. Banish me, cast me away, make me penniless. Do whatever you want. Just don't kill me."

The word 'please' danced on my tongue, but I swallowed it back.

*I'm not weak.*

I wouldn't give him the satisfaction of begging.

"You've heard the tales. You've seen the proof of why we live such strict lives. You know I can't do that, Jethro. It's better for everyone this way. You're firstborn. I cannot legally grant my estate to Kestrel while you're still alive."

"I'll sign whatever you want renouncing my claim."

"Jet—" Cut growled, stepping closer, calm and resigned. "What's done is done. Time to suffer the consequences."

He discussed taking my life as if I were the household trash and not his flesh and blood.

I turned my back on him and looked out the window again, reliving the procession of cars that'd stolen Nila from my world.

She'd given me so much, yet taken more than I could bear. It wasn't fair.

*Life is never fair.*

I snorted.

*My life is over.*

"Jethro—" His temper snapped my name in half. "Unless you want a bullet in your brain, I suggest you come with me. As terrible as you think of me, I don't *want* to hurt you."

I spun around. "What?"

My heart raced in false hope.

Moving closer, he waved the gun. "Come without a fuss. You don't want your sister to see a mess in here...do you?"

Whatever hope had gathered in my heart ruptured. I flinched at the thought of Jaz witnessing a gruesome dispatching.

"I'll come with you." Crossing the distance between us, I wrapped my hand around the muzzle of his gun. "Put it away. It's not needed."

Silence webbed around us.

Cut sighed and holstered the weapon in the back of his trousers. "Good boy." The compassion in his eyes was so wrong. He *did* care for me—more than he would admit.

Normally, my condition meant I had no choice but to listen. To feel. To understand.

Not this time.

My body shut down, already killing off sensitivity and accepting fate. Thoughts of beating him up and running filled my mind. It didn't have to end this way. But if I left Hawksridge, I would still have to live with the nightmare I'd been born with. And after falling for Nila, my reserves were empty. I wanted a rest.

I was fucking tired of everything.

Cut stood aside, waving at the door. "After you."

"No, after you. I'll follow. I gave you my word."

Cut scowled but finally nodded. Wordlessly, he made his way to the door and looked over his shoulder to ensure I obeyed.

This was it, then.

On the cusp of winning, I'd lost everything.

*So be it.*

I followed.

# Nila

"STOP THE CAR. Please, stop the car."

The policeman shook his head, gripping the wheel and taking me further away from Jethro. "Sorry, Ms. Weaver. The next place we'll stop is London."

The sway of the vehicle sent goosebumps over my skin. Every spin of the tyres thickened my blood with dread.

*What will Cut do to him?*

How could I leave?

Straining in my seat, I winced. The bruises on my ribcage from CPR, the flaring heat in my throat from drowning, and the headache from confusion all competed with the fisting sensation around my heart.

I tapped the policeman on his shoulder. "Please, this is all a big misunderstanding. Take me back. I *want* to go back."

*Now. Immediately. Before it's too late.*

"Don't worry. Just relax. Everything is as it should be," the officer said.

I just walked away! How could I *do* that?

"No, it's not. I don't have time to explain, but I need you to take me back." Debts and death and diabolical Hawks didn't scare me anymore.

Only the thought of what Jethro would face scared me.

I wouldn't let him suffer alone.

*What can you possibly do to help?*
I ignored that thought and the panic it brought. I was useless, but I had to try. It was the least I could do. He cared for me. He sent me away and put himself in my place.
*Damn him for sending me away!*
The officer lost his cordial nature, turning stiff with annoyance. "Miss, I understand that you've lived through a great deal, but the Hawks are not a family to be trifled with. We've acted on the wishes of the media and your family, so don't say you did not wish to be rescued when the world knows what you're tangled in."
My eyes bugged. "The world knows what?" When he didn't answer, I pried, "How did my father get you to come?"
The policeman glared at me in the mirror. "Your father and brother didn't *make* us do anything. *We* went to them—we had to do something. Your sibling was out of control."
My heart hurt. My head hurt. I couldn't make sense of this mess.
Pressing my fingers against my temples, I begged, "Please, whatever you've heard, pay no attention. They have it wrong. Just—please take me back."
*Take me back so I can save him. He needs me!*
My soul cried for lying about my brother—the one person who had my wellbeing in mind—but my loyalties had changed. Somewhere along the way, I'd chosen Jethro over everyone. He was my curse, my challenge, my salvation, and I wasn't going to leave him when he needed me the most.
I'd forced him to notice me. I'd forced him to lean on me.
*And now I've left him without any help.*
The car didn't slow. We kept driving...mile after mile of rolling hills, grazing deer, and dense forest. The car remained silent.
Fear gave me palpitations. Frustration gave me shakes. I *hated* that I wasn't in control. I hadn't been in control my entire life, and this was just another instance in which men believed they knew better.

First my father. Then Jethro. Now these assholes.

I wanted to scratch out their eyes and slam on the brakes. I wanted to scream and teach them just how capable I was.

*Breathe. Calm down.*

*You're free!*

*You should be happy!*

To prevent myself from combusting, I glanced out the window. Our speed blurred tussock and seedlings. Acres and acres of woodland and fences. No wonder Jethro had let me run for my freedom. I would never have made it to the boundary.

Miles already separated me from the Hall, but I couldn't stand another metre without Jethro.

Gripping the door handle, I tried to open it. "Let me out. This instant." It remained locked and impenetrable.

A cough caught me unaware, residual liquid still in my lungs.

The policeman glanced at me, eyebrow raised. "I'm afraid I can't do that, Miss."

"Why? Am I under arrest?"

The further we drove, the more my body hurt—I could no longer distinguish if it was from drowning or leaving Jethro in the hands of evil.

A smidgen of relief came unwanted. I was free. Despite everything, I'd gotten out alive—at the cost of another. *I'm safe.*

The officer smiled thinly. "You'll be fully debriefed when we get to London. I suggest you have a rest."

Every new distance, my diamond collar grew heavier, colder.

Every metre we travelled, my fingertip tattoos itched with spidery scratches.

It was as if the spell Hawksridge had over me tried to suck me back—gravity throttling me with diamonds and ink bursting from my skin to return to its master. As much as I despised being a prisoner of the Hawks, I'd found love with Jethro. I'd found myself, and every hill we ascended, I lost more and more of who I'd become.

My stomach churned as I remembered the gravesite with my family's tombstones. Voices filled my head, flitting like ghosts.

*You said you'd be the last.*
*You promised you'd end this.*
I glowered at the policeman driving.
*It isn't over. Not yet.*
*I will go back and save him.*
*I will stop this!*

My eyes widened, noticing the two policemen wore bulletproof vests. Why were they wearing raid gear on a simple 'rescue' mission? Were the Hawks seriously that crazy? Would they shoot men of the law?

The men remained silent as we coasted beneath the gatehouse and archway of the entrance to Hawksridge estate.

I craned my neck to look at the family sigil of hawks and a nest of women. "You're making a mistake." I pressed my hand against the window, wishing I could run back to the Hall where I'd spent the past couple of months trying to flee.

The policeman muttered, "Tell that to your brother."

The conversation faded, leaving a stagnant taste of trust and confusion. What had V done? What did the cops think happened to me?

My stomach once again somersaulted.

*You're doing the right thing leaving.*
*You're doing the only thing you can.*

Jethro knew that. It was because he cared for me that he sent me away. In his mind, it was the only solution. But in mine, it was a dreadful mistake.

*He'll pay for setting me free.*
*And it'll be all my fault.*

Sighing, I rested my forehead on the coolness of the glass.
I ached.
I burned.
*I didn't even get to say goodbye.*

# Jethro

I FOLLOWED HIS every footstep.

Down corridors where I'd played as a little boy, through rooms I'd investigated, and past hidey holes where I'd played hide-and-seek with my brothers and sister.

The house held so many memories. Past centuries lived in its walls with births and deaths, triumphs and tragedies. I was just a speck in history, about to be obliterated.

My heartbeat resembled an inmate on death row as we made our way through the kitchen toward the cellar. The ancient door leading beneath the Hall was hidden in the walk-in pantry. Hundreds of years ago, the cellar stored barrels of beer and freshly slaughtered meat. Now abandoned, it housed a few lonely wine racks and cases of expensive cognac resting beneath blankets of dust.

We descended the earthen steps and traded the dry warmth of the Hall for the damp chill of the catacombs.

A cool draft kissed our skin as vapours rose from exposed earth. My black jeans and t-shirt clung to my skin, growing heavy with mildew.

Cut didn't stop.

We made our way from the food storage area to a locked metal gate. The staff weren't permitted past this point. Secrets were stored down here. Deep, dark, dangerous secrets that only

Hawks could know.

Electric lights flickered like candles as Cut unlocked the rusty mechanism and guided me onward. The screech of the hinges sounded like a skeleton dragging its bony fingers down the claustrophobic walls.

Just like the natural springs where I'd revived Nila, this warren system of circular tunnels and crudely hacked pathways was found by accident while renovating Hawksridge.

Why did previous generations toil so hard in pitch dark and dripping ice?

To build a crypt.

Weavers were buried on the chase, exposed to whipping winds and snow; my ancestors were entombed below the feet of the living, howling their laments and haunting the hallways of their old home.

It was morbid. Depressing. And I *despised* it down here. The stench of rotting corpses and tentacles of ghosts lurked around shadowy corners.

"Where are we—"

"Silence," Cut hissed. His voice echoed around the cylindrical chambers.

My sluggish beat turned frantic as Cut continued onward, leaving the crypt behind and stepping foot into the one place I'd avoided all my life.

The memory came thick and fast.

*"Wait up!"*

*Kes charged ahead, hurtling down the cellar steps and disappearing into the dark underground pathways beneath the house. These tunnels went to all areas of the estate—to the stables, Black Diamond garage, even the old silos where grain was stored back in the day.*

*It was also dark, damp, and rat infested.*

*We had no torches, no jumpers. Being a hot summer's day, we'd been searching for spots of shades, only to end up getting bored and playing tag.*

*"Come on, scaredy cat," Kes taunted.*

*I couldn't see him in the inky blackness, but I kept running with my hands outstretched just in case I ran into something.*

I came to an intersection and narrowly missed ploughing headfirst into dirt. Fumbling along the wall, my heart flew into my mouth. The wall surrounded me…three sides, soaring higher and tighter as claustrophobia kicked in.

The clank of heavy metal suddenly rang deep and piercing behind me. "Kes?"

"We'll play dungeons and guards. You're the prisoner." Kes laughed as he rattled the bars he'd just slammed over the entranceway I'd stupidly entered.

It was so black.

I couldn't see a thing. But I could hear everything. My breathing. My heartbeat. My terror. So, so loud.

"What do you have to say for yourself, prisoner? Do you plead guilty?" Kes asked, his eight-year-old voice deepening with fake authority.

I moved toward his location, arms outstretched until I found the cold iron bars. "Let me out, Angus."

"Don't use that name."

"I'll use whatever name I want unless you get me out of here." My body itched for fresh air, light, freedom. It felt as if the walls were crumbling, folding in, and burying me alive. "Not funny. Let me out."

"Okay, okay. Jeez." He yanked on the bars. The awful clanging noise jangled around us.

I pressed from my side of the cell.

Nothing happened.

"Err, it's locked."

"What do you mean it's locked?" My soul scratched at my bones needing freedom. "Find a key—get me out!"

"Stay here. I'll go get help."

Kes's body heat and the sound of his breathing suddenly disappeared, leaving me all alone in the pitch black, locked in a prison cell where men had been tortured and died.

I shuddered, breaking the memory's hold.

Since that day, I'd never returned. Kes had dragged our grandfather to free me, and after he'd unlocked the cell, he'd forbidden us from returning to the dungeons past the crypts.

I'd readily obeyed. Never again did I want to step foot in a place still reeking with ancient pain and suffering.

But now my father carted me to the same fucking place, only this time there was light illuminating the deep scratches on the walls from people burrowing for freedom and messages to loved ones who'd never see them.

It took all my strength to follow him around bends and duck where the ceiling hung too low. Scurries of vermin echoed up ahead, and it took everything I had not to break my father's neck and run.

Was I weak not wanting to kill my father? Was I a fucking pussy or justified for being a loyal son? He'd given me life…wasn't it fair he could take it away?

My rationality couldn't temper my panic. My nostrils flared, inhaling damp air.

"Get in, Jethro." Cut came to a stop, waving at the same cell where Kes had accidently imprisoned me for two hours while our grandfather located the key.

The electric sconces glinted off new bars—not the thick, rusty ones of my childhood. My eyes fell to the lock—that was also modern with a number pad rather than an old-fashioned key.

I stepped backward. "You want me to go in there?"

Cut nodded, waving the gun threateningly. "In."

"Why?"

"No questions." He cocked the weapon, sliding a bullet into place.

Swallowing hard, I brushed past him and entered the cell. There was no bed, no facilities, no comfort of any kind. Just earth and mould and puddles.

I turned to face him. Why the hell had he brought me down here? To feed my deceased body to the rats? Or perhaps he meant to starve me to death and not waste a bullet?

Cut stood in the doorway, pointing the gun at my chest.

I sucked in a breath, fisting my hands. "Why bother bringing me here? No one would've heard the shot upstairs—not with so many rooms—and even if they did, no one would interfere." We all knew our place—Hawks and servants included. "I would've appreciated my last view to be of something enjoyable rather than this godforsaken place."

Cut narrowed his eyes. "What makes you think I want this over so quickly?"

I froze.

Footsteps echoed like doomsday percussion off the tunnel walls.

My heart beat faster. "Who else will witness this?" It wasn't Jasmine, that I could be sure—unless someone carried her.

Fuck, would he be that cruel? To make her watch me die after everything we'd done to her?

My mind ran wild with questions and regrets. There was so much I never did, so much I wanted to do.

Now, it was all over.

"What makes you think they're a witness?" Cut's cold voice sent shackles of numbness around my limbs.

Staring into the shadows, out of range of the light, we both waited for the mystery guest to arrive.

The moment a figure materialized from the gloom and golden eyes met mine, I bared my teeth. "What the fuck are you doing here?"

Daniel snickered, moving to take his place beside Cut. Equal breadth and height, they matched in their leather jackets and complementing smirks.

"I'm here to teach you a lesson, *brother*."

Fuck. All the tormenting and lording my firstborn status came back to haunt me. *This* was my true punishment. Not being shot or maimed but being disciplined by my fucking brother.

My gut churned. I had to will every cell to stay upright and stoic. In my mind, I conjured Nila. She possessed my thoughts—not in the everyday attire she'd worn around the Hall—but in the black feathered couture from Milan. Her skin was faultless. Her ebony eyes depthless. She'd been utterly perfect.

Then I'd stolen her. Degraded her. Fucked her. And ultimately loved her.

I pushed her image away as fast as I'd invoked it. It hurt too much.

"I don't understand you, Jethro." Cut entered the cell, his boot scuffing a pebble. "You were so fucking close to throwing away, not just a fortune, but sentencing your sister to the grave as well as yourself."

My blood turned from liquid to rock. "Leave her out of this."

"You're saying you believe Jasmine doesn't deserve repentance? After all, it was *she* who convinced me you could be fixed. She's the one who gave her livelihood for yours that day...or have you forgotten?"

I breathed shallowly. "I haven't forgotten, and it's not her fault. Don't fucking touch her."

"Oh, we won't touch her...if you do everything we say." Daniel brushed past Cut, encroaching on my space. His aftershave of spice and musk overpowered me. My gullet fought to retch—to vomit right on his shiny black boots.

I glowered. Everything about this felt wrong. As if we were boys again playing games we didn't understand. "What do you want?"

Cut chuckled. "Isn't it obvious, Jet? I want a firstborn that I can trust. I want a man who will oversee my empire. I want a fucking heir who isn't some sort of fucked-up delinquent."

I straightened my spine. "Life is full of disappointment."

"Yes, but at least I can get some enjoyment out of this." Looking at Daniel, he nodded. "You're up, Buzzard. Teach him a lesson."

My eyes flashed to Daniel's. I kept my expression blank. I refused to beg for mercy or let him see the fear percolating inside.

Daniel smiled, cracking his knuckles and slinking out of his jacket. "Hear that, *Kite*? Time for a little payback. And I have to say, it's gonna taste fucking sweet."

Tossing his jacket into the corner of the cell, he clenched his fists and danced like a seasoned fighter. I instinctually raised my arms, preparing to spar. Daniel was third born—the mistake—he was also the smallest out of all of us, but he was still strong. Plus, he had something I was missing: savage with no mercy.

"Ah, ah, ah, Jethro." Cut tapped the gun against the bars, sending a god-awful *twang* around the cell. "You aren't to fight back."

I snarled, "You expect me to let him pummel me and not defend myself?"

Daniel laughed, circling me like some rabid hyena.

"I have a deal to offer you, Jethro." Cut's words fell like stones. Everything had new meaning. That ridiculous hope swelled in my heart again.

"What deal?"

"Last chance," Daniel sneered, never stopping his aggravating circles.

Cut ran a hand through his hair. "I was fully prepared to kill you, son. Ready to put you out of your misery because—let's fucking face it—you're not happy." Sympathy coated his features, confusing the shit out of me.

"You're saying you were prepared to put me down like some rabies-infested dog? For *my* sake?"

Cut frowned. "After everything that's happened between us, you still think I'm some kind of monster. I care for you. I care for all my children."

*Bullshit.*

"It's only natural that I want to help you."

Crossing my arms, I tried to ignore Daniel and understand this new development. "What do you propose?"

"It comes in stages."

"Go on."

"First, you need punishing. I won't tolerate any more disobedience." Toying with the gun, his eyes bored into mine.

"Part one of this new deal is..."

"Let me beat your ass with no retaliation." Daniel laughed, socking a punch into my kidney from behind.

White-hot heat scorched my system, setting fire to every organ. I gasped, holding the throbbing bruise. Sickly sweat sprang over my skin. I sucked air between my teeth. "You can't be serious."

Cut's eyes narrowed to slits. "I'm more than serious. Fight back or try to harm your brother, and I'll put a bullet through your skull with no hesitation."

Daniel threw another punch, right into my intestines. A grunt escaped as I staggered forward, bending over to spit on the slimy floor. Only once I'd straightened, trembling with adrenaline, did Cut grant me the next part of his rehabilitation. "When you've accepted a thrashing to what I deem payable, then I'll tell you the next part of the deal."

Coming forward, he pressed the gun under my chin, holding my eyes on his. "You say you hurt. That life is a constant hardship. Well, I have news for you. It's not enough for me that your innards fucking hurt. I want your body to scream, too. It's fitting and a worthwhile punishment for the son of a nobleman."

Transcriptions of such punishments executed hundreds of years ago came to mind. Aristocrats dealt in different conduct when a crime had to be paid. Fists were a gentleman's weapon rather than stocks or floggers.

Daniel's fist collided with my jaw, snapping my head sideways. I groaned as my equilibrium turned to shit. I stumbled sideways, fighting every instinct to defend myself.

Cut stepped back as Daniel round-housed me, planting his boot squarely in my chest. With flaring pain, I tumbled to the earthen floor. Fuck, it hurt. Every inch of me was on fire—pounding with agony.

"Take your sentence like a man, Jethro. Then we'll see if you deserve my proposition."

I scrambled to my feet.

Daniel cackled as he kicked my ankle, sending me face-planting into dirt. I braced myself on all fours, presenting a soft target of my belly in line with his boot.

He kicked me like a fucking animal, breaking a rib and hurtling me into Hades.

I would've given anything to fight back. I howled inside—handcuffed by the illusion of leniency. I took each blow, not for my downfall of being what I was, but for what I'd *done*.

Every strike was my penance for what I did to Nila.

Each kick was a purging for my disastrous behaviour.

I nursed Nila in my heart and found a strange healing, even in such unjust brutality.

My eyes watered as Daniel yanked my hair and cracked his knuckles against my cheekbone.

Cut muttered, "I want you bleeding in apology, son. Only then might you deserve another chance."

# Nila

"WE'RE HERE."

Powerful buildings and iconic landmarks replaced the rugged landscape of Buckinghamshire's countryside. There were no trees or sweeping hills, no foxhounds or horses.

London.

"Bet you missed your family, Ms. Weaver." The policeman driving had tried small talk over the course of our three-hour drive. I'd ignored every topic.

Instead of focusing on grey concrete and overpasses, I thought of Jethro.

Where was he? What were they doing to him?

My emotions split into an unsolvable jigsaw puzzle. I was smooth edges, crooked edges, and awkward corner edges. I was cutthroat and fierce, betrayer and deceiver, loved and lover.

Only a few hours had passed since I'd left Jethro, yet I felt as if I'd been adrift forever.

*I have to go back.*

I was no longer a girl who would bow to her father and submit to her brother. I wasn't content with letting others be in charge.

I was a fighter.

And I owed Cut Hawk payment for what he'd done.

A fog rolled in over the busy cog-work city of London as

we journeyed through ancient streets and new.
Every streetlamp and road sign spoke of home.
*My* home.
My old home.
I knew this place. I'd been born here. Raised here. Trained here.
*You also met Jethro when you were too young to remember here.*
The car came to a halt outside my family's sweeping Victorian manor. The whitewashed bricks looked fresh and modern. The lilac windows decorated in my mother's favourite colour. It was quaintly feminine despite its three-story grandeur.
*It's a dollhouse compared to Hawksridge Hall.*
I missed the gothic French turrets and imposing size. I missed the richness and danger that breathed in its walls.
I missed Jethro.
The glass of my window on the second floor winked through the grey drizzle, welcoming me back.
The driver pressed the intercom on the wrought iron gate, barring the Weaver Household from the rest of society. We lived in an affluent end of town. No one asked for a cup of sugar here. Everyone guarded themselves behind camera systems and armed fences.
"Yes?"
The moment my father's voice came through the speaker, vertigo swooped in and held me hostage. The world spun.
"We're here, Mr. Weaver."
A crackle then a panicked bark, "Do you have her?"
The driver threw me a smile. "We have her."

# Jethro

SOMETHING HARD THUMPED against my chest.

It roused me, dragging me from the bowels of hell and back into a body sobbing with pain.

"Open your eyes, Jet."

I flinched, fearing another kick or punch. How long had Daniel punished me?

Long enough to break a couple more ribs and swell my left eye completely shut.

"He's gone." A presence squatted in front of me—a blurry figure obscured by blood and dirt.

I tried to swallow, but my throat was too dry. Incredibly, a water bottle was pushed into my lifeless hands. When I almost dropped it, Cut wrapped his warm fingers around mine, clasping the bottle tightly.

A wave of compassion and sympathy lapped around my sodden form, forcing my vision to focus. "Tha—thank you," I whispered brokenly.

Cut nodded, sitting on his haunches while I sipped from the already open bottle and slowly wrangled my body into life.

Struggling to sit upright, Cut moved so I could spread out my legs and recline against the frigid, dripping wall.

"Better?" he asked. As if he cared about my welfare only moments after beating me to a pulp.

*Still alive, unfortunately for you.*

I fought my sarcastic response and glared instead. "Did I pass your little test, Father?" In that second, I hated him. I fucking despised that this man was my patron and relation.

He didn't reply. Only motioned to the thing that'd landed on my chest and rolled to the side with an odd rattle. "That's the second requirement of this last chance."

I couldn't make out what it was. My eyes flickered as my system organised my pain into filing cabinets of life threatening, throbbing, and liveable.

"Pick it up."

Swallowing my groan, I slipped sideways against the wall and scooped up the small white bottle. I squinted, trying unsuccessfully to read the label.

"What—what are they?"

Cut shifted, bringing my attention to the gun resting on his knee. It still pointed at me, like it had during the beating Daniel gave me. "I told you. Your final chance."

I scowled at the gun. "And if I don't agree…to whatever you want me to do next?"

"It ends. Here and now. I put you out of your misery and life moves on."

My heart raced, dragging Nila back into existence. "If you kill me, does that void the Debt Inheritance?"

Could I somehow free Nila from this by sacrificing myself?

Cut pursed his lips, anger shading his features. "You're saying you would die for a fucking Weaver? Come on, Jethro. Be a man and accept what I'm trying to give you." He opened his arms, signalling Hawksridge. "This will be all yours. The companies, trade routes, mines…all *yours*. Is one woman worth all that?"

Silence was syrupy, its only companion the chilled dampness surrounding us.

*Yes.*
*She's worth that and more.*

"So that was a yes?" My voice croaked. I took another sip

of water. "If you kill me, the debts are done. You need a firstborn. That's why there's only been seven Weavers claimed over the centuries. Things go wrong; life interferes. What did you tell me? That raising a Hawk and Weaver to age requirement without one dying, going missing, or failing in some way was a fucking miracle? Kill me—end this so-called miracle. Another generation would be safe."

Cut shot to his feet and kicked my leg. Normally, such a blow wouldn't hurt, but it landed on multiple bruises already given courtesy of Daniel.

I hissed, fisting my hands around the bottle and spilling water down my bloodied clothes.

"Ordinarily, Jethro, you would be right. With your death comes her salvation. She'd walk free. She wouldn't be claimed because the firstborn didn't survive."

The biggest wash of relief enveloped me. That was the answer then. The only way. I could avoid any more hardship and Nila could avoid death.

*I can give you that, Nila. I can give you a long life free from me.*

"Do it," I commanded, my voice firm with conviction. "It seems our wishes have finally aligned, Father. I wish to die. You wish to have a different heir. There's only one logical conclusion."

Gathering my threadbare energy, I somehow climbed to my feet. I used the wall as a cane and swayed like a drunkard, but I was on two feet—equal to Cut standing before me.

Cut raised the gun, pointing at my heart.

All fear was gone. I was happy with this sacrifice. I finally found a purpose for my screwed-up life, and Nila would be safe to live without being beheaded.

*It's the right thing—the noble thing to do.*

And thanks to Daniel's beating, perhaps I'd paid enough tax to find my way into heaven, rather than purgatory.

"You truly are twisted," Cut snarled. "How can you piss me off and make me proud all at the same time?"

I stiffened. I didn't need his mind games anymore. I

needed an ending. *I want it over with.* "Just do it." I held out my hands, one clutching the water bottle and the other the white container that rattled with who knew what. "You know you want to."

Cut paced away, dragging a hand through his hair. "No, I do *not* want to! I'm not a fucking monster, Jethro. I'm trying to save your fucking life, not end it!" He stormed back, waving the deadly weapon in my face. "You know what? Death is too easy for someone like you. You're too damn strong, and I refuse to put an end to a man who could rule our name as it needs to be ruled. Kestrel is a good man, but he isn't steadfast like you. And Daniel—" He rolled his eyes. "He's a fucking maniac who would whittle away our fortune in years." Tapping the gun against his chin, his eyes came alight with a plan.

My gut twisted.

*Fuck.*

"There's a new condition to my offer."

I'd been so close to saving her.

I fought the urge to hunch in defeat. "Spit it out."

"If you die…if you kill yourself, plan an accident, or find some other way to end it thinking you can protect that little Weaver Whore, then I'll give her to Daniel. Do you hear me?"

My temper roared. "But he's not firstborn—"

"I don't care about the fucking rules anymore, Jet. Because of you, all of this is a complicated fuck-up. That girl *will* pay. She wears the collar. It will come off. And the Debt Inheritance will be paid—with or without you."

I didn't bother to ask how we'd sort out the media mess and get her back. My family was entirely too resourceful. Her escape was merely an interlude, and I was fucking kidding myself if I thought differently.

My heart galloped with hatred. "What are you saying?"

"If you do what I ask, you can continue to extract the debts. No one will lay a hand on her unless you command it. She'll remain yours and in your protection until the Final Debt."

My bruised hands tightened around the bottles. "And how do you propose I do that?" I laughed, the dark chuckle sounded like insects in the catacombs' echoing chambers. "Let's end the bullshit, Father. You know what I am. We both know I can't change. Why bother keeping me alive when I'll only cause more fucking hardship? Just get it over with. Forget about the Weavers. Forget about me. Just forget all of it and put an end to this madness."

Cut grinned; the evilness I was used to overshadowed his pity for me. "I'll never forget, Jet. A true Hawk never forgets." Pointing at the white bottle in my hand, he muttered, "That will fix you. Make you my true son instead of this diseased creature before me."

I winced as if he'd struck me again. Nothing like a few kind words from a father to make a kid feel adored.

"Get yourself under control. No matter what you think of me, I *want* you to inherit."

Putting the water bottle down, I summoned strength and twisted off the lid of the small vial. I glanced inside. It was hard to see with the meagre light, but the tiny moon-shaped tablets gave me equal measure of despair and hope.

I looked up. "Drugs?"

Cut nodded. "Before this shitty debacle, you'd impressed me the past few years. You listened and obeyed. You showed such promise. I can't dispatch you when I still believe you can be cured."

I blinked. Was this my father? The man who'd threatened me all my life. He'd had a sudden change of heart?

"You know these don't work on me. We've tried enough in the past." Nothing worked. From antipsychotics to beta-blockers and downers. They were all the same—useless.

Cut put the safety on and shoved the gun down his waistband. The cocky confidence of winning already infected him. "These are different. Not even on the market yet."

"How did you get them?"

"Doesn't matter. All you need to know is they're stronger

than anything you've tried and come with a guarantee of success."

Suddenly, I had choices. Before, I had the daily toil of self-harming to give myself something to focus on. I had death to look forward to in order to save Nila. But now, I had to stay alive if I had any chance of saving her and putting an end to the Final Debt. I also had an option to help me survive in order to do that.

That same taunting hope fluttered with new wings. *Will they help?*

For a moment, I was selfish. Could it be possible after all this time? To live a normal life? To be free?

I couldn't stop the overwhelming rush of gratefulness. The past couple of months in Nila's company had been utter torture. She'd forced me to change—to grow—to look for other ways to exist.

*But this…*

What I held might be the end to all my problems.

"You believe them? That they'll work?"

Cut shrugged. "We can only hope." Picking up my water bottle, he held it out to me. "We won't know until you've taken a course. Five a day, every few hours. Take more if you need to. Don't worry about the side effects—not if you want to survive in order to keep Nila in your control."

The threat was there—disguised as a helping hand but still an ultimatum. Drug myself and become everything he ever wanted, play puppet master with the life of the woman I was in love with, and carry out his wishes…or perish at his hands and have her subjected to Daniel's murderous plans.

I hated all those choices.

"And you won't let me leave? Disown me and give the estate to Kes?"

*Then I can have Nila and live far away from here.*

"No negotiation." Cut crossed his arms. "You take the drugs and embrace your proper place, or you die and she lives a life of horror until her death. Your choice."

I stopped breathing.

"Get that bitch out of your mind and heart, son. Take the drugs, find your way back, then we'll see if you get to live."

Could I be strong enough to obey Cut all the while double-crossing him by loving Nila? Could I last to my thirtieth birthday, so I could tear up the Debt Inheritance and eradicate it once and for all?

*I have no choice.*

I had to try.

I tipped a tablet into my palm and tossed it onto my tongue. Locking eyes with my father, I took a swill of water and swallowed the first drug of many.

Nila had my heart.

But my father had my very existence.

# Nila

THE CAR ROLLED through the gates.
The tyres inched closer to the front porch.
The front door opened.
My brother appeared.
*V.*
Before I could take a breath and prepare, the car door was jerked open.
He hadn't changed.
His black hair still fell roguishly over one eye. His body was fit and toned—wiry with model-perfect lines. He sported a slight beard—tight and dark—it made him seem like some modern day Robin Hood stealing me from the Hawks and returning me to my rightful place.
"V—" I wanted to say more, but my throat gave out. Tears spurted from my eyes.
Vaughn was here.
He could fix this. He could mend my broken heart. He could fight for me so I wouldn't have to.
*We have to save Jethro. Before they do something terrible.*
His hands captured my cheeks, holding me firm as his mirroring black eyes drank mine. "Threads." He pressed a kiss against my temple. "Threads. Fucking hell, you're here."
I sucked in a breath, fumbling with my seatbelt. I wanted

to be closer to him. To let him erase my breaking pieces.
Because I was breaking.
Jethro had stolen my everything.
But this was my brother.
The brother I'd betrayed.
A sob latched onto my lungs, making me cough, making me relive what the Hawks did to me in the lake.
I coughed again. More tears fell.
V groaned under his breath, tearing off my seatbelt and dragging me into his arms.
My legs dangled as he crushed me to his chest. His heartbeat was steady and strong as I cried into his white shirt.
*Steady and strong.*
Jethro's heartbeat had been irregular and terrified.
I cried harder. Not just for how royally I'd screwed everything up but for leaving Jethro when I'd promised I'd stay.
*Please, please let him be alright.*
"It's okay, Threads. I gotcha. You're safe now. Those fucking bastards will never come near you again. You hear me? Never." His voice was harsh with promise.
He sounded so young compared to the scratch and scrawl of Jethro's immaculate eloquence. Swear words were something Jethro only resorted to when he couldn't control himself—whereas my brother used them as punctuation.
"Nila."
My body stiffened at my name...at the way my father breathed it so lovingly.
V unwound his arms. I raised my head and looked into my father's eyes. Archibald 'Tex' Weaver looked a hundred years older. His toned physique was gone, replaced by a sagging middle and even worse sagging eyes. His effortless style of slacks and shirts had been switched for baggy jeans and stained polo shirts.
His despair—the complete abandonment of everything he'd been—was better than any spoken apology. More poignant than any beg or plea for understanding.

"I'm so sorry, Nila," he choked, tears glittering.

I was livid. I was distraught. I had so many unresolved issues toward my father but we were *family*. Forgiveness was utmost.

Another sob escaped as I shuffled closer. V never let me go. Instead, Tex came to us. He wrapped his strong arms around his son and daughter and crushed us to the bone. His cheeks grew damp with sadness, and his signature smell of Old Spice tore up my nose and ripped my brain into ribbons.

*Oh, God. Oh, God.*

The world spun.

Faster and faster and *faster*.

In my family's joint embrace—the same embrace where I'd found such comfort before—now I only found sickness and horror.

I screeched as my ears roared; my eyes slid to the back of my head.

Round and around and around.

I suffered the worst vertigo spell in years.

I trembled so much, no one could hold me. They let me go, leaving me to suffer alone. They had experience dealing with me—they knew when I became like this, touch was the worst kind of torture.

V and my father guided me to the floor where I knelt with my head on my knees, trying to hold on to the world that'd suddenly gone mad.

Down was up and up was down.

Their voices plaited into concern, rushing around, making the spinning worse.

Sickness became nausea which became overwhelming.

I couldn't get it under control. I was completely at the mercy of my broken mind.

I threw up.

A small, tiny voice in my head squeaked. *Vertigo or pregnant?*

I threw up again.

*Never. Not possible. I couldn't be.*

"Shit, Threads." Vaughn squatted beside me. His hands twitched to touch me. To rub my shoulders and tuck my hair behind my ear. But he knew to stay away. If he rocked me or tried to comfort me, my body might hurl me into another episode.

It was *me* who had to stand—me who had to heal.

The vertigo wave spun faster, stealing my ability to think. My body bellowed from my other injuries.

My father stood over us, his scruffy jaw clenched. He used to be such a support system—such a much-needed part of my life. Now, he made me shatter. My newfound strength slowly siphoned into a cesspit of misery.

The world continued to swing like a crazy pendulum, sending my brain sloshing.

V whispered, "You're here. You're safe. Those motherfucking sons of bitches will pay for what they did. Starting with Jethro Hawk."

*Don't touch him!*

His voice had a duplex effect. My past personality sank into his capability and brotherly strength—grateful that he was now in charge. While the new Nila cringed from relying on anyone but herself.

I had him to thank for my freedom.

I had him to thank for my misery.

I lifted my head. Vaughn's black eyes stared into mine, and the love I felt for my twin broke through. I hated myself for my previous thoughts.

I was safe. I should be so grateful.

But every minute that ticked past, I vowed to go back. Not because I'd been brainwashed into accepting torture or pain, but because death had tried to claim me only for love to save me instead. Jethro had brought me to life. I wouldn't leave him behind.

*We'll both break free. We have to.*

My heart twinged thinking of Jethro. I was lucky enough to be loved and accepted by a family who cared for me, even if

they never really knew me.
    What did he have?
    A prison cell that'd existed all his life.
    A future that might destroy him.
    Collapsing to my side, I wrapped my arms around myself and heaved. My throat howled from drowning. My head pounded. And through it all, all I could think was…
    *This would never have happened if Jethro were here.*
    His very soul was an anchor.
    The one I needed the most.
    I groaned at the horrible irony.
    I was free at Hawksridge in a way that I could never be free in London.
    I couldn't live without him.
    I didn't *want* to live without him.
    *I need to save him.*
    *And soon.*

# Jethro

THE CURE BEGAN slowly—whispering across my thoughts.

The unravelling Nila had achieved slowly stitched itself back together. The love, the panic, the pressure...it all faded.

My intense world became shrouded. The glare of intensity diminished and, tablet by tablet, I grew delightfully numb.

I liked this new blanket.

I was grateful to my father.

Without him, I would've resorted to opening the scars on my soles and living in pain to survive. What he hadn't factored in was my conviction to save Nila. The drugs gave me strength to do that.

So I took another and another...believing they would be my salvation and her key to surviving.

How fucking stupid was I?

Seventy-two hours.

Three days since Nila left.

My injuries from Daniel's beating were stiff and mottled. I refused to look at myself in a mirror, as I couldn't stomach the yellow and purple bruised asshole staring back at me.

Whereas my body hurt, my soul was miraculously floating. Every day the overwhelming hazards of my disease bleached further and further into a watermark rather than a vibrant stain.

Cut let me leave the dungeon under the condition of medicating myself. The choice between dank darkness and pills was no hardship.

I kept to myself. I didn't visit Jasmine to protect her from my appearance. I didn't go on shipment runs or seek out my father. I spent the days in the stable, finding solitude in Wings' silent presence and slipping deeper into the drug's embrace.

However, lying in bed at night couldn't stop my mind filling with her.

*Nila.*

I missed her smell, her taste...her heat.

I craved to be inside her, to hold her in silence and find the gift that she'd given me by falling in love. She'd used me to help her. She'd manipulated me in a way I couldn't refuse, but in the end, we were both losers...or winners—depending on my frame of mind. Her heart belonged to me. And my heart belonged to her.

I'd fallen for her.

I'd tried to become a better person for her.

But the drugs were so much more powerful than me.

I wanted to rejoice at finally finding something that worked. I should bow to the doctors for creating this miraculous cure. I needed everyone to know how incredible it felt to be cocooned by the gentle fog of intoxication.

Nila had obeyed me when she left—taking my heart and sanity with her. But now, I had a rare opportunity to fortify myself. I would become the man she needed, so when the time came to claim her, we would both be ready.

One hundred and twenty hours.

Five days since Nila left.

My injuries were healing—my ribs remained strapped and

sore, but my face didn't look as swollen or grotesque.

Five days equated to thirty-seven tablets. I'd become attached to my rattling bottle, devouring the promised fog as if each drug was exclusive caviar.

Nothing affected me anymore. Not loud noises, overpowering scents. Not even raised tempers or malice. The fog was thicker...the insulation between them and me growing deeper by the day.

The tablets were working.

They were stealing, healing.

But they hadn't solved me completely. I still ached as if my heart had been ripped out. Every night I throbbed to slide inside Nila and have her come apart in my arms. My tattooed fingertips mocked me—reminding me she'd branded me and I'd branded her but for now...we were apart, even if we belonged to each other.

*But soon I can collect her.*

Soon I could save Nila, Jasmine, Kestrel, and myself.

So many futures rested on me. I couldn't let them down. So, I popped another tablet, I said goodbye to another ounce of feeling, and I prepared myself for the ultimate finale.

I should've seen it coming.

*Why didn't I see it coming?*

I'd begun taking my new tablet friends to save me from myself, to save Nila from a worse fate designed by Daniel, and to guard the goodness Nila had conjured inside me.

That was my goal...but I'd underestimated Cut.

I didn't pay close enough attention to my evolution as the drugs took me hostage.

It started slowly, methodically.

The man I knew slowly sank deeper and deeper inside, leaving a husk—a husk living with men like my father and brother—twisting the hologram of the man I once was.

It began like before: Cut put me back in charge of the

mines and shipments. He returned my responsibilities and praised me for doing a good job. Security and finances filled my day, leading me further away from the soft tenderness Nila had nursed.

At night, I would be summoned to my father's quarters to talk about what would happen now I was back in control. He made me drink from his convoluted perception and made me eat his disgusting morals.

Slowly but surely, I became angry. And that cultivated anger was given direction.

The Weaver twin.

Vaughn was to blame for *everything*.

He stole her from me. His fucking meddling hadn't ceased. He brought shame and suspicion onto my house. His tampering couldn't be allowed.

Nila had been free for days—there was no reason to continue to spread gossip—in his mind, he'd won. I hadn't made any attempt to contact Nila under another of my father's conditions.

*"Stay away until the drugs have worked."*

I should've guessed then that the drugs had two targets: help me, but collar me. I could no longer remember why I wanted to help Nila. Yes, I had feelings for her…but they felt so long ago. She was a Weaver. My family's mortal enemy. Why would I deviate from my destiny when so many others relied on me?

Every breakfast, my father would turn on the news, YouTube, and every social media platform available today. Slowly, he filled my heart with hate.

He showed me disgusting lies and slander all originating from Vaughn. Twitter ran rampant with hashtags of #BastardHawks and #InnocentWeavers. Facebook hosted debates and surveys on their opinions of the Debt Inheritance.

Everyone had a hypothesis.

Everyone was wrong.

But they all had something in common.

They wanted our *blood*.

It was Vaughn who put me back into the icy blizzard I'd escaped from. His twin had thawed me, but he froze me all over again.

He'd gone to every journalist and reporter imaginable. He'd divulged ancient tales of filthy deeds and contracts and debts. He spilled our private affairs to the fucking world.

Every day the phone rang for interviews. Our sources with buyers on the black market grew wary—not enjoying the slander our family suffered—in case it smeared them, too. Our staff began whispering. Our fucking lives started to unravel.

We had money. We controlled police, Customs, and made a livelihood of manipulating those in power for our own means, but we had no clout when it came to strangers on the internet.

Vaughn Weaver harnessed this new age influence and brought a mob to our door, and in doing so, he made my family rally together. Hawk against Weaver. Just like before.

He proved we weren't untouchable, after all. Cut didn't deal with the knowledge well. He fucking raged at how little he could do to stop this storm of antagonisers. He never had to worry about social media when he had Emma Weaver—but in today's society, it was a bigger beast than we ever anticipated.

Our empire was built on greased palms and ancient 'blind-eye' agreements. We all knew whatever contract we had giving us ownership of the Weavers was bullshit.

Nobody could own another.

Only imbeciles believed such a thing.

But I did believe in our power. Our wealth. Our status.

The tales of our rise from rags to riches had been told so many times, they'd reached phenomenon status within our family—spoon-fed the same crap since birth and believing in the power of a binding parchment that gave us *carte blanche* to do what we pleased. Not because it granted us immunity, but because it showed just how many people obeyed us now that we had control.

But what good was control when it unthreaded with a fucking rumour?

All of this was a game. Only Vaughn had changed the rules by bringing in spectators demanding answers.

I'd kill Vaughn for that.

He was already dead—just a nail in my rapidly freezing coffin as I popped pill after pill.

Hour after hour, I slowly gave in.

Day after day, I slowly felt nothing.

I was done being the man everyone thought was weak. I lived with a disease, but I wasn't a cripple.

I didn't need snow anymore. Or ice. Or pain.

I had drugs.

I was stone.

# Nila

I'D LIKE TO say life returned to normal.
But I'd be lying.
I'd like to say I slipped back into my previous existence as entrepreneur, seamstress, and daughter.
But I'd be bullshitting to the highest degree.
Every day was worse than the one before it.
I was lost.
Alone.
Unwanted.

Life was a death sentence.
The press hounded me for interviews on my disappearance. My assistants pestered me with hundreds of new designs and orders. My father tried to talk to me about what happened. And my brother suffocated me with love.
It was all too *much*.
It drove me to boiling point.
In the beginning, I suffered physical healing from the Second Debt payment. I coughed often, doctors checked me for pneumonia, and the bruises on my chest took forever to fade. I used the pain as a calendar, slowly ticking off the hours

Jethro left me all alone and unresponsive. I waited for a message from Kite007. I became obsessed with daydreams of him swooping in and taking me away from the mess of the press and envy of misguided people.

At night, I lay in a room that'd been mine since I was born. The purple walls hadn't changed. My unfinished designs draped on headless mannequins hadn't vanished, yet nothing was home anymore.

I felt like a stranger. An imposter. And the sensation only grew worse.

The strength and power I'd found on my own dissolved. My joy at suffering fewer vertigo attacks disappeared as I went from managing the incurable disease to suffering the worst I'd ever had.

Yesterday, I'd suffered nine.

The day before, I'd had seven.

I had more bruises on my knees, elbows, and spine in just a week of being a true Weaver again than I *ever* endured at Jethro's hands.

Every second the same questions hounded me.

How was I supposed to return to my old life?

How was I supposed to forget about Jethro?

How was I supposed to give up my strength in order for my brother to adore me?

And how was I supposed to forgive my father and be grateful to him for rescuing me?

How.

How.

*How?*

The answer...

I couldn't.

For a week, I tried. I slipped seamlessly into my previous world. I toiled in our Weaver headquarters, answered emails, and agreed to fashion shows two years from now. I painted on a mask and lied through my teeth.

I became a master at ignoring what my body told me.

Throwing up was a bi-weekly occurrence and my dreams were full of accusations. Memories of Jethro coming inside me played on repeat—hinting at one thing:
*Am I pregnant?*
Or had I just escalated to vertigo-cripple?
Everywhere I turned there were magazine articles, newspaper speculations, billboards, and BBC broadcasts. I had to face banners of my dead mother and grandmother in Piccadilly Circus. I had to close my eyes as buses drove past with the Hawk family crest painted on their sides. And I had to swallow back bile as advertising for the latest 'must-have' accessory plastered park benches and taxi stands.
What was the 'must-have' jewellery?
My diamond collar.
*Everyone* wanted one. Everyone wanted to see mine, touch mine—ask me endless questions about the unopenable clasp and the meaning of such a beautiful but despicable piece.
I was a living specimen. Plopped into a goldfish bowl and made to perform like some circus freak. I was the 'unfortunate Debtee' and Jethro Hawk was the 'loathsome Debtor.'
Vaughn had destined us to a life of gossip about family feuds and incomprehensible contracts.
Every night when we gathered to eat in floundering silence, I wanted to stab my twin with a steak knife. I wanted to scream at him for announcing to the world how ludicrous our two families were.
People *laughed* at us.
People gawked—not only had V brought to light the evil insanity of the Hawks, but he'd also shown what a cruel, vindictive race our own bloodline had been.
It didn't seem to matter to him. He'd freed me. He'd turned a private agreement into an international affair. As far as he was concerned, I should be grateful.
I would've preferred to deal with rumours Jethro had put into play the first night he stole me: the photos of him holding and kissing me—doctored and delivered in a perfect alibi of a

relationship turned elopement.

*That* was reasonable.

This was unbelievable.

Now everyone had those photographs—printed over tacky magazines and exposed in newspapers with headlines: *'The Man and His Toy.' 'How Far Can Legacy Go?' 'Multiple Murders Go Unpunished.'*

Every sordid detail of my family was unearthed and published. However, the facts on the Hawks were extremely vague. The press hadn't uncovered that a motorcycle club lived on the grounds. They didn't mention diamond smuggling or their massive wealth.

All it would take was for me to agree to a private interview and announce to the world about Cut's underworld dealing, his meticulous record keeping, the Weaver Journal, and the videos of debts extracted. That evidence would buy them a one-way ticket to jail.

But their lives belonged to *me*. I wanted to be the one to take them down. I wanted to watch them perish—not waste away in a cell where I couldn't reach them to make them pay.

*That's not the only reason you're staying quiet.*

I sighed. The main reason was because I was in love with a Hawk and would stay silent to protect him.

I'd gained my freedom. Jethro would, too. I would make sure of it.

Throughout the torture of the first week, Vaughn was in his element. He smiled with model good looks, wrapped his arms around me as he performed for the cameras, and showed the world the bruises on my wrists from the ducking stool.

I'd done my utmost to hide my hands from my family— keeping my tattooed fingertips from worldwide knowledge. But I couldn't hide the Weaver Wailer.

Everyone knew what it meant.

The first day I was back, my father made me sit for hours while he tried to remove it. He'd used every micro-tool available to work the hinge free. V even tried to pry the collar off with tiny pliers. But the mechanism was too well made. The diamonds too well set.

It didn't work.

Jewellers and diamond merchants put their hands up to try. They all failed.

As I lost the new Nila and stumbled with awful vertigo, my father slid deeper and deeper inside himself. After living with the constant questions and insinuations of how his wife died, he became a hermit. I no longer recognised him. We no longer had anything in common.

All of that was my life now.

I supposed I was lucky.

I supposed I should be *grateful*.

After all...

At least I was free.

# Jethro

"KITE?"

I looked up from my desk. Jasmine wheeled herself into my room, her tiny hands wrapped around the stainless steel rims of her chair for propulsion.

It'd been ten days since Nila Weaver had left.

Two hundred and forty hours. Sixty-one tablets.

I was immune to everything.

Blank to everyone.

I couldn't think about my life before without shuddering in pain. How had I withstood it for so long when this was so much better?

The past ten days I'd finally, *finally* earned what I'd hoped all my life: Cut said he was proud of me. He'd been wary at first—never stopped watching—searching for a weakness…a chink in my surrender to my new addiction.

But this wasn't a lie.

It was better this way. Easier this way. *Survivable* this way.

I had no fears of making it to my thirtieth birthday anymore.

When he saw the truth, he gave me more and more control. He praised me for my clear-headedness and ruthless behaviour.

My siblings, on the other hand, weren't pleased. They

didn't understand what it was like to live with my condition, and I was done being judged. I pulled away. I put up walls and fastened locks. I stopped visiting Wings as I became too busy to ride. I ceased my visits to Jasmine and put an end to late night chats with Kes.

All I needed was silence and my little rattling bottle of pills.

Nila had done me a favour.

She'd shown me how diseased I truly was. And with her disappearance came my cure.

If I had any feelings left to be dispensed, I would still have a fondness toward her. But I was happy being empty. I was free being immune to the insanity of life.

"Go away, Jaz." I turned back to my task. Running my fingers over the paper Nila had signed the night of Cut's birthday, I shook my head at my scrambled forward thinking.

I thought I could circumnavigate the Debt Inheritance by forcing Nila to sign another binding contract. I'd planned to brandish it as a weapon the day I turned thirty and stop the Final Debt in its twilight hour.

I smirked.

Stupid idea and so much fucking work.

There was no point fighting the inevitable.

"What are you doing?" Jaz asked, wheeling closer, the swish of her chair softened by thick carpet.

Grabbing my sigil-engraved lighter, I flicked it open and held the Sacramental Pledge over the naked flame. The thick parchment crackled as I teased it with flickering heat.

"None of your business." I brought the fire closer.

Jaz slapped my desk, jerking my eyes to hers. "We need to talk. I'm worried about you."

I laughed softly as the fire suddenly caught hold, licking up the parchment. I became hypnotised as flames rapidly devoured the last of my madness.

Jaz eyed up the pledge. "What is that?"

The orange glow danced in my retinas. "Nothing."

I tensed, expecting to feel some sort of regret at destroying the one piece of assurance I had over Nila's soul. The night she'd signed this, she'd agreed to give me all rights over her—to *belong* to me. But there was never any chance of a happy ending.

Not for us.

Not for me.

Fire blazed, gathering strength the more paper it devoured. The black ink cindered to ash, falling like black petals onto the desktop.

"Stop burning it," Jasmine demanded, trying to knock my hand and dislodge my hold.

The paper continued to hiss and vanish.

I didn't look at her. I didn't argue.

I felt nothing.

Jasmine puffed out her cheeks, trying to blow out the fire, but it was too eager, too fast.

"Give it up, sister. Some things you cannot change." In a matter of moments, the contract between Nila and me was no more. My stupid planning and ideas that I could win against my father no longer infected my brain.

It was so *liberating*.

Wiping the charred remains into the rubbish bin, I finally looked at my sibling. Her cherub cheeks and sultry lips were wasted on her broken body. She was a stunning woman, yet she would forever remain a spinster ensconced in this house under Bonnie's control. "What do you want?"

Her eyes flickered in pain. Shouts and curses painted her skin, but her bluster faded before she even opened her mouth. Sighing sadly, she shook her head. "Why won't you tell me?"

"Tell you what?"

"What he did to you."

The air became stale. I pinched the bridge of my nose. "I don't have time for this."

"You have plenty of time, Jethro. Answer me." Her face flushed red. "What's happened to you? Why don't you seek me out anymore? Why are you so remote?" She reached for my hands, but I shifted quickly, scooting backward in my chair.

Anguish weighed heavily on her shoulders, but I felt no guilt. Jasmine had a rough start in life. She continued to deal with her own demons, but they were *her demons*. Not mine. I'd finally found a way to be free and I wished to *remain* free.

"Is that all you want?" Cocking my head at the paperwork of the latest machinery upgrades needed for our warehouses, I pursed my lips. "I really am busy—"

"Kite, you listen to me and you listen good." Waggling her finger in my face, she glared. "The day she left, I was so sure he would kill you. I suffered a panic attack thinking the one woman you loved—the one girl who could give you a place to hide—left you to die. But then I heard from Kes that you were alive. I waited for you. I waited *three days* for you to come to me—to ask for a fixing session or just to talk." Dropping her head, her midnight bob hid her eyes. "But you never came. Ten days and you *still* haven't come."

I remained silent.

Jaz looked up, her eyes wet with tears. "You're scaring me, Jethro. I miss my brother. I want him back. Tell me what happened, so I know how to find him again."

*Poor deluded sister.*

Standing, I bent and kissed the top of her head. "Nothing happened. And I don't want to be found. If you love me like you say you do, then be happy for me. I've finally found something that works and will never go back."

Tapping my pocket, the gentle rattle of my pills said hello. I relaxed knowing if life ever got too much, if the tears of another drove me to breaking point, all I had to do was swallow a tiny friend and I would be fine.

"Goodbye, Jaz."

Without waiting for her reply, I strode out the door and left my sister behind.

My phone vibrated its way across my bedside table at three in the morning.

I didn't jump or tense.

In a way, I'd been expecting this to happen for days.

Picking up the device, I swiped the screen and read the blinking message.

I'd wondered how long she would stay away. She'd lasted longer than I anticipated, but I had no doubt that was down to the circus of stories and endless hounding by reporters—not to mention, her brother would've done everything in his power to keep her from contacting me.

But just like my father had said, Nila had reached out.

Unknowingly, she'd just begun the next stage and walked right into a perfect trap.

Needle&Thread: *I've been staring at this phone for over a week, wondering what to say. I still can't find the words, so I'll stick with simple ones. Kite, I love you. I miss you. I'm here for you. I've become a prisoner in my own family. They watch me, guard me. I've traded one captivity for another. I need you to come claim me. If we work together, this can all be over. Please...I need you to fight for me like I've fought for you. I need to know you're alive and uninjured. Jethro, I want you to take me from this place. Let's leave. Let's runaway where no one will find us.*

This was the true test. The ultimate trial on the numbing fog I'd ingested for the past ten days. I waited to see if her words would make me step outside the comforting blankness I now embraced.

They didn't.

I was empty. Nothing could make me go back to the way I was. Not Nila. Not my sister. *Nothing.*

This game had turned into a fishing expedition, and as all good fishermen know, you have to let the fish nibble the bait before they swallowed the hook and sealed their own fate.

*Swallow away, Nila Weaver.*

*Let me catch you.*

Tossing the phone to the floor, I left her message unanswered.

I'D MANAGED TO last over a week before I sent him a message.

But once that boundary had been crossed, I couldn't stop myself from crossing it every day.

I lived only to send more messages, hoping that one day, he would reply.

Monday...

Needle&Thread: *Please, Jethro. I'm begging you. Don't throw me away like this.*

Tuesday...

Needle&Thread: *Are you okay? Did Cut hurt you? Please...I'm going out of my mind with worry.*

Wednesday...

Needle&Thread: *Message me, Kite. Please tell me this doesn't change what happened between us.*

Thursday...

Needle&Thread: *I tried to ditch my security detail today to come save you. But they chased me down the motorway. I can't get free. I need you to come get me if I mean anything to you at all.*

Friday...

Needle&Thread: *What did they do to you? Why won't you reply?*

Saturday...

Needle&Thread: *Answer me, Jethro! Just a simple message to let*

*me know you're still alive. You owe me that at least.*
   Sunday...
   Needle&Thread: *The world thinks we're certifiably crazy. I agree with them. What your family has done is wicked. But you aren't. Don't let them take you away from me...*
   No matter how many messages I sent, no matter how much I poured my heart into them, Jethro ignored me.
   He'd cut me out completely.

   Seventeen nights since I'd seen him.
   Seventeen days since I'd talked to him.
   Eighteen days since he'd loved me, cum inside me, and shown me how much I meant to him.
   And now, *nothing*.
   I lay in my queen-sized bed, staring at the ceiling where a purple chandelier glittered from the moonlight streaming in through open curtains.
   Anger overrode my self-pity, and for the first time since I'd been home, I cursed Jethro Hawk.
   "Damn you!" Staring again at my blank phone, I gave it one more moment to chime. *Come on...*
   It never did.
   With a wail, I tossed the device across my room. It clunked against the rug outside my private bathroom, glowing in the dark.
   My room was big, but not nearly as large as my quarters at Hawksridge, and despite the strange blend of comfort and stress of being home, I couldn't find peace.
   My eyes drifted over my top-of-the-line treadmill in the corner, to my overflowing walk-in closet.
   This room was a part of me.
   But now it was an enemy.
   *Everyone* was an enemy. From work to strangers to family. I didn't fit in anywhere. I didn't even fit into my own thoughts.
   Why was I grieving for a man destined to kill me?

Why was I so determined to return to a household of murderers?

Why did I panic every time nausea took me hostage?

*I know why.*

*Because you're more in love than afraid.*

*Because you can't stand the way Tex looks at you.*

*And because you're afraid you might be pregnant...*

My father tore apart my heart every damn second we were together.

We couldn't talk anymore—not about trivial things or important things. Our awkward conversations were stilted and fake. He couldn't take his eyes off me, even though they were exhausted and ringed with shadows as deep as darkness itself. He shrunk beneath a lifetime of regret over me, over my mother.

And I hated that I couldn't console him.

Why hadn't he gone after her?

Why had he let them come for me?

Those questions were never voiced, but I knew he felt them, lashing the air with contamination.

My family were adrift, and I had no clue how to fix it.

I dug my tattooed fingertips into my eyes, banishing the thoughts of my father and pressing back the tears that never seemed to leave.

I huffed, the silence rejecting any noise and swallowing my sadness. I couldn't stomach the quietness—the lifeless darkness.

I was *safe* here.

No one to hurt me, fuck me, or transform my soul with wings.

*I am safe here.*

And I didn't know how to cope with that anymore.

My ruby-encrusted dirk lay beside me on the silver and lace bedspread. It belonged to the Hawks...yet it was the only thing I'd brought with me. I'd left everything at Hawksridge, including my phone. My father had banned me from getting another—he blamed the press hounding us for constant interviews, but I knew the real reason.

He wanted me to be cut off, untouchable.

But it hadn't stopped me from commandeering a new one, and, like the love-struck moron I was, I knew every digit of Kite's number perfectly.

Countless times, I messaged him.

But not once did he reply.

*I miss you.*

*I curse you.*

*I love you.*

He left me empty and all alone.

"JETHRO."

I looked up from a small pile of diamonds on my desk and brushed overgrown hair from my eyes. My father stood in the doorway to my study; his stance was relaxed and open, a camaraderie between us evident after the past few weeks of my impeccable behaviour.

Placing the loupe onto a velvet case in front of me, I smiled. "Need something?"

Cut cocked his head toward the corridor. "Only a word. We've all been busy with preparations this last week. I think a debrief is in order, don't you?"

My mind prodded at the plans we'd made. The strict timeline when Nila would be ours again. The retaliation we'd lined up to dismiss the fading interest in my family's name. Vaughn was losing power as each day passed. Social media was a feral beast baying for blood, but it was short-lived, quickly moving onto juicier gossip.

The longer we waited, the less power the Weavers had. We'd also fortified our alliances with the local police, who ensured they would stay out of our way this time—otherwise…well, they knew what would fucking happen.

Scooping the diamonds into a soft pouch and storing them in my top drawer, I didn't worry that there were over three hundred thousand pounds worth of stones amongst ballpoint and fountain pens.

Strolling over to Cut, I tapped my pocket to make sure I had my vial of friends with me. The comforting rattle sounded, and with another smile, my father and I walked side by side through the bachelor wing, up the stone staircase, and to his office on the second floor.

My eyes flickered to Jasmine's door. I hadn't seen my sister again. I didn't like being estranged from her, but I was above silly dramatics now. I had no feelings to spare. It was her problem not mine. I wouldn't dwell on it.

The moment we were locked and secluded in his chambers, he motioned to his private stash of rare Rémy Martin cognac. "Please, help yourself to a drink."

"Want one?" I asked, moving to the small bar and uncorking the decanter. My mouth watered as a generous amount splashed into a crystal goblet.

Cut sat in his favourite black chair and placed his feet on the coffee table housing the bleached bones of Wrathbone, his dog. My fingers twitched around the bottle as I remembered the last time Nila had been in here. We'd done the Tally; I'd inked my initials onto her body.

"Please." Cut relaxed into the leather. Our dealings with one another had become highly civilized—businessman to businessman rather than delinquent son and disappointed father. "Untether him for me, too, will you?"

Depositing my drink on the coffee table, I prowled to the window and the beautiful bird perched on its stand. "Hello, Finch." I stroked the breast of Cut's pet hawk.

The bird preened under my attention. Its autumn feathers glinted in the waning sunlight, and its beady eyes remained hidden beneath its blinding cap. A horrible life really—to spend so many waking hours in the dark.

The silkiness of Finch's feathers sent me into a trance. It was funny to think that all three of Bryan Hawk's sons had bird of prey names, yet he never used his. Being the president of the

Black Diamonds meant he used his brotherhood name. However, his nickname had always scared me as a boy. I could imagine him stripping the bones of his enemy's carcass, just like his namesake: the Vulture. Bryan 'Vulture' Hawk. It was apt.

"Free him," Cut ordered.

Tugging on the little tie, I released the blinding cap and Finch immediately traded quiet stroking for violent flapping. The bell around his ankle tinkled as he tried to take off only for the tether to jerk him back.

"Steady, steady," I murmured, undoing the bow and freeing the bird. Finch had been named after his first kill. He hadn't gone for the gerbil we'd released onto the lawn. Instead, he soared high and plucked the tiny prey from the sky and ate it in a few strips.

"Finch," Cut said. "Cast off." He raised his arm, already wrapped in a supple piece of leather. No one wanted a talon through his or her forearm.

In a rustle of burnished feathers, Finch launched from the perch and soared across the room.

Cut grunted as the weight of the large raptor landed on his arm. He grinned, his lined face looking younger and carefree. Stroking the plumage of his pet, he caught the creance and wrapped the cord around his fist to keep him in place.

Heading to the small refrigerator by the wall, I opened a Tupperware container and brought back a delicacy of raw rabbit liver. Finch instantly hopped and snapped his beak as I handed the meat to Cut. He grabbed a bloody piece and tossed it at the bird.

Sitting down, I sipped my cognac.

For a few minutes, we let Finch entertain us, the occasional bell slicing through the squelch of raw liver. Finally, Cut cast off the hawk and let him navigate the room wherever he wanted.

Toasting his glass to mine, his eyes shadowed.

*Finally getting to the point, Father?*

Clinking glasses, I settled back, waiting.

"You know I saw everything that happened between you and Nila. I've shown you the tapes of you fucking her. The close-ups of your face when extracting the debts. I've listed all the times you disobeyed me and went behind my back. You had feelings for her."

I shrugged. Once upon a time, I might've panicked and done everything to deny such a revelation. Now, it didn't matter. I was above all that.

"All in the past, as you well know."

Cut nodded. "I know. That's why I'm bringing this up now. You've seen the light, and I think it's time you know a bit more of the legacy you're upholding."

I crossed my legs, nursing my goblet. "Go on."

"Did you ever stop to think about other Hawks and Weavers who had to pay the debts?"

My forehead furrowed. "No."

"You never thought others might've had the same issues you did?" Nostalgia shaded his face. "I won't deny I had a soft spot for Emma toward the end. She was nothing like her daughter—not insubordinate or stubborn, but she enticed me all the same."

My heartbeat kicked just the tiniest bit.

Without disrupting the conversation, I pulled the small bottle free and tipped a tablet into my palm. "I had no idea." Chasing the pill with a healthy dose of cognac, I added, "I suppose it's logical for any man and woman to have feelings if they're forced together long enough."

Cut stared into his drink. "I suppose."

He always did this. Always hinted at a topic in a roundabout way, waiting to see if I would trip up and reveal things. It might've worked in the past when I had things to hide and nervousness to feel, but now I had nothing.

Blank. Blank. Blank.

My voice was soft. "You did what you were tasked with. Just like I hurt Nila, you hurt Emma."

His eyes connected with mine. "Exactly. You made her

bleed in the First Debt. And I have no doubt you're capable of carrying this inheritance to its conclusion."

A few weeks ago, there was no chance in hell I would've been able to complete the Final Debt. But things were different now.

My loyalties were to the Hawks. I would do my duty. I would inherit what was mine.

"Of course."

I would commit murder.

It was what I was born for.

Cut shook his head, almost in awe. "I wish that drug had been around years ago. I'm so happy to have you on my side after all this time. Not to mention, Bonnie is delighted that you no longer harass Jasmine from her studies."

I smiled, taking another drink. "Yes, we both know it was time for me to grow up."

Finch suddenly flew overhead; his russet feathers a rainbow of orange, brown, and taupe.

Cut sighed, running a hand through his white hair. "There is one thing I need to bring up, before we can put the past behind us." His body tightened. "You can probably guess what I'm about to say."

*Could I?*

I wracked my brains.

What had he hated about me the most? My inability to obey? My endless problems? Or was it the fact I'd slept with Nila with nothing barred and somehow lost a piece of myself that I would never get back—no matter how numb I was?

"You'll have to enlighten me. I have no idea what you mean."

"I must admit, you were beyond stupid. If those pills hadn't worked, I would've put you down for that infraction alone."

My eyebrow raised. "Oh? This will be interesting. Don't torture me with suspense—what did I do?"

He grinned. "I'd hoped you would be able to tell me why.

Explain in your words what the fuck was going on in your screwed-up mind. But I guess that won't happen now that your insanity is cured."

*Insanity.*

That annoying little word. Out of everything, it still had a smidgen of power over me. I hated that label. All my life, I'd been called insane, broken. My father had sent me away as a young boy to undergo counselling and get psychiatric help. The conclusion came back stating I was demented, mentally unsound.

Every day of my childhood, Cut reminded me of my flaws. I'd come to hate those words. *Despise* those words.

Cut laughed again, dragging me back to the present. "Can I ask if you did it because you truly didn't think, or were you more clever than I gave you credit?"

A slight headache began. "I honestly have no idea what you're getting at."

*What the fuck?*

Until I had a guess, I wouldn't say a word. I'd learned how to hide, and those habits were hard to break.

Cut laughed—a full belly chuckle dancing with pride.

My heart swelled. I'd never get tired of having him be proud of me.

"Your balls are iron, Jet. I'll give you that. I always hoped having your own pet Weaver would fix you." Leaning forward, he clasped my knee. "I like this man before me. I'm honoured to call him my son."

*Shit...wow.*

Clearing my throat, I raised my glass to him. "Appreciate that, Father. More than you know."

Reclining back in his chair, Cut said quietly, "Let me give you a quick history. You've seen the tapes of what I did to Emma, so you know what is required of you. In turn, you know what *isn't* required of you." He tilted his head. "The men of our family are weak when it comes to their Weavers. They fucked them—same as you. They fell prey to their charms—same as you." His voice darkened. "However, unlike you, your forefathers saw what the Weavers were doing by enticing them into their beds. Nila is just like her ancestors. She was using sex to get to you—using her body to screw up your mind, and it fucking worked."

My glass was empty. I wanted another.

Cut grew angry—the same mask I recognised slipping into place. "I have no issues with you fucking her. But what *does* make me rage is you did it without protection."

I froze.

Conveniently, my mind had buried that titbit beneath all the other crap I'd been dealing with. No protection equals...

"Every time you sank inside that little whore, her face screamed victory. For her it wasn't lust or love for you, Jethro, it was happiness at being the winner. She used you and it worked."

Memories of her claiming to win made their way through my druggy fog.

*He's right.*

Cut continued, "If your plaything is attractive, it only makes sense to use her for pleasure. As I mentioned before, Hawks are weak in that area and the Weavers somehow carry that knowledge in their bones. Didn't you think there'd been accidents? Birth control wasn't around at the start of this contract. Did you stop to wonder if there were half-breeds born of both Hawk and Weaver bloodlines? Impure abominations?"

My heart went from slow to interested. "No, I hadn't." I honestly hadn't contemplated much of our heritage or history. Would that void the contract then? Firstborn carrying both genes?

*I guess not, because it's still in effect.*

"What happened to them?"

Cut smiled cruelly. "Same thing that happened to their mothers."

The alcohol I'd consumed oozed through my blood.

He leaned forward. "When Nila returns, when the time comes to extract more debts, you're free to do whatever you want with her. I'll put an end to any illegitimate offspring, and as long as you teach that whore her place, then I give you my vow that on your thirtieth birthday, I will gladly hand you the keys to everything I own. It will all be yours, Jethro."

Finch majestically landed on the back of the couch, his beak sharp and deadly. Cut stroked the bird as if no threat echoed in his words.

I raised my empty glass. "Her tricks won't work again, Father. Consider my eyes open and my heart firmly aligned with the Hawks."

"Good to hear." His gaze locked on mine. "Because if you disappoint me again, there will be *two* bodies in Nila Weaver's grave. Mark my words, Jet. I love you, but I won't hesitate to kill you if you screw this up again."

Twenty-one days.

Five hundred and four hours. One hundred and twenty-seven tablets.

I hadn't relapsed. I'd taken my medicine religiously, and Cut had tested me thoroughly.

I'd passed.

I was ready.

To celebrate the next stage of our plan, my father took the brotherhood off the estate to a local pub in the village. He hired out the entire place and bought each Black Diamond member dinner along with an open bar.

The night was full of laughter and drunken idiocy. Kes remained cool but friendly, and Daniel drank far too much, as fucking usual. I enjoyed myself, growing in my role as heir and basking in the way my men watched me. They looked at me the same way they looked at Cut—with trepidation and respect.

I'd truly taken my place, and there was no mistaking I was next in line for the throne.

After a four-course dinner and plenty of crude innuendoes, Cut stood at the head of the table, clinking a knife against his half-empty beer.

The low ceilings of the 16$^{th}$ century pub pressed down on us with hops drying in the rafters. It was quaint and country—so different to the imposing halls and artifacts of Hawksridge.

"Attention." Cut tapped his glass again. Men continued to snicker and drink. Cut slammed his glass down, making the dirty plates rattle. "Attention!"

Silence fell; all eyes zeroed in on Cut. "Time to toast. Listen up."

A few men saluted while others sobered.

"Stand up, Jethro."

The past three weeks had changed us. His face had lost its pinched anger. I'd lost my defiant hatred. We no longer looked at each other like we wanted to kill and maim.

We were equals.

I got my wish. I found a place in my family. I became... *him*.

Cut raised his arms. "Tonight is a special night, boys. Not only have we expanded across Sierra Leone this month and done more trades than ever before, but I believe luck has finally granted us a true successor."

I'd done everything he'd asked. Put everything into place like he wished. And tonight, I'd earned his ultimate respect.

He tilted his glass to me. "The newspapers are bored with shredding my name. The black market dealers are back to buying in bulk, and our notoriety has only strengthened. The Weavers think they've won, but this is only the beginning."

I planted my heavy boots on the ancient floor, mirroring him in a toast. "Here, here."

The men followed, murmuring ascent.

We'd all seen the newspapers, the broadcasts of Vaughn Weaver telling secrets that should never be told. He thought he'd ruined us. That any moment we'd be arrested and convicted.

*Stupid, stupid idiot.*

Dressed in black leather with our stitched emblem of Black Diamonds on the pocket, I felt invincible. Nothing could stop us now. No one could even try.

I was untouchable. And it was fucking magical.

"To Jethro." Cut's voice softened. "To my son. To Kite. I'm so glad you've finally seen the error of your ways. I always knew you had potential and have no doubt you'll earn everything I have to give before this is over."

I nodded. "You can trust me."

The men stomped their feet, sloshing their beer onto the table.

Kestrel patted my back. "I hope you know what you're doing."

Daniel gave me a signature smirk. "Roll on the next debt, brother."

I was firstborn.

This was my legacy.

After weeks of preparation, I'd agreed once and for all to prove it.

By killing Nila Weaver.

# Nila

LIFE MOVED ON.

I learned to live with a broken heart and stopped jumping at shadows.

No one came to steal me back, and the threat of destroying my family's life went unresolved. However, I had one question that never left: *Are they just biding their time?*

In my mind, I lived in a fake world of normalcy and safety. But somewhere out of sight, clouds were forming—growing heavier and more powerful every day.

I no longer trusted that the police could help or that publicity could keep me safe.

If the Hawks weren't done with me, there was nothing anyone could do.

Hour after hour, I wondered why I stayed. Why I headed into the factory to work under crazy deadlines and demanding buyers. Why didn't I just run?

The passion to create had gone.

I had no wish to sew.

I hated my listlessness.

I hated the coldness inside that no one could touch.

I lived in constant trepidation; serpents gathered in my gut, hissing with premonition. I missed Jethro with every fibre of my being. He was dazzling sunlight and now I lived in endless darkness.

I was dying without him.

But it wasn't finished.

The debts weren't done.

Vaughn wanted me to fly to Asia and hide. Father wanted me to enter witness protection and escape.

I didn't want to do any of those things and worried about all of us—about what this had done to my family. But despite my worries, my clothing brand exploded overnight.

*Nila* went from exclusive couture to being the most wanted garments in all major department stores. Vaughn became the face of menswear and even dabbled in design himself.

And me...

I went from Weaver Whore to a slave for the Weaver Empire. I didn't have the drive I once did but didn't have the heart to tell my family.

The only time I had to stand still was to wobble with a vertigo attack.

I was paraded before media.

I was the centre of a worldwide scandal.

I was a marionette.

All I could do was clutch my brother as my life spiralled out of control.

I missed the tranquillity of Hawksridge.

I missed the lavender-scented breeze when I sat out in the gardens and sketched.

But most of all, I missed the soul-deep connection with Jethro.

I'd continued to bombard him with messages, but he didn't text back.

Not once.

Not a single time.

My gut churned as the world laughed. Questions followed me wherever I went:

*How could they get away with that?*

*Why didn't they tell someone?*
*Why didn't they run?*
Even I felt that way.

Yes, the Debt Inheritance was used as a tool to wield power. Yes, it granted certain privileges to our pain. But none of that was the real reason.

There was nothing to stop Jethro or his family setting up a sniper rifle on the building opposite our home and firing rounds of ammo through our windows, slicing our lifespan in a blink.

They didn't need the Debt Inheritance to kill us.

This was something more.

A game.

Something I felt was more to do with Jethro than with me. I was just the unlucky target. Just like any employee had to prove their loyalty and skills before a promotion, I had a horrible feeling I was Jethro's final test.

Needle&Thread: *I don't know why I keep messaging you. You've cut me out of your life completely. Three weeks, Kite. Three long weeks of nothing. You've hurt me worse than anyone. I miss talking. I miss our messages. I miss...*

I pressed send before I could delete it.

I shouldn't miss him—not when he obviously felt nothing for me.

*Try telling my stupid heart that.*

My stupid heart fed me worry. I feared for his life. I had no way of knowing if he was alive or dead.

Waiting for a new message reminded me of the very beginning when I first started messaging him. I'd hang on a thread for one tiny response—waiting for a sliver of his attention. It seemed I'd gone full circle.

I leaned over to dump the phone into my bedside drawer when something miraculous happened.

It vibrated.

*Oh, my God!*

Fumbling with the lock screen, I swiped it on and stared greedily at the first text from Jethro in almost a month.

Kite007: *That's cruel, leaving the message unfinished.*

My heart thundered. Resting against my pillows, I replied:

Needle&Thread: *You're cruel, not replying to any of them.*

Kite007: *Cruel is my middle name.*

I glanced at my fingertip tattoo and its inked JKH.

Needle&Thread: *No, it's not.*

Kite007: *Believe what you want to believe.*

Needle&Thread: *What happened to you? Tell me. You seem different.*

Kite007: *I am different.*

My chest deflated, sorrow drowning my veins. He'd let them win. He'd changed.

Needle&Thread: *You might believe you're different, but I know what happened between us. It's not over because you care for me.*

Kite007: *That's in the past. But you're right. What happened between us isn't finished.*

My spine whipped straight. What did he mean?

Needle&Thread: *The world knows. I heard they questioned your father. It's only a matter of time before he's convicted. The debts are over. It means we can be together—truly with no horrible ending hovering over us.*

Kite007: *Still such a naïve little Weaver.*

Tears bruised my eyes. In a few words, he'd successfully tarnished my memories of him and made me doubt.

My hands shook as I responded.

Needle&Thread: *You said you'd tell me everything—who you are...what you suffer. I'm asking you...tell me. Don't let them win.*

I couldn't stand the thought of Jethro going to jail for what he'd done. Even though he deserved punishing—he'd been under the control of Cut. If he let me help him...he could stop his family and finally be happy...with me.

Kite007: *I'm not that man anymore. There's nothing to tell.*

My heart fell out of my chest.

Needle&Thread: *Don't do this, Jethro.*

Kite007: *It's not up to me, Threads.*

My world screeched to a halt. That nickname. It wasn't his to use.

Needle&Thread: *How do you know that name?*

Kite007: *Come on, silly girl. You think I don't know everything about you? You think the past month you've been free of me? That I'm not there...watching you?*

Goosebumps splattered across my arms. If his tone was nicer, I would've been thrilled to know he'd been watching me. That he missed me and had to stay close.

But his tone was sinister—reminding me all too much of Milan.

I tried to reply, but I had nothing left.

My silence encouraged another text from him.

The phone came alive in my hands.

Kite007: *Your time is almost up, Nila Weaver. Enjoy it. I'm coming for you.*

*I'm coming for you.*
I couldn't think of anything else.
*I'm coming for you.*
But when?
Work the next day did nothing to ease my state of mind.

I suffered three vertigo incidents before lunch, and when I finally had time to eat, I threw it all up again.

*Please. Please...don't let my sickness be what I think it is.*

I pressed my forehead against the cool porcelain of my private toilet in my office as more nausea tore through my system.

I couldn't ignore it any longer.

Dreadful horror crept over me.

I had unprotected sex.

Jethro came in me.

*Twice.*

I moaned as the room spun again.

*I can't be pregnant. I can't!*
Doctors had always told me I ran too much. My periods had stopped coming a year ago, and they said I'd tricked my body into believing it was in starvation mode; therefore, it wasn't strong enough to have children.
I'd been careless.
I'd been fucking stupid.
*Why did I think I could ignore it?*
Stumbling to my feet, I grabbed my purse and charged out of the warehouse with its steampunk vibe and countless cubicles all with private sewing machines. My bodyguards that Tex had commissioned were somewhere close by, but I didn't want them following me.
Not for this.
I didn't take a breath until I'd run down the stairs and dashed down the road to a local pharmacy. I didn't think people might witness me buying a pregnancy test, and I definitely didn't think I would bump into my twin as I came out with a little paper bag clutched in my hands. All I focused on was getting answers. Answers I should've learned weeks ago.
*I can't be pregnant!*
I slammed into his hard bulk.
V's dark eyes widened, his arms automatically coming out to catch me. "Threads! Been looking for you. I have a new idea for the backlog and—" His gaze dropped to my fingers, concern etching his brow. "Eh, you okay?"
My cheeks heated.
*No, I'm not okay.*
I nodded, backing away from him and hiding the test behind me. "Yes, I'm fine. I have to return to work. See you later, alright?"
Pushing past, I bolted across the road, summoned the lift, and flew into my office in record speed.
The moment I was safe, I locked the door and charged into the bathroom.
"Please. *Please* don't let me be pregnant."

The mantra wouldn't stop echoing in my head. There was no logical way I could be pregnant. *Surely!*
It was explainable. *I'm not pregnant.*
My hands trembled as I ripped open the baby-blue box and read the instructions. I'd never had to do this before. It was almost as embarrassing peeing on the testing strip as it was making myself come by a showerhead.
My head pounded.
Was that only last month? Had I gone from writhing with fantasies of Jethro Hawk to spiralling into panic thinking he'd knocked me up?
*Oh, God.*
"Please, don't let me be pregnant!"
Shaking, I fumbled with what I had to do. Once done, I placed the cap back on the wet strip and tossed the test into the sink. I couldn't touch it any longer. I couldn't look.
*Oh, God.*
*Oh, God!*
I stepped away.
I stepped so far away.
I backed up against the wall, bracing myself against the cool grey tile.
*I'm not pregnant.*
*I would know if I was pregnant.*
*You've been throwing up a lot.*
*That's explainable.*
*You suffer from vertigo.*
*You. Are. Not. Pregnant.*
My inner thoughts henpecked and argued, swinging between screaming for being so stupid, to planning how to kill myself just to get this nightmare over with.
Five minutes ticked past, and I still didn't have the courage to look.
*Go on.*
*Get it over with.*
"Nila?"

Oh, my God, this couldn't get any worse. What was my brother doing in my office? I locked the bloody door!

*He has a key.*

Two seconds later, he rapped his knuckles on the bathroom. "Threads? You okay?"

My throat closed up. I wanted the ground to fissure and swallow me.

"Nila, answer me. I'm worried about you."

Swallowing back a sudden avalanche of tears, I pushed off from the wall to open the door.

Only the door swung wide, presenting my perfect brother in jeans and a white t-shirt. He looked as if he'd stepped off a runway, while I looked like a homeless ragamuffin.

His eyes went first to the damn pregnancy test in the vanity, then swung to me.

His dusky colouring went ashen; his eyes darkened. "Please. Please. *Please* tell me that animal didn't fucking *rape* you." Prowling forward, he seethed in the small space. His temper bounced off the tiles, ricocheting with violence. "Nila, tell me right now. Did that cocksucker fucking touch you?!"

I laughed. If only it had been that easy. That *awful*. I would have an excuse for my stupidity. This was all on me.

V's lips twisted in horror as my laugh turned into a sob.

*It wasn't rape. It was glorious. It was everything I ever wanted and can never have again.*

More tears erupted, giving way to the avalanche.

"Threads, hey. It's okay. We can get you help." Vaughn closed the distance and tugged me into his arms. "It's okay, sis. Honest. I've got you."

His concern was worse than his anger.

More tears.

More sobs.

I struggled. I didn't want him touching me. Not when I didn't know if I could live with myself. But his gentle warmth—so unlike Jethro's frostiness—seeped into me. I sagged. I hadn't let myself cry since the morning I'd been taken from Hawksridge. But now, I couldn't stop.

I let it all go.

Somehow amongst my tears, I stuttered, "He—he didn't ra—rape me, V."

Just admitting I'd brought this on myself filled me with another wave of shame, of remorse.

V stiffened. His arms bunched as he pulled back, looking into my eyes. "What do you mean, he didn't..." Understanding suddenly swamped his face. "Fuck, Nila! You *slept* with him?" Tearing his hands from me as if he were contaminated, he snarled, "You slept with that motherfucker—*willingly?*"

My tears dried up. I hung my head. "Vaughn, don't."

"*Don't?*" He stormed to the vanity and swiped the pregnancy test into his fist. He shoved it in my face, hiding the viewing window so I couldn't see if I'd just ruined my life by being impregnated with Hawk spawn.

"You slept with him unprotected!" He snorted. "Bet Tex will be so happy to know all his energy at keeping you sheltered was in vain. The first guy you're around and you have to fucking screw him and get pregnant!"

"I don't know if I'm pregnant yet!"

"Should we find out then?" He presented his palm, holding up the test. "I can't believe you. God, Nila!"

I didn't want to see.

I wanted to see.

The results were upside down.

V noticed at the same time I did. He rolled his fingers so the test bounced upright.

One little line.

One.

*What does that mean?!*

I quivered with terror. "The packet—what does the packet say?"

Vaughn looked behind him, returning to the vanity to pluck the discarded box from the bowl. Passing it to me, he threw the test into the bin and washed his hands. As he ran the water, it gave me time to figure out this mess, while he got a hold on his temper.

I flipped the box.

*"Congratulations, you're pregnant if you see two blue lines."*

Two.

I slithered into a puddle.

*Thank you. Thank you. Thank you!*

V spun around, his face losing the angry glare and melting into regret. "It's negative?"

I nodded.

*No baby.*

Suddenly, I didn't know how I felt about that.

I eyed the rubbish bin. I couldn't leave the test in there. I couldn't run the risk of prying staff or my father jumping to conclusions.

The moment V left, I'd take it to the bin in the park opposite our factory.

He sighed. "I'm sorry, Threads. I was out of line." He came by my side, sliding down the wall to wrap an arm around my shoulders. "You okay?"

I tilted my head, resting against his shoulder. He was so good to me. How could I resent him and Tex for saving me?

"Yes," I whispered. "I'll be fine."

V squeezed me. "Talk to me, Threads. You haven't said one word about what they did to you. Every time I bring it up, you change the subject." Sighing again, he added, "If you don't talk to me, you have to talk to someone. I can feel that you're unhappy. I'm feeding off your vibes." Nudging my shoulder with his, he smirked. "Twin link, remember? I could always tell if you were hurting."

Something about what he said tickled my brain, trying to connect dots that I couldn't follow.

"I'll be okay soon. I promise."

*Let me mend my broken heart in peace.*

He couldn't know I'd fallen for Jethro—not after his campaign of death and destruction against the firstborn Hawk.

We sat there in silence for a few moments. V gave me quietness with no judgement, allowing me to put myself back together again. Slowly, my heart rate calmed, shoving away the panic.

V's touch was like a butterfly, whispering sweetly over my shoulder. He'd always been so gentle with me—so different to the man I'd fallen for. Jethro had been anything but gentle. He'd whipped me, fucked me, and adored me in his own dark way.

*He scarred me.*

I flinched to think what Vaughn would do if he saw what existed beneath my teal blouse. The scars Jethro had painted me with from the First Debt blemished me forever. V wouldn't be happy. Shit, I'd go so far as to say he'd tie up Jethro and give him the same punishment—only a lot harder.

Squeezing my eyes, I tried to push away those concerns. Vaughn would never know because I would never show him.

V stiffened, his fingers digging into my skin.

"What? What is it?" I shifted in his hold, peering into his eyes.

"Nothing. Forget it."

I paused. Normally, if V had a thought, I could pick up on his idea. We were in tune with work, with life. But this time, I had no clue.

Pinching him, I said, "Come on. You can't leave me hanging like that. Give me something else to think about other than this catastrophe."

Vaughn shook his head, looking as if he wanted to tear the thought from his brain. "I—no, you don't need to hear it."

"And you don't have to feel my sadness, yet you do." Sitting up, I untangled his arm from around me. "Tell me."

He sat taller, running a hand through his glossy black hair. "What if you *had* been pregnant?"

I froze. "What do you mean?"

He looked away. "This madness with the Hawks is over. The police are involved. The media know everything. You're as safe as I could make you by telling everyone what I know. But...what if it's not enough."

Tremors captured my limbs. Jethro's text came back to haunt me.

*I'm coming for you.*

"What do you mean?"

V looked at me, his eyes tight and grave. "What if you had his kid? What if you gave birth to a girl?"

My mind raced. "She'd be a firstborn girl. She'd suffer the same fate our mother and I did. I would *never* put her through that."

V shook his head. "She'd be firstborn. She'd be a girl. She'd be a Weaver." He leaned closer. "But she'd also be a Hawk."

V's epiphany changed everything.

I couldn't stop thinking about alternatives, imagining an entirely different conclusion to the Debt Inheritance, to Jethro, to our future as enemies.

Jethro said he was coming for me.

I didn't know when and I didn't know how...but what if I let him?

What if I went back with him *willingly*? Instead of saving him and running, why not do something to end the debt completely? I could *end* this—like I'd promised my dead ancestors.

Would it work?

Would my scheming of seducing him over and over again until I became pregnant be abhorrent or justified?

Did it make me a terrible person to contemplate bringing another life into this madness—all in the hope of breaking the debts hold?

Could I even stomach becoming pregnant with a firstborn of mixed blood? Would Jethro agree to something so drastic—so crazy? Would I go to hell for trapping someone that way?

My mind whirled with more and more questions.

If I *did* do all of those things—would it destroy everything? Put an end to debts being collected because the debts were now merged? Why had no one thought of it sooner? *Is it even possible?*

There were dreadful flaws to my plan. Cut barely tolerated his own children. I couldn't see him decreeing the Debt Inheritance null and void just because the firstborn of both houses was *made* from both houses. I couldn't see him giving up that easily.

But Jethro...he might.

If he had something of his own...for the first time in his life...

Would he fight to protect it?

Would he finally give me his heart and choose me over them?

He could change.

He could save me.

He could save himself.

# Jethro

THE NIGHT BEFORE everything changed, my phone buzzed.

Two a.m., but I was still awake.

The tablets had numbed me to everything, but I still had issues sleeping.

Opening the message, a slow smile crossed my face.

Needle&Thread: *You said this isn't over. That you're coming for me. Well, I want you to come. I'm here waiting, Jethro. Hurry up.*

My cock twitched. Her message was almost perfect. Could she sense everything was in place? Could she tell that her home was here...with me...and it was time she returned?

Kite007: *I appreciate the invitation.*

She took her time replying. The longer it took, the harder I got. A side effect of the pills was my libido had dried up. But here...lying in the dark with no one to see or judge, I cupped my length and squeezed.

Needle&Thread: *It's not an invitation. It's an order. I'm waiting for you.*

I pinched the head of my cock, wondering how to reply. Another message arrived.

Needle&Thread: *I'm wet for you. Kiss me, Jethro Hawk.*

My cock jerked in my hold. Fuck.

I growled under my breath.

My father's wise words came back. *"Nila is just like her ancestors. She was using sex to get to you—using her body to screw up your mind, and it fucking worked."*

I fisted harder. Not this time. She wouldn't manipulate me again. I knew my place. I liked this new world, and I had no intention of stepping out of it.

Kite007: *You know I don't respond to orders.*

Needle&Thread: *Would you respond if I begged you?*

My hand worked harder, dragging pleasure up my shaft and radiating in my balls.

I didn't want to reply. I wanted this charade over with. If I fucked her again, it would be part of a debt—not breaking the rules like I had.

I'd been idiotic. A rebel son who didn't appreciate all that he'd been given.

In her absence, I finally saw the truth.

In my tablet fog, I finally found my home.

And it wasn't with her.

Kite007: *What would you beg for?*

If she were smart, she'd beg me to forget her. To run across continents and try to hide. But she wasn't smart, because she was still governed by inconvenient, uncontrollable emotion.

Needle&Thread: *I would beg for your tongue to kiss me deep. I would moan for your fingers to stretch me and make me wet, and I would get on my knees and suck you for the chance to have you inside me again.*

My eyes rolled back as I worked myself faster. My breathing puffed in the silence of my room.

What was she doing? Debts had dragged us together, but life had given us that magical spark that made even the simplest of touches or barest of smiles cataclysmic. It was fucking dangerous, and I had no intention of playing with fire again.

I had other things to chase. *Better* things.

Kite007: *If you're lucky, I might let you taste me again.*

Only while she was paying the Third Debt and nothing else. And I doubted she'd want anything to do with me by that point.

Needle&Thread: *All of you?*
Kite007: *Don't get greedy, little Weaver.*
My hand bruised hot flesh, jerking with violence as I crested and craved. My dick hardened. A release grew stronger, just out of reaching distance. Picking up my pace, I thrust into my palm, driving myself toward the goal.

The residue of the last pill I'd taken five hours ago faded, letting me live in bliss for a short moment. Falling back into insanity, I typed:

Kite007: *I'm fucking myself. Are you jealous?*
Needle&Thread: *Obscenely jealous.*
Kite007: *Rub yourself. I want to hear you moan.*
Needle&Thread: *If I were in your bed, you'd hear me scream.*
Goddammit.

I gritted my jaw; my hips drove faster into my hand. My breathing accelerated until my bed creaked with my thrusts. In a few short hours, I would collect her—not because she'd 'invited me' but because it was time.

Our plan was in place. It was time for execution. *In more ways than one.*

Needle&Thread: *I'm so close, Kite. So close to coming. I need you to collect me. I want to be fucked by you again.*

I came.

I couldn't help it.

With a loud groan, ribbons of white shot through the air and splattered against my naked belly. Wave after wave, I rode through vicious pleasure. The foggy haze dispersed just long enough for me to twitch and moan with the first sensation I'd had in weeks.

Breathing hard, I typed one last message:

Kite007: *Don't go into the dark alone, little Weaver. Monsters roam the shadows, and your time is officially up.*

With a cold smile, I tucked the phone inside my drawer and wiped down my stomach with a sock. My breathing slowly steadied as I rested my head on my pillow. Taking the small bottle from its safe place beside me, I swallowed a pill and felt the change instantly.

Whereas before there was sensitivity, now there was nothing.

I was back to being blank, and the next time I saw her, she'd finally understand the errors of her ways.

She'd had me and lost me.

Now it was time to suffer the consequences.

It was cold tonight.

My breath billowed as I shrugged into my leather jacket and straddled my new Harley. My gloved hands were warm, my uncut feet toasty in my heavy boots.

I no longer had to hurt myself to stay sane.

I had something better.

Pulling out the small bottle, I popped another tablet of the best medicine in the world. I'd taken an extra dose today—just to be sure—and welcomed the familiar blanket over my thoughts.

My heart was a lump of snow, my extremities their usual ice.

I pulled down the black visor on my helmet.

I was no longer human but a black shadow.

The Grim Reaper.

A Hawk about to steal what was rightfully mine.

I left at midnight.

Leaving Hawksridge behind and driving at crazy speeds from Buckinghamshire to London, I counted the minutes until she'd be mine again.

I doubted she'd planned on this when she'd texted me last night. I couldn't wait to see her face and for her to finally understand what'd changed in the month we'd spent apart.

There were three of us on the road.

Me, Kes, and Flaw.

They flanked me and had my back—just in case the Weavers got any ideas. After all, we'd bided our time to make them complacent, but I wouldn't underestimate them again. Not after the sneaky fuck up Vaughn had created.

The entire journey, I thought about Nila's text messages.

I grew hard again, knowing that soon she would belong to me and I could once again prove to my father that his leniency toward me was justified.

Nila was nothing to me. Not anymore.

Time flew as we tore through the night with a roar of engines and smoke. The smell of gasoline filled my nostrils.

I was high on octane, and soon I would be high on thievery.

I was stealing what was rightfully mine.

I was claiming her, exterminating her.

Her fate was mine. There was never any other way. No alternative ending.

She was a Weaver.

I was a Hawk.

*This is it.*

I was outside her house.

I killed the engine.

# Nila

I WOKE TO a dangerous darkness.
My heart rate exploded the moment my eyes tore open.
*He's here.*
I knew it as surely as I knew my name.
*He's in my room.*
I couldn't see him.
I couldn't smell him.
But I *sensed* him.
Coldness and anger and bite.
"Jethro—?"
I blinked, peering into dark corners.
*He's come for me.*
I knew it stronger than anything.
*It's not over.*
But this time...I had a plan. I wasn't the victim. I wasn't some stupid girl who'd been sheltered by her family. I'd stared death in the face—I'd been in its clutches—and I knew how to survive.
"Hello, Ms. Weaver."
His silky, icy voice whispered beneath my sheets, hardening my nipples to rocks. My core clenched, feeding off his power, getting wet on the sheer deliciousness of having him near.

*Oh, God.*

After so much time apart, he was visceral, mystical, *mythical* in his power over me.

He had a magic—a spell that softened me, even while fear percolated in my blood. I knew he wasn't safe, knew that I ought to scream and stab him, rather than grow wet and want him.

But I'd made a pact. *I will be the last Weaver.*

I had the strength to stand up to Jethro and his family. He was mine. I just had to make him accept it.

"I told you I would come for you."

The shadows twisted, revealing him as he stepped from the pitch black, moving closer toward my bed. He was dressed in leather and denim; an outfit I'd seen Cut and Daniel wear but never Jethro. He was no longer an aristocrat but a biker. The embroidery on his jacket glinted, and his large boots were whisper-quiet on the carpet. He looked like the devil—a deliciously dark sinner who'd come to ravage and possess me.

Another ripple of desire shot through my belly.

The closer he came, the more the past month faded. The lostness, the incessant vertigo, the lack of conviction I'd suffered ever since leaving just *disappeared.*

It was as if I'd never left Hawksridge. I couldn't imagine why I would.

*I can think why.*

A torrent of torture and threats filled my mind. Cut and Daniel and Kes. They were my true enemies. Did I really want to go back there? I doubted I would get a second chance to escape.

*I know what I have to do.*

I knew how to end this. I knew how to save Jethro. And I was prepared to do anything to make that happen.

"Hello, Kite," I murmured.

Jethro sucked in a breath, his chest expanding as he closed the final distance and towered over my bed. His heavy clothes couldn't hide his sensual bulk. Every time he breathed, a soft creak of leather filled the silence. The thread used to stitch the diamond on his front pocket glinted in the moonlight.

I'd never seen him in full motorcycle regalia.

It did terrible things to my core. I couldn't stop my craving—the heat in my blood or the wetness gathering between my legs. My mouth tingled to touch his, to bite his bottom lip and suck his tongue.

The room turned static. The hair on my arms stood up at the very thought of Jethro shrugging out of his jacket and climbing on top of me.

He swallowed, his eyes glittering dangerously. Holding up a small packet of powder, he whispered, "Do I need to drug you again, or will you come willingly?" He bent over me, his long fingers tracing my leg beneath the covers.

I trembled, frozen...desperate for him to drop the act and end the chilliness between us.

We'd been so close. *Connected.* Something sinister slipped over my thoughts. *Something's wrong.*

"I asked you a question, Ms. Weaver." His gaze dropped to my legs, his fingers tugging at the sheets. Inch by inch, he pulled, sliding the warmth down.

I didn't say a word as he revealed my camisole, black satin shorts, and legs; the same legs itching to wrap around his hips while he took me hard.

"I missed you." I couldn't look away. The night beneath Hawksridge—the way he'd touched me in the springs and brought me back to life—made my heart swell.

He hadn't said the words. But I'd felt his submission.

He'd fallen, too.

Just as hard as me.

Removing his hand from my covers, he tucked the drug packet back into his breast pocket. "Let me explain what will happen if you don't honour your invitation and come with me." His voice slipped into emotionless chill. "Vaughn and your father are asleep inside this house. They no longer have the interest of the press or media, and it would bring me great pleasure to teach your twin a lesson. Two seconds is all it would take to remove them from any future problems." He bared his teeth. "They deserve it after the mess they've caused."

Anxiety crept higher up my spine. His temper swirled around us as if we stood in the centre of a blizzard. I was used to that with Jethro. But whereas before I could sense something warm beneath his rage...now, there was nothing.

*Touch him. Thaw him.*

Swinging my legs out of bed, I gripped the edge of the mattress. "I said I would come with you and I meant it." I did my best to hide my building terror. "Leave them alone. This is between you and me." Taking a deep breath, I stood, bracing myself for a vertigo attack.

So many times over the past month, I would stumble whenever I stood. But this time...I remained stable.

My eyes widened, drinking in Jethro.

*He* does *fix me.*

He gave me too much to think about. Too much to analyse and read into. My brain was too frantic trying to see between his words to give into a useless imbalance.

"Did you come last night?" I murmured, remembering our messages.

His jaw clenched. "What happened last night or any other night no longer has any relevance in your future."

I shook my head, my heart smarting with pain. "What happened to you?" I reached for him, wanting to clutch his forearm and reassure myself that our bond was still there.

With a sneer, he sidestepped, staying out of reach. "What *happened* to me?" Smiling coldly, he made me seem as if I were some idiot child asking for the universe's secrets. "I got better. That's what happened to me."

"I don't—I don't understand. You weren't ill."

"You wouldn't understand. No one can understand another's problems. All you need to know is that I'm cured and I won't make the same mistakes again."

I took a step back, goosebumps scattering over my body.

"Don't say that. I'm in love with you. Something like that cannot be undone—"

"Love is a chemical imbalance, Ms. Weaver. I am no longer imbalanced." He came closer. "Don't get cold feet on your invitation. You promised you would come, and you don't want to give me a reason to punish you so soon...do you?"

My skin pinpricked with panic. That sentence should've dripped with eroticism. But it wasn't. It was cold...lifeless...*like him*.

Snapping his fingers, Jethro held out his hand. He kept his digits curled slightly so I couldn't see the tattoo marks on the tips. "Come. I want to be back at Hawksridge before sunrise."

I eyed his hand, taking another step backward. My instincts blared that all of this was wrong. My careful planning of seducing him and carrying his baby was obsolete if he'd turned back into the monster who'd stolen me from Milan.

"What did they do to you?" I breathed. "This can't be real."

He snorted. "They?" Stalking forward, he snatched my wrist. "*They* did nothing." Yanking me forward, he slammed me against his body. "*You* did this, pretty little Weaver. Don't blame anyone else for your flaws. I no longer do. I've accepted them. I've dealt with them. And now it's time to go."

He pulled me again, knocking me off balance. Pressing a hand against the chilly zipper of his jacket, I said, "I'll come with you. I've *told* you that. But first let me write a letter to V."

Jethro sneered. "No. No more letters or scams. The whole world believes they're privy to our private business. Your family has done enough damage without telling your brother how to rescue you again."

I shook my head, my knees shaking.

What had he done?

*Why is he so different?*

He was scaring me and not in a good 'I want to blow you and then let you fuck me kind of way' more of a 'I'm thinking of stabbing you in the heart to see if you've misplaced it' kind of way.

"It's for those reasons that I'm leaving him a letter." Twisting my wrist, I broke his hold and beelined for my wardrobe.

I was about to leave this house, this bedroom, this world. *My* world.

For good this time.

I had no intention of coming back.

I would either win or lose.

My destiny was elsewhere. I had no urge to pack anything—most of my things were still at Hawksridge anyway. Seeing as Jethro was in leather, I assumed he'd come on his two-wheeled death machine.

Rifling through my drawers, I quickly pulled on a pair of black skinny jeans, a black sweater, and tapered leather jacket to match his ensemble. We were both creatures of the night.

Jethro crossed his arms, glaring as I slipped on a pair of knee-high boots and stomped past him. "I'm leaving a note, and then we'll go." Not waiting for Jethro to reply, I headed toward my desk and tore off a piece of paper from my sketchpad. With my scalp prickling, I selected a ballpoint and tried to concentrate.

A rustle of denim sounded as Jethro came closer. His large bulk seethed behind me, watching my every move.

I waited for that spark—the lust that was always beneath the surface. But once again, there was nothing but ice.

Sighing heavily, I wrote:

*Dear V and Dad.*

*I love you. I hope you know that.*

*The past few weeks with you have been tough, but I love you both so much. I don't want to seem ungrateful for your hard work rescuing me, but this is something I have to do.*

*Don't come get me.*

*Don't worry on my behalf.*

*I have a plan.*

*If it works, then I'll see you again.*

*If it doesn't, then I'll forever be your Nila.*
I didn't sign it. I just folded it in half and left it unaddressed on the table.
I spun to face my kidnapper for the second time in my short life. At least this time, I wasn't petrified of the unknown. I knew exactly what I'd agreed to and how hard it would be.
Jethro clenched his jaw. "What plan, Ms. Weaver?"
I suffered a mental image of him thawing and falling in love with me all over again—no hidden lies, no secrets. I imagined him holding a black-haired baby girl with a combination of his perfect white skin and my tanned heritage. A Hawk-Weaver. A new legacy that would erase the sins of her forbearers.
*Am I strong enough to make that happen?*
"No plan. Just a hope."
"Well, whatever hope you have, you might as well leave it here. It's useless baggage that will only upset you." Silently, he stole my wrist again and carted me from my room.
I'd thought he'd sneaked in using my window—after all, it was a fairly easy climb up the façade of the manor—but he'd been bolder. He'd used the front door.
The two servants we employed had their rooms downstairs. It was sad to think even now, in this day and age, our help was still housed in the basement. Had we learned nothing from our past transgressions?
*They have an apartment down there. Private suites, a bathroom...it's not as if it's a dank cellar.*
That was the truth, but it still couldn't hide that they lived below us. Below our high and mighty rank as Weavers.
Perhaps this was my karma.
For all *my* wrongdoings and not my ancestors.
Without a sound, Jethro opened the front door and guided me out. I looked one last time at my childhood home before the door clicked shut, casting me out.
Jethro didn't give me time to mourn. Dragging me down the front steps, he nodded at Kes. The front courtyard housed

three bikes and two darkly dressed men.

Kestrel touched his temple in greeting, his light coloured eyes looking like moonbeams in the darkness. "Nila. Pleasure to see you again."

I smiled once, still dreadfully unsure if Kes was on my side, his brother's, or his father's.

Jethro tugged me close. Grabbing my hips, he tossed me onto the back of his bike. A small puff of air exploded out of my mouth at his rough handling. My skin tingled where he'd touched me, but he seemed unaffected.

*I'll break you again, Jethro Hawk. I did it once. I can do it a second time.*

*And then I'll save both of us.*

I swallowed hard as the reality of my pregnancy scheme slapped me with doubt. It would take nine long months to hatch. I doubted I had nine months to *live*—let alone breed in the hope it would keep us alive.

*I need a back-up plan.*

"We're done here," Jethro muttered, throwing a glance at Flaw before taking his helmet from the handlebars and jamming it on his head.

Flaw said, "If we're done. Let's go." His gloved fingers wrapped around his throttle.

I was back with the men who'd claimed me.

Back with my enemies.

Back in power and ready to destroy them.

# Jethro

DAWN.

The new sun painted the sky a glowing pink as we drove beneath the gatehouse at the entrance of Hawksridge. Kes and Flaw accelerated, pulling away and speeding up the long driveway.

I slowed down, steadying the bike and Nila's weight behind me.

Her torso plastered against my back, her hips as close to mine as possible. She was the exact opposite from the first time I'd collected her.

Back in Milan, she'd been respectful in her fear. She'd kept her distance and didn't try to break through my carefully constructed walls. Now, she was pissing me off taking liberties she was no longer entitled to. Her hands hadn't stopped roaming as I drove down motorways and country lanes. Her heat seeped through my jacket, infecting my skin below. She thought things were the same—that I secretly wanted her to touch me.

She couldn't be more wrong.

Slamming my bike to a halt, I planted my legs on the road and twisted to face her. "I'm going to give you a choice." Tearing her arms from around my waist, I held up a blindfold that I'd stuffed into my pocket.

Nila frowned, her eyes flickering up the hill where the road disappeared toward Hawksridge. "What choice?"

Rubbing the silk between my fingers, I said, "I can either blindfold you or not. It's up to you."

Cut was confident this imprisonment would be a lot smoother than her first, but he still didn't want her knowing the way off the estate—unless she gave a guarantee. I smirked. "Decide, Ms. Weaver."

"How is the choice up to me? And besides, I saw the driveway when the police took me away."

"Fair enough." I let the blindfold fall from my fingers and onto her thigh. "Are you going to try to run again? Or have you accepted that your home is now with me?"

I hadn't meant to word it like that. I'd meant to say had she accepted that she would die on this estate. That her life out there—her home in London—was over, done.

*Forever.*

Nila's gaze delved into mine. I felt her probing my soul, looking for answers and hope.

I didn't have to stop her or hide.

There was nothing inside that shouldn't be there. Not anymore.

I was proud of who I'd become.

And it was all thanks to the little white tablets in my pocket.

After a long minute, she replied, "My home is with you, Kite. I know that. I think I've always known that." She licked her bottom lip. "I won't run. I won't leave you. Not again. Whatever happened to you the past few weeks, I'm willing to look past it because I know what we found together is true and this…" She waved at me as if I offended her. "This is a lie that I don't buy."

My heart skipped—just a small skip—before settling into its wintry shell. Her power over me was gone. It'd just been tested and proven.

"You don't have to buy anything for it to be the truth."

She sighed. "No, but I can hope."

"Hope is as useless as love, Nila Weaver." Shoving the blindfold back into my pocket, I gunned the bike and took her the final distance home.

The underground parking garage housed thirty or so bikes for the Black Diamond brothers. We'd built the bunker especially for our MC, hidden away in case the police ever raided us, which until last month was never a possibility.

Now it might be thanks to the fucking Weavers and their lies to the local papers. Our bribes worked perfectly to keep the law on our side. But when strangers started moaning and demanding justice, it wasn't a simple matter of turning a blind eye anymore.

Luckily, we had a plan. Damage control was in full swing, and after a few weeks out of the limelight, Nila would be forgotten and the world would continue.

We also had a trump card.

The one thing Vaughn couldn't get his sister to do: a private interview.

Later today, Nila would answer all the questions the world wanted to know. She would shed her silence and feed the media a story that would put an end to the disgusting rumours in a carefully scripted pantomime, then she would go back to belonging to us. To *me*.

Plucking my captive from my bike, I discarded my helmet and jacket.

She was back where she belonged, but first there was a simple matter to attend to. One that my father had pointed out and shown me how important it was after my indiscretions.

He was wise, my father. I hoped to rule like him when it was my turn.

"Come with me." Taking her wrist again, I half-escorted, half-dragged Nila through the underground garage and into the private elevator that spat us out by the stables.

Neither of us spoke as we traversed the grass beneath the pink-silver light of dawn. The Hall loomed before us, its turrets glowing with sunrise and stained glass windows looking as if blood ran down the panes.

Flaw and Kestrel had gone—no doubt already snoring in their beds.

I hadn't slept much last night, but I wasn't tired. Far from it. I was awake and ready to prove my worth.

My fingers itched to open my tablet bottle. It wasn't time for another dose, but the way my heart skipped back at the gatehouse proved the fog needed reinforcing.

Now Nila was back in my vicinity, I would have to keep an eye on my dosage—increase the prescription to remain immune to whatever tricks she might play.

"Where are you taking me?" Nila asked as we stepped into the hushed world of Hawksridge and prowled through its sleepy corridors.

I didn't reply. She had no right to know. She would understand the moment we arrived.

It didn't take long, another few minutes before I stopped and opened a large carved door in the north wing of the house.

The space wasn't as big as many of the other rooms, but it'd been staged with the equipment required.

My lips twitched into half a smile as Nila crossed the threshold.

The moment her eyes landed on the medical table in the centre of the room, her mouth fell open in horror. "What—what is this?"

She struggled in my hold while I reached behind her and locked the door.

She wasn't stupid.

She knew this wouldn't end well.

The light in her face went out. Her eyes widened in horror. I'd been right to suspect her motives. Did she not think I would see? That her messages weren't so fucking obvious?

"I'm not someone you can manipulate, Ms. Weaver." I

patted her arse as I moved forward. A reclining chair suddenly swivelled around, revealing my father.

His eyes landed on Nila, glowing gold with triumph. "Ah, welcome, my dear. So glad to see you after this dreadful time apart." He raised his tumbler of cognac. "It wasn't the same without you here. Was it, Kite?"

I no longer hated my bird of prey nickname. I no longer despised my father using it. In fact, it was an honour. Before, it was a constant reminder that I was born and bred to be something I could never be—now it was a badge of distinction. I'd somehow achieved the impossible and become the perfect fucking son.

Smiling at Nila, I answered, "No. It wasn't the same without her."

If only she knew what'd happened while she was off playing seamstress with her brother. If only she knew what Cut had done to me, what I'd done in return. She wouldn't have come willingly. She would've done anything to avoid being my prisoner again.

"Jethro…" Her voice trailed off, her eyes never leaving the table. "What is the meaning of this?"

Cut laughed. "Come now, child. You can't play that card with us. You know as well as I do what you've done to deserve this."

"Please!" Nila plastered herself against the door, jiggling the doorknob with her hand. It was pointless. I had the key in my pocket. "You don't have to do this."

Cut slowly placed his empty glass on the table and stood. Undoing his cufflinks, he rolled up his sleeves, systematically and refined, never rushing. "I think you'll find, my dear, that we do."

Nodding in her direction, he ordered, "Jet, enough dallying. Grab the girl and let's get on with this."

"Be my pleasure." I advanced on Nila.

Blues and greys decorated the room. The wallpaper was an oriental silk that was so vibrant, the indigo pattern bounced off

Nila's black hair.

"Stop it," Nila snarled. "Don't."

Standing in front of her, I held out my hand. "This can be easy or hard. Your choice."

"I hate it when you do that! Can't you see I don't want a choice?!"

I narrowed my eyes. What the fuck did that mean?

Cut chuckled. "You want us to take full responsibility for what's happening to you, is that right? When will you admit that you're the same as us? Doing something willingly doesn't mean you're going to hell, pretty girl. But fighting us at every step doesn't mean you'll go to heaven, either."

I waved my hand, openly revealing the tattoos on my fingertips. "Your choice, Nila. Own free will or restraints."

Nila visibly trembled. A curtain fell over her face, blocking all thoughts.

In a quick move, as if her courage would desert her, she pushed off from the door and brushed past me.

I smiled, dropping my hand. "Good girl."

"Where?" Nila snapped when she stood by the table, her body vibrating with tension.

"Climb on," Cut said.

With ferocity coating her face, Nila scooted onto the table and lay down. She lay there as if she was in a coffin. Her hands clasped tight on her lower belly, her chest rising and falling with panic.

She refused to look at either of us, glowering at the ceiling.

Cut patted her arm. "See...that wasn't so hard now, was it?"

She stiffened, her fingers turning white.

Cut stroked her gently. "I must admit. I missed your presence in my home." He smiled wider. "You're such fun to torment." He traced her collarbone. "However, these past few weeks have been rather enlightening. In fact, I'm delighted with the outcome and only have you to thank for it." Throwing a look my way, he grinned. "You gave me my son. My *real* son.

And for that I will always be grateful to you, my dear."
　　Bending over, he pressed a soft kiss on her mouth.
　　Nila shuddered, twisting her head to the side.
　　I just stood there.
　　No feeling.
　　No jealousy.
　　No remorse.
　　"Don't fight it," Cut murmured. "Don't ruin what you've started."
　　Nila pressed herself deeper onto the table, no doubt trying to become invisible but not succeeding. I moved closer, taking the side opposite my father. Her eyes met mine, wide and feral. She sent a silent message, so loud and obvious I was sure my father saw.
　　*Why are you doing this?*
　　*I thought you cared for me?*
　　I had no intention of replying. If she opened her naïve little eyes, she would see my answer without me spelling it out for her. This was what happened to those who broke promises. She was a true Weaver. And I was finally a true Hawk.
　　Cut continued to drag his fingertip along Nila's throat, following the contours of the diamond collar. "As much as it's a pleasure to have you living under my roof, Ms. Weaver, I do have one requirement. I hope you don't begrudge me my small request."
　　Cut reached into his pocket and pulled free the single reason why we were here. He held up the item for her to see.
　　Gritting her jaw, her eyes popped wide.
　　The syringe glinted in the lowlight chandelier.
　　Fight and flight filled her body. "Wait. You don't have to drug me. Jethro, tell him. Tell him you don't have to drug me. I came on my own accord! I already promised I wouldn't run. I won't. I give you my word." A single tear rolled down her cheek. "I'll behave. You can trust me. God, please trust me. I'll behave now." Her breathing turned shallow and fast. "I don't want to be drugged. I don't want to be lost. Please!"

Cut laughed, hushing her spew of words. "I know all that, my pet. Calm down before you give yourself a heart attack."

Nila paused, hope lighting her gaze.

Cut smiled softly. "This isn't to subdue you."

"What—what is it then?"

"I'll let my son tell you that." Brushing some hair that'd fallen over her eyes, he pressed another kiss against her mouth. She tensed but permitted the touch, not twisting her head away.

The fear of being manipulated by a substance had well and truly subdued her. I'd have to remember that. If only she knew that some drugs were better than life—that they made existing so much more *pleasurable*.

Cut stood tall. "I'll leave you two lovers alone." Stroking between her breasts, he smiled. "You're free to do what you please for the rest of the morning, but I expect to see you dressed and presented for your meeting at noon."

Handing the syringe to me, he said, "I'm watching you."

Taking the implement, I nodded. "You don't need to. Consider it already done."

Cut stared, searching my reply. He would find no lie in my tone. No secrets in my voice. I meant what I said: it was already done. Being around her for a few hours hadn't changed me. I was stronger than that and wouldn't relapse.

He clapped me on the back. "I believe you."

And there it was. The one thing I'd wanted all my fucking life.

Trust.

*Acceptance.*

There was no trace of animosity or disbelief. He'd fully accepted me. I couldn't be more grateful. *I have no intention of jeopardising what I've waited so long to gain.*

Not for Nila. Not for anyone.

With a fatherly squeeze, Cut moved toward the door and left. The moment he'd gone, Nila turned her glassy black eyes on me. "Please, Jethro. Whatever he's told you to do—please don't do it. You know me. I know you. What we have—don't destroy it."

Ignoring her, I tapped the glass of the syringe, making sure there were no air bubbles.

"There's nothing between us, Ms. Weaver."

"Please!" She sat up, clutching my forearm. "You don't believe that."

My temper boiled over. Grabbing her throat, I growled, "Self-control or I will restrain you. Lie. Back. Down."

Shivering, she shook her head. "What *happened* to you?" She tried to capture my cheek, but I dodged her grasp.

"Touch me again and you won't like what happens." I snatched her bicep. "If you move, this will hurt a lot more than if you're still." I poised the needle above the fleshy part of her arm. "And to answer your repetitive question, nothing happened. I'm not doing this because he told me to. I'm doing this because *I* want to."

Piercing her skin, I pressed the plunger.

Tears fled to her eyes, twinkling like black stars. She winced as the cool liquid fled from syringe to flesh.

It only took a second to empty the injection. The moment it was gone, I withdrew the needle and tossed it into the stainless steel tray beside the table.

A small droplet of blood swelled from the puncture wound.

Plucking a tissue from the box on the sideboard, I handed it to her.

Taking it reluctantly, she asked sadly, "What is it? What did you just give me?"

I ran a hand through my hair. "Call it a pre-emptive."

Nila frowned. "Pre-emptive against what?"

"Any plans you might have."

My temper glowed as I remembered her note to her brother. Had she come to the same conclusion my father had, or was she still blindly believing I felt something for her? *Silly, girl.*

"I have no plans. I don't understand." She swung her legs

over the table, rubbing her arm.

I moved closer, pressing both hands against her cheeks, imprisoning her. She shied away, but I slid my fingers behind her skull, wrapping them in the thick strands of her hair.

The touch wasn't meant to be kind or gentle. It was meant to show who was in power and it was about fucking time she learned that.

"It's pre-emptive; to make sure the Final Debt will be repaid."

Colour washed from her cheeks. "What do you mean?"

I cocked my head. "Come on. Don't continue to play me when you've already lost." Running my thumb along her bottom lip, I whispered, "You were clever, I will admit. But not clever enough. There is nothing you can do to hinder my plans."

She gasped, her soul falling from her eyes.

She finally understood. "How could you? How could you be so...*heartless?*"

Tugging her hair, I kissed her jaw. "It was you who saved me from such a stupid notion of feelings. The day you left, I thought my life was over. But then I found a new way—a better way—and I'm no longer your toy to play with." Pressing soft kisses down her throat, her pulse throbbed beneath my lips. "No more plans. No more games. It was a contraceptive, Nila. Now do you get it?"

Silence.

Her heartbeat exploded, blood gushing, heating her paper-thin skin below my threatening kisses.

"I've stolen what you hoped to steal from me, Ms. Weaver. There will be no children. No half-breeds. No saviour. I've won."

# Nila

"MS. WEAVER, SO nice to meet you."

My attention snapped to the man wearing designer jeans and a cream tailored shirt. His hair was artfully coiffed, and he'd rimmed his baby-blue eyes with kohl. Thin and handsome, he was obviously gay and perfect for the role of jotting down gossip.

*"There will be no children. No half-breeds. No saviour. I've won."*

I stared blankly, unable to do anything but listen to the echo of Jethro's voice inside my head.

*"I've won. I've won. I've won."*

Tears pricked my eyes for the hundredth time since I'd arrived back at Hawksridge. How could he say that? He'd lost. We *both* had. Somehow, Cut had turned Jethro into his lap dog and the connection we'd shared gurgled down a drain of despair.

What if I had been pregnant? Would the contraceptive have hurt the baby?

How could Jethro do something so terrible?

*I hate it here.*

*I positively* hate *it here.*

I'd *always* hated it here.

How could I return with such stupid plans? How did I think I could save Jethro and kill Cut? What an idiot!

*Jethro doesn't even want saving.*
Not after what they'd done to him.
"Ms. Weaver? Are you quite well?"
I shook my head, sniffing back unshed tears and doing my best to focus.

Gay Reporter's assistant smiled, her purple fluffy pen tapping her chin in concern. "Can we get you a glass of water or something?"

"She's fine," Jethro murmured in his signature soft voice. I'd forgotten how smooth and precise he was. Forgotten how rigid he held himself, how restrained and contained and arctically frigid.

I shot him a look full of venom. "Actually, I would love a glass of water."

Jethro pursed his lips as the blonde-haired woman who looked like a delicious cupcake in her pale pink dress and curves sprang from her chair.

She giggled. "I can't believe I get to play hostess in this place." Moving to the sideboard where an array of drinks and hors d'oeuvres had been set by invisible staff, she poured me a glass and came back. "Truly, it's an incredible home you have here, Mr. Hawk."

I smiled in thanks, taking the offered water.

Jethro shifted on the settee beside me, his temper gathering a tempest. "I'm so glad you like it." Clasping his hands, he glowered at the reporter. "Are we quite ready to begin? I have a few other appointments that demand my attention."

Gay Reporter nodded, sitting higher on the mirroring settee opposite us. "Yes, of course." Revealing tic-tac perfect teeth, he began his well-rehearsed speech. "First, we want to say what an honour it is to be chosen for the exclusive interview. I have no doubt that our readers at *Vanity Fair* will highly enjoy such an intriguing piece. My name is George, and this is Sylvie."

His eyes bounced between Jethro and me. "I predict the

interview will go on for about thirty minutes, followed by a short tour of the grounds and anything else you wish to share with us for the article. Does that sound satisfactory?"

Sylvie scooped out a voice recorder, iPhone, and notepad and arranged her arsenal on the coffee table.

"Fine," Jethro murmured, playing with a diamond cufflink. He looked resplendent in a grey cashmere suit and open-necked white shirt. His salt and pepper hair caught the light with distinguished old-world wealth and his shiny Gucci shoes were pristine.

The sun streamed in through the windows, stencilling the carpet with happiness I didn't feel.

I was cold. Aching. Confused.

Once again, my fingers returned to the bruise on my arm. I flinched remembering the pain of the needle piercing my flesh. The skin still stung from the contraceptive as if he'd only just done it—not a few hours ago.

How could he *do* that?

How could he obey Cut and dismiss me from his heart?

He'd shattered my dreams so damn quickly.

*Why oh why did I come back here?*

*You know why.*

*To save Jethro, kill the Hawk bastards, and end this.*

George's eyes darted around the lounge. Jethro and I rested on a loveseat with silver swans gilded on white satin. Purple velvet-flocked chairs encircled the seating area, lending a richness to the oriental charm of the day parlour.

The décor was feminine with its intricate jewelled music boxes enclosed in glass-domed cases and ancient grandfather clocks chiming the hour. I would've liked to relax in this room and I guessed Jasmine used it, too—judging by the faint wheel marks in the thick lavender carpet.

I was tired. Terribly tired.

For three months, my life had been anything but normal and I needed to rest. I needed to stop and get my bearings, because I no longer knew where I was. I thought I understood

Jethro.

How wrong was I?

A vertigo wave danced in my brain. I moaned, pressing my fingertips against my temples.

Jethro inched closer, resting his cool hand on my thigh.

My skin reacted instantly, craving him, seeking more. I cursed myself for reacting that way. It took everything in me not to shove him away and sprint from the room.

What a traitor.

What a *bastard.*

"Ms. Weaver, you don't look entirely well." George looked at his wristwatch. "We can postpone for an hour or so if you wish. To rest?"

"No." Jethro's eyes locked on George's. "She'll be fine." His fingers tightened on my knee, biting uncomfortably. "Won't you, Nila?"

Once upon a time, my heart would've fluttered if he used my first name. Now, it tore off those wings and plummeted to hell.

Leaning into me, Jethro whispered in my ear, "You know what's expected of you. Behave and everything will remain cordial, got it?" Pulling away, he put on a show for the reporters. "I'm so worried about you, darling. For days, you've been saying how excited you are to reveal the truth to the world. You don't want to ruin your chance now, do you?"

George clapped his hands. "Yes, please don't let us down, Ms. Weaver. We are so excited to hear your tale." He picked up an expensive camera with a zoom lens. "If you feel restricted sitting down, we could always conduct the questions by the window over there. Be a great spot for some pictures."

"Oh, yes," Sylvie said. "It would be such a romantic shot with the two of you. Our readers would love it."

Another vertigo spell teased my vision. I didn't trust my legs to stand and shook my head. "Perhaps in a little bit. I'm happy to answer whatever you want here." I stretched my face into a smile, but it felt heavy, sad, *fake.*

George and Sylvie didn't notice.

But of course, Jethro did. Pinching my knee again, Jethro cleared his throat. "My apologies. My love has been rather overworked the past few weeks." He leaned forward with a conspirer's smile. "She went home to her family, you see. A bit of a disaster—as you might've heard."

Sylvie giggled, completely buying the lies Jethro spilled. "We did hear a rumour or two."

His commanding fingers stroked my thigh, looking like a caress but feeling like a punishment. "Those rumours were started to thwart our love. Her family doesn't approve of mine. They think she can do better than me and never approved—even though we were born for each other."

My heart thudded to a stop. The words could've been so perfect. So full of promise. Instead, they reeked with deceit and dripped with lies.

*We were born for each other, that's true.* But only for him to kill me in his quest for whatever Cut promised.

I sank further into the loveseat, wishing the swans on the fabric would come alive and fly me away from there. I missed the sanctuary of the Weaver quarters. After the awful injection, Jethro had left me to reacquaint myself with the space. I'd showered and tried not to cry over my gullible heart or naïve hopes smashing to dust in the face of Jethro's new behaviour.

I'd dressed in a blood-red A-line skirt that I'd made while here previously and shrugged into a slouchy jumper with a rose hand-stitched on the front. I hadn't bothered with makeup or my hair. The damp strands hung down my back adding to the chill in my soul that I doubted would ever thaw.

Sitting beside Jethro in his immaculate attire, I truly did feel sick. Dying cell by cell until I would be nothing but a corpse.

"Sounds like an awful predicament to love a man your family doesn't approve of, Ms. Weaver," George prompted.

*This is it then.*

The interview had officially begun.

Placing my hands in my lap, I struggled to think up an approved reply. When Cut came to collect me for the reporters, he'd given me strict instructions:

"*Act heartbroken but happy. Paint your family as the bad guys and us as the victims. Make the Hawks shine, Ms. Weaver, or else.*"

*I'm so sorry, Vaughn.*

After everything he'd done to save me, I was about to undo it all with a few awful sentences.

Jethro suddenly wrapped an arm around my shoulders, crushing me into his body. His lips landed on my ear in a whisper-kiss. "Play the damn role. It's not hard."

Pulling away, his eyes burned into mine. *You wanted to come back. You invited me to take you. Now you have to play along if you want to survive.*

Looking away, I answered George's question. "It is hard. I love my father and brother so much, but when I met Jethro…I just knew. He was it for me, and no matter what they say or do, I can't change something that's written by fate."

My voice hovered in the room, quiet, unsure, but resonating in just the right frequency to melt George and Sylvie. Their postures changed, their interest flared, and Jethro relaxed a smidgen. "Good girl," he murmured into my hair.

I shivered as his breath warmed my nape. I wanted my words to be real. I wanted it so much.

*Then make it real.*

Just because Jethro was damaged again, didn't mean I couldn't win him back.

Where was my strength? My conviction? I'd come back not to wallow in misery but to *end* this.

Power shot into my blood; I sat straighter. Pinching my cheeks, I willed colour to paint my skin and dispel any sign of weakness. "True love is a curse, don't you think?" I smiled for the first time, shoving aside my worries and throwing myself into this new challenge.

*You want me to play my part, Jethro Hawk?*

*Fine.*

I would play it so well, I would have the press eating out of *my* hand—not the Hawks'.

"I agree. Falling in love can be the most dangerous thing anyone can do." Sylvie smiled.

Stealing Jethro's hand, I looped my fingers with his and brought his large palm to my lips. I kissed him. I breathed in his scent of leather and money. I grew strong again.

He didn't move. Didn't inhale or twitch.

*It doesn't matter.*

*I'll get him back.*

"So your brother felt so strongly that the Hawk family wasn't good enough for you, he spread vile rumours of debts and deaths...all to break you up?" George asked, his eyes gleaming.

Jethro faded into the background.

*Please forgive me, Vaughn.*

"Yes. V and I were very close growing up. I would tell him everything. But then I met Jethro, and I didn't want to share my secret. I kept our affair hidden. I suppose that was a betrayal in my brother's eyes. He felt like he lost me. And took it out on my love."

Jethro smiled like the doting partner. "I will admit, it's been hard."

"I can imagine." George grinned. Conferring to his notes, he perched higher. "How about, before we discuss other topics, we clear the confusion about those rumours. Would you mind?"

Jethro answered before I could. "By all means. We have nothing to hide." His lips stretched over his teeth in a cool smile. "It would be beneficial to clear the air on the disgusting rumours Vaughn Weaver spread."

My shoulders rolled at my twin's name. I should've listened to him—not about running away, but arming myself with weapons and fighting the Hawks with violence rather than my idiotic idea of getting pregnant.

*That's over anyway.*

I didn't know how long the contraceptive would work, but I remembered a staff member having the injection and saying it lasted anywhere from three to six months.

*I won't be alive in six months.*

Sylvie pulled an *Elle* magazine from her satchel beside her. Passing it to me, she asked, "Have you seen this particular article?"

I leaned forward, taking the glossy weight and forcing myself to remain detached as I stared at the cover. The model pouted for the camera, eerily close to my dusky colouring and black eyes. However, where I had long hair, hers was cut short—a sleek bob revealing the full impact of the heavy stones around her neck. The intricate design of the choker was missing the barely noticeable W's hidden in the rows of diamonds, and the filigree work around the stones was ordinary compared to the workmanship in mine. Plus, my diamonds were bigger.

I smiled smugly, stroking my collar as if it no longer heralded my death sentence but linked me to a man who belonged to me.

"No, I haven't seen it."

"Would you mind if you read some of it aloud, Ms. Weaver? Elaborate on a few key points?" George pointed at a Post-it note sticking from the pages. "I've bookmarked it for you."

Flipping the magazine open, I gasped as the same model from the front smouldered in a centrefold. She wore a dress very similar to the feathered couture I paraded at the Milan show.

The title blazed in diamonds:

*The Truth Behind the Weavers as told by Daphne Simons, Employee at Weaver Enterprises.'*

"Do you know that employee?" Sylvie asked.

I looked up, shaking my head. "No. We hire too many people to know them all."

The room turned silent as I skimmed the ridiculous article.

Nila Weaver, the daughter of the conglomerate company Weaver Enterprises has recently been spotted back in London after a stint outside the limelight. Gossip has spread over the past few weeks that her family are victims of an age-old dispute that defies all logic and rationality. A world where promises are kept and oaths are never broken. Her brother, Vaughn Weaver, recently broke his silence when his efforts to have his sister returned went unheeded.

Turning the tables on the leaked photographs depicting Ms. Weaver with a young man unknown at the time, and the rumour that she'd had a mental breakdown and run off with her mystery lover, the world was shocked to discover the man in the photographs wasn't her lover, but her kidnapper.

How could they print such heresy?

Upon Nila Weaver's return to London High Society, she's been repeatedly asked to tell her story, but has remained silent on the matter. However, here at Elle, we have an exclusive interview with one of her employees.

Elle: *Thank you for meeting with us, Daphne. Care to tell us what you know?*

Daphne: *Well, all I know is she returned to work last month. She's always been rather quiet. Too work focused and always stumbling into things. But now, she's even worse.*

Elle: *You mentioned she seems different? Can you elaborate?*

Daphne: *It's common knowledge about the collar. She never takes it off. She's constantly touching it. The staff room is a buzz with conspiracies that she suffers that problem when a captive falls for her kidnapper...you know what I mean?*

Elle: *You're saying she's in love with the man who collared her?*

Daphne: *Yep. For sure. My theory is the debt stuff is just a cover up. I reckon she's into that freaky business...you know like S&M? Not to mention the diamond collar is an obvious ode to belonging to a master when in those types of relationships. She's changed.*

Elle: *How do you mean?*

Daphne: *Well... she used to be sweet, shy. It's a family company, so we see the Weavers interact a lot. But now she's shut down around her brother. Her love for the industry has gone.*

Elle: *And you believe this is due to a Sadomasochistic relationship?*
Daphne: *I believe she's changed too much to fit in anymore. Mark my words. She won't be in London long.*

*And there you have it; our very own textile heiress has returned bearing a collar, bruises, and a history of intolerable cruelty. I suppose we won't get answers or know the full story until justice has been served.*

"So, tell us," George said. "Is any of that true? Are you in an S&M relationship?"

Jethro sat taller, chuckling under his breath. "You honestly expect us to answer questions about our sex life?"

Sylvie laughed. "Sorry if it sounds like we're prying, but our readers love to know that stuff."

Stroking my collar, I smiled coyly. "All your readers need to know is Jethro completes me both in and out of the bedroom."

George laughed, slapping his thigh. "Now, that's a politically correct reply, if I ever heard one."

Jethro reclined, spreading his arm over the back of the loveseat. "The rumours about death and debts are complete lies. However, some parts are indeed true."

I didn't know how he did it, but in a few short sentences, he'd enraptured George and Sylvie.

"Oh, how so?"

"People no longer accept the idea of arranged marriages. They like to think we're all free to do what we like, when we like, but realistically, we are all still governed by class, income, our family tree." He ran a hand through his hair. "My family has known the Weavers for six hundred years. We've effectively grown up together, crossing paths and healing feuds, and ultimately agreeing to come together to form a strong alliance."

George frowned. "So you're saying this so-called Debt Inheritance is what? A marriage contract?"

Jethro shook his head. "Not quite. It's an agreement of debts between two houses that strive to support each other with payments in different forms throughout the years."

I blinked stupidly, unable to believe the way Jethro spun

three weeks of rumours. It made people seem ridiculous—clutching at straws and jumping onto a witch-hunt they knew nothing about.

He sounded so reasonable, so *justifiable*.

His speech was too perfect not to be scripted...perhaps by Bonnie.

*Bonnie.*

Did she tell Jethro to come and collect me, or was she against this development? After all, she'd kicked me out. She was the one who wanted me gone.

"And you, Ms. Weaver. That's how your family sees this Debt Inheritance, too?" George pinned his baby-blues on me.

"Yes, of course. What else could it be? To think that one family owns another is completely ludicrous. We support one another. Sure, at times there's some unrest and rivalry, but for the most part, we're one big happy family."

Maids arrived with fresh tea and a three-tier cake stand with cucumber sandwiches and éclairs.

George grabbed one, jotting down a few notes. "So really...it's the age-old 'mountain out of a mole hill' kinda thing."

Jethro crossed his ankles, ignoring the finger food. "Yes. Not that it's anyone's business, but our two influential families have always prospered by linking our history. It's such a shame that after centuries of friendship, it's come down to Mr. Weaver spreading such terrible lies."

I sucked in a breath. I wanted to tell the truth but what good would it do? Would it stop the Hawks from breaking countless laws—would it save my life?

Vaughn had told the world, yet even with so much gossip, it was still his word against the Hawks. And they sounded so much more believable than him. A sure way to disband the Twitter posters and bury old Facebook shout-outs under new intrigue.

George swallowed a bite of cucumber sandwich. "Are you happy to be back? After the time away?"

This was it. My turn to lie as spectacularly as Jethro.

Swooning into Jethro's side, I snuggled against his chest and sighed dramatically. "Oh, yes. Every night we messaged each other. And every night we professed our belonging and knowledge that we wouldn't let lies come between us."

Jethro stiffened then slowly wrapped an icy arm around my shoulders.

My body trembled with the need to be hugged—for real. Having the weight of his body cloaking mine did nothing to ease the inconsolable pain inside my heart.

I wanted to hurt him as much as he'd hurt me.

I wanted him to wake up!

But how?

Then suddenly, I knew *exactly* how. How to get back at him for what he'd done to me. How to announce to Cut that his plan to steal my right to bear children wouldn't come without consequences.

Placing my hand on Jethro's chest, I sought out the flat-line and uninterested beat of his heart. "It was agony being apart." Dropping my voice to a breathy whisper, I said, "I was so homesick for Jethro; I threw up almost every day."

Jethro's heart remained steady and unaffected.

*Try ignoring this, you monster.*

"But it turned out I was throwing up because I was pregnant."

Jethro's heart screeched to a stop. He went deathly still.

George clapped. "Oh, that's wonderful! So if the Debt Inheritance is kind of like a marriage contract, then they have to let it take place now that you're carrying!"

I swallowed my morbid giggle.

*You* want *them to cut off my head?*

If only they knew what it meant.

"That's amazing. I call first dibs on coming to the wedding and baby shower!" Sylvie laughed.

Jethro never looked at me; his gaze remained locked on the other end of the room. He struggled to plant a smile on his face, nodding at the ecstatic interviewers. "Yes...it was quite a surprise. But of course...a welcome one."

Letting tears spring to my eyes, I murmured, "I was so happy. I couldn't wait to start our family and create something that was just ours. But..." I played up the hitch in my voice.

Sylvie leaned forward. "What—what happened?"

Jethro tightened his arm around me. "Yes, *Nila*. What happened?" His voice was whip-sharp.

George passed me his handkerchief. I accepted it, dabbing my dry eyes. "I lost the baby!" I sniffed loudly, making sure I sounded extra pitiful. "The stress of all the rumours made me sick, and I lost the best thing that could've ever happened to us."

George slapped a hand over his mouth, totally forgetting his notepad and pen. "Oh, that's tragically awful." Getting up, he came to squat in front of me.

Jethro glowered at him as George took my hand and kissed my knuckles. "It's okay though...that little one wasn't meant to be, but you can try again. You can have other babies." His gaze flashed to Jethro. "Can't you? You're both young. It's only natural to create your own family and make this love story complete."

"Yes, quite," Jethro muttered, tugging me away from George's caressing fingers.

I fought Jethro's hold, clutching onto George. If Jethro wanted the world to believe we were together and happy then it was his turn to play along with my farce.

Letting a sob free, I wailed, "That's the problem. Something happened...." I narrowed my eyes at Jethro, letting him see my wrath and hate for what he'd done.

*You took away the one weapon I might've had to free us.*

George clutched my fingers tighter, completely buying my story. "Oh no, not more bad news?"

Imbecile.

Leech.

As lovely as he seemed, I couldn't stand what he

represented. He was there to make my family look like liars and the Hawks to smell like roses. They would tarnish my brother, break my father's heart even more, and make me seem as if I was a scatter-brained lovesick child completely out of her depth.

*I mean to change all that.*

"I was told the conception was a miracle. That I have a rare disorder that might mean I'll never conceive again. The doctor said I might die if I ever carried a child full term, but he knew I wouldn't give up. It's my ultimate dream—the one thing I have to have."

Jethro growled, "Nila, no need to tell the world our—"

"Jethro's father, Bryan Hawk, loves me like a daughter. He arranged for the doctor to give me a contraceptive, completely against my will. He said if I tried to bear the child of my soulmate, I might die, and he couldn't have that on his soul!" I let ugly, wet sobs spew forth, hurling myself into the performance.

George went white, his face half enthralled with having a delicious story to tell and half full of heartbroken sorrow. "Oh, you poor thing. You poor, poor—"

Jethro sniffed, physically untangling George's fingers from mine and pushing him away. Pulling me into his body, he snapped, "It's been a hard time for all of us." Standing, he yanked me to my feet.

His eyes shot a warning.

*What the hell are you doing?*

Anger radiated, but beneath it all was the faintest shadow of horror. Did he believe my tale? How did he feel to know what he'd done when I might've been carrying his child?

*Does it make you sick?* I blazed my own silent message. *Does it rip out your insides to think you might've killed your own flesh and blood?*

Before I could seek answers in his eyes, he looked away.

"I'm sorry, but the interview is over." Jethro stood to his full height, his suit looking crisp compared to his ruffled exterior.

I'd come into this as a victim, but I'd stolen the show. I felt redeemed.

They might've stolen my plans of pregnancy, but I'd just stolen theirs.

I was no longer the meek little woman. I was the strong barren woman destined to live with a man she adored and never get pregnant. The media would direct their sympathy onto me—they would be kinder to my family, less likely to slander my last name.

And should all my scheming fail and it came time for me to pay the Final Debt, I might have some chance of rallying them to save me.

George stood up, his fingers fluttering over his camera. "Ah, can we bother you for some pictures? Before we conclude for the day?"

Jethro's nostrils flared. "No, I think my girlfriend needs to lie down. This has—"

"Now, *honey*, don't hide the truth from them." I wiped beneath my eyes, hoping he saw my challenge.

*I'm not done with you yet.*

Jethro's eyebrows knitted together. "We haven't hidden anything, *my love*." He smiled thinly, pinching my arm where George couldn't see.

"Wait—what are you talking about, Ms. Weaver?" Sylvie asked.

I smiled radiantly. "I'm not just his girlfriend."

Jethro sucked in a breath.

George bounced on the spot with anticipation. "What do you mean?"

Beaming at Jethro, I said, "I'm his fiancée. We're getting married."

# Jethro

WHAT IN THE ever-loving fuck was she doing?
My mind scrambled; a terrible lancing pain stabbed my temples.
*Was* she pregnant?
Did she miscarry?
What the fuck did it mean if she *was* pregnant? What would the contraceptive do?
I shook my head, trying to get my erratic breathing under control. I couldn't think about those things—not while the reporters were here, watching our every move.
Pills.
*I need another pill.*
Nila suddenly nuzzled into my chest, wrapping her bony arms around my waist. Collecting her last night, I'd noticed she looked skinnier than normal. But I knew her well—I knew she would've run every night on her treadmill, knew she would've overworked herself to forget.
*But what if she's telling the truth and* was *sick?*
Did that become an extra issue with what my father had planned? And why did I even care? I *shouldn't* care.
*Do something about it.*
Shoving her away, I fumbled in my pocket and yanked out the bottle. Tapping two tablets into my palm, I threw them

down my throat and swallowed them dry.

My heart raced as I tucked the bottle back into my pocket and jerked my hands through my hair. Knowing I had something that helped—that the drug's fog wisped through my blood—allowed me to regain control on the flapping mess Nila had created.

"Headache?" George asked, his eyebrow raised at my pocket.

Nila narrowed her gaze, too, incorrect conclusions filling her sniper glare. With the way she was behaving, I didn't want her anywhere near my newfound cure. Slipping back into welcome numbness, I gathered her close and smiled for the damn journalists. "Yes, sorry. While Nila has been going through some terrible ordeals lately, I've suffered my own stress."

Sylvie came closer, her eyes pooling with sympathy. "Oh, I'm so sorry to hear that."

*See, Nila, two can play at this game.*

I waved it away as if I was a martyr only focused on the love of his life. "Only a few headaches, but I can't tell you how happy I am to have her home." I jostled Nila closer, planting a kiss on her forehead. "I missed you so much."

Nila squirmed, her lips thinning with frustration. "Me, too. I just wish you'd been there when I lost the baby instead of on business."

Our eyes locked—the challenge in hers made my fingers dig into her side harder than I intended.

*Watch what you bloody say.*

I hoped she got my message because I was at the end of my patience. Cut would be watching somewhere—making sure I didn't fucking fail. Once we were free of our audience, she had a shit-load of explaining to do.

Ignoring Nila, I smiled at George and Sylvie. "But that's all in the past, and we've dwelt too long on that already."

George looked like he might argue, but I used the same trump card Nila had. "Let's discuss something a lot more exciting." I narrowed my eyes on my target: Sylvie would help guide the conversation to safer ground. "We're getting married. Let's talk about that."

# Nila

NO, LET'S TALK *about those drugs you just swallowed.*
Was it true he had a headache? Or was there something more sinister in that tiny bottle?

Sylvie clutched her heart, swooning a little. "It's so romantic. Star-crossed lovers reunited after lies and a miscarriage split them apart."

I let her turn my attention back to the stage-show but made a mental note to steal Jethro's pills the first chance I had. I had to know what they were.

"It's so tragically perfect." Sylvie's eyes were dreamy and dumbstruck by Jethro's undivided attention. He held the poor woman enraptured with his piercing golden gaze.

I nodded.

It *was* perfect.

Love and wealth and family.

*Pity it's all a heinous lie.*

"If *Vanity Fair* would be interested, you're more than welcome to an exclusive when I've finished designing my wedding gown." I hadn't even thought of saying that. My own lie snowballed, gathering faster and faster momentum.

If I had a future engagement with the magazine, it might make my untimely death more suspicious. If the debts took me, would they dig a little harder and uncover the truth? Then again, knowing the Hawks, they would spin some plausible tale, and I would be forgotten.

"Wow, that's a fantastic offer. Thank you, Ms. Weaver," George said. "We'd be delighted, of course."

"Excellent."

Jethro ground his teeth.

Despite his attempts to manipulate the conversation, he was in my shadow this morning. I had no intention of giving him the limelight. Jethro and his father had forced me to do this. But I would do it *my* way. I hadn't broken any of Cut's rules. I'd played along. I'd painted a picture for the world to eat up.

I'd just been smarter than they gave me credit for.

"When will the ceremony take place?" Sylvie spun on the spot, eying up the beautiful parlour. "Will you get married here or in a church?"

Jethro pinched the bridge of his nose, struggling to plant a smile on his lips. "It wasn't going to be announced for another few months, but I suppose it's out now, so we can spill a few of the details. We'll most likely have a garden wedding."

"I can imagine how happy you are," George said, fiddling with his camera and preparing to move from questions to pictures.

Jethro beamed, looking so young and carefree he took my breath away. "Extremely. I've never been so happy." His eyes landed on mine; a thought flew over his face. Then he grabbed me, dipped me as if we were on a dance floor, and before I could breathe, his lips slammed against mine.

The world switched off. Completely. Utterly. *Everything* disappeared.

There was no sound.

No colour.

No fear or stress or panic.

Just *him*.

Crackling, sparking, all-consuming lust. His taste, heat, smell. My skin hummed, my lips melted, my core clenched.

For weeks, I'd wanted nothing more than to kiss him. To hold him and find that combustible connection. To bind ourselves together even in the face of debts and danger.

I moaned as his tongue nudged against my lips.

I opened for him, sighing into the passionate kiss, suspended in his arms in front of the press. He didn't seem to care we had an audience. I *loved* that he didn't care.

He'd changed so much—lived through something I didn't understand. He'd become a stranger all over again. But no matter how he changed his thoughts and mind-set, he couldn't change his body. That part of him I knew. His body belonged to me as surely as my body belonged to him, and I had no doubt that would enrage and petrify him. Because no matter what distance he tried to put between us—it disintegrated whenever we touched.

With another soft moan, I slinked my fingers into his thick hair, jerking his mouth harder against mine. His tongue dived deeper, wrestling for dominance. His muscles trembled, holding me in the dip as the coolness of his mouth switched to heat and for the barest of delightful moments his teeth nipped my bottom lip.

Then sound came back.

Colour returned.

Awareness of the outside world drove a wedge between us.

The kiss was over.

Jethro swooped me back onto my feet, his mouth glistening.

*It was a set-up.*

My heart hardened. He'd kissed me for the reporters.

George stood with his camera, busily clicking, capturing every second of our sexy 'staged' slip-up.

*Good.*

At least people would have half of the story.

The part not drowning in bullshit.

There *was* love between us; there was a story about

connection beneath all the fakery. If only love was enough, I could be free. Jethro could be free. It could all be over if only love was stronger than debts.

"That was some kiss. Hot with a capital H." George laughed, fanning himself. "I can see why your brother wouldn't want you anywhere near Mr. Hawk, Ms. Weaver."

My tummy flipped. "Why?"

Jethro stiffened, paying strict attention.

George grabbed a tripod from his duffel. "I have a younger sister myself and if I saw her kissing a man like that, I would want to break them up, too."

Sylvie frowned, asking the question floating around in my head. "But why? It's a dream come true for any woman to have such a compatible partner."

George snorted, waving at Jethro and me with his camera. "Maybe women see it different, but from a guy's point of view, I know what I just witnessed, and it scares me."

Jethro cleared his throat, his natural intensity suffocating the room with power. "Explain. I'm not quite following."

George rolled his eyes. "Come on. You don't get it? Passion is incredibly dangerous if it's not respected and you two…" He shrugged. "Forget it. I'm overstepping. All I mean is chemistry like that can't be contained. It can bring great happiness but also destroy."

A shiver ran down my spine. His words sounded oddly prophetic.

Dragging his tripod over to the window bay, he clapped his hands. "Now, Ms. Weaver, if you wouldn't mind standing here. I want a picture of you with your diamond necklace in the sunshine."

For some reason, my feet remained planted on the carpet. What did he mean? That Jethro and I were freaks of nature governed by sex and nothing else? That we were idiots in a game we didn't understand?

George came toward me and manhandled me over to the window. "Perfect. Stand right there." His fingers slipped into my hair, fluffing the now dried strands, then brushed a powder over my brow and cheekbones that magically appeared from nowhere. "I don't know many women who look as stunning as you do without makeup."

I had no reply as he backed away and clicked a few test images, moving the tripod around until he was happy.

*Passion is incredibly dangerous if it's not respected.*

"If you could gather your hair to show off the choker?" George paused. "By the way, what does the choker symbolise? Were the rumours right that it portrays ownership...a wedding ring if you were?"

I opened my mouth to reply—with what, I had no idea— but Jethro jumped in. "It's a Hawk family heirloom. It's given to the woman who bewitches the first Hawk."

"Bewitches, that's an interesting word." Chuckling to himself, George turned his attention back on me.

*Did I bewitch him?*

My eyes drifted to Jethro as I cascaded black hair over my shoulder and angled my neck so the diamonds caught the sunlight. Instantly, rainbows drenched the carpet around my feet.

Jethro sucked in a breath, his hands fisting by his sides.

If what George said was true...did I have more power than I realised? Did that mean Jethro had more control over me than I thought? *Passion can be dangerous... I already tried to rule him with sex—but what if it worked both ways?* Had I dug myself into this hole without even realising it?

Too many questions. And really, answers wouldn't help. I would still be in the same situation.

"Give me a half smile. Look mysterious," George commanded, ducking to take angled pictures.

I pouted and preened, doing my best to come across secretive and coy.

If I was running out of time, I meant to be talked about for years after my death. I wanted to be known as the woman who brought down an empire—even if I had to sacrifice my life to do it.

A macabre thought made me swallow a laugh.

*I'm living a real life Romeo and Juliet saga.* Montague and Capulets, fighting an ancient battle. Would it end like that tragic tale, too?

Five minutes later, George had taken a gazillion pictures and grabbed his tripod. "Before we go, we would appreciate some photographs with the two of you outside."

Sylvie packed up the gear and made her way to the exit. "We'd love a tour as well, if that would be possible?"

Jethro drifted close to me, stealing my hand. My heart stuttered. I couldn't stop the overheating prickle of his skin against mine.

"I'm afraid the Hall is undergoing some renovations currently. Very few rooms are useable."

There were no renovations. Just lots and lots of things to hide.

Smiling to soften the blow of his rejection, Jethro added, "But I'm more than happy to invite you back when Nila has finished her wedding gown and you can see it then." His fingers squeezed tighter around mine in a silent reproof at my earlier comment.

Looking down, he gave me a calculating look. "Isn't that right, *darling?*"

I nodded. "Sounds perfect."

*If I'm still alive.*

"Follow us to the gardens." Jethro strode past George and Sylvie, dragging me with him. His long legs ate up the corridor, putting a couple of metres between us and our entourage.

Once out of hearing distance, he whispered harshly, "You're doing very well so far, Ms. Weaver. I'm impressed. However, if I were you, I'd stop overstepping boundaries."

Leaning into him, I murmured, "What boundaries are those? I don't remember boundaries when I was last here. Oh right, yes I do. No going on the chase where my family is buried. No going on the second floor. No running away. No talking to Vaughn. However, I don't remember you ever telling me to stop touching you or telling you how I felt."

His shoulders bunched. "Don't get cocky, Nila. No more games. I'm done trying to win—"

"That's because you always lose."

Jethro's eyes flashed. "I *never* lose. Unfortunately for me, my opponent hasn't been playing fair."

"What do you mean?" My forehead furrowed. "Everything I've tried to do—"

"Was to manipulate me. I was stupid to believe otherwise, but my eyes have since been opened. Regrettably for you, I will no longer be so easy to control."

Leaving the Hall by the main entrance, we stepped down the imposing stairs and crunched onto the gravel below.

"You were never easy to control, Jethro, and it was never about that. It was about finding someone I never thought I'd find. It was about falling in love—"

He yanked me to a stop. "Don't mention love in my presence again. You don't love me, and I certainly don't love you." Grazing his knuckles over my jaw, he smiled frostily. "Never underestimate my desire to fit in with my family, Ms. Weaver. And remember that I'm now immune to your distractions. Life at Hawksridge is going to be a lot different from now on."

I wanted to shout and scream. I wanted to attack him and kiss.

"You don't know anything, Jethro Hawk."

"Ready?" George appeared with his incessant camera.

Jethro wrapped his arms around me. Our tense standoff was silenced for a moment. He gave me no choice but to liquefy in his arms, smile demurely, and pretend everything was perfect for one of the fakest photographs ever taken.

"I know more than I need to," Jethro murmured, his breath hot and enticing on my neck. "I know everything I need in order to complete my task."

George darted forward. Sylvie, with her bouncing blonde

hair, checked the sunlight with handheld sensors. The day was cool but bright; a brilliant autumn backdrop for *Vanity Fair's* extravaganza.

"Perfect. Don't move," George said.

"Oh, I hadn't planned on it," Jethro whispered just for me. He rocked his hips into my arse as he cradled me in his arms. His head bowed as he nuzzled my hair. "You smell just as good as I remember."

"Oh, you remember that, do you?" I cocked my chin, glaring at Hawksridge and doing my utmost to remain unaffected by Jethro rubbing himself on my lower back. "And here I thought you'd forgotten everything to do with me."

"I haven't forgotten a thing."

"That's not true," I whispered sadly. "You've forgotten what I said to you the night you brought me back in the springs. You've forgotten that I said I was in love with you. That it didn't come with conditions or commands. That I couldn't hate you for what you did yesterday or tomorrow." I sighed, nursing the pain deep inside. "Don't you see what I'm offering you? Cut doesn't love you, Jethro. *He's* the one controlling you. Choose me. *Love* me. And we can be free together."

Jethro growled under his breath. "Stop wasting your time. It's not going to happen."

George pranced closer, clicking his camera, capturing us for eternity.

"You'll see, Kite. Eventually, you will see, and I hope for both our sakes it isn't too late."

That was the last time we talked while we became the perfect models for George. For the next hour, we were told where to stand, how to smile, what to do. Photographs were taken in front of Hawksridge, in the stables with the foxhounds threading around our feet, and beneath the apple trees in the orchard.

With each click of the shutter, my heart fell a little more. I had no doubt the pictures would turn the world from suspicion

to adoration. The rumours would die. The questions would disappear. And life would move on.
Exactly as the Hawks intended.

# Jethro

SCREW HER AND her conniving plans.

I wanted to fucking throw something, punch someone, and surrender to the rapidly building hailstorm inside.

*You need a top-up.*

I thought my dosage was perfect, but it was useless against her. The intensity she projected—the feral energy and righteous anger. It was enough to fucking cripple my walls and blow away my numbing fog.

*Not going to happen.*

I'd come so far. I wouldn't go back. I *couldn't*. I wouldn't survive and not just because Cut would kill me, but because I couldn't live that way any longer. I wasn't fucking built for this disease. I'd done my penance. Twenty-nine long years of it.

Pulling the small bottle from my pocket as I entered my quarters, I placed two pills on my tongue and swallowed them back.

Nila hadn't even been back a day and I'd already tripled the amount I normally took.

And when I kissed her.

Fuck!

What was I *thinking*?

To get so close to her? To taste her again?

I'd planned on an impromptu ad-lib for the article, but it

fucking backfired on me.

I stormed into my bathroom and tore off the grey suit I'd worn for the *Vanity Fair* interview. Cold sweat drenched my back. Goosebumps covered my skin as I stripped the rest of my clothing and stepped into the shower.

As soon as the meeting was over, I'd left Nila in the parlour and stormed to my room. Being around George and Sylvie had been easy. Their reactions and opinions didn't lash at me nearly as much as Nila's did.

What was it about her? Why couldn't I block her out?

Hot water rained over me, burning my flesh. Instead of washing away the tension of the morning, all I could think about was Nila pleasuring herself with the showerhead a few weeks ago. The way her face had tightened and pleasure made her glow. She'd never looked so goddamn beautiful.

My cock thickened, demanding I do something about the ache.

I couldn't let her do this to me. Not again. Not after I'd had the best month of my life with my father. I'd finally found something that could work. I'd finally tasted freedom.

I just had to stay out of Nila's clutches and do what I was born to do.

Fisting my cock, I thrust into my palm.

"You won't win this time, Nila," I growled. "I want you out of my head. Out of my fucking heart."

*Get out.*

My quads tensed as bliss danced with pain. I was rough, punishing my cock for having the audacity to want the one thing that could destroy me. My balls tightened, delicious pleasure gathered in my belly.

Fuck, I wanted her. I wanted to be inside her.

I needed to stay far away from her.

My fingers squeezed harder.

*You can't have her.*

Not if I wanted what Cut promised. Not if I wanted to rule.

My mind raced. I might not be able to have her physically, but Cut would never know what fantasies I allowed inside my broken brain.

I could have her like this—and still win.

With one hand braced on the tiles and water cascading over my shoulders, I imagined Nila spread-eagled on the bed, tied to four corners and panting from an orgasm I'd just given her with my tongue.

Her taste filled my mouth as I climbed on top of her and slid deep inside her wet pussy.

*Goddammit.*

Her moans echoed in my ears as I thrust inside her, giving into her tightness, dropping every restraint and shackle.

I came.

It was the fastest orgasm I'd ever had. Ribbon after ribbon, I spurted over my knuckles.

Jerking beneath the water, I rid my body of the insanity she'd conjured and slowly…interminably slowly…I could breathe again.

"Where are we going?"

Her melodic voice was anything but soothing. After a night of tossing and berating myself for how weak I turned out to be, I wasn't in the mood to deal with her—*especially* with her looking rested and fresh in jeans and an off-the-shoulder jumper with her hair plaited and just begging to be fisted while I took her from behind.

She didn't look nervous or fearful—she looked defiant and ready to battle.

"So, you're ignoring me now?"

"Not ignoring you, just filtering out your useless questions." I didn't turn to face her. Instead, I kept driving. Guiding the four-seater Ferrari FF away from Hawksridge Hall, I looked into the rear-view mirror.

I'd made the mistake of sitting Nila in the front with me. I should've put her in the back with Kestrel.

He caught my gaze, smirking a little as if he knew exactly what I was dealing with but didn't give a toss. Awful thing was he *did* know exactly what I was dealing with and whatever sympathy he'd given me in the past had long since dried up.

It fucking hurt to have my closest ally wash his hands of me.

Nila spun in her seat, the tan leather creaking beneath her. "You tell me, Kes. Why was my morning spent sketching my so-called 'wedding dress' interrupted by a mysterious trip off the estate?" Her voice lowered. "You've only just gotten me back—why am I being given outings when I was told I would never leave again?"

Kes chuckled, his silvering hair longer and slightly shaggy. "That's a lot of questions."

Nila deadpanned. "I have a lot of confusion."

Kes had changed a bit since I'd last seen him—withdrawing from me just like I withdrew from him.

Our fight came back with crystal clarity. It'd been two or three days after Cut had given me the ultimatum: *Drugs and keep Nila for myself. Die and give Nila to Daniel.* Kes had raged at me. He wanted me to give in and trust that together we could find another way. Only, he didn't know the sentence Cut had given. It wasn't his business. It was *my* curse. *My* responsibility to stay alive in order to protect Nila even while being cruel to her. And I had to use the tablets to remain sane enough to do that.

*I don't need him anymore—just like I don't need my sister.*

Kes laughed harder. The friendship between him and Nila sprang instantly back into place as if she'd never gone. How could they have such a bond when they were practically strangers?

I'd lived all my life with these people and still wasn't comfortable in their company. The numbness from my tablets meant I'd deliberately distanced myself from the people I was closest to, so their feelings and thoughts wouldn't sway my conviction. But to have Kes laugh so easily with Nila, when he was stilted and removed with me, hurt in a way I would never admit.

"Perhaps if you practice patience, you'll find out soon enough," I snapped.

Kes scowled, his hands clasped between his legs, his leather jacket and jeans filling up the rear of the car with authority only wealth can bring. "Everything is different now, Jet. You know that. If she asks, we tell her. Cut's orders."

Nila twisted further in her chair, eyes wide. "What does that mean?"

"It means that things have changed and our secrets...well, they're not just ours anymore." He leaned forward, his bulk crowding the centre console. "Try me. Ask anything and I'll answer."

I ground my teeth.

Nila bit her lip. "Okay...answer my first question. Where are we going?"

Kes didn't hesitate. "Diamond Alley."

"Diamond Alley?" Her mouth popped open. "What is that?"

I glanced warningly at Kes in the rear-view mirror. He was right. The rules had changed. But it was still my call what she learned, where she went, who she interacted with. I was both her protector and jailer. Confidant and confessor. Even though I didn't want our connection to hurt me anymore, she was still mine until the end.

Kes scowled at my reflection before giving Nila his full attention. "You want the truth, Nila?"

Her lips thinned. "I've been asking for the truth for months. Of course, I want it."

"The truth is sometimes worse than reality," I murmured under my breath.

She sent me a look, but the question in her eyes assured me she hadn't heard.

Kes settled back in the Ferrari bucket seat. "Okay, here it is. We're taking you to one of our shipping warehouses.

Diamond Alley is where most of what we mine enters England. We have a few distribution centres all over Europe, Asia, and America, but this one is closest to home and where we run the others overseas."

And just like that Nila became an honouree Hawk.

*I hope you're ready for this ride, Nila, because once you know, you can never forget.*

Nila absorbed that for a second, discounting hundreds of questions fleeting in her eyes. Taking a deep breath, she nodded. "Alright...and what does this have to do with me?"

I answered before Kes could. "What you're about to see is the truth. You will know where the stones come from. What they look like. How much we earn. Who works for us. Where the rocks end up. How we pay off the police. How we run fucking England. There will be no more secrets on who we are or what we expect of you. Answers will be given on every topic."

I glared at her. "You'll know *everything*. Every scrap of history, hope, dream, and disaster of our family and yours."

Nila's eyes glowed. "And what did I do to deserve such trust?"

My fists tightened around the steering wheel.

*Because you're special.*

Kes smiled sadly. "Because you proved yourself."

She tensed. "How exactly?"

"You spoke to the reporter. You dug your own grave," I murmured. "And no matter how much you want to, you won't be leaving Hawksridge again. Cut has made sure of that. Bonnie has made sure of that. You have nowhere else to go."

Nila's face went white, finally realising what she'd done. Kes and I stayed silent, waiting for her to verbalize her fate.

Her voice shook. "You no longer need to hide anything from me, because I won't be around much longer to share it."

*Bingo.*

I groaned quietly as a despairing cloud filled the car. The unhappiness, regret, and anger resonating from Nila was too much. Flicking the button on the steering wheel, I wound down the windows, blasting cold autumn air into the car.

I inhaled greedily, trying to dispel the lacerations of her anguish.

Nila shivered, hugging herself with white fingers.

Kes said, "You see...the truth is a bitch, but you've earned the right to know everything. Any question you want answered...we'll tell you. Every facet of our enterprise and brotherhood, you'll know."

Placing his hand on hers, he smiled softly. "You're one of us now, Nila. Forever and always. The world knows it. Your father and brother know it. There is nothing else to say on the matter."

She twisted in her seat, looking to the left where the moor and the graves of her ancestors rested. A chill scattered down my spine.

"So I'll be buried on your land to hide all the secrets I'll be privy to. Just like them." Her head fell forward. "I'm so *unbelievably* stupid. About everything."

I opened my mouth to agree—to dig the blade of unhappiness a little deeper. But...I couldn't.

No amount of drugs could make me kick her when she was already bleeding. I wouldn't be able to withstand the backlash, not to mention the rapidly building agony in my heart.

I thought the tablets would save me. Nila wasn't the only one who'd been stupid.

*We're both fucked, and it's up to me to hide my issues so Cut leaves her alone.*

I couldn't stand the stagnant sadness in the car. Unable to stop myself, I whispered, "You'll like what we have to show you, Nila. You'll see. You're one of us now, and it's time you understand what my family has been fighting to protect for generations."

Diamond Alley.

Nicknamed centuries ago by an ancestor who no doubt graced Hawksridge walls in some depressing painting. It'd gotten its name due to the four huge warehouses facing each other, creating a narrow road between them.

Driving here took a couple of hours, but it was worth it to have our very own port—unwatched and unmolested—yet another example of being above the laws governing the masses.

No light entered, only shadows. Electric fences, keycards, and passwords fortified the entrance. Located on the coast between sleepy seaside towns where the police force was entirely owned by us, we guarded our domain carefully. Greased pockets and yearly bonuses, we paid the coppers handsomely but we required strict loyalty.

I'd bloodied my hands a few times over the years teaching one or two traitors who didn't follow the rules a lesson.

Slowing to enter a key code at the front gate, conversation remained scarce as I drove through the compound and parked the Ferrari. The only cars and motorbikes here were those of trusted employees. No sightseers or holidaymakers. No one had any reason to visit, and it wasn't on any map. The two long fingers of warehouses looked derelict on the outside, but top-of-the-line security equipment, heat sensors, and bulletproof glass guarded their contents.

We protected our investment.

Pity the Weavers didn't do a good job protecting theirs.

The moment the car was stationary, Kes tapped Nila's shoulder. "Shall we?"

She unbuckled her belt and scooted out of the bucket seat without a backward glance. Kes climbed out and slammed the door.

I was left all alone.

*Thank fuck for that.*

I stretched my arms in front of me, rolling my neck and exhaling the magnitude of emotions I'd absorbed in the journey here. We hadn't spoken since leaving Hawksridge, but Nila's thoughts bombarded me mile after fucking mile.

Nila and Kes drifted away, heading toward the warehouse. With shaking hands, I fumbled for my pills and took another before climbing from the vehicle and locking it.

I had a horrible thought that I'd need a tranquiliser in order to make it through the journey home. It made me contemplate turning to alcohol and nicotine for other escapes—finding respite in chemicals and false highs.

Running my hands over my face, I trailed after my brother and little Weaver. Today was a simple transaction of overseeing a new arrival. Normally, Daniel would take care of it, but there was something else lined up. Something I'd agreed to unbeknownst to Cut and entirely on my own head if it didn't work out.

My Black Diamond jacket kept the sea breeze away, and the watery sun did its best to warm up the cool day. Stringy grey clouds shadowed the bland concrete beneath my shoes. It didn't matter that it was gloomy and bland outside—inside Diamond Alley, we didn't need sunshine.

We made our own.

A few metres away, Kes held out his arm for Nila to take. I waited for her to accept. I waited to see what I would feel. But she shook her head and kept her distance, preferring to glance at the gentle lapping ocean to our right and inhale the seaweed stench of kelp-covered rocks.

We made our way toward the entrance of Diamond Alley. The shadows of the huge buildings swallowed us as we traded open space for cramped alleyway.

My dress shoes clipped regally against the concrete while Kes's biker boots crunched and stomped. Nila made no noise at all, drifting forward in her flat ballet shoes, so young and innocent.

For a month, I'd lived without her. I'd visited the Weaver quarters often and fingered the half-finished designs she'd been working on.

The place had been empty, howling with injustice. I

couldn't stay in there long, too attuned to her smell and lingering presence. I'd told myself it was to desensitise myself for when she returned, but in reality, I was looking into the future—trying to see how I'd feel when she'd be gone for good.

Her room would be even emptier.

Her soul vanished forever.

Kes stopped halfway down the alley at a door. He knocked three times in a systemic code, and looked above the bombproof veneer to a camera.

A screen lit up with the face of one of our trusted guards. He glanced at us, nodded, then switched the screen to a keypad that scanned fingerprints as well as demanded a nine-digit passkey.

Nila remained silent as Kes entered everything he needed and the large mechanism unlocked, permitting entry.

Together we moved forward, leaving behind cramped laneways for the most dazzling sunlight imaginable.

"Wow," Nila breathed, squinting against the brilliant light.

It was blazing.

Far, far too bright.

Kes and I came prepared.

He chuckled, placing Ray-bans on his nose. "Rather cool, huh?"

Sliding my sunglasses from my front pocket, I placed the aviators over my eyes. Snapping my fingers, I held out my hand for the guard to give me a spare pair.

Instantly, a girlish retro pair was pressed into my palm, which I passed to Nila. "The lights are necessary."

Nila took the glasses, fumbling to put them on. "I've never been somewhere so bright."

"You'll see why it's like this."

"I'll get going," Kes said. "I'll come find you when I'm done." Patting his pocket, he moved away. "Got my phone if you need me. Have fun, Nila." With a wave, he prowled down the centre corridor of the huge open plan warehouse and disappeared.

Nila looked left and right. We stood in the centre of the four-story building where track lighting and halogen spotlights dangled like false suns. Not only had we traded a dreary autumn outside, but we'd also traded the cold for muggy heat.

Sweat already prickled my lower back beneath my leather jacket. I used to hate wearing this thing. I was a businessman, not a thug in a gang, but Cut wanted me to take over not just our Hawk legacy but the Black Diamonds, too.

And what Cut wanted, I was determined to deliver.

"Stop standing and staring, let's walk." Placing a hand on her lower back, I guided her forward.

She instantly sucked in a breath at the contact.

I waited for my fingers to burn and my heart to jolt...but I felt nothing.

The extra dose finally did what they should.

Nila drifted forward, her eyes taking in the rows upon rows of tables. They faced each other like little cubicles, some manned with staff, others empty. But all of them had numerous trays, tweezers, magnifying glasses, loupes, and black velvet covering the table-tops.

"Why is it so bright in here?" she asked, keeping pace with me.

"You're in a diamond warehouse. Light is the one tool to highlight flaws from perfections, clarity from cloud."

Despite the size of our operation, only thirty full-time staff worked for us in Diamond Alley. They'd been vetted, tested, and knew when they'd started working for us that it wasn't a simple position. Once they signed on the bottom line, there was no quitting or second-guessing their profession. They were ours for life.

To ensure we had no mutiny or unrest, we increased their salary every year, gave them room for promotion, and even compensated their families.

We'd never had an unhappy staff member. But then again, if they were caught stealing, pilfering, or tampering with the merchandise...well, a human life wasn't worth as much as a diamond.

Nila edged closer. "They're all in their underwear."

I eyed the staff members who didn't bother glancing up—too engrossed in their task and eager to hit their bonus for the day by clearing a certain amount of stones. Various skin colour, contrasting sizes, different sexes—but all one similarity—they all wore black underwear provided by the company.

I nodded. "A condition of employment."

"Why?"

"I thought it would be obvious? Fewer hiding places. Not to mention, they don't need clothing with the amount of heat generated from the lights."

Sweat moistened my brow as we reached the end of the warehouse and climbed the metal steps to the office above. Our footfalls clanged with every climb, shuddering the framework.

"And you sit up there and play God, I suppose," Nila muttered as we ascended toward the glass-fronted office with its bird's eye-view down the length of the building.

"It's a shared office for managers, but in a way we do. After all, we provide a livelihood to the people below us. We treat them well as long as they behave."

"A bit like me then." She darted ahead, opening the door and slinking into the office.

Following her, my eyes drank in the glistening sweat on her upper lip and tendrils of hair from her plait sticking to her nape. "You look warm, Ms. Weaver. You could always strip, you know. You are, after all, technically a Hawk employee."

She bit her lip, the air flaring between us with static electricity.

*Shit, why did I say that?*

She lowered her gaze, not hiding the way she ogled me. "Perhaps I should."

Instantly, my cock twitched.

"But only if you strip, too."

I slammed the door and brushed past her. "Not going to happen."

Never again. I couldn't afford to sleep with her. Not if I wanted to stay in my drugged-bubble.

The office was sparse. Bare metal floors, filing cabinets bolted to the walls, a cowhide couch, and a desk in the centre.

Nila stalked me, moving toward the desk I placed between us. "Do you want me to strip because you don't trust me around the stones or because you want me naked?" Her hands tugged at the jumper cascading off her shoulder. Pulling it further down, the swell of her breast and the tantalizing hint of black lace appeared. "Get naked with me, Jethro. Or don't you trust yourself around me anymore?"

I gritted my teeth, forcing myself not to react. My cock completely ignored me, thickening to a steel fucking rod in my pants. Doing my utmost to seem unaffected, I switched on the desk lamp and picked up one of the many Post-it notes and memos stuck to the walnut desk. "Don't flatter yourself. I told you before, I'm not interested anymore."

Nila came closer, her fingertips dragging over the table-top. "Not interested...or not allowed?"

My head snapped up. "Be careful."

"No."

"*What* did you just say?"

She narrowed her eyes. "I'm tired of being careful. Being careful only brought me heartache. All my life I've been careful, and you know what? I'm *sick* of it."

With an erotic twist, she grabbed the hem of her jumper and tugged it over her head. Her plait draped down her back and the tiny white camisole she wore didn't hide the lacy bra beneath.

*Fuck.*

It also didn't hide her pebbled nipples.

"Does this count as being careful, *Kite*?" Nila dropped the jumper onto the desk, cupping her breasts. "Does this count as acceptable to you?"

I couldn't breathe.

Everything I'd been running from made my head pound, my cock beg, and the drugs in my system to fucking disintegrate.

What was it about her? Why did she have this control over me? And why was I utterly, ridiculously helpless around her?

*God fucking help me.*

Didn't she know the more she antagonised me and made me slip, the more likely Cut would give her to Daniel and fucking slaughter me in my sleep? I wanted to strike her—hammer the precariousness of our situation home.

"Why did you bring me here?" she murmured, skirting the desk.

I couldn't tear my eyes away from the hard pinpricks on her chest. She couldn't be cold—not in this furnace. That meant she was turned on.

My mind instantly went to one question. *Is she wet?*

"Kes told you. Our secrets are now yours."

"I don't think that's the only reason." Closing the distance, she licked her bottom lip. "I think you wanted me off the estate, so you could have me without anyone seeing." Her voice layered with sex and invitation. "You wanted me away from the cameras, so you could drop the act and show me the truth."

*Fuck.*

I cleared my throat. "What truth?"

"That all of this is a lie. That you're still the man I fell for—playing the same game you said you were sick of before I left."

Shaking my head, I tried to clear my thoughts. "You're once again delusional." Swallowing hard, I ordered, "Go down to the sorting floor. I have a meeting to take care of—"

"No," she breathed. "I'm not going anywhere until you stop being an asshole and show me the real you." Closing the final distance, she stood beside me, crackling with mischief and lust.

Locking eyes, she undid the button and zipper of her

jeans. "Don't hide from me, Jethro. I can't stay strong if you cut me out."

My legs bunched to push the swivel chair backward. One heave and I could launch myself free and run from her web. But somehow, I couldn't. I remained tethered in place; breathing fast, fear swamping my lungs.

She grabbed my wrist. "Don't fight it. You can't fight the inevitable." Without a word, she pressed my hand into her trousers.

*Holy shit.*

My heart catapulted through my ribcage; my jaw locked as the scratch of her lacy underwear rubbed my knuckles.

Our eyes never looked away as she guided my fingers lower. I tugged half-heartedly, trying to remember why this was wrong when it felt so fucking right.

"Don't…" She rocked her hips, twisting my wrist so my hand cupped her wetness.

She moaned, her head falling back. Her breasts were proud, jutting out, begging for my teeth and tongue. "That's what you were wondering, wasn't it?" She bent over me, licking the rim of my ear. "If I was wet for you?"

I groaned as she deliberately rubbed herself on my fingertips.

My eyes snapped shut as she eased her underwear aside, guiding my finger inside her.

I stopped breathing. I stopped worrying. I couldn't do anything but give in.

My cock punched against my belt. Pain existed everywhere. It took everything I had not to grab her and fuck her over my desk.

Her plait dangled as she breathed in my ear, "Take me, Kite. Fill me like you did in the spring. I'm yours and you belong inside me. Nobody can change that." She rocked again, moaning softly. "I want you."

"Nila…"

*I want you, too. I want to tell you everything. I want to fucking run away and never look back…*

"Well, this is an interesting sight."

Nila shot upright. "Oh, my God."

Yanking my hand from her jeans, I shoved her behind my chair. "I told you I had a fucking meeting," I growled.

She fumbled with nerves, struggling to do up her trousers. Her eyes narrowed at our guest, anxiety waking off her in droves.

For once, I didn't mind. I rather enjoyed her flustered need. Her unsettled confusion.

Spinning my chair around, so the man in the doorway wouldn't see, I raised the finger that'd been inside her and ever so slowly, sucked it clean. Her taste exploded on my tongue. I could've come right there if we didn't have an audience.

Nila stumbled, her hands crossing over her chest to hide the sheer camisole and bra.

"I have a feeling I interrupted something. However, I'm not going to be the gentleman and say sorry. I'm just going to stand right here and wait." The man laughed quietly. "By all means, continue if you must. I'm a patient guy."

Nila looked over my head, swallowing desire and frustration. "Not at all. I was just leaving."

Moving fast, I latched my damp fingers around her wrist and tugged to whisper in her ear. "Whatever you just started…it's not over."

Her eyes widened as I let her go.

I spun back to face my guest. "Hello, Killian."

Nila sneaked forward to snag her jumper. I chuckled under my breath. How could she be so sensually confident one moment and so flummoxed the next? "Nila Weaver, seeing as you delayed me, please say hello to my business meeting."

The man in the doorway nodded, filling the frame with his large bulk and brown leather jacket. The stitching of his MC glittered with the words 'Prez' and 'Pure Corruption.'

Nila blushed, slipping into her top. "Pleasure to meet you…"

"Kill," the man said, stalking into the room and holding out his hand. A smirk spread his lips, remembering what he'd interrupted. "On second thought, perhaps I won't give you my hand. I don't know what you'll do with it."

Nila turned a deeper pink. Her eyes hit the floor.

I laughed.

*Serves her right for unsettling me.*

Standing, I crossed the room and shook hands with the president of Pure Corruption. Standing taller than me with muscles bigger than Kestrel and black hair brushing his jaw, Killian screamed violence and influence. He wasn't someone you messed with.

His huge grip clasped mine. "Nice to see you again, Hawk."

Nila sized him up, interest glowing beneath her shyness.

It pissed me off, but I wasn't worried. It was well-known that Arthur Killian of the Florida Pures didn't go after women. He wasn't gay, but for some reason he avoided the opposite sex.

Kill dropped my hand, crossing his arms with a creak of leather. "Now that the intros are out of the way...shall we begin?"

# Nila

I COULDN'T TAKE my eyes off the new intruder.

I wanted to back away to become as invisible as possible.

The entire atmosphere of the room changed the moment he'd stepped inside. Jethro was sleek and cool—as flawless as ice and as deadly as poison, but Arthur Killian was like a tank. A weapon reeking of biker oil, sunshine, and fearlessness. My body completely belonged to Jethro, but I couldn't deny Killian's massive arms, untamed hair, and glowing emerald eyes didn't flutter my stomach.

Coming toward me, his clothing rustled as he held out his hand. "No matter how much I fear for my hand's safety, I can't ignore such a stunning woman." The air hummed with fierce intensity.

My gaze flickered to Jethro as I looped my fingers with his. Jethro stiffened but didn't retaliate. My cheeks burned as Killian's grip wrapped tightly around mine.

He was so *warm*.

An oven compared to Jethro. And his eyes. Oh, my God, I'd never seen such green, green eyes.

"It's not *your* hand that should be worried."

*Only yours, Kite.* I shot the silent message to Jethro.

Killian laughed. It sounded like a rumbling earthquake. He shook his head almost sadly, glancing over his shoulder at

Jethro before looking back at me. "In that case, I don't know if I should be jealous of Hawk's hand or regretful for my own." His deep voice was rhythmic—an accented drawl different to Jethro's crisp English loquacity.

"You're American?"

Kill took a step back, running a hand through his jaw-length dark hair. He looked wild, ferocious, but with a brokenness about him speaking of unpredictability.

What hurt him? Or *who*?

The vulnerability hiding beneath his rough exterior called to the nurturing side of me. I wanted to protect him from something. But what? There was nothing in the world that could hurt this mountain of a man.

Kill nodded. "Yes, ma'am. Born and bred in Florida."

"What are you doing so far from home?"

His large boots clopped across the metal floor as he sat on the cow-print couch by the door. Bright spotlights shone behind him, casting him in a fuzzy silhouette. His eyes narrowed, tone turned dark. "Business, mainly. And new connections."

The way he said it didn't sound just about business.

I'd been around dangerous men enough to recognise one with a vendetta. "And Jethro is going to help you with that?"

"Nila...don't pry." Jethro appeared by my side, wrapping a chilly arm around my shoulders. His strength suffocated me, tightening like a boa constrictor instead of a simple embrace.

My eyes shot to his. In the presence of a man who wore his vitality and emotions in full view, Jethro seemed even more remote. A damn island surrounded by shark-infested waters with ice for waterfalls and snow for sand.

Stepping out of his hold, I crossed my arms. "Does Killian know what you've done to me? What your family has done to mine?" It was a ridiculous move and one I would never normally do. But Killian made me bold.

Jethro froze.

His eyes turned deadly. "Enough." Pointing at the door,

he growled, "Time for you to leave."

Kill laughed. "She your old lady?"

Jethro turned his temper on the burly man commandeering the entire couch with his bulk. "We don't have misses or old ladies in our MC. We're more of a business enterprise rather than a brotherhood."

Kill shook his head. "Doesn't matter. I run the Pures as a business, too. But we're still family."

I jumped in. "The Black Diamonds aren't family. They're employees."

Kill cocked his head, pinning his vibrant emerald eyes on me. "And you...are *you* an employee?" His gaze drifted down my front, drinking me in.

My heart beat faster, subjected to his scrutiny. His interest was visceral, but it wasn't sexual.

I stood taller, balling my hands. "No, I'm—" *His Weaver Whore. The woman destined to die for ludicrous debts.*

"She's not an employee," Jethro snapped. "She's a pain in my ass and needs to leave." He herded me toward the door. "You've pushed and pushed me today." Lowering his voice, he added, "Wait till we get home. You'll pay the price."

I spun in his hold, causing his hand to go from my lower back to my belly. I gasped as his long fingers brushed my bare midriff below my jumper.

"That threat doesn't scare me."

"Oh, no? It should."

I inched closer, cursing the wetness building between my legs. "It doesn't because I'm brave enough to give myself over to you. You're terrified of me and all I need to say is 'Kiss me, Jethro Hawk' and we'll see who wins again."

He sucked in a harsh breath. "You'll pay—"

"Watch me." Tearing my eyes from his, I looked at Kill again. "To answer your question, I'm not his employee. I'm so much more than that." My heart broke a little for a dream I would never have. "I could be his everything, but he's too stupid to see what I'm offering."

Killian's face seemed to shatter, his own heartbreak slamming into mine. I felt a kinship with him. A mirroring echo to our hidden desires. He'd been hurt by someone just like Jethro was hurting me.

Fists and kicks and bullets might maim and destroy, but love...love tears out your insides and leaves you hollow, leaving you destined to live an empty existence until death. Lucky for me, I wouldn't have to live long knowing Jethro could never love me.

Jethro pinched the bridge of his nose, fumbling for something in his pocket. "Goddammit, woman. Get out."

Kill perched on the edge of the couch, a black shadow shading his face. "Wait, you love him?"

My heart lurched. I couldn't look at Jethro as I confessed, "I do. And believe me, if I knew of a way to stop it, I would."

Jethro turned into a vibrating ice sculpture. He tipped something into his palm—something small and white.

Kill glared at Jethro, his temper eddying around the room. "Did you know she loved you?"

Jethro sucked in a breath. "What the fuck sort of question is that?" Throwing the pill into his mouth, he swallowed.

*What the hell is he taking?*

Kill crossed his arms. "A simple one."

I looked at Jethro, waiting for his answer, begging him to snap out of whatever his father had done and *admit it*. What was the harm? Why couldn't he put me out of my misery and profess he felt what I did?

"Kite..." I whispered. "Answer it."

Jethro's eyes latched with mine. He trembled.

*Please...stop pushing me away.*
*Stop being so cruel.*

"There is no simple answer." Jethro's voice was strained, full of rocks.

Kill stood up, a huge wrecking ball about to decimate us. Ignoring Jethro, he brushed past and cupped my cheek so tenderly, it broke something that'd been festering inside me for months. "Love is something that strikes without warning to the most unsuspecting. It's a fucking gift and so goddamn priceless, but only the worthy realise what they have. Only the ones truly deserving fight every fucking day to treasure it. And those who don't...they end up alone."

Dropping his hand, he glowered at Jethro. "I pity people who can't be true to their hearts. But I'm done prying into your private lives." He stormed back to the couch. "Leave, Nila. Hawk and I have business, and I want to get it over with."

Jethro glared. His voice skittered into my ear. "Thanks a lot. Good fucking work."

He shoved me out the door. "Go play with diamonds, Ms. Weaver, and leave me to worry about what repercussions your little stunt has caused."

Before I could say a word, he slammed the door and yanked down the inner shutters. He left me stranded and alone, drenched in spotlights, dancing in rainbows from precious stones.

An hour passed.

A full hour of waltzing down rows upon rows of diamonds while wearing sunglasses indoors. I'd never seen so much wealth in one place and in so many varieties.

There were cloudy, uncut rocks that looked like any old stone. There were brilliantly faceted marquise, cushion, and princess.

Each and every one sent my heart throbbing, because each and every one symbolised just how much wealth the Hawks had and the lengths they would go to protect it.

I snorted. *They value rocks more than human life.*

My mind skipped back to Jethro and the tablets he'd taken. Were they the reason for his dramatic change? And if so...what could I do to detox him and make him mine again?

The staff smiled as I made my way through the middle of the warehouse. I walked strictly down the centre, not wanting to get too close to the desks and black velvet just in case I was accused of stealing.

I would never do such a thing, but for now, I had no clue what went on inside Jethro's head. Cut might be biding his time for me to screw up to hurt me. This might be some crazy test.

I dawdled as long as I could, before turning and making my way back toward the office. Looking into the heights of the building, I frowned. The shutters were still in place, no hint of life.

*How much longer is he going to be?*

"You can touch, you know."

My attention whipped to the side. A man with a beer gut and goatee motioned me closer. "They're not poisonous."

I shook my head, keeping my hands behind my back. "It's okay. I'm more of a looker than a toucher."

The man grinned, showing a gold-capped tooth and lines around his mouth. With stubby fingers, he chose a stone from the tray in front of him and placed it on his palm. The brilliant lights highlighted the dull quartz, and despite myself, I drifted closer.

"Give me your hand."

"No, really—"

"Look, you came with the owner. You wear millions of their diamonds around your neck. I think they'll let you hold a boring rock like this."

My hand shot to the collar. The diamonds were warm beneath my touch, humming with vitality—almost as if they recognised their kin.

"When you put it that way." Taking my sunglasses off, I pushed them on top of my head and hesitantly held out my hand.

"There you go." He plopped the rock into my palm. I tried to ignore how strange it was to be talking to a half-naked man in a sweltering diamond factory.

When I just stood there, fearing that any moment Kes would arrive with a gun or Cut would chuckle and hurt me, the man shook his head. "Nothing to be scared of." He pointed at the stone. "Roll it between your fingers, feel the smoothness even though it hasn't been cut yet."

I obeyed, stroking the cloudy diamond and feeling the same strange warmth emitting as my necklace. "It feels alive."

The man nodded. "The heat from the lamps keep them temperate, but it also comes from the diamond itself. There's an old tale that true diamonds could heat the world. That they hold enough life and love in each stone that we would never be cold again."

Sadness fell over me. Jethro worked with heat-giving diamonds, yet I'd never known anyone so cold. "If that's true, I should be forever hot."

The man chuckled, reaching to stroke my collar. His chair squeaked as his belly dug into the table. "That you should." His head cocked, eyes feasting on the Weaver Wailer. "I've seen those stones before. They're old...very old." He frowned, then his face shocked white as he stole the rock from my hand.

My heart raced. "When...when did you see them?"

He pursed his lips, keeping his eyes downcast. "Never mind. Forget I said anything. Go on, carry on looking...there are much prettier rocks a few trays away."

I touched his knuckles, sickness and dread swimming in my veins. "You saw her, didn't you?"

He froze. "Saw who?"

I sighed heavily as my mother appeared in my mind. She'd been here. She'd lived through everything I had—a carbon copy of myself. "A woman with shoulder-length black hair, dark eyes, and high cheekbones." My voice trailed to a whisper. "I've been told we look similar...you don't need to deny it. You saw my mother."

The man swallowed. "I don't think I'm allowed to talk about the past, Miss." His eyes shot upward to the office. "Shit."

His curse was out of character. I looked up.

My heart fell into my toes.

Jethro.

He stood on the metal staircase, halfway down. One hand on the banister, the other in his trouser pocket. His requisite diamond pin glinted on his lapel looking small compared to the size of some of the stones surrounding us. The lights dazzled, causing his golden eyes to sparkle like the champagne diamonds on the tray before me—just as unique and perfectly cold. Unlike the diamond I'd held, there was nothing flawed about this man.

*Apart from his mind, of course.*

The more time I spent with him, the more confident I was that Jethro and I were the same in that respect.

I had a physical imbalance. My body hadn't mastered the art of equilibrium and occasionally malfunctioned. Jethro, on the other hand, had a mental imbalance but in what I hadn't figured out.

*You have a sneaking suspicion, though.*

Ever since speaking to Vaughn when we watched one line instead of two appear on the pregnancy test, I'd wondered. Could it be that obvious? Or that surprising?

*I need to see Jasmine again.*

I hadn't forgotten the way she'd sobbed as I left—not for me, but her brother. She knew everything, and it was time she shared that knowledge.

Jethro descended the stairs, his eyes never leaving mine.

"Best move along," the man whispered.

I didn't want to get him in trouble, but I couldn't move.

Jethro glided toward us, his gaze narrowed against the glare of the lights.

"Are you enjoying your time inspecting the merchandise, Ms. Weaver?" Jethro smiled curtly at the man beside me. "Christopher, I hope you are indulging my guest's every whim."

Christopher swallowed, a droplet of sweat running down his naked chest. "Um, yes, sir." He shot me a glance, awkwardness all over his face.

I felt sorry for him but furious for my mother. Grabbing

Jethro's arm, I pulled him away from Christopher's table. Anger bubbled in my veins. "He was kind and helpful and under no circumstances will you discipline him, but he told me something interesting." Looping my fingers beneath my choker, I growled, "He said he'd seen my collar before."

Jethro stopped breathing.

"I'm assuming that meant my mother was brought here."

He didn't reply.

"She was given the same privileges, wasn't she? Because everything she learned was destroyed when Cut took her life."

He balled his hands.

Suddenly, it was all too much. I sighed. "Don't worry. I won't force you to talk. I won't ever attempt to make you do anything again. Can we just leave? I want to go home."

The minute I said it, visions of my quarters at Hawksridge came to mind...not home in London with Vaughn. I groaned under my breath. Even my memories had replaced my past with all things Hawk.

Jethro still didn't say a word, his pale skin growing whiter the longer he stared.

I stared right back.

His body vibrated the longer we stood in silence.

Then, he snapped.

Stealing my wrist, he stormed down the aisle, dragging me with him. "Goddammit, why must everything in my fucking life be so hard?"

"Wait." I tugged on his hold. "Where are we going?"

"Quiet."

I looked back to the office; perhaps that massive Pure Corruption biker could save me? If I told him everything— would I stand a chance at getting free? "Where did Kill go?"

"Gone."

"Back to Florida?"

*Would I be safe from you if I flew to America?*

"No, to the next warehouse to pick up what we promised."

I stumbled; the pace Jethro set was manic. "What did you promise?"

"Something in return for something else."

"What something else?"

"He's a genius with numbers—hides dirty money in many ways."

"And what does he get?"

Jethro groaned under his breath. "Questions. Always bloody questions with you."

I shrugged. "As Kestrel said, I've dug my own grave. My questions can be answered now."

*Including the ones I really want to know. Like who you truly are and why you won't let me in!*

Coming to the end of the warehouse, he opened a door and dragged me down an empty corridor. At the end of that, there was a single exit. It looked like a janitor's closet, but the moment he opened it, it revealed a ginormous silver barricade with a keypad and spin dial.

Letting me go to enter in codes and spin the dial, he scowled. "Fine. You want to know? I'll tell you." The mechanism *snicked* open and the air pressure shifted a little. With a grunt, he yanked the thick vault open and motioned me to enter.

Deciding to obey and avoid his biting fingers, I entered the large safe.

Jethro followed, sighing in relief at the temperature change. Inside was bright but cool—the buzz of air-conditioners kept the space chilly compared to the warm warehouse.

I expected to see stacks of cash and precious gems, but all that existed were walls of gunmetal grey safety deposit boxes.

"You asked. I'll tell." Waving at the space, Jethro said, "All of this is to control the world we live in. We're untouchable because of these tiny pieces of rock. We've built an empire on wealth accumulated from a single incident in our past that enabled us to leap over the heads of the Weavers and prove that they might've owned England back then but *we* own it now."

"But how? Surely a mine would dry up after a time?"

"We don't just have one mine, Ms. Weaver. We have dozens all around the world."

Having my questions answered was a novelty—a saving grace. I never wanted to stop. "Where?"

"We mine diamonds in Africa, rubies in India, sapphires in Thailand, emeralds in Pakistan. We have the world's most exclusive catchment of Alexandrite—one of the rarest stones—and we also have this…"

Jethro moved to the back wall and used a key to open a safety deposit box. Pulling it out, the drawer went on for ages—a long grey finger sliding free from a wallpaper of squares.

Another twist of a key and the lid opened.

Without a word, Jethro reached into the shallow box and pulled out a red velvet pouch. Stitched into the plush material was the emblem for the Black Diamonds with his initials on the front.

The JKH was exactly the same as the one on my fingers.

My heart raced as he undid the strings, moving toward me. "Hold out your hand."

I didn't hesitate.

Jethro tipped the velvet pouch, plopping into my palm the blackest, richest, most incredible stone I'd ever seen. It looked like the devil's apple from the Garden of Eden. Large and gleaming and wrong. The weight alone made me grasp it with two hands. "Wow."

"The largest black diamond ever found."

The stone was uncut but still shone as if it were alive—as if it sensed me holding it and had eyes looking back at me. My skin tingled. I wanted to put it down—somehow I knew it didn't like me. "How big is it?"

"Six hundred carats." Jethro came closer, his spicy aftershave clouding around me. "It's the reason why we are what we are."

I blinked. "What do you mean?"

Jethro stole the stone, holding it up to the spotlight in the ceiling. "It was the third diamond my ancestors ever found. They didn't know what it was—we didn't know then that diamonds come in colours—pink, yellow, blue. They thought it was obsidian. But they knew they had something special. When they returned to England, they researched it. They had the top specialist from the Crown Jewels make an assessment."

He twisted the rock, his face pensive. "When they were told it was a black diamond, the name stuck. The men who'd helped my ancestors find it immediately became known by that name." He smiled. "Fancy that...a piece of history and you didn't have to pay a debt to hear it."

Chills scattered down my arms.

Up until that second, I'd revelled in hearing how the Hawks came into power. But he'd ruined it. Just like everything.

"How did your family go from serving my ancestors to mining massive rocks?"

Jethro shook his head. "That piece of information will come with a price."

"What price?"

Jethro pulled me into his body, his hardness instantly igniting my blood. "A debt, naturally."

I winced. "Can we not mention those again? Not when it's just us."

His eyes fell on my lips. "When it's just us, it's even more dangerous to talk...about anything." His head bowed; a lock of tinsel hair kissed his forehead. "I have something I need to ask." He tensed. "Not ask...demand."

"I prefer it if you just asked. You should know by now if you give into me, I'd do anything for you."

He let me go. "I need you to watch what you feel around me."

My mouth parted. "What?"

His eyes darted around the space, searching for help in

silent corners. "I can't explain it, but whatever you think of me, whatever you think of the way I've treated you since you came back, keep it to yourself. Don't hate me. Don't love me. Don't fear me. Put up a wall and just stop."

"You're asking me to stop feeling?" I gasped. "That's like asking someone to stop *breathing*, Jethro. It's not possible."

He dragged a hand over his face. "Things changed, Nila, and if you want to remain mine—you have to do this for me."

Ice water replaced my blood. "Remain yours?" Drifting forward, I touched his forearm. "He threatened you, didn't he?" My heart lurched, blooming bright with the love I'd tried to smother. Whatever Jethro was or did, he *did* care for me, and that was why he suffered. "What did he do?"

Jethro backed away, his face twisting. "Nothing. That's one question I won't answer. Just do as I ask and your existence will continue without hardship."

I laughed softly. "You don't get it. Having you distant from me is the worst hardship of all." Taking his hand, I placed it over my heart. "You can't see the scars you're leaving on me but they're there, Jethro. As surely as the scars on my back from your whip."

"I can't keep doing this," he breathed, his shoulders caving.

"Can't keep doing what?"

"I can't keep doing *this*." He pushed me away, holding up the dark stone. "A black diamond is completely different to a white one."

I struggled to switch topics.

*Why is he changing the subject?*

"They have a different crystalline structure. They don't sparkle because they don't refract light." His eyes glittered. "They absorb it."

*Where is he going with this?*

"Like you? Absorbing Weaver lives."

He didn't answer, sadness darkening his face. "White diamonds are windows for light to bounce and reflect. Black diamonds are souls—sucking in everything, ingesting their environment and giving nothing in return."

His voice bristled with depth—it wasn't just about the stone. *He's trying to tell me something...*

My hands twitched to grab him. My lips burned to connect with his.

*Tell me!*

He couldn't look at me. He couldn't even admit what he revealed. However, the diamond was no longer an innate object—but him.

*He* absorbed and ingested. *He* was a direct product of his surroundings.

"You've absorbed me..." I breathed.

My voice shattered Jethro's confession, snapping him into ice. "Time to go." Slipping the mysterious black diamond back into its home, he locked the safety deposit box and took my hand.

I never mentioned the stone again.

Not during the long drive home with Kes.

Not lying in bed that night.

Jethro had finally admitted the truth.

And I had no idea what it meant.

# Jethro

TWO DAYS PASSED.

Two days where I avoided Nila, took copious amount of drugs, and tried my utmost to swim back into numbing fog.

The meeting at Diamond Alley with Killian and Nila in an enclosed space had been sheer fucking hell.

Both of them were so opinionated and strong willed. When Kill asked Nila if she loved me and Nila had fractured into pieces of grief, I'd almost snapped.

*Almost.*

She must've guessed what I was by now.

I couldn't seem to keep it a secret.

I was at the point where if she asked me again, I would tell her. I would spill every sordid detail and bullshit diagnosis. I couldn't hide it anymore.

The night after dropping her back at Hawksridge, Kestrel and I had dealt with a dispute with one of our traders on the black market. They wanted more stock for less money. We wanted more money for less stock. The age-old upsets between businesses.

The negotiations hadn't gone smoothly.

The tension between both sides drained me of my rapidly dwindling energy, and by the time we returned home, I wanted nothing to do with people and fled.

I'd hidden until the moon rose and I could escape without consequence. I needed fresh air. And I needed it now.

I revved my bike down the long drive, heading away from Hawksridge. Turning right off the estate, I leaned into a corner, speeding up until inertia became an enemy trying to steal me from my vehicle.

The rumble of the machine soothed me. The cool wind on my cheeks gave me room to breathe. And the power from the engine made me invincible.

But it was lacking.

*I miss it.*

I gritted my teeth.

*You miss nothing.*

I refused to admit that I missed my fucking horse.

I hadn't ridden since Nila paid the Second Debt. I doubted I would ride again. Not now I was the perfect son and life stopped playing me for a fool.

Every mile I travelled, the fog I craved wisped behind me until I was clearheaded for the first time in weeks. Out here with only squirrels and owls for company, it didn't matter. I sighed in relief as I reached the outskirts of Buckinghamshire and pulled over onto a verge.

I wasn't far from home, twenty minutes at most. But the rock walls and overhanging trees of the country lanes could've been centuries ago—so far removed from humanity and technology.

Killing the engine, I took off my helmet and fumbled for the pills in my leather jacket. I had no intention of going home without more drugs barricading my system.

"Goddammit," I growled, unable to open the bottle with my gloves on. Biting the middle finger of my glove, I yanked it off with my teeth.

The two tattoos of Nila's initials shone in the moonlight.

They sucker-punched me in the gut.

*Fuck.*

Everything I'd kept buried rose up unhindered on the

desolate side of the road.
*You're ruining everything.*
*I'm ruining nothing.*
I was protecting my sister, my brother, myself. I was walking the line I'd been born to walk. I couldn't do any more than that, and if Nila expected more from me, then tough shit. I had nothing left to give.

A rustle and twig snapped in the field behind the mossy rock wall I'd stopped beside. My ears twitched for more; my eyes tried to see through the darkness.

I couldn't see a thing.

Ignoring the noise—putting it down to a badger or fox—I tipped a tablet into my hand and tossed it into my mouth. Already, my head pounded and hands shook. Withdrawal was a fucking bitch.

I went to swallow.

I never had time to swallow.

Something hard and brutal struck the back of my skull. I slammed forward, crunching my nose on the handlebars, gushing with blood.

"Shit!" I didn't know which pain was worse—my nose or the back of my head.

"Travelling on your own, motherfucker?"

I stiffened. This was why we didn't go for midnight excursions alone. This was why I had bodyguards and ran a fucking biker gang.

Thieves and vagrants.

Blinking through the pain, I shoved off my handlebars and glared into the night.

Three bikers from the Cannibal Chainmen MC climbed over the wall and landed on the road surrounding me.

Every muscle tightened.

"You." These assholes had ambushed our deliveries for years. They knew never to step foot in Buckinghamshire. This was our fucking territory. They belonged in Birmingham—dirty scum.

"Get off our turf," I snarled, drinking blood and wiping the remainder on the back of my hand. Swinging my leg off my bike, I stood in their circle, turning slowly to inspect each one. "You know the consequences."

They were lowly ranked members, patched in, but held no position of authority.

"Oh, we know the fucking consequences, alright." A guy with a shaved head and knuckles wrapped in red tape sneered.

"Messing with the Black Diamonds is a sure way to die." I spat a wad of blood on the ground, wishing the throb in my skull would fade. "I suggest you fuck off. Our turf. Our rules."

The biker laughed. "Ah, but if we take out the Vice President of the Blacks, then doesn't that make it *our* turf?"

*That doesn't even make sense.* Fucking idiots had to take out Cut for that to become a possibility. And that would never happen.

They continued to circle. Even though I was trapped in the centre, I guided them toward the middle of the road—away from the wall and my bike.

I needed open space to win.

I needed silence and darkness and no interruptions.

My hands curled, stretching knuckles and tendons, preparing to fight. I hadn't been in a battle for months. And…I needed one.

Fuck, I truly did.

I needed something to let off steam. To get rid of everything inside. To finally scream and rage and fucking give into the hatred I never seemed to be free of.

These men had no idea what they'd just walked into.

The intensity I'd lived with all my life remained on a leash, but I slowly let it affect me. Drinking in their violence and bloodlust—I became infected.

In that moment, drenched in moonlight and starshine, I was free.

Free like I was on a polo field. Free like I was when I slid inside Nila.

*Fuck, I've been so cruel to her.*

Away from the Hall and the pressures of my life, I could see clearly. There was no fucking excuse for what I'd become.

"Made your peace, asshole?" the bald man said, smiling at his two accomplices with dirty brown hair. They slipped out of their jackets, revealing grimy tank tops and tatted arms.

I cracked my neck, smiling with bloody teeth. "Have *you?*"

They laughed.

I laughed.

I moved first.

A shout fell from the leader's lips as I slammed my shoulder into his chest and bowled him to the asphalt. The moment his back smashed against the road, I punched him.

Over and over and *over.*

Face, nose, temple, throat.

I wasn't one to drag out a fight. Once I made up my mind, I did it. No second chances. No second guesses.

A rain of fists came down on my back and skull. I rolled off the leader, shooting to my feet.

The men threw a worried look at their unconscious comrade. "You'll die for that."

I shook my head. "Wrong."

They attacked together.

I wasn't expecting that. They seemed sloppy and unorganised, but they moved as one. I covered my head as they attacked.

It hurt.

The pain was good.

But their anger and feral temper was better.

It siphoned into my blood, feeding me, charging me.

I let loose.

I did what I'd fought against all my life.

My walls came down.

I drank in their poison.

And I killed those motherfuckers piece by fucking piece.

# Nila

"IT'S ME. CAN I come in?"

I knocked again on Jasmine's door.

For the past two nights, I'd sneaked up the stone stairs and knocked. And for the past two nights, she'd ignored me.

I knew she was in there. The light shone beneath the door and the camera blinked above the frame. Occasionally, a shadow would roll past, but she never opened it.

I even tried the door handle to barge in uninvited. It was locked.

"Jasmine. I really need to talk to you." I pressed my forehead against the wood. "Before it's too late."

Time had a horrible way of ticking faster here.

Already, the month I'd spent away from Hawksridge faded into scratchy memories. Vaughn and my father messaged me continuously—neither satisfied with my response that I had to return. That I knew what I was doing.

Why would they believe me? Even *I* didn't believe me.

I had no clue how I would do what was needed.

Jethro avoided me. Cut laughed at me. And Daniel lurked in the background like fungus waiting to consume me. Every night hurtled me quicker toward another debt. The final one would soon be on the horizon, then all my options would be gone.

I couldn't afford to be blasé or slow.
I had to be smart and act fast.
I knocked again. "Please. Let me in."
Nothing.
I couldn't walk back to my room, not again. The past few nights, I'd turned into an insomniac and suffered every morning with a vicious vertigo attack.

I hadn't thrown up since leaving London, but every time my thoughts strayed to the contraceptive shot Jethro administered, my gut churned with sadness and rage.

Not that it mattered, seeing as he'd made no move to kiss me after the magazine picture—let alone sleep with me.

If I didn't win, I would never know the joy of having a child or being held in a man's arms while I grew big with his unborn baby. Vaughn would never have a niece or nephew and my father...I couldn't think about him without suffering awful anguish.

He would never have a grandchild. But I think...I think he'd always known that. He'd kept me away from men all my life, so I would never have the opportunity to fall in love and conceive—like my mother did before the Hawks took her.

She'd found her soul-mate before horror found her.

I'd found mine the day I'd been taken.

"Jasmine, I'm not leaving. Not this time." With a heavy heart, I turned around and slid down her door to the carpet.

I wasn't leaving until she came out.

I'd be there all night if I had to.

*"Nila..." Jethro's eyes burned as bright and golden as the sun.*

*I melted in his arms, raising my lips for a tender, love-filled kiss. His lips were like sherbet—sweet and tingling and delicious. "I love you, Kite."*

*He squeezed me harder, his tongue entering my mouth to lick and taste.*

*I trembled. Pushing him backward, the field of daisies and clovers swayed magically in the summer breeze. We were all alone in this idyllic*

meadow; there was no one to ruin it.
No Hawks. No debts. No Weavers.
Just kisses and love.
Our clothes suddenly disappeared, and I ran the tip of my finger down his breastbone, along his defined stomach, following the small trail of hair to his groin.
Sliding down his body, I hovered my mouth over his erection. "I love bringing you pleasure."
His back shot upright as I guided him into my mouth, swirling my tongue and inhaling his taste.
His strong fingers slinked through my hair, holding me firm. His hips raised to meet my lips, pushing gently, pleading for more.
I didn't deny him.
I let him set the rhythm, growing wetter with every stroke of his cock in my mouth. Then I was moving, gathered in strong arms, and placed on top of his naked body.
He didn't speak as I straddled him, positioning myself over his cock.
We both cried out as I sank down his length.
Down and down. Deep and deep.
Planting my hands on his chest, I rocked on his huge size, shivering as he sheathed himself completely. Only once he'd claimed me did I open my eyes and look down.
The joy on his face.
The adoration in his gaze.
The blistering love in his every thought.
Tears bruised my eyes as he held up his hands and intertwined our fingers together. "I'm your anchor now, Nila. Ride me. Use me. Control me. I've always got you. I'll always catch you if you fall—"
I fell backward, tumbling through a wormhole, falling, falling.
The delicious dream shattered.
My spine collided with soft carpet and my eyes shot wide. Gleaming silver wheels and narrowed bronze eyes welcomed me back to reality.
"What the *hell* are you doing?"
Scrambling to a sitting position, I wiped my eyes and

hoped my cheeks weren't flushed. Having an erotic fantasy was one thing. Having an erotic fantasy about the brother of the woman now glaring at me was entirely another.

"Normally, if a person doesn't answer their door, it's because they don't want to be disturbed."

"You ignored me. I had to take drastic action."

Jasmine sighed. Her dark hair was flat on one side, her skin rosy from sleep. Looking past her, I noticed the covers of her bed were turned down and her nightgown of white cotton and forget-me-not blue ribbons covered her from head to toe.

I climbed to my feet. "If you don't want to talk to me, tell me where his room is."

"Where whose room is."

I rolled my eyes. "Come on, don't play that game. You know who. If I knew where to find him in this godforsaken place, I'd go and camp outside his door instead of yours."

She huffed. "Firstly, he's not on this floor. Secondly, I wonder how long that would be permitted until Cut dealt with you." Leaving me on the threshold, she wheeled herself back to bed.

I closed the door and followed. Standing awkwardly at the foot of the mattress, I whispered, "Do you want some help?"

Her head snapped toward me. "Do I *look* like I need help?" She waved around the empty room. "Do I have a maid to help me? Do you think I can't manage even the simplest of tasks by myself?"

I flinched. "No, of course not."

Keeping my fingers together, preventing any chance of reaching out, I stood fixed to the carpet as Jasmine locked the wheels and placed her hands on the bed.

It wasn't high and with a small grunt, she hoisted herself from the chair and into the covers.

With brisk efficiency, she slid against her pillows, reached down to direct her legs from twisted and dangling to laying perfectly straight, then covered herself with the duvet.

"See?" she sneered.

I drifted forward, perching on the side. "You're very proficient at that."

A wry laugh escaped her. "I've had many years to get used to it."

Awkward silence fell; I struggled for another topic. "Were you born this way?"

Her eyes glinted. "No."

My heart banged at her simple but very revealing answer. Deciding I had nothing left to lose, I murmured, "Did someone do this to you?"

Her face shut down. She pointed at the door. "I want you to leave."

"No. Not until you tell me where I can find Jethro." *And explain what happened while I was gone.*

She crossed her arms, pouting like a little child surrounded by yellow-lemon pillows. "You come into my room and demand to know where my brother sleeps. God, you've got some nerve." She cocked her head, her bob slicing her jawline. "What? So you can kill him or fuck him?"

I coughed with surprise. "You sound just like him. He said the exact same thing when he dragged me up here for the Tally Mark."

Jasmine sucked in a breath. "Well...which one is it?"

I sat straighter. Now might be my only chance to get Jasmine on my side. In order to find the truth, I had to give it. No matter how revealing it would be. "I'm in love with your brother. I hate him most days, but that doesn't stop my idiotic heart from loving him. I love the goodness buried inside. I love the way he wants to be better but can't. I love the way he touches me. And I'm not ashamed to admit I love sleeping with him."

My cheeks flared, but I continued boldly, "He's mine as much as yours. I'm not your enemy, Jasmine. I want to be your friend."

Silence fell, thick and cloying.

She never stopped glaring.

Fear darted down my arms. "What happened the day the police came? Before that, you were...nice to me. You were welcoming. But now...you hate me." Hanging my head, I said, "I didn't leave of my own free will. You know that."

Animosity swirled thicker, webbing us together.

Finally, she sighed. "I know you didn't go freely."

"Then why punish me? My brother meddled in things he doesn't understand. I know it cost Jethro hugely, but it wasn't my fault."

She stared at the ceiling, battling a sudden glisten in her eyes. "But it was. It was both our faults. I pushed him to let you inside him, and you won by making him care. We both made him so vulnerable. Cut..." She looked away, biting her lip.

I inched closer, patting her knee. I didn't know if she could feel it, but I squeezed anyway. "What did he do to him?"

Jasmine plucked the bedspread. "I don't know. Kite won't tell me. I can't get through to him. Not like I used to." Her gaze latched onto mine. "He won't talk to me. He won't even come see me. He's cut Kestrel out, too. He doesn't ride anymore. It's like everything that made him my broken brother has been lost."

My soul cracked at the thought. "It can't be lost. There must be a way to change whatever Cut did."

Jasmine shook her head. "I've never seen him this cold, this remote. He's exactly like our father, and it terrifies me to think I've lost him." A tear rolled down her cheek. "I suppose in a way, I should be grateful. At least he's still breathing."

My world stopped. "What do you mean?"

Jasmine scowled. "Oh, don't look so surprised. You must've guessed what would happen when you walked out of Hawksridge and never looked back."

"He *told* me not to look back," I snapped. "He forced me to obey by using my love against me."

Her face turned frigid with anger. "Yes, but you could've found a way to come back sooner. You must've believed

Bonnie when she said you'd earned your freedom at the cost of another."

I didn't want to hear anymore.

Jasmine scoffed. "My father is doing everything in his power to destroy your line because of some stupid ancient vendetta that should've been dismissed centuries ago. If he can do that to innocent people, what does that mean for the ones being groomed to take over his throne?" She suddenly leaned forward, snatching my hand off her knee. Her French-manicured nails dug into my skin. "Whatever Jethro has done or whatever Cut threatened him with is the last resort. I thought I would never see my brother again. I thought the moment you walked out of Hawksridge Jethro would disappear, too. But he didn't. He's still alive—but God only knows what stipulations Cut placed on him."

She jerked me closer. "Just stay away from him. Don't try to find him. Don't try to love him. Don't try to do anything to upset whatever balance he's been able to find. I miss him, but I'd rather have him unattainable and alive than caring and dead."

She threw my hand away. "Now leave, before I call security."

I stood, moving quickly to her door. I needed to go before I burst into tears at the sheer hatred she had for me. Every word was delivered with fury and dislike. I was no longer a friend but foe.

How could she switch so easily?

How could she give up on Jethro when I knew he was so close to snapping back?

*She's protecting him. She thinks there's no hope.*

"Oh, and Nila?"

My eyes met Jasmine's. She said in a monotone, "Don't ever come back here. Leave my brother alone. Let this madness end. I'm begging you."

It wasn't until I'd descended the stairs and entered my own quarters that I unravelled the message in her final words.

Let this madness end.
*She's asking me to let them win.*
*She's asking me to die.*

# Jethro

SLINGING A TOWEL around my waist, I exited my steamy bathroom and stalked across my bedroom to get the first aid kit.

My knuckles were torn, I could barely see out of my right eye, my lip was split, and countless bruises mottled my torso. But fuck, I felt better than I had in months.

I shook like a damn junkie needing another fix, but I relished the win and adrenaline of playing God over someone else for a change.

Passing the full-length mirror, I cringed at my reflection. It didn't look like I'd been the victor, but I was still here and they weren't.

*Suck on that, assholes.*

Grabbing the first aid kit from the 17th century dresser, I returned to my bed to begin repairs.

I didn't need stitches or serious medical care, but I did need antibacterial cream and a few butterfly strips to hold the cut on my forehead together while it healed.

Damn fucking Cannibal cunts—thinking they could kill me when I was alone. Their president would have a nasty surprise tomorrow when the local farmer inspected his potato field and found three new varieties sprouting instead.

I'd left a calling card on each—a single worthless diamond.

Courtesy of my family and our power over immortality.

There would be no retaliation. They were on our turf—fair and fucking simple.

My muscles ached, my head pounded, but my mind was blessedly clear. I could think straight—free from emotions and pressure. I hadn't run into anyone since my arrival.

A new prescription for pills rested on my bedside table. As much as I loved this clarity, I couldn't stomach it come morning. I made a note to take one the moment I'd finished patching myself up.

Sitting on the edge of the bed, I popped the lid of the first aid kit and selected a tube of antiseptic.

My door flung wide.

*Shit, I forgot to lock the damn thing.*

I looked up, expecting to see Kes, my father, or even Daniel popping in for a three a.m. chat. Instead...Nila fucking Weaver stood frozen on the threshold.

I dropped the tube of cream.

She brandished her stolen dirk and a brass candlestick from one of the tables lining the halls. Her hair was untethered—a curtain of midnight—and her black camisole and shorts made my mouth instantly dry up.

*Fuck, fuck, fuck.*

What the *hell?*

I stood up instantly.

The first aid kit slammed to the floor, spewing its gauze and bandages to all corners of the room.

"What the fuck are you doing in here?" I stormed forward, ready to slam the door in her face. She couldn't be here. Not with my appearance or condition.

"Oh, my God. I found you."

I grabbed the doorknob. "Go back to your room, Ms. Weaver."

"No, wait!" She darted inside before I could block her. Dashing to my bed, she ran around the large mattress, placing it between us and brandishing her weapons. "I've been looking for hours. I've tried every room on the ground floor. I almost gave up when I found a secret door in the parlour."

She'd been running around all night? *Alone?* Shit, didn't she know how fucking dangerous that was?

Daniel wouldn't hesitate. My father wouldn't, either.

"You're a reckless, naïve little girl." Slamming the door, I stalked toward her. "Do you have *any* idea what might've happened if you'd been seen?"

Her eyes skittered around my space, taking in the soaring high ceilings, old-fashioned priceless toys and artifacts, and Chinese woven carpets. "I have an idea." She raised her chin. "But it was a risk I was prepared to take. After all, what else could I do?"

Tossing the candlestick onto the bed, she rolled her wrist from the weight. "You avoid me for days after telling me something cryptic about black diamonds and absorbing light. You tell me to stop feeling around you. You shut me out all while swallowing a drug you never took before. All of that brings me to one conclusion, Mr. Hawk."

"Oh? And what conclusion is that?"

*So, she did understand my half-assed attempt to make her understand.*

Why couldn't I just come out and tell her?

Why did I have to continue to hide?

"A conclusion that needs testing." She sighed softly, "I have a theory, you see. And if I'm right…well, it means things are going to change between you and me."

My heart tap-danced a crazy step.

*You have no idea how much I want that.*

"That will never happen."

"You don't even know my theory."

"I know enough to ask you to leave."

*Before you destroy your own life and get me fucking killed in the process.*

Having her here, in my space, with no fog to protect me, I tasted everything she felt like fine wine, expensive truffles, rich desserts. Anger, desire, fear...and most of all, love. Beneath her temper, she glowed with it. Vibrated with it.

It was all I could do to remain standing and not buckle under the waves of unconditional acceptance.

I groaned, "Nila, you have to leave."

"No. Not until I find out what you are."

I shivered, forgetting my bodily aches and pains and suffering emotional ones instead. She was breaking me—smashing the rules Cut had fashioned. If she could be so strong, why couldn't I?

Couldn't I indulge for just one night?

"You don't understand." I moved forward. "You can't be here."

"Tell me, then." Placing the dirk on my bedside table, she dropped her hands. In a single move, she went from warrior to sacrifice, inviting me to take her. "*Make* me understand, Jethro."

My head swam. I needed time to decide if I was stupid enough to put us both in danger. If I was going to give into her, it could only be for one night.

Inching closer, I murmured, "To find my room, you must've gone through my entire quarters."

Her eyes narrowed at my subject change, but she nodded. "I did. Your room is the last one along the corridor." Her body softened. "You have so many spaces. Game grottos, offices, a gym. I must've peeked into a dozen rooms after slipping through that secret door."

A lot of space for a man who needed a lot of distance.

It looked like luxury; in reality, it was a gilded cage.

"And doesn't that tell you something?"

She frowned. "Tell me what?"

"That this part of the Hall is private. I don't want guests. I don't want company. I keep my life removed from my family, even though we live in the same house."

She trembled as I continued to close the distance between us. Each step I took, I fought to be strong enough to send her away. She would remain unhurt as long as I could fake the perfect heir.

The longer she stood in my quarters, the more I struggled to deny her.

Almost as if she followed my thoughts, she whispered, "It doesn't matter. I've found you. Now I know where to come when you disappear and avoid me."

My hands fisted as delectable thoughts filled my head: sneaking her into my quarters, sleeping beside her, fucking her without cameras reporting to Cut just how disobedient I was.

My jaw clenched. "There won't *be* a next time, Nila." Pointing at the door, I growled, "You have to leave."

"Why? Give me one good reason and I might consider it." Abandoning her position by my bed, she came toward me.

I sucked in a breath as her gaze danced over my body. Her fingers twitched as she took in my bleeding forehead and knuckles. "You're hurt."

"I'm fine."

She lingered over my split lip before her eyes drifted down my still-damp torso to the towel around my waist.

An image of us walking back from the springs dressed only in towels came swift and strong.

I'd never been so free. Never been so happy at the thought of telling her everything and finally admitting that Nila was it for me. That I might have a chance.

It was a pipe dream. And one that got us both into this mess.

"Fuck." I couldn't have her in here, and I definitely couldn't have those thoughts.

I tried to grab her, but she darted away. Jumping onto my bed like fleeing prey, her tiny feet disappeared in the feather duvet as she pranced across the mattress. She leapt down, once again placing the bed between us.

A headache throbbed and the bruises on my ribcage smarted as I ran a hand through my wet hair. "I don't want to play any more games."

Never taking her eyes from mine, she placed her palms on my bed. "Neither do I. We've both established that." Her voice lowered. "You're hurt, Jethro. Let me help you."

"No. You need to go."

*How many times do I need to tell you?*

My eyes flashed to the pills on my bedside. If I took one, the numbness might give me enough reprieve to kick her out.

"Who did this to you?" she murmured, inching closer again, forgetting that her intention was to stay away from me, not comfort me.

Her concern was like a mink blanket, soothingly warm and so, so soft.

I wished she would stay away. Her concern might be a blanket, but her love... Shit, her love was a blade slicing me into pieces.

She kept coming closer, no longer trying to flee.

I held up my hand. "Stay right there."

"Jethro...don't do this."

"No, *you* don't do this," I snarled. "You don't know what you're risking."

Nila didn't reply, and she didn't stop.

My throat dried up. I was stuck between the wall my father had erected and the chasm she created. *I need help.* My hands shook as I charged toward my bedside and scooped up the bottle of pills.

My body blared from the fight, but it was nothing to the way my mind bled being around her. It was like claws on a blackboard, forcing me to listen—regardless if I wanted to or not.

The tablets offered quietness. Peace.

I needed that.

"No!" Nila sprinted forward, knocking the bottle from my hand. The tablets spewed all over the carpet.

"What the fuck?"

"Whatever they are—don't take any more."

My temper bubbled. "They're painkillers!" I held up my

torn knuckles, shoving the evidence in her face. "See."

She scowled. "No, they aren't." Rummaging in the first aid kit, she brought out some anti-inflammatories and paracetamol. "*These* are painkillers." Snatching my hand, she dumped the blister packet into my palm. "Whatever those others are—they're hurting you, not helping you."

Throwing away the pills, I ran a hand over my face. Being this awake after a month of listlessness, my old concerns came back. I missed Jasmine. I missed Kes. And fuck, I missed Nila. So damn much.

I looked at her beneath my brow, unable to fight anymore. She wanted to talk? Fine. I'd talk.

We'd played cat and mouse too many fucking times. The trap had sprung, and if death was the reward, then I sure as hell would make it worthwhile.

Capturing her hips, I dragged her closer. She gasped as I circled my thumbs on the cool satin of her night-shorts. "You came here for a reason. What was it?"

Nila blinked, lust blazing in her black eyes. "Eh…I came to…"

I tugged her closer, fitting her small frame against mine. "Yes?"

My heartbeat raced. My cock thickened. Giving in was an ultimate aphrodisiac, and the pain dissolved in favour of my intense need to fuck her.

I cocked an eyebrow, dragging my gaze down her body.

She had magic. I didn't deny that. Magic that we hadn't managed to take even though we'd treated her like a witch with the ducking stool.

Swallowing hard, I slinked my fingers into her hair, curling them around her nape. She bit her lip as I pressed my thickening erection on her belly. "You didn't come to talk, did you? You came for this." I rocked again.

Her eyes snapped closed.

"Admit it," I purred. "Admit that all of this is our version of foreplay. We argue. We fight. And then…" My fingers tightened around her neck. "We fuck."

She made a breathy noise that made my heart crack and bleed. "You're right..." Her hand disappeared between us, latching around my cock through the towel.

I bit back a growl as her thumb pressed the crown, shooting electric bolts into my balls.

Her nipples peaked beneath the black satin. The lust she'd conjured in my office at Diamond Alley came back in full force.

"Goddammit, you test me." Fisting her hair, I jerked her backward, supporting her spine as I ducked to suck her nipple.

She cried out, her hand releasing my cock to tug on the knot in the towel. "Yes...Jethro."

"You truly are the worst kind of punishment," I panted, sucking, grazing her with my teeth.

She squirmed. She was as fucked as I was—sex-hazed and drunk. Lust infused the very air—desire became oxygen and hunger became life.

We were both destroyed. And the only cure was to give in.

"I'll give you what you're looking for." I walked her backward to the bed.

She looped her arms over my shoulders, leaping into my embrace. "Give me everything. I beg you."

I caught her, holding her weight as her legs wrapped around my hips. She thrust against me.

"Fuck, Nila."

A few more steps and I'd have her on the bed. If I could fucking walk. My entire body vibrated with need. "Why did you come here?"

Her lips parted. Her black hair shimmered in the lowlights of my bedside lamps. "You want the truth?"

I nodded.

Pressing her breasts against my chest, she whispered in my ear, "I came here to be filled, taken, *ridden*. I came to find you again. I came to remind you of what we have. I came for so many reasons, Jethro, but most of all, I came to save you."

My soul swelled as the mattress hit my knees. I folded her

backward, drinking in her flushed skin and sparkling eyes. I couldn't speak. What was there to say to that?

*I don't need fucking saving?*

*I don't want you to come for me?*

Of course, I wanted that. Anyone after a lifetime of loneliness would dream of someone accepting them unconditionally.

All I wanted to do was crash to my knees and beg—fucking beg for her to finally understand—to see the only way to exist was to let me be who I was born to be. I had to take her life. I had to stay alive. One of us would die—if not both.

She wanted hope—the belief that this could have a happy ending.

*But it can't.*

And that was too much to fucking bear.

She scooted toward my pillows, spreading her legs. With sexy boldness, she hooked her fingers into the waistband of her shorts and shimmied out of them.

I swallowed. Hard.

I prowled toward her on hands and knees, unable to tear my eyes away from the dampness between her legs. "You want to be ridden? Let me make your wishes come true."

I reached out to touch her, but she rolled away.

I blinked; the urge to chase her hammered at my skull. "Come here."

She sat up, tugging the hem of her top, wrenching it over her head.

Naked.

Gloriously fucking naked.

I reached for her again, but she scrambled over my sheets.

A fleeting thought came. That quote to *Vanity Fair* about miscarrying. Was it true? *Could* she have been pregnant with my child? My heart fisted. I couldn't unscramble how that made me feel.

"Come here," I growled again.

"Come and get me."

I trembled with the idea of her becoming more than just a woman I'd fallen for but *family*. If she carried my baby, we would be joined forever.

*And you know what Cut would do.*

My heart shut down.

I focused on sex—trying to separate emotional from physical gratification. I lied to myself, but it was better than asking her what truly happened while she was free.

"You want to play? Fine, I can play."

She'd upset me without even trying. I wanted payback.

With a vicious yank, I untied the towel and hurled myself across the bed. I snagged her waist, slamming her onto her back.

Naked skin against naked skin.

I'd never felt anything so delicious.

She cried out as we bounced and collided, coming to rest on top of the blankets. Instantly, sharp unbridled lust laced around us. She smelled so good. Felt so good.

So warm.

So right.

Her chest rose and fell, teasing her nipples against my skin, twining her legs with mine.

I swooped down and bit her throat below her collar. "See what happens when you run?" Her incredible smell punched me harder than any of the bastards on the side of the road.

"You're crushing me," she breathed, her stomach fluttering against mine. Her fingernails dragged along my naked arse. "It's not enough."

Her talons sent shivers up my spine. I was so close to diving inside her. I snagged her wrists, pinning them above her head.

"Do you enjoy being spread-eagled beneath me?" I nuzzled her neck. "You're my prisoner, yet you keep thinking you can win."

She stiffened. "I think it's time we agree we're on the same side." Her gaze darkened, a mask slipping into place. "I don't want to win or lose anymore." Struggling in my hold, she pressed a kiss on my jaw. "I just want you."

My cock twitched, agreeing wholeheartedly.

I no longer wanted to be on anyone's side but hers. That included my own.

*Fuck, what a mess this has become.*

When she'd left, I'd been willing to sacrifice my life to save hers. I would've died if it meant the Debt Inheritance had been void. But now—now I had to stay alive to ensure the Final Debt was paid.

I rocked against her pussy. "I agree..." Adjusting my hold on her wrists, I locked both with one hand and trailed the other over the delectable lines of her body. "Same team."

She shuddered beneath my touch. "You mean it?"

I grabbed her breast, pinching her nipple. "I mean it."

Her lips fell wide. A sigh escaped. And I took full advantage.

I kissed her.

She moaned, her mouth submitting to mine. Within a moment, the kiss went from a connection of lips to something deep and ravenous.

A kiss was a disaster.

A kiss was power.

A kiss was love and togetherness and faith.

It was so many, many things.

But this...this was something so much more.

*More.*

*I want more.*

*I want everything.*

She moaned again as her tongue dove into my mouth, taking control of the kiss and rocking her hips, seeking more just like me.

I kissed her deep. I kissed her hard.

Her knees fell wide, welcoming my body to claim hers. We both needed to join. Become one.

My fingers skated down her hip to her inner thigh. She

bucked, trying to free her wrists as I dipped further with questing traces.

"Jethro...let me touch you."

"No. *I'm* touching *you*." With no hesitation, I thrust a finger inside her, mirroring the action with my tongue.

She groaned, her back flying off the bed.

Our lips never unglued, driving each other to galaxies beckoning with freedom and sanctuary.

"Oh, God." She rode my finger, her body wet and wanting. "More. Give me more."

I bit her bottom lip. "Your wish is my command." I inserted another finger, driving deep, stretching wide. She was wet but so damn tight.

I wanted to fuck her so badly, but it wasn't a simple matter of climbing on top. It never was for me. I had to prepare—had to make sure she was ready—even when it drove me to agony.

I wanted her hard and ruthless. This wasn't making love. This wasn't even a battle—this was a ceasefire. An admittance that we couldn't keep fighting, but it didn't mean we were dead.

"Kite...please, fuck me. I need you," Nila begged between kisses.

*Shit, she called me Kite again.*

Every time she did, goosebumps scattered down my spine. All those nights of messaging her, getting into her head and heart—playing a game I never should've started—all crescendoed.

She'd slept with me as Jethro, but she hadn't slept with me as Kite.

I lost all sense of self as I tore my fingers from her wet heat and shifted my body higher. Our eyes locked as the tip of my cock found her heat. The world stopped spinning.

There was so much to say and no words in which to speak.

Gritting my teeth, I nudged inside her.

The second I entered her, all decorum went out the fucking window.

I let go of her wrists and her hands flew downward,

digging her nails into my arse and dragging me forward. Her knees came up, opening wide. "Yes. Oh, God, yes." Her cheeks were rosy red, eyes wild.

Clutching the sheets, I thrust without warning, driving too fast and deep inside her.

She screamed.

"Shit!" I clamped a hand over her mouth, pulling out. "Be quiet."

She vibrated in my arms, eyes glassy and lust-stricken. Dropping my hold, I growled, "No one must know you're here." Finding her wetness again, I climbed inside—slower this time, pushing, pressing, invading.

The tight unforgiving muscles of her body resisted me, but I was too far gone to care.

"Feel that?" I grunted as I slowly conquered her.

She moaned, her breath coming in short pants. Her eyes squeezed tight as I relentlessly filled her. "Yes."

"Does it feel good?"

"Yes…so good."

"You want more?"

"I want everything."

I thrust hard and fast, sliding all the way inside. *I'm home. I'm never fucking leaving again.*

I'd killed three bikers tonight with no second thoughts. I was a killer, defender. So why couldn't I be the same for Nila? Could I become a traitor to my family? Could I kill my father and Daniel in order to save the woman I loved?

I drove again, rocking her body deeper into my mattress. *Do I have a choice?*

She threw her head back, hair fanning over my pillow. "You belong inside me, Jethro." Her hand cupped my cheek, transfixing my soul to hers with irremovable super glue. "Never forget that."

I just got my answer.

Pills and debts and empires.

Utterly worthless compared to this creature who'd stolen

my heart.

Sighing, I gave up. I surrendered to the inevitable. *I have to kill to protect.* She was mine. It was my duty.

"I ache when you're not inside me," she murmured, dragging my mind back to her.

I smiled sadly, consumed with a gruesome future I didn't want. Her face was in shadow from my body suffocating hers. She looked like she might vanish any second.

Tilting my head, I licked the seam of her lips. She opened, welcoming me inside. She was silk and sugar. Despair and happiness.

How could I be so happy yet so broken at the same time?

Her hands fell to my hips, pulling me into her with every thrust. Our chests stuck together, our bellies glued. Her legs wrapped around the back of my thighs, using her ankles to push up and meet me thrust for thrust. "Harder, Kite. Harder."

Once again, that tiny voice filled my head. *Would you be so rough with her if she was pregnant? Shouldn't you ask?*

But the fear of the unknown and what it would mean silenced me. I obeyed instead, driving hard.

Her head fell back as I fucked under her command.

"I missed you." Her voice broke. A single tear rolled down her cheek.

And that was it for me. I knew there was no going back. Never again.

"Nila." My voice was lost.

She opened her eyes, anchoring me to her.

"I need you to know that I feel what you feel. This—" I never broke my rhythm, diving inside her over and over. Loving, fucking, claiming. "—this, it's right. I see that now."

Anger blossomed in her eyes. "How long will you see it? Tomorrow? The day after? Or once tonight is over, you'll cut me back out and leave me stranded all over again?"

My pacing stuttered, my cock twitched. "You're right. To you it must seem as if I'm schizophrenic."

*Insane.*

*Just like everyone said.*

She was silent for a moment, before brushing her thumb over my lips. "You seem troubled. That's all." Wrapping her arms around me, she sandwiched our bodies together.

*I am troubled. More than you know.*

The urge to be close—as close as humanly possible—forced my arms to wrap around her and thrust hard. I rode her like that. Arms locked, bodies merged into one. My balls slapped against her as my cock rubbed against her clit.

Pleasure supernovaed into a raging black hole, waiting to consume us.

I picked up speed, chasing the finale.

"Oh, don't stop," she moaned.

Her body bucked beneath mine, jousting and submitting in equal measure. I felt her pleasure as surely as my own. I drank her bliss like nectar.

"Am I hurting you?" I fisted the pillow behind her, rocking faster.

Her forehead furrowed. She nodded a little. "It's a beautiful pain, though. A belonging sort of pain. Don't stop."

"I can't take you without hurting you," I said into her hair. "In a way, it's only fair."

Her fingernails dug into my lower back. "Why…why is it fair?"

I groaned. I didn't want to answer that.

*Because you hurt me when you take me, too. When you give me no choice but to let you inside me.*

She rolled her hips, rubbing against me. "I'm angry with you. So damn angry at the way you treated me."

I kissed her, forcing her to drink my words. "I know."

Speaking through our kiss, she groaned, "I can't control myself around you, but it doesn't mean everything is fixed between us."

"I know that, too." I rocked harder, driving us to insanity. "But no matter how angry you are, your feelings won't stop you from coming."

I pinned her delicate frame with mine and let loose.

No more talking. No more thinking or feeling or planning. Just fucking.

She gave in, moulding her body to mine, sighing heavily as my groan echoed around the room like a serrated blade.

She tormented me. But by God, I fucking loved her.

I didn't understand her. I didn't trust her. But my instincts plaited with hers and we fed off one another.

My balls cramped, desperately needing to come.

"Please, Kite. Give me what you're hiding."

Needing this over, craving silence from her all-consuming emotions, I drove faster.

Nila moaned as I reached between her legs, rubbing her clit while fucking her with no mercy.

It took two seconds for her to detonate.

Her eyes rolled back, she stopped breathing, and every molecule of her body exploded.

"Fuuuuck," I grunted as her pussy contracted hard and strong around my cock.

I didn't stand a chance.

I came.

Bliss and pleasure hurtled me into the stratosphere where no thought existed. Together we unravelled, spiralling deeper into chaos.

I didn't care about anything. We journeyed to fucking utopia in each other's arms.

Our hearts thundered against each other, speaking in Morse code just how precious this was. However, beneath the blistering contentment, I cursed myself to hell.

As my seed splashed inside her, all I could think about was the way I'd stolen her right to be a mother. I'd injected her to save her. But now it felt like a coward's actions.

The Grim Reaper himself danced over my spine as another thought came to me.

If she *had* been pregnant, her child—*my* child—would've been murdered.

And nothing on earth could ever make that okay.
*This has to end.*
When our orgasms faded, I fisted her hair, forcing her to open her eyes. "Look at me."
She breathed hard, staring into my gaze with melted heaven and sweetest satisfaction. "I'm looking, Jethro. And despite everything you do...I *see* you."
"I know you see; that's why I need you to promise me something."
"Anything."
Familiar ice filled me at the thought of what I had to do. I had to be smart. I had to win. Because there would be no second chance—for either of us.
"Outside of this room, I will continue to be cruel. I will continue to do what is expected of me. You have to trust me."
She stiffened. "You're saying after what just happened, things are going to go back to the way they were?"
I nodded. "They have to. Until I can do what's needed."
Her eyes narrowed. "And what are you going to do?"
I kissed the tip of her nose and hoped to God I'd made the right choice.
*Please, give me strength.*
"I'm going to do what I should've done a long time ago."
*Kill my motherfucking father.*

# Nila

LIFE SETTLED INTO a temporary rhythm.

By day, I either sewed or spent it with the Black Diamond brothers learning all there was about carats and mining techniques. I was told where the mines were located. I memorized the wealth extracted from each location and the brand they laser cut onto every stone. By night, I shoved away infrequent vertigo waves and sketched new designs I might never create.

I learned that every few months, one Hawk brother would travel to Brazil or Africa or Thailand to inspect the mines and assess the managers left in charge. They would go with an entourage from their brotherhood, acting as support, discipline, and protection.

I was wrong when I thought the only brothers in the Black Diamonds were the ones who'd licked me at my welcome luncheon. There were factions all around the world—all controlling the empire that belonged to Bryan 'Cut' Hawk.

*And soon Jethro.*

After our night together, things had become strange between us. He avoided me as much as possible. He didn't come to my quarters. He didn't seek me out for my morning run. And when we met in the dining room with his family for breakfast, he would find subjects to discuss with his father and be detained far longer than I could wait.

His eyes, once glowing with lust and togetherness, became dead, lifeless. Every few hours, he would swallow a white pill and give me a smile that said a hundred things all at once.

*Trust me.*
*Wait for me.*
*Don't hate me.*

The Black Diamond brothers continued to be kind and generous. If I came upon them in the library, we'd chat like old friends. If I bumped into one of them in the corridors, we'd discuss the weather and any titbit of interesting information.

I never went to visit Jasmine again, and my brother and father never ceased in their rally to get me to reply. I'd never been around so many people—all impacting my life in some small measure.

Whenever I moved around Hawksridge, I took my dirk—jammed in my waistband or hidden in the garter around my leg. I'd seen Daniel once on my own—it'd been around nine p.m. He'd caught me strolling back to my quarters after visiting the kitchen for some orange juice.

I knew then why Jethro was so livid that I'd hunted the house for his wing. The look in Daniel's eyes reeked of rape and lawlessness. His hissed promise when the first tally was made came back in full volume. *"The moment you're alone..."*

He'd come toward me, a sneer on his lips. I didn't think, just reacted. I'd thrown my glass at his face, splashing citrus juice all over irreplaceable carpets and tore back to the kitchen.

And there I'd stayed until Flaw returned from a late night delivery and escorted me back to my chambers.

I didn't tell Jethro what'd happened, but he must've seen it on the cameras, because the next day he found me and whispered that from now on his rooms would be locked. That there was no point in going to him because he wouldn't let me in.

I knew he did it for my protection—to stop me recklessly patrolling the halls—but at the same time, it killed me to think the one chance we could be together had been taken away just like the rest.

The dynamics in Hawksridge Hall had changed. Cut had thawed considerably toward Jethro. I caught them laughing together one afternoon and Cut slapping Jethro on the back the next. The stronger the father and son bond grew, the more Kestrel faded into the background.

Daniel didn't seem to notice or care about the alliance that'd sprung between firstborn and ruler. He carried on as if life was fine and dandy with no cares apart from which club bunny to screw that night.

Kes, on the other hand, stopped being his jovial self. He stopped smiling at me. Stopped smiling period.

And despite not knowing who he truly was, I missed him.

I missed the ease and togetherness I enjoyed when I'd first arrived. I missed having him as a friend—even if that friendship came with conditions and hidden motives.

One day, as I made my way outside for a run, I saw Kes disappear over the front garden dressed in a tweed jacket and woollen trousers with a shotgun cocked over his arm.

*Where is he going?*

Jogging down the portico steps, I zipped up my fleece and was glad I'd put on leggings as the wind howled in welcome.

Autumn was losing every day to winter. Summer was long since forgotten, and I craved the sunshine and greenery of the first few months that I'd arrived.

Kes looked up as I traversed the gravel.

His eyebrows rose. "Nila. What are you doing out here?" He peered at the sky. "It might rain...or snow, feels fucking cold enough." His skin was white, but the tip of his nose was painted red. He'd had a haircut recently and it was trimmed and neat at the side with an unruly mess on top. He looked younger, sadder.

"I'm going for a run. Want to join me?"

I forced away the memory of running with Jethro and ultimately finding my ancestor's graves. Jethro had wounded me too many times over the past few weeks. I wanted to hate him but couldn't.

The way he'd begged me to trust him the last time we were together. The way he looked so close to crumbling under the weight he carried.

He had a plan. I had no choice but to trust him.

It took a strong conviction to trust someone who rarely talked to me and went out of his way to come across as a drug-induced robot.

I blew on my frostbitten fingers. My chill was partly due to the freezing cold day, but it was mainly thanks to living in a historic tomb. Hawksridge Hall was decadent and majestic, but it was damn cold when moving around cavernous corridors. Only the rooms were heated, and even then, the ceilings were so high it was never toasty.

"No, I don't run." Kes jostled the gun over his arm. "Thought I'd go for a hunt. Shoot a pheasant or two for dinner."

We fell into step together. I wrapped my arms around myself, retaining the small amount of body heat I had. "I couldn't think of anything worse—killing something."

*Will Jethro kill someone? Cut, Daniel...me?*

Grey clouds and a faint dusting of mist dulled the vibrancy of the estate. It was magical as much as it was depressing.

Kes noticed my shivering. He stopped.

Holding out the gun, he waited until I took it, then shrugged out of his thick tweed.

The weapon was morbidly heavy. I was only too happy to trade it for the soft wool of his blazer. "You don't have to—"

"I know." He slung the tweed over my shoulders, encasing me in his masculine scent of musk and heather. "But I want to."

"I can't take it." I tried to slip it off. "I won't need it when I start running."

"Fine." He narrowed his eyes. "Only trying to be kind."

The pain flickering in his gaze made me keep it on and place an icy hand on his forearm.

His head snapped up.

"Kes...are you okay?"

He snorted, shoving aside his melancholy unsuccessfully. "Yes, of course. Why wouldn't I be?"

I looked back at the Hall. It sat ominous and frightening, casting shadows over the hibernating gardens. "You miss him, too. Don't you?"

His nostrils flared. "We shouldn't talk about it."

"Why not? You said all secrets were mine to know." I smiled, despite the awfulness of the circumstances. "I'm not going anywhere, and I have no one to tell. The world believes I'm marrying into your family. My brother's reputation is ruined, and my father is a ghost of the man he used to be. What would be the harm in trusting me?"

"You have a point." For a moment, he looked disgusted. With what? What his family had done to mine? Or that I had the audacity to ask him to trust me?

Finally, he sighed. "I wouldn't say this in front of anyone else, but..." He inched closer, ducking to whisper in my ear, "I'm sorry. For everything that's happened."

For the tiniest moment, my heart fluttered. He was so *uncomplicated* compared to Jethro. He kept things hidden—his true agenda being one—but I felt as if he only had one layer beneath his exterior, not thousands.

I placed my hand over his, squeezing in gratitude. "That means a lot. Thank you."

The moment stretched on for longer than it should; we both jumped away guiltily.

Clearing his throat, Kes asked, "I'm going to get the foxhounds. Want to come to the stables?"

Huddling deeper into his jacket, I nodded. "Why not? Perhaps it's not a day for running, after all."

"Well...if you're not going for a run, I have a much better idea."

Holding out his arm, he waited for me to loop mine with

his. His smile was still tainted, but life sparked in his eyes. "Let's go do something fun."

Fun.

I envisioned a drink in a warm *boudoir* or hanging out with friends while playing a board game, or even watching a movie with popcorn.

But apparently, that wasn't what Kes had in mind.

Entering the stables, he placed the shotgun in the tack room and motioned for me to follow. We headed into the long cobblestone-paved building where countless horses rested in cubicles. The floor was scattered with sweet smelling hay and the air temperature was warm and inviting. Scents weaved with the comforting aroma of horse and leather.

My tension dissolved, slipping down my spine and leaving my shoulders free from the choke of worry and deliberation.

Jethro said he would save me.

But Kes saved my mental state by reminding me normalcy still existed. Animals were still there to lick away my sorrows, and the sun still rose on days not so bleak.

I needed reminding of that.

Considering I'd never been around horses growing up, something about them tamed my anxiety, giving me a place to hide and regroup.

Kes smiled, moving between the stalls; horses watched with glossy gazes and pert ears. He stopped halfway down the aisle. A long, grey face and the gentlest black eyes popped over the railing. The horse nuzzled his pockets, nickering softly.

*Moth.*

I moved faster, still madly in love with the dapple grey that I'd travelled to the polo tournament with.

Kes grinned as Moth switched her attention to me. Her velvet nostrils huffed, seeking oats and other treats as I reached out to stroke her powerful neck. "Hey, girl."

She pawed the ground, the metal of her shoe clinking

against cobbles.

"Wait there." Kes disappeared to the end of the stables, then came back holding a rosy apple. "Here you go."

I took it.

Moth followed the fruit with sniper-like attention.

"I just feed it to her?"

Kes nodded. "Put it on your palm and keep your fingers flat. You don't want her to bite you accidentally."

*Great.*

I eyed Moth hesitantly. Her neck strained over the railing, trying to get at the apple. When I didn't move, Kes chuckled.

"Don't be afraid." He stole my hand, bent my fingers till they were flat, then shoved me forward. "Can't tease the poor girl."

The second I was within biting distance, Moth pinched the apple from my hand. A loud crunching noise filled the stables. Every other horse pricked its ears, alerted to the sound of treats and the fact that they weren't getting any.

Apple juice dripped from her lips, plopping onto the dusty floor.

Kes laughed. "She'll do anything for sweets. She's a nutcase for molasses."

I raised my hand, patting between her eyes. Moth nudged closer, demanding more cuddles, telling me exactly how she wanted it.

"She's lovely," I said softly, imagining owning such a magnificent animal.

"She is, I agree." Kes never took his eyes off me. His words hovered between us, not entirely innocent. Something stronger than friendship emitted from him.

I had the insane urge to wrap my arms around Moth and use her as a crutch in this suddenly precarious position.

"Kestrel…"

He cleared his throat. "Sorry."

We both stood awkwardly. I continued to stroke Moth and the yips of foxhounds in the kennel next door reminded me all over again of the first night I'd spent here and the kindness Squirrel had shown by licking my tears.

There was goodness in all of us. Human, equine…canine. We were all capable of good and bad. We were all redeemable—no matter what we did.

Kes rubbed his jaw. "You know…"

I looked up, waiting for him to continue. "Know what?" I prompted.

His gaze narrowed. He suddenly cleared his throat, shaking his head. "Eh, don't worry about it."

I frowned, scratching Moth around her ear, straining on tiptoes to reach. "Okay…"

A few seconds ticked past before he exploded. "You know what? Fuck it. It's *his* fault he can't bloody cope. I'm done with how he's treated me and sick to fucking death of him reneging on everything we agreed." He punched himself in the chest. "*I* was there for him from the beginning. I kept his bloody secrets. I deserve to know what the fuck is going on, but he's cut me out."

I froze. "What do you mean?"

Kes chuckled darkly. "It means, I'm *done*. That's what. I'm sick of waiting for him to crawl back and apologise. I'm also sick of him threatening me to stay away from you—even though I know he's ignoring you as much as me."

What on earth happened between Kes and Jethro to warrant their relationship turning so sour?

He dragged a hand through his hair. "Jethro approached me after the polo game last month. He asked if I wanted a new horse."

I gasped. "Oh, no! You can't get rid of her." I leaned into her, pressing my face against her neck. "She's perfect. Don't ever say such a thing."

Kes smiled, patting the mare. "I know. She's a great girl. She's only eight years old, so she's not going to the glue factory anytime soon."

I grabbed Moth's ears, squeezing tight. Speaking to the

horse, I said, "Pretend you never heard of glue or factory. That will never happen to you. I won't allow it."

Even as I said it, I wanted to burst into insane tears. Moth would outlive me by decades. I was the one on the countdown to be put down, not her.

*Unless Jethro figures out his plan.*

Kes's finger pressed against the underside of my chin, raising my eyes to his. "I don't know why I'm telling you this, because it just makes him look good all over again, but...he wanted to get me a new horse, so *you* could have Moth."

My heart stopped. *"Me?"*

He nodded. "He was going to give her to you the night after the Second Debt. But of course..." He trailed off, both of us aware what happened the next day.

Kes gritted his jaw. "And if I'm completely honest, I'm glad he didn't have the chance to give her to you." A cloud fell over his face, twisting his features with anger. "She's *my* horse. I should be the one to give her away if I choose."

I stroked his arm, hoping to reassure him that no one was taking his horse. And even if Jethro *had* given me Moth, I couldn't have taken her because she already belonged to Kes. "Don't worry, Kestrel. She's yours. No one—"

"I want you to have her."

The air solidified.

Moth huffed, nudging me as I stood mute.

I spluttered, "I—I can't."

Even as I said it, the thought of owning this incredible beast blistered my heart. To have something of my own, while surrounded by things that could never be—it would be...wonderful.

Kes clamped strong hands on my shoulders, staring deep into my eyes. "She's yours. She responds to you more than she does with me. You're meant to have her, Nila."

Gratefulness and overwhelming amazement filled me. "I—I don't know what to say."

Kes smiled. "Say nothing. It's already done." Squeezing

my shoulders, he stepped back. "You're the proud new owner of a dapple grey by the name of Warriors Don't Cry." Patting Moth on the neck, he grinned. "I'll find the pedigree papers later, so you can keep them safe, but for now...let's go for a ride."

My eyes bugged out of my head. "I've never been on a horse before."

*Not counting with Jethro when he carted me back on Wings, of course.*

Kes ignored me, heading toward the tack room. "Doesn't matter. I'll show you."

An hour later, I sat atop my first ever horse.

*I'm freaking.*

*I'm terrified.*

*I'm beyond exhilarated.*

I couldn't remember the last time something affected me so piercingly.

*Even Jethro?*

Well, apart from him.

It seemed the older I grew and more jaded by life I became, the more I lost the heightened extremes of newness. No longer enjoying the catapulting happiness or devastating lowness. These days my highs and lows were more hills and valleys rather than mountains and chasms.

But looking down and seeing the ground far below, feeling the unyielding metal stirrups beneath my borrowed boots, and the leather reins in my hands, I'd never been more alive. More joyous.

This was Christmas on crack.

This was birthdays all in one.

*I own her.*

*I own this majestic animal.*

I couldn't sit still with excitement. Leaning forward, I patted Moth's beautiful grey neck. From up here, I had full view between her ears at the rolling fields and sweeping dark forest.

Kes led his mount from the stables and swung his leg over an inky black horse. Its coat gleamed in the autumn gloom, its velveteen nostrils flaring with huge gusts of breath.

Before Kes could get his seat, the horse skittered sideways with a clatter of hooves.

"Whoa, you damn animal." He jerked the reins, forcing the horse to submit.

"Who's that?" I asked, clutching my own reins as Moth tossed her head at the fiery beast prancing beside her. Her flanks rippled with indignation.

Kes's face pinched in concentration. He swatted the horse with his whip as it bucked and nickered. The horse's ears flattened, eyes rolling in a mixture of hell-bound fury and eagerness.

"This is Black Plague. He's technically my father's horse, but he's in-between purse races right now. He always gets like this if he isn't trained every day." He stroked the pitch-black pelt. "Don't you, boy?"

"Rather you than me."

"Plague definitely isn't for beginners." Raising his eyebrow, Kes pointed at my helmet. "Check that it's on tight. I'm not a conventional teacher and need to make sure you're protected."

I laughed, forcing a finger beneath the strap below my chin, showing him that if it were any tighter, I'd choke. I also waved at the bracing corset he'd made me wear, along with the borrowed jodhpurs and boots. "Completely protected."

I felt like royalty—an equestrian princess who knew exactly what she was doing.

*I don't have a clue what I'm doing.*

For the past hour, Kes had taught me how to clean out Moth's hooves, curry her coat, saddle her, tighten a girth, and slip a bit into her mouth.

So much to do before going for a ride and so much more

to do once we returned.

But every single thing I adored.

I didn't think I'd ever been so happy than standing in the stall listening to Kes's deep voice as he joked and teased and congratulated me when I copied correctly.

He was patient and kind and we got along easily. Being with him made my heart weep for Vaughn. The ease in which we chatted reminded me of the relationship I'd had with my twin.

My heart also cried for another.

A rolling black cloud shaded me whenever I thought of Jethro.

He should've been the one teaching me.

He should've been the one laughing and joking and kissing me in the hay.

I hadn't seen Jethro today, and the lovesickness I suffered whenever I thought of him became a constant sabre to my chest.

How could I love someone with so many demons?

How could I love someone who didn't share those demons with me?

*I don't have a choice.*

If I did—I would choose Kestrel. He was kind and sympathetic. He made me feel better about myself, rather than condemned me to fear.

"Who are you, Kestrel?" I asked before I had time to censor myself.

He stilled, his hands tightening around his reins. "What do you mean?"

"Well, you seem to have a gift at hiding whatever you're thinking—just like your older brother. However, unlike him, you don't seem afflicted. Jethro responds to you. He obeys you when there's tension and looks to you for help." I squinted beneath my helmet. "Why is that?"

Kes lost his smile, filling with seriousness. "Do you know what he is yet?"

His question slapped me.
*I know about black diamonds and absorbing. I know about feelings and pain.*
"I'm beginning to understand." Moth shifted below me. "I don't have a name for his condition, though. Do you?"
"I do, but it's not my place to name it." He laughed softly. "Come back to me when you've figured it out. When Jethro tells you what he is—I'll tell you who I am. Fair?"
*No, not fair. I doubt he'll ever tell me.*
Tipping his helmet in salute, he added coyly, "However, there really isn't much to tell about me. I'm an open book."
Kicking Black Plague, he moved forward. Moth automatically followed. The *clip-clop* of hooves echoed off the kennel as we left the stables behind.
The rocking of Moth and the sheer power of her muscles sent fear skittering down my spine. What if I had a vertigo attack and fell off? What if I didn't steer properly and we ran into a tree?
"Uh, Kes...perhaps this isn't such a good idea." My legs trembled. "Maybe I should learn to ride on something smaller?"
Kes turned around, planting a hand on Black Plague's rump. Ignoring my concerns, he said, "Remember how I said I'm not a conventional teacher?"
I nodded slowly, nervousness billowing in my chest. "Yes..."
"Well, here is your crash course in riding. Hold your reins tight but not too tight. Don't jerk on her mouth. Pretend you have a twenty-pound note between your arse and the saddle and under no circumstances is it to fly free. Keep your heels down and back straight, and if you fall, roll away and *don't* hold onto the reins."
The more he spoke, the more my heart raced.
"Got it?"
Everything he just said went in one ear and out the other. "No. I don't have it. Not at all."

Kes threw me an evil grin. "Too bad." Raising his whip, he kicked Black Plague and shot away as if this was the Championship Derby. "Hold on, Nila!"

I pulled on my reins as Moth bunched and collected beneath me. "No...you are *not* going to follow him, damn horse. I like my neck being attached to my body."

Moth tossed her head, snatching the reins from my hands.

"No. Stop!"

A moment later, I went from standstill to full-blown gallop.

I became a blur of grey.

I became the girl from my past who believed in unicorns.

I became...free.

# Jethro

THE PAST FEW days, I'd done nothing but conspire on how to end this mess. I played my role, took my pills, and avoided the love of my fucking life.

Every time I thought up a plan, I researched each angle and plotted. But each time there were flaws, hurtling me deeper into despondency. The longer I couldn't solve my problem, the longer I avoided Nila.

I was so fucking close to destroying everything.

I *missed* her. So much.

So far, I'd discounted eleven different ways of murdering my father.

Option four: Invite him to go for a hunt. Shoot him and make it look like an 'unfortunate accident.'

Flaws: *Too risky. Witnesses. He would have a weapon to retaliate with.*

Option seven: Invite him to dinner. Poison the bastard's food with cyanide—just like he'd threatened me all my life.

Flaws: *Dosage might be wrong. Contamination to others.*

Option Nine: Arrange a mercenary to attack mid-shipment, dispatch him and keep my hands free from murder.

Flaws: *Kes might be with him and get hurt in the crossfire.*

Each one seemed plausible enough until deeper inspection. But all of that was shot to shit the afternoon he called me into his office.

Once again, he somehow knew.

*How the fuck does he always know?*

Was it his uncanny sixth sense? Constant monitoring of my behaviour?

*How?!*

What gave me away? The look of disgust I could never quite hide? The sneer of hatred I could never wipe away?

Whatever it was, I was once again fucking screwed.

In his office, with rain pelting on the windows, he'd shown me his prized and protected Final Will and Testament.

It was a tome the size of the Royal Decree. Pages upon pages of notary amendments and appendixes. And buried in the fine print were two highlighted areas.

Primogeniture: the section on myself, my role as firstborn, and what I stood to inherit. That part went on for sheets and sheets.

His death: Most importantly his *untimely* death.

Cut was a businessman. He was also cunning, ruthless, and smart.

The clause stated that any unnatural death, be it from bee stings or drowning, horse riding fall or car accident—even as simple as dying in his sleep—would make his entire Will null and void.

And not just for myself but for *all* of us.

My siblings would be tossed out. Jasmine would be sent to a convalescent home against her wishes. The Black Diamonds disbanded. Kestrel cast away without a penny.

What did it mean?

Simple.

Cut had noted that if he died from anything other than cancer or a medically proven condition, Hawksridge was to be demolished. Any death that could potentially be maliciously faked, our mines would be detonated. Our wealth donated to causes that had no right to receive charity.

It would be the end of our lifestyle.

It was his ultimate sacrifice and safeguard to ensure we stayed loyal.

Unlike him, I didn't care about money or ancient rubble. If it meant I could be free, so be it. But no amount of drugs could stop me from caring about my siblings.

And Cut knew that.

He showed me his trump card.

Along with Jasmine's imprisonment in a disabled rest home—her power of attorney stripped away—and Kes's renouncement, I would become a ward of the crown, placed in a straitjacket, and thrown into a padded room.

He had authentic documents stating my mental wellbeing. A sworn oath bullet-pointing testimonies and histories, proving I was legally unfit to represent myself. All decision-making was to be at the discretion of my enlisted doctors—doctors who'd been bribed and coerced for years and knew my past. I would have no power—no room to argue.

The documents were submitted with a letter to his lawyer, stating if anything unseemly happened to him, to look no further for the smoking gun, because all fingers pointed to me.

I would be thrown in an asylum—one I could never escape.

Needing fresh air, I threw down my pen and crossed my office.

*There has to be another way.*

"Fuck!" I hissed, stepping onto the Juliette balcony the same way I'd done countless of times before. The cool breeze whistled down my back, and the ache in my chest deepened.

Yet, unlike countless of times before, my heart fucking shattered into a trillion pieces.

Below me, with her hair streaming behind her and the happiest, slightly terrified smile on her face was Nila.

She was a grey comet. A thundering silver-shooting star.

She couldn't have been more majestic or sublime.

Moth's elegant legs chewed up the lawn, heading toward the paddock I'd galloped over many times on my own.

Horse and rider merged in utmost perfection.
Only, she wasn't alone.

The ring of male laughter came over the breeze as Kestrel shot past her on Black Plague, his hand in the air and a grin plastered to his motherfucking face.

The picture they presented tore out my heart, turning it to dust.

All this time, I'd worked my ass off to protect Nila, Kes, and Jaz. All this time, I'd distanced myself and done what was required.

And how was I fucking repaid?

By being *forgotten*.

Nila hunched further over Moth's withers, galloping faster. Together, they tore off into the distance, leaving me stricken...hollow.

No amount of pills could stop me feeling the wave of crashing desolation.

The numbing fog couldn't help me.

This was my breaking point.

My utter grief.

*I'd* wanted to experience that with her.

I'd wanted to make her smile and laugh and slide inside her in the dark, secretive world of the stables.

I'd wanted to grant her the gift better than any material thing.

But that'd been stolen from me.

By the one man I thought had my back forever.

*Betrayer. Stealer. Forsaker.*

I turned around and went back into my office.

But I returned empty.

My heart was left tagging along like a kite, its strings tied to Nila as she galloped further away beneath the cloud-filled sky.

# Nila

IT WAS FINISHED.

The centrepiece of my Rainbow Diamond collection.

I stepped back to inspect the gown, making sure it hung just right.

The mannequin presented the crinoline dress as if I'd stepped through time and created something my great-great-grandmother would wear.

The hoop in the thick petticoats forced the rich grey dress to flare in an elegant bell-like swish. There were no layers or feathers or tulle—not like the corset highlight of my Fire and Coal show in Milan. This was understated and sleek—like a smoky waterfall shimmering with secrets and mystery.

Around the cuffs, I'd sewn cream lace that I'd found in a rusted-shut cupboard in my quarters. The lace held the W sigil. My ancestors must've painstakingly created it decades ago; it was fitting to adorn a gown such as this.

The bodice gleamed with panels of midnight silk, creating a prismatic effect. Tiny black beads decorated from décolletage to hem in a glittering asymmetrical pattern, just like the black diamond Jethro had shown me at the warehouse.

There were no rainbows on this dress.

Only darkness.

But it filled me with terrible pride, along with immense

sadness. *This might be the last headline piece I make before leaving this world.*

Instead of becoming more optimistic as my time continued unmolested, I became less and less sure. Jethro couldn't hide his frustration. Breakfast, he barely talked. Dinner, he barely ate. He watched Cut with a mixture of obedience and feral rage. But beneath it all was helplessness.

I'd bumped into Bonnie twice since being back. Each time she stretched thin red lips into a smile so cold my blood iced over. She hadn't summoned me. She didn't want anything to do with me. However, I had a horrible feeling that would soon change.

Moving away from the mannequin, I stretched my lower back. My hands were pinpricked and sore. My eyes achy and tired.

I'd worked nonstop for four days—ever since Kestrel took me for my first ride.

I still had bruises on my inner thighs from gripping so hard, but I hadn't fallen off. I hadn't had a vertigo attack. And I hadn't thought of Jethro once as I soared over the fields and escaped everything that hounded me.

And that made me absolutely wretched.

I didn't think of him. *Not once.*

Kestrel had given me so much that day, and I'd taken it with no thought as to how it would affect my relationship with Jethro. I was guilty, full of shame.

I felt as if I'd betrayed him.

And the longer he stayed away from me, the worse it became.

The next night, I entered the dining room and bumped into the firmest, most delectable chest in Hawksridge Hall.

The moment I touched him, I melted into his body. The tears and guilt I'd been storing inside sprung up to strangle me.

"Jethro…" My fingers swooped to bunch in his t-shirt.

"God, it's been days. Such long, awful days."

I looked into his golden eyes, seeking the love I'd witnessed when I'd sneaked into his chambers. However, I recoiled at the angry agony glowing in them.

My skin prickled.

He swallowed and for an enchanted moment, we stood together. Breathing, touching, *living*. Then his mask slipped into place, the emotions in his eyes vanished, and his hands captured mine, tearing them away from his chest.

"Hello, Ms. Weaver."

Was his coolness because of the low murmur of voices of Black Diamond brothers eating behind him? Or was it the drugs he'd once again befriended?

"Don't." I shook my head. "Don't keep doing—"

He took a step back. "I can imagine you've worked up quite an appetite."

"Excuse me?"

"Then again, I would think now that you have your own horse, you'd be out more often—yet you haven't left your quarters since."

My heart fell through the floor.

Freedom. Laughter. Friendship with Kestrel.

"You saw that?"

He sneered. "You mean did I see you riding the horse *I* wanted to give you? Did I see you laughing the way *I* planned with my brother? And did I see the way you revelled in the freedom *I* wanted to show you—then yes." His eyes narrowed. "I saw all of it."

Before I could say a word, he left.

Needle&Thread: *This was a mistake, V. I don't know what possessed me to come back here without a thought-out plan. I need to think of another.*

I did have a plan: get pregnant with his child and nullify the debt.

219

And look how that turned out.

Last night, Jethro showed me just how much I'd hurt him by living the best I could within the parameters he'd set. I'd found happiness with Kes. I'd proven I wasn't broken and still found joy in simple things.

I wanted to find happiness with Jethro. I wanted to runaway together. To prove that our love transcended duty and family honour—but Jethro wasn't prepared. How could one person be so committed to finding another way, when the other was stuck in the same warped trap from his childhood?

I was angry, upset. But most of all, stricken for the way I'd made him feel. It wasn't logical, but I felt responsible for his pain.

And until we'd talked and made amends, I couldn't rest.

The moment the Hall retired to slumber, I tiptoed to his chambers and tried to enter. But the private door in the parlour leading to the bachelor wing was locked. And no matter how much I poked and prodded, I was no expert on lock-picking.

I'd returned, mournful and frustrated, to welcome the sunrise of a new day.

All I could think about was the mistakes upon mistakes I'd made. With my brother, father...my lover.

What power did I have if I cut myself off from everybody? What hope of survival could I wish for if I was all alone?

Sitting in the silk upholstered loveseat beside my window, I drowned in dysphoria.

I didn't want to eat or sew or read.

I just wanted to...exist.

To pretend I had a simpler life and one not so tangled in treachery.

My phone remained silent in my hands, the screen glowing with invitation to mend bridges between Threads and Kite.

A text said a thousand things. It allowed the reader privacy and time to absorb. Good news and bad were easier to face. Easier to accept.

Uncurling my legs, I opened a new message.

I had no idea what to write, so I turned off my mental critique and let my fingers decide for me.

Needle&Thread: *Kite...how did everything change? My heart beats for you, my soul craves yours. During the Second Debt we shared everything. We were free. I hate this distance now. Talk to me. Tell me what you're thinking. You give me nothing, but I see everything. Trust me. Come to me tonight. Let me show you I'm yours forever. This doesn't have to be complicated. I love you. Love is simple, kind. Love is forgiveness. Can we forgive each other before it's too late?*

Tears ran silently over my cheeks as I pressed send.

# Jethro

"JETHRO."

I looked up from my phone. My father came into my quarters, fastening a diamond cufflink through his black shirt.

I couldn't stop reading Nila's text. Over and over again. Her words embedded into my soul, and no matter what happened in the future, I couldn't carve them out.

Once again, she'd proven her power over me was undeniable, forcing me to face the conclusion I'd finally admitted to myself yesterday.

Nothing would work.

No one would fix me.

I couldn't continue to be responsible for my brother or sister.

I couldn't continue to live in constant fear of being murdered or cast out.

It was time to take what was mine—regardless of the aftermath, and I couldn't do it on my own.

Last night, I'd swallowed a tablet and visited my sister for the first time in almost two months. She'd been cross and short-tempered, but once I laid out my plan, she'd thawed.

Like the perfect sibling, she'd forgiven me and gave me what I needed to face what must be done.

Then, I'd visited Kestrel. I'd apologised, admitted my

douche-bag behaviour, and asked for help. Just like Jasmine, he'd granted absolution and listened to my struggles. I hid nothing, revealed everything. For the first time since we hit adulthood, we were completely in-tune and equal.

Lucky for me, after my bout of honesty, he was only too happy to agree to my ludicrously ambitious plans.

Killing Cut wasn't an option—for now.

We had to be smarter

We had to be shrewd.

The time had come.

Hawks against Hawks.

Cut finished securing his cuffs. "Tonight, Jet. I want it done."

My body seized. *What?*

No way.

Every fucking time.

He'd guessed I was breaking and came at the perfect moment with his proverbial hammer to smash me into pieces.

"Not tonight." I clutched my phone. I had a hair-brained concept, but it was still in its infancy. *It can't happen tonight. I'm not ready.*

"Yes, tonight. I want this whole process sped up." He dropped his hands stiffly by his sides. "Those pills are working. You've impressed me more the past few weeks than you have in your entire life. You've killed to protect our family. You've remained distant from those you don't need, and you've cut that Weaver Whore out of your heart."

He came forward and patted my shoulder, harsh respect glowing in his eyes. "I don't want anything to jeopardise the new connection we've found, son. And she's the cause of it all. Let's get the Debt Inheritance over with. Complete your final test and take your place fully by my side." His voice dropped. "When the time comes, I'll gladly hand over the crown because you've earned it."

Despite my hatred for him, relief slithered around my heart. Relief because I'd *finally* been worthy of the gift I'd been fighting to receive for twenty-nine years.

Pity, it was just empty words.

"I'm proud of you, Kite."

I bowed my head, squeezing my phone until the casing cracked.

I would have to be ready...there was no other way.

"Now, tell the lady's maid to prepare the girl. Tonight, we inch closer to the finish line." His teeth glinted with an evil smile. "Tonight, the Third Debt will be paid."

# Nila

I FOUND TEX *in the lounge, nursing a brandy and looking as if he hadn't showered in days. He didn't look up as I perched on the arm of his favourite chair.*

*Something had changed between us. We no longer had a close bond—it was taut, strained—full of accusations and denials.*

*I missed him.*
*I feared for him.*

*But I didn't have the strength to bring up what I truly wanted to know. So, I sat there, rubbing his forearm with my tattooed fingertips, hoping he knew that I forgave him. He might be my elder, but he wasn't faultless. He needed to let his guilt go before it killed him.*

*Without looking into my eyes, he spoke. His voice was cracked and brittle, his brandy glass long since dry.*

"She told me to hide you."

*I knew instantly he spoke of my mother.*

"I had plans. I'd booked flights for all of us. I had a whole new life arranged in America. There was no way I was going to let those bastards have two of my girls. I would've died to protect you, Threads. You have to believe me."

*My father's head bowed as the weight of wrong decisions pushed him deeper into his chair.*

"The night before we were due to leave, I had a visitor. He showed me...things—" He swallowed hard, squeezing his eyes as if he couldn't bear to remember. "He made me believe that no matter where I took you, no matter how well I hid you, they would find you. And if they did, the debts would be twice the repayment. Twice the pain. He made me a promise that if I let his firstborn take you easily, that you would be given a good life. A life that might go on for years."

A tear rolled down his cheek. He clutched my hand so hard blood ceased to flow. "By God, I believed him, Nila. He had too much...too many things to prove he spoke the truth. I couldn't refuse. I couldn't subject you to that. The things they've done—"

Taking a deep breath, he stuttered, "So I cancelled our new life and remained, knowing that one day you would be taken from me." A horrible sob escaped him. "I'm so sorry, little one. I only did what I hoped was right. I chose the lesser evil, do you see? I chose the one with a longer timeframe so I could get you free."

He looked up, his black eyes watering and bloodshot. "I couldn't save your mother, but I'm going to save you. I will. I swear it."

His confession wrenched silent tears of my own. I kissed the top of his head, granting absolution. "I trust you, Dad."

He collapsed in on himself. I didn't have the strength to ask him what I *desperately* wanted to know.

Where did he think my mother was buried all this time?

And what did Cut show him to leave his wife in the hands of monsters?

"Miss?"

The dream shattered.

Not that it was a dream, but a memory. The one time Tex spoke honestly while I'd been back home. He'd then wiped it from his history by drinking so much, he didn't remember the next morning.

"You awake, Miss?"

I stretched, wincing at the crick in my spine. "Yes. Yes, I'm awake."

*How long did I nap for?*

My phone rested on the floor and a damp patch where I'd

drooled on the silk loveseat hinted at a while.

I shivered, rubbing my arms to ward off the chill. The archaic central heating in this place was intermittent at best. Scrambling to my feet, I eyed up the marble fireplace. Cold ash and black soot looked back. I'd set it last night, but I sucked at making a decent heat-delivering flame.

Picking up my phone, I checked the inbox.

*Nothing.*

I'd hoped after my message, Jethro would've replied or at least come to see me. I needed him again. I needed him every damn day. The lust in my blood never ceased.

The maid bustled about, picking up scraps of material and tossing them into the wicker basket where my cut-offs ended up. "You have an hour, Miss. Time to get ready."

"An hour?" I rubbed my eyes, chasing off the cloudiness from my nap. "For what?"

The maid with her brown ponytail and pink lips never stopped tidying. "Wasn't told. I only know you have to get ready."

My heart unfurled. Could it be Jethro's way of asking me to prepare for a long overdue conversation?

*Could he be taking me on the date he promised the night of the Second Debt?*

I hugged myself at the thought. *Finally.* After weeks apart, we could finally connect and be true. Like we should've done at the start.

He'd admitted we were on the same team, yet he'd avoided me ever since.

*Teams have to stick together, Kite.*

He'd been raised with siblings but always so alone. However, he wasn't alone any longer.

*He has me.*

"Tell, Mr. Hawk, I won't need an hour."

Without waiting for her reply, I charged into the bathroom.

Fifty-one minutes later, I stepped from the misty steam back into my bedroom.

I'd never been so diligent in my appearance before. I'd used the expensive soaps and lotions stocked in the bathroom. I'd showered, shaved—ensured my legs were silky smooth, and the hair between my legs manicured into a perfect strip hiding just a little but not a lot.

I wanted to be perfect for him.

I fully intended to seduce him and force Jethro to admit who he was, what it meant, and to finally accept that I wanted him—faceted flaws and all.

To ensure I looked the best I could, I'd straightened my glossy hair and shaded my eyes with a mixture of blacks and pewters. My lips however were left virginally pink with just a swipe of clear lip balm.

I wanted Jethro to drop to his knees the moment he saw me. I wanted him panting and so rock-hard, he forgot to be gentle and slammed me against the wall in his rush to take.

I was already wet imagining everything we'd do.

The maid had disappeared, leaving me free to strut around naked if I wished. Instead, I clutched a towel around me and made my way to the imposing carved wardrobe. Swinging open the doors, I inspected my choices.

I'd made a few dresses while here, but nothing screamed first date with the man I would spend the rest of my life with.

*However long that might be.*

A tentative knock came.

"Come in." I tightened my knotted towel, deciding on a fuchsia pink wraparound dress that would set off my tanned skin.

"Ah, Miss. You don't need to choose. Your outfit has been arranged."

I spun around. *Jethro picked out a dress for me?*

I tripped a little bit more in love. "Really?"

Keeping her eyes downcast, the maid came toward me holding a large zipped clothing bag. "This is the chosen outfit."

My heart did an excited two-step, dying to see what Jethro had chosen. It was romantic. Sweet, in a way. And also telling of his preferences—a glimpse into his inner desires. I shadowed her as she placed the garment on my bed and unzipped it.

"Once dressed, your presence is required in the gaming hall."

*I can't see.*

I moved around her, eagerness making me rude. She hadn't pushed aside the bag, still hiding the contents. I reached to move it, but she said, "Did you hear me? You're to go to the gaming hall."

My heartbeat switched to a sombre *thud-thud.* Jethro wanted our first date on Hawksridge land? Surely, there were more enjoyable places than a stuffy cigar-fumigated den?

"Did he say why?"

She shook her head. "No, sorry."

And why would he? Jethro was kind and gentle beneath layers of complexities, but he was still a rich, powerful man, and she was but a lowly servant. Such things wouldn't be shared.

"You're running out of time. I was told to help you dress." Frowning a little, she pushed aside the bag and withdrew a simple cheesecloth shirt and...breaches.

The sombre *thud-thud* turned to a more panicky drum. My eyes swooped up to hers. "He said I had to wear this?"

*Is Jethro into weird kink that completely escaped my notice?* Whenever we slept together, I got a feeling that missionary and the more conventional methods weren't entirely his taste. He held something back—but *this*?

*What on earth is erotic about breaches?*

She shook her head. "Nothing, ma'am. All I know is I'm supposed to help you dress and get you there within the hour."

She reached for my towel.

I backpedalled. "No...that won't be necessary. I can dress myself."

*Please...*

A silent beg began in my soul, gathering volume with every breath.

*Please...*

The beg became a prayer, tiptoeing through awful conclusions.

*Please don't let this be what I think it is...*

The maid nodded. "Okay. I'll just wait outside." She headed for the door, but turned around. "Oh, I almost forgot. There were two instructions. No bra or knickers and tie your hair up."

*Oh, my God.*

My heart slammed to a stop.

*Please. Please, don't let this be...*

My beg was no longer a scared prayer but a raucous in every limb.

"Why?" I choked, suffocating on knowledge.

The maid shrugged. "Again, Miss. I wasn't told. But they do expect your presence quickly so..." She nodded at the items. "Best to hurry."

She stepped from the room, shutting the door behind her.

*They.*

*Not him.*

*They.*

The pain came from nowhere. A crippling ripping *tearing* deep inside. It felt as if my body tried to evict my soul—every cell shredding with agony. A silent scream billowed, succumbing to the horrific knowledge, battering me with violence—almost as if I could commit suicide just from fear.

*Run, Nila.*

*Climb out the window and run.*

I folded in half, clutching my heaving midriff.

Vertigo swooped like bats of hell, flapping in my hair and

screeching in my ears. I toppled to my knees, not stopping my cantilevered descent until my forehead touched the carpet. I stayed that way—with my arms locked around me in a useless embrace and my head at the foot of some deity who refused to save me.

*It might not be what you think.*
*It might not be the Third Debt.*

A sob crawled up my throat.

Lying to another was doable. Lying to myself was impossible.

Trembling, I sat up and grabbed the clothes from the bed. They slid from the sheets, scattering on the floor. The material was scratchy, rudimentary.

The urge to bolt grew ever more incessant.

*Don't let them do this.*

I vaguely knew where the boundary was now. I could make it. I had a beast with four legs ready to carry me away. But even if I made it to the stables and to Moth—even if I made it to the boundary and galloped all my way to London—no one would believe my tale. Not after the press. The interview. Not after the online websites and gossip columns placing wagers on when our big day would be and how the world had been used in an elaborate hoax between family rivalry and an overprotective brother.

Cut had cleverly strengthened my bars to a worldwide level—locked in by hearsay and propaganda.

Swallowing the sickness from vertigo, I slowly stood. The room still spun. The nausea still battered. But I had no options. Deliver myself willingly and pray I was strong enough to get through it. Or wait for them to claim me and administer a worse punishment.

Tears clawed my lungs as I dropped the towel.

An ant's nest of hatred and helplessness crawled over my skin as I picked up the breaches.

A shudder hijacked my muscles as I pulled the abrasive wool over my feet and up to my hips. Instantly, I itched—

rasping claustrophobia within the primitive trousers.
*Keep going.*
Gritting my teeth, I slipped into the cheesecloth shirt, cursing the see-through fabric and my dark nipples. I might as well be wearing nothing.
*I can't go out like this.*
The maid suddenly appeared without knocking. Her eyes cast over me. "Great, you're almost ready." Pulling a hair tie from around her wrist, she gave it to me. "You need to tie up your hair, too. They said in a bun."
I couldn't speak.
It took all my power to keep from murdering her and bolting.
Taking the elastic, I gathered my straightened hair and twisted it into a rope before twirling it up on top of my skull and fastening it in place.
"You ready to go?"
Ignoring the maid, I padded over to the full-length mirror, hating the fact my chest was in full view beneath the cheesecloth.
My reflection.
A wild moan keened. I slapped my hands over my mouth.
*I look...*
*I look...*
My heart decided it would no longer beat. No longer strum to keep me alive. It turned into coal—no longer flesh or blood or diamond—just dirty, dusty coal splintering into kindling.
All my fears had come true.
I was about to pay the Third Debt.
And I knew who I was paying it for.
The Hawk ancestors had a family. I'd already paid for the husband's trial for stealing by whipping. I'd paid for the sins of Mrs. Weaver by drowning the Hawk daughter for witchcraft. And now I was to pay whatever curse befell the Hawk son.
The little boy who worked so hard only to be rewarded

with starvation.

I knew that with utmost certainty.

My reflection told the terrifying truth.

Dressed in breaches and a basic shirt with my hair scraped back, I no longer looked like a woman who wanted to seduce Jethro Hawk.

But a little boy about to be ruined for life.

The maid led me down the corridor, through countless living rooms and dayrooms, before stopping on the threshold of a smoke-hazed billiards den.

She didn't say a word, just nodded at the open door. Pirouetting, she left me standing with my arm over my chest, trying to hide my freezing nipples. I couldn't stop shaking. Couldn't stop fearing.

"God's sake, come in, Nila." Cut snapped his fingers, never glancing away from the cards in his hands. The Hawk men sat around a low poker table in leather-studded chairs. The snooker table with its apple green velvet and low hanging Tiffany chandeliers was utterly ignored in favour of gambling.

Unwillingly, I stepped from corridor to room.

"Shut the door; there's a good girl." Cut glanced up, puffing on a cigar dangling from the corner of his mouth. He looked me up and down, his eyes lingering on my hidden chest. "Well...can't say you look very attractive. Drop your arm; at least let us see some tits, so we know you aren't truly a fucking peasant boy."

My teeth clamped together as I fought every instinct to run. Forcing myself to ignore Cut, I focused on the man I loved—regardless of his mistakes, chilliness, and icy words.

Jethro sat with his family but somehow looked so removed. His eyes locked on mine. His face ashen and tight, cheekbones were blades, slicing through stretched skin. His posture spoke of a bound animal seething with the need to kill, while his jaw held a permanent clench of desolation and regret.

It hurt too much to look at him.

Kes caught my attention.

He gave me a sad smile, hiding everything he felt behind the incredible gift of illusion. He was a magician, deleting anything that might give him away. Even the connection we'd built the day he'd given me Moth didn't let me see his thoughts.

Daniel, on the other hand, snickered, leaning back on two chair legs, chewing the end of his cigar. "Can't say you're pretty dressed like that..." His tone lowered. "But I'd still fuck you."

Jethro tensed.

A gasp fell from my lips.

I stepped back, wishing I could ignore common-sense and run. Bolt down corridors and charge through doors. But there was no *point*. I would be caught. I would be hurt. And I would have to survive the debt regardless.

Jethro and Kes weren't smoking, but they had a large tumbler of amber liquid beside them, glowing in the warm sidelights that cast more shadows than illumination. The room lurked in colour palettes of brown, maroon, and earth. Forest green drapery obscured the windows, while the carpet was a thick motif of a huge chessboard with black and white squares.

It truly was a parlour where games were played—the debts being the ultimate game of all.

"Jet, are you going to say something to our guest?" Cut narrowed his eyes.

Jethro's knuckles turned white around his glass.

I stood motionless on the carpet, waiting...waiting for him to doom me to his heinous family once again.

Jethro tore his eyes from mine, glaring at the table. Kes nudged him subtlety.

Sucking in a heavy breath, he pinched the bridge of his nose. Without looking up, he murmured, "Your job is to serve us while we gamble, Ms. Weaver." His eyes landed on mine only to dart away a second later. "You are to do as we ask in all instances. Understood?"

I didn't listen to his words but his eyes. They shot their

own message—but it was scrambled, hectic, unfathomable.

"Grab a fresh ashtray from the sideboard and replenish the peanuts," Cut commanded.

I couldn't move.

Cut twisted his body to face me. "Why are you still standing there? Did you not hear me?"

*Oh, God. Oh, God.*

My hands fisted and I tried to obey, but my legs seized with terror.

Kes stood up, scattering a few nutshells. "I'll show—"

Cut slammed his palm on the table, toppling stacks of poker chips. "Sit down, Angus, and fucking behave." Glowering at me, he snarled, "Do as you're told, Ms. Weaver, or this gets a hundred times worse."

Jethro hung his head, dragging a hand over his nape. His eyes infernoed with hatred, blazing at his father.

Cut bellowed, "Now!"

Kes hastily sat back down. I somehow found the strength to move. Silently, I made my way barefoot to the sideboard where staff had left an expensive bottle of cognac, more cigars, crystal ashtrays, and an array of nuts and crisps for the game.

With shaking hands, I grabbed a bag of honey-roasted peanuts and hugged them. Suffering another vertigo tilt-a-whirl, I spun to face the men.

Four Hawks.

One of me.

I baulked.

I didn't want to go anywhere near them. The table had an aura of evil around it, dangerous and foreign, screaming at me to run. Even Jethro was shrouded, neither granting me strength through his love nor soothing me that somehow he would save me.

Cut snapped his fingers, cigar smoke wisping toward the ceiling. "We don't have all fucking night."

The grandfather clock chimed the hour.

The heavy gong reverberated like visible notes, rippling

through the air.
*Clang.*
*Clang.*
*I'll move when it ends.*
*Clang.*
*Clang.*
Four chimes. I forced courage into my veins, even though I'd used every drop. I couldn't bear to look at the clock to see how many were left.
*Clang.*
*Clang.*
"Shit, girl. Get over here now!" Cut yelled.
*Clang.*
*Clang.*
Jethro looked up. His golden eyes had been cloaked before with chaos, but now they screamed with everything he wanted to say.
*I read your text.*
*I'm sorry.*
*Clang.*
My heart cracked open as Jethro's lips formed two words. Two words that asked so much of me with no hint of deliverance.
*Trust me.*
*Clang.*
The final chime hung in the air like a cymbal crash, giving me nowhere else to hide. Ten p.m. and the night had only just begun.

Dropping my gaze from Jethro's, I steeled my heart and trusted not in *him* but in *me*.

I was strong enough.

I was brave enough.

I trusted I could survive.

Straightening my shoulders, I moved toward the Hawks to serve them.

# Jethro

FUCK, SHE WAS beautiful.

I couldn't tear my eyes away from the see-through shirt and awful trousers she wore. Instead of turning her into a scullery boy—an unwanted little heathen—the billowing material transformed her into a pixy. An ethereal creature barely fitting into human clothes.

*Please, let this work.*

I hadn't had much time. I didn't have the assurances I needed.

But I'd done all I could to protect her.

*Trust me, Nila.*

I waited for her to raise her eyes, but she kept them downcast as she approached the poker table. It was a proper gaming platform with cup holders, chip placers, and leather cushioning for hiding our winning hand.

'Poker Night' used to be a weekly occurrence. The Black Diamonds, my brothers, and my father would set up multiple tables and play until those tables morphed into one. The stakes of each game were high. Buy-ins were fifty pounds, and it wasn't uncommon for a pot to reach five figures before anyone won.

But now, this was a private affair. Four Hawks and one lone Weaver. Along with the disgusting knowledge of what would happen tonight.

Nila leaned over to restock the bowls, trying her best not to get too close. Her smell wrapped around me, spilling rich, fresh scents entirely too sensual. She looked so good. Her eyes were darker, her lips so fucking kissable.

Damn her for being so pretty. She might've been protected if she wasn't so tempting. Just like my family had damned her to this fate, her own genes ensured it would be worse.

"Thank you, Nila," Kes whispered as she moved around the table.

She flinched, not acknowledging him.

My cock twitched; I gritted my teeth. I couldn't handle my brother talking to her.

I couldn't stomach what would happen next.

The intentions leeching off my father were too hard to ignore. Lewd excitement and salacious greed. A lecherous asshole who thought of nothing more than stealing money and pleasure from those vulnerable.

*Fuck!*

Breathing hard, I forced myself to slip back into the drug-riddled fog.

I'd tripled my dose.

Cut made the mistake thinking they kept me clearheaded enough to be controlled. I'd learned that they granted clarity to seek other paths. They gave me enough peace to look past the abominable thoughts existing in this house and become as wily as him.

His Will and Testament sewed up my future as a lunatic in some psych ward if I ever tried to dispatch him. But he didn't have a safeguard if I played politics with politics…

Kes nudged me under the table.

I glanced at him from the corner of my eye, pretending to shuffle the deck. I hoped to fucking God I'd done all I could.

I hadn't had enough time to prepare. What would happen tonight would be improv and sheer fucking luck.

If I didn't pull it off…tonight would be a bloodbath. There would be no way to stop myself from slaughtering my entire bloodline—including myself.

So many things could go wrong.

So many unthought-of issues that could destroy my hard work.

*Trust me, Nila.*

*Because you have no other choice.*

Without a word, Nila took the used ashtray and spun to return to the sideboard.

Cut grabbed her around the waist, keeping her locked to his side. "I like this on you, Ms. Weaver. It looks rather…provocative." He raised his hand to cup her breast. The wash of lust springing from him overrode my triple dose.

I shot to my feet, showering the table in fifty-two cards.

Everyone froze.

My chest pumped. My fists clenched. My body howled for fucking murder.

Cut cocked his head, glaring deep into my eyes. In a heated challenge, he twisted Nila's nipple through the gauzy shirt.

*Shit, shit. Do. Not. Deviate.*

"Something you want to say, Jet?" Cut hissed, imprisoning Nila as she wriggled. Her lips pursed, sickness swimming over her face.

I couldn't look at her without drowning in everything she felt. Horror, hatred, hopelessness. She expected me to be her champion. To save her at the final hour.

*I will.*

*I'm trying.*

Daniel cackled, stubbing out his cigar. "If what father says is true, brother, perhaps you should leave. After all, you've already had a taste which was against the rules."

Kes stood up beside me. His hand planted on my shoulder. "He has nothing to say. Do you, Jethro?"

I never looked away from Cut. This was between him and

me. No one else. We were the main players; everyone else was collateral in our war. Unlike Cut though, I meant to keep everyone alive in the aftermath.

A headache sprang from nowhere. The standoff vibrated stronger and stronger.

It was Nila who broke the tension. "Sit down, Kite." Her voice was raindrop soft and just as watery. My eyes tore to hers.

I had so much to say and no time to speak.

"She calls you Kite now, huh?" Cut shoved her away.

"That's a disappointing development."

My heart seized.

Kes's hand pressed on my shoulder, forcing my knees to buckle and deliver me back to my seat.

*Keep it together.*

"Not an important development, I can assure you." Swallowing my rage, I methodically scooped up the scattered cards. "I think the table needs another drink, Ms. Weaver."

Cut relaxed a little; Daniel laughed.

Nila bit her lip, tears glossing before turning her back on all of us to collect the cognac.

I sighed, shuddering under the tangled thoughts coming from all three relations. Each emotion fucked me up inside until I couldn't fathom my own conclusions.

It was easier to drink from the poisoned well than reject it. I would have to slip a little in order to win.

What Nila was about to go through would break her.

What I was about to go through would destroy me.

And no amount of pills could save us.

I just had to hope. Had to pray. Had to scheme.

Had to motherfucking implore that tonight I would win over Bryan 'Vulture' Hawk.

*Clang.*
The final chime struck midnight.
Two hours of torture.

Two hours of gambling.

Only Daniel was out; his chips distributed between Kes, Cut, and myself. My own stack dwindled, calling for drastic measures of going all in with an unbeatable hand. Kes was the winner, keeping Cut chasing as they puffed like chimneys and drank thousands of pounds worth of cognac.

Every few seconds, my attention wandered to Nila. She hovered like a ghost, jumping at my father's commands and pre-empting his requests by stocking crisps and emptying ashtrays.

Her presence distracted the hell out of me, but the fact that she refused to look at me drove me insane. She wouldn't let me silently explain or encourage.

She'd cut me out. In fact, she'd shut down emotionally. The only hint of feeling was dismal resignation.

"Your turn, Jet," Kes prompted, pointing at the flop.

I ran a hand through my hair. My mind wasn't on the game, only the fucking chimes of the clock.

One a.m. was the starting bell.

One more hour to go before the catastrophe began.

"I fold." Throwing the cards face down on the felt, I took another sip of my drink. The liquor formed a decent barrier with the drugs in my system, relaxing me enough to remain myself and not fester on Cut's intentions.

We continued to play.

Nila lingered in the background, and second by second, we all inched into the future. The setting was slightly different to what'd happened that fateful night—we weren't in a local drinking hole and Nila wasn't a tavern wench—but her role as waitress was the same.

Kes dealt the next hand.

He'd stopped smoking and slowed his pace on the cognac. His eyes were clear, hands steady. He'd fortified himself just enough with liquid courage but hadn't slipped into drunk.

I'd been an asshole to him the past few weeks, yet he'd forgiven me before I'd even apologised. He was a true friend. A

steadfast ally.
*But will you ever be able to look at him again without killing him after tonight?*
That question gnawed at my heart until I was riddled with holes.
I honestly didn't know. In order to save Nila, I might lose my brother.
But it was a chance I had to take.
Another round ensued.
The solid *ticks* of the grandfather clock pierced my eardrums. All I could think about was the time.
I flopped. Kes raised the stakes. Cut won. Daniel continued to guzzle.
New round.
I was the dealer. I handed out cards, waited for bets, did my part, then delivered the river. My hand was shit. The worst all evening, but I couldn't play this fucking farce any longer.
"All in." I shoved my small chip pile into the centre and glanced at the clock.
12:55 a.m.
I sighed.
*Shit.*
Kes threw me a look, his back tensing. Our knees touched, agreeing that from now on, I was on my own.
Nila sucked in a breath, dragging my attention to her. Her eyes were wide, confusion painting her cheeks from our shared message. She shrank further into the borrowed clothes she wore.
The last few minutes ticked past. We kept playing as if we weren't all exceedingly aware of what was about to happen.
"All in," Kes mumbled, shoving his substantial pile into the centre.
Cut glanced at us, rubbing his chin. "You boys are playing with fire." Backhanding his own chips, he spread them over our tidy towers and slapped his cards face up. "All in. Show me the final card."

Daniel chuckled. "This will be interesting." He leaned forward, pinched the deck, and slammed down the rest of the river.

The moment I saw who won, the clock chimed one.
*Clang.*
Kestrel.
He'd won.
*Of course, he did.*
Just like he'd won the girl.

# Nila

THE SINGLE TOLL of the clock sent mayhem racing through my blood.

One a.m.

Closer to the witching hour than daybreak—curtained by deep darkness where sins and perfidious acts occurred with no repercussion.

Fear.

Endless fear.

It compounded, amalgamated until I couldn't breathe.

Time screeched to a halt as the four Hawks discarded their game and turned their eyes on me.

I backed away, clutching my heart.

*No!*

My voice became a dried-up riverbed with no words to flow.

Jethro placed his elbows on the table, running his hands through his tinsel hair. His shoulders heaved as he fortified for whatever came next.

Cut slapped him on the back, muttering something beneath his breath.

Kes glanced at me then away. His body stiff and bristling.

*He knows.*

He knew what was about to happen. He knew and

couldn't look at me.

*Oh, God.*

My fear turned to petrified terror.

Daniel stood up first.

Cut nodded as the little creep moved toward me.

"Come here, Nila Weaver. It's time."

I shook my head, backing up until I bumped into a blood-red wingback. "Don't touch me." My gaze shot to Jethro. He stood bowed like an ancient tree that'd weathered far too many storms. His body was knotted and twisted, eyes tight and strained.

"I said, come *here*." Daniel lunged, grabbing my arm and jerking me against him. "Oh lookie. I'm touching you."

I bared my teeth, struggling in his foul grip. "Get your filthy—"

"Nila..." Kestrel stood, clearing his throat.

I paused, waiting for him to say something more. If his older brother wouldn't stop this atrocity, perhaps he would. Maybe I should've put my faith in Kes all along.

However, he only shook his head, his face once again hiding everything.

Cut reclined in his chair, snapping his fingers. "Proceed, Daniel."

"No, wait!"

Daniel dragged me forward. "Come along, whore." Yanking me to stand in front of him, he snatched my hands and secured them behind me with a silk sash. "Can't have you scratching or running now, can we?" He laughed under his breath.

Jethro trembled.

*Please, stop this!*

He didn't see my silent message as he tossed back another finger of cognac and warily turned to face me. The binds around my skin were tight, already cutting off blood supply.

Cut watched his son closely, not giving instruction but overseeing his every move.

Planting his legs on the chess piece carpet, Jethro said, "Nila Weaver, tonight is the night you will pay the Third Debt. Do you have anything to say before we begin?"

I fought against my restraints as Daniel hovered behind me. He'd secured them too well—they wouldn't budge. "Please...whatever you're about to do. Don't do it."

Cut laughed softly. "Such a waste of words, Ms. Weaver." Nodding at Daniel, he ordered, "Seeing as she has no respect for speaking. Gag her."

"Wait!" I turned feral. "No!" I darted forward, but Daniel dragged me back. I squirmed in his hold, turning into a snake hoping to slither from his trap.

But it was no use.

Within a moment, his wiry strength caught me, subdued me, and threaded a piece of red cloth through my lips. I bit down on it as he tied the knot behind my head, effectively bridling me like a domesticated pony. The material pressed uncomfortably on my tongue.

"Can't speak now, can you, Weaver?" Daniel tapped my cheek.

*Jethro!*

Jethro ran a shaky hand over his face.

How could he permit this? Didn't I mean *anything* to him?

"Now you have no option but to listen; it's time for your history lesson." Cut angled his chair, looking like a king on the carpet chessboard about to slaughter a simple pawn with no concern. "Listen carefully, Nila. Understand your sins. Then the night will proceed exactly as it did all those years ago." He looked at Jethro. "Continue, son."

With lethargic steps, Jethro took his place in centre stage. He looked paler than a vampire and just as ridden by death. Daniel's body heat repulsed me; I rode the ragged gallop of my heart, trying to calm down enough to persevere.

Jethro's measured, chilly voice filled the smoky room. "Many years ago, your ancestors loved to gamble. As happenstance would have it, most of the time the gamble paid off. Weaver possessed luck and used that luck in business, pleasure, and monetary gain." His voice thickened but never faltered. "On occasion, the head of the Weaver household would visit the local pub to play two-up, rummy, and poker."

My eyes drifted to the finished game of littered chips and empty glasses, seeing the scene and understanding whatever happened to me would be a direct correlation to that night.

"However one not-so-good year, the Weavers' luck ran out. Not only was his wife accused of witchcraft and the Hawk daughter sacrificed for her sins, but his skill at cheating cards was no longer a talent but a flaw.

"The news got out that he was a conniving thief, and the local gentry invited Weaver to a game at the local establishment to trip him up. Weaver went—as he always did. And cheated—as he always did.

"When the game was over, however, Weaver hadn't won. The cards had been switched, and Weaver folded with no money to pay back his losses. His playing companions demanded he pay his debts right there and then.

"Of course, he had no funds. He had a profitable business and textile enterprise. He owned silk shipments and exotic inks worth thousands of pounds, but his pockets were lined with lint and buttons, not paper and coins."

Jethro took a breath, his back straightening the longer he talked. I didn't know if it was anger at what my ancestors had done giving him power or that he somehow had a plan.

"They gave him an ultimatum. Pay the debt or lose his hand like so many other thieves. The police weren't there. It was late. Alcohol had been consumed, and men were at their worst. Lust. Greed. Hunger. They wanted blood and wouldn't settle for less.

"Weaver knew he couldn't pay. He stood to lose an appendage if he didn't provide something worthwhile to make up for his lies. That was when his eyes fell on the servant boy he'd brought with him to help tend to his needs during the game. The underling to the butler, the ragamuffin who worked in the cellars. The Hawk son—last offspring of my ancestors."

If I wasn't gagged, I would've lamented in horror for such a plight.

Poor boy. Poor, hungry existence. Whoever he'd been, he'd suffered an awful upbringing watching his father punished, mother raped, and sister drowned. He'd lived through enough strife to last a hundred lifetimes only to end up sisterless—*hopeless*—all alone and dealing with a mob of intoxicated men.

Jethro growled, "He was only thirteen. And small for his age."

His harsh voice dragged my eyes to his. His fists clenched; anger shadowed his face. "A deal was struck. Weaver offered an alternative: a debt paid in human flesh rather than money. When the men argued they had their own servants and didn't need a sickly, scrawny boy, Weaver sweetened the deal." Coming closer to me, Jethro murmured, "Want to know what the agreement was?"

I shook my head, sucking on the gag as my mouth poured with horror.

Jethro whispered, "Weaver offered up his servant—not for cleaning or fetching or menial tasks—but for one night. Twelve whole hours to be used at their discretion."

My knees gave out.

Daniel held me up, wrenching my shoulders with the sash around my wrists. My back burned, but it was nothing to the way my brain fried listening to such grotesque stories.

"The men pondered such an offering and...after much deliberation...agreed."

My spit turned sour, knotting with a vertigo spell and wobbling the world.

My mind swam with sickening thoughts.

Daniel whispered hotly in my ear, "You can guess what that meant, can't you?" He pulled me back, rubbing his erection against my spine. "I've been waiting for this night ever since you arrived."

Tears leaked from my eyes.

I moaned around the gag, begging Jethro to snap out of whatever stupor he existed in and slaughter his family.

*Save me. End this.*

The second he saw my wordless message, he turned away. His voice fell further and further into a mournful monologue. "A night of buggery for a few hundred pounds of debts. Weaver got off scot-free. He returned to his home safe and sound in his horse and buggy, leaving behind his faithful servant."

Silence hovered, pouring salt on flayed wounds.

Cut said, "The payment began at one a.m., and by one p.m., the boy was returned." He laughed blackly. "Alive. But unable to walk for a week."

My heart shattered. That poor, wretched boy. The humiliation, the pain, the degradation. The soul-destroying catastrophe that wasn't his to bear.

Jethro came forward.

I flinched as he cupped my cheeks with cold hands. His chest rose and fell, but no air seemed to fill his lungs. He looked furious, disgusted, entirely not coping. How could he stand there and say this? How could he contemplate making me pay?

Tears cascaded silently from my eyes, drenching the gag.

"In this debt, you shall be used. You shall be shared. And payment will be taken from your body any way we see fit. There are no rules on where you can be touched and no boundaries that won't be crossed."

He swallowed hard, pressing his nose fleetingly against mine. "As firstborn, I will be the last to partake in this debt. This is my sacrifice for my sins, too. You belong to me, and I must sacrifice you in order to earn my place."

Daniel hissed in my ear, "Time for some fun, little Weaver."

My entire body prickled with heaving fury. I didn't have time for fear anymore—not when the very thought of what would happen threatened to switch me from sane to insane.

Jethro's nostrils flared, torment and misery quarrelling over his face. "Do you repent? Do you take ownership of your family's sins and agree to pay the debt?"

I could barely stand up. I couldn't speak. I couldn't even think properly.

"Don't make him repeat the question, Weaver," Daniel muttered.

Jethro crossed his arms, looking as if he'd throw up any moment. "Say it, Nila." His voice was so quiet but throbbed with such sorrow.

How was I supposed to speak when I was gagged?

Cut smiled. "The sooner you agree, the sooner it's all over." Standing, he came toward me. I'd never been so uncomfortable, sandwiched between Daniel and Cut, knowing that this time they were allowed to touch me. That Jethro couldn't stop them from sharing because he was debt-bound to hand me over on a silver platter.

Cut stroked my cheek, his fingertips branding my skin. "Three places to violate you, my dear. And three men. We'll draw straws to see who will claim your pussy, mouth, and arse."

Vertigo plunged me into a rollercoaster roll, sending me stumbling into Cut.

He chuckled, holding me against his chest. "I never knew you were so eager."

The moment I could see without the whitewash of nausea, I growled and fought to get free.

Cut let me go, smiling as I backed away only to end up in Daniel's arms.

*This can't be happening!*

A sob escaped through my gag. My heart was supersonic—a dying piece of muscle about to combust at any moment.

"Fuck, Nila. Agree to the damn debt!" Jethro suddenly exploded.

The room froze. More tears torrented. More pain imaginable cleaved me in two.

I narrowed my eyes, funnelling my disgust fully into his gaze. *You want me raped by your fucking family? Fine.*

Raising my chin, I hoped he saw just how badly he'd screwed up. I was prepared to forgive him everything. His ice. His lies. His closed off arctic behaviour.

*Everything.*

But not this.

Nothing could absolve this.

*Ever.*

*You understand, Jethro Hawk? The love in my heart for you. It dies. Right now.*

*It's over!*

Jethro flinched, bumping into Kestrel.

Kes clutched his brother's hand, squeezing it hard. Jethro wiped a hand over his mouth as if he could prevent any more monstrous things from escaping.

Kes's voice was strained and sharp. "Do you consent, Nila Weaver? Answer the question."

I never looked away from Jethro. I was the queen on this carpet chessboard. I was the most powerful player in the entire long-winded game, yet my king had just ended the game with one colossal mistake.

Tearing myself from Daniel's arms, I moved forward to stand in the centre of Hawks. With my shoulders proud and body vibrating, I nodded.

One single nod.

*Yes.*

*Yes, I'll pay your sick and twisted debt, but I will never be the same. I will never be so soft and stupid. I will never let love convince me of goodness in others. I will be hatred personified, and I will fucking slaughter every single one of you when you're done.*

"That's it, then." Jethro swayed to the poker table. He moved like a soldier who'd been shot in battle—a warrior about to die. Snatching the lid off the cognac bottle, he angled the liquor and drank. His powerful throat contracted, guzzling fast, before he tore it away, slammed it down, and stormed to the exit.

In a moment, he was gone.

*What?!*

He wasn't even going to be there to *watch*? To have his heart torn out witnessing the awfulness he'd befallen?

My tears dried up in complete shock.

I shut down.

Everything inside turned to ruins.

Kestrel sighed heavily. Silently, he retrieved the bottle Jethro had slammed on the table and poured three fingers into fresh glasses.

Daniel and Cut drifted forward as Kes held out each goblet. The men ignored me—knowing I would wait. That I couldn't run. That I had nothing left.

With a grim smile, Kes held up a toast. "To paying debts and being worthy."

"To debts," Cut muttered.

"To fucking," Daniel cackled.

All three clinked and slammed the liquor down. However, Kes was the last to drink. It was only a fraction of a second, but he watched Cut and Daniel finish first before tipping the amber liquid down his throat.

Tossing their empties on the poker table, the men once again pinned their attention on me.

I stiffened, fighting uselessly in my binds.

Kes was the first to move.

He came forward. I moved backward. We danced slowly around the large room.

He didn't say a thing.

He didn't have to.

Jethro wasn't in control of this debt. He wasn't even here. This was Kestrel's time to shine.

"Before you came here tonight, Nila, we had a bet. The opening round of poker was to secure the right for first choice."

I bumped into a padded chair, changing directory to inch

around the pool table.

Kes murmured, "Any idea who won that round?"

My heart thundered. I shook my head.

Something flashed in Kes's eyes—too fast and swift to be understood. "It was me. I won. I get to choose."

Charging forward, he caught me effortlessly and wrapped his bulky arms around me. In his embrace, I didn't find friendship or liberation. I found a prison cell where the man who'd laughed and chased me over the paddocks on horseback became my rapist.

Breathing into my ear, he whispered, "I get to choose. And I want to go first."

# Jethro

I COULDN'T FUCKING do it.
I couldn't watch.
I couldn't hear.
I fucking *refused*.

The entire time we'd played poker, Cut had watched me. He knew what this would do to me. He knew how I would struggle and cripple and potentially unmask myself completely.

He'd come to the game with the same gun he'd threatened me with two months ago—hooked into his waistband, glinting off the chandeliers—nonchalantly promising death if I disobeyed.

It'd been fucking torture waiting for the time to creep closer, but it'd been nothing compared to leaving Nila with my family.

I hated leaving. But I had no choice.
Discussing what would happen was one thing.
Watching it come to pass was entirely fucking another.
My skin itched. My heart burst. My thoughts were a turbid wreck.

*I need help.*

I couldn't live with myself knowing what would happen to Nila.

*You could overdose.*

Take a handful of pills and slide into a coma, so I would never have to face the consequences of what this debt would do.

I fisted my hair and kicked the wall.

The small act of violence simmered some of my rage.

I kicked it again.

The pain I used to seek before swallowing tablets flared into being.

I kicked for the third time.

Throbbing agony graced my toes. It calmed me. Helped me focus on the bigger picture, rather than the next few hours.

Finding a certain peace in my fury, I went rogue.

I let down my walls and turned into a beast.

Whirling around, I embraced every inch of my anger—the parts I'd always suffered, the parts I'd barely acknowledged—all of it.

I showed my true insanity.

Nila was right.

I suffered a madness.

And she'd doomed me forever with no cure.

*She fucking hates me.*

"Shit!" I stalked down the hall and plucked a music box that'd been my great-great aunt's from a side table. Hurling it onto the floor, I felt a sick satisfaction as springs bounced free and twangs of music serenaded with broken notes.

"Shit!" I speared gold-gilded candlesticks at the tapestry-draped walls.

"Shit!" I kicked over a priceless French *caquetorie*.

"Shit, shit, *shit!*"

Throughout my tirade, all I could think about was what Kes would do.

And how Nila would react. Through trying to save her, I'd lost her forever.

*She hates me.*

*She despises me.*

*She loathes everything about me.*

And I didn't fucking blame her.

# Nila

MY WORLD WENT dark.

The blindfold secured around my head.

Kestrel's fingers were soft and firm as he tied a knot, careful not to catch my hair. Once fastened, he ran his fingers over my diamond collar. "Relax, little Weaver. It will all be over soon."

Cut chuckled. "Yes, soon you can go to sleep and pretend none of this happened."

My ears strained for one other voice. The voice of the man who controlled my heart even if he'd thrown it back in my face. *Please, come back, Jethro.*

But only silence greeted me.

Daniel snickered, licking my cheek. "Time to pay, Weaver." A moment later, he undid the gag from between my lips and massaged my cheeks to encourage the numbness to recede.

Cut clapped. "It's time for the Third Debt. Take her, Kes."

I prepared to spit and bite, but Kestrel suddenly picked me up, scooping my legs out from beneath me and toppling me into his arms as if I were a bride on her wedding night.

I might not be gagged by material anymore, but my terror kept me muted as Kes carried me a short distance and closed a door behind us. Another few strides and he placed me on my feet.

He didn't speak and didn't attempt to remove my blindfold.

The awful anticipation stung my very being. My ears ached for the barest of sounds. My wrists throbbed from the tight sash binding me.

Large hands landed on my shoulders.

I tore away from his touch. "Don't!"

He sucked in a breath, letting me put distance between us. However, he stalked me, stepping in sync, chasing me through the darkness.

Something pressed against the back of my knees.

*A bed.*

I whimpered, hanging my head.

Kes came closer, his body heat so much warmer than Jethro's. "Don't fight me, Nila. Okay? Let me do this. Then it will be over and life can go on."

*Life can go on?*

"For you, perhaps. Don't you see this is the worst punishment for a woman? You're not just taking what you want from my body. You're invading my very soul." Injecting a plea, even though I wanted to spit in his face, I murmured, "Please, Kes. Don't do this to me. I know you're a better man than they are. Please, prove me right." A sob strangled my voice. "*Please*, don't do this."

His hands fumbled with the front of my cheesecloth blouse, swiftly undoing the eyelets and tearing the fabric down the front.

"Wait!" I bowed my head, trying to ward him off like a bull with no horns. He kept me trapped by the bed with no vision to run.

"It's *because* I'm a better man that I'm doing this." He dropped before me to yank the coarse wool from around my hips.

I cried out as cool air licked my itchy skin.

*I'm naked.*
Naked and shaved and bound for the wrong man.
If I didn't hate Jethro enough, it was ten times worse now.
I sniffed back tears as Kes stood up and wrapped his arms around me. My breasts pressed against his chest.
His *naked* chest.
Goosebumps broke out all over.
*My nipples are against his skin.*
I moaned in despair as he cuddled me like any normal lover. "Don't worry, Nila."
I gasped, drowning all over again. "Please, Kestrel...*please*, don't do this."
Kes ran his hands through my hair, tugging on the elastic holding my bun in place. His touch was gentle but persistent. He managed to free the rope of hair, and, with tender fingers, fluffed out the thickness so it blanketed my shoulders and back.
I shivered, comforted somehow.
Ever since he'd secured the blindfold around my eyes, I'd been borderline catatonic. Every few seconds my heart threw in an extra beat, turning my internal balance into a gyroscope with no direction. But somehow, not seeing him kept my mind distanced.
I was free to float away—to leave my body and slip into the darkness of anonymity.
"Do everything I say and you'll get through this." His lips skated over my jaw. His touch was so different to Jethro's—dominating and soft—but lacking sparkle, connection...*love*.
I arched my chin away from his mouth. "You're asking me to obey you while you rape me?" A morbid laugh escaped.
Kes's breath whispered over my exposed breasts. "Yes. It's the only way."
"Only way for what?"
My heartbeat boomed in my ears as he took my hand, guiding me from the pool of woollen trousers around the edge of the bed.
"Only way to make this work."

I scowled behind my blindfold. Make *what* work?

The debts?

His twisted fantasy?

I hated moving around naked. I hated him seeing me.

My skin pinpricked with nervous sweat; I was lightheaded with panic. And that was just with Kestrel. He didn't scare me nearly as much as Daniel or Cut.

If I couldn't survive this, how would I survive the other two?

Another moan echoed in my chest. This couldn't happen. It was the worst nightmare imaginable. Three men. Three rapes.

And Jethro. Where the hell was he? Why wasn't he here to oversee what his family would do? What would he claim once everything had been taken from me?

*My heart?*

He lost that the moment he made me consent to this god-awful condemnation.

Kes kissed my cheek, pushing me so I fell onto the bed. The mattress sprung beneath me, cushioned and fresh. I winced as I bounced against my tied wrists.

"I'm going to place you in the centre." His strong arms caught me, manhandling me until I was where he wanted. His every touch caused my skin to crawl. My stomach rolled as I kept my legs pinned together.

I lay in the middle of the mattress like a corpse riddled with rigor mortis.

Kissing my shoulder, Kes climbed beside me. The heat of his naked thigh brushed mine; something heavy and hard nudged my hip.

*Oh, God!*

"I'm going to place you on your stomach." His voice was soothing; his words were *definitely* not.

I bucked as he tried to flip me over. "No! I can't—not that!"

He stroked my side, his fingers way too close to my breast.

"It's okay. Don't worry. Just roll over for me." He pressed me harder.

"No!"

*He wants to steal your anal virginity.*

Horror possessed me. I kicked and wriggled. I was no longer an atrophied skeleton but a furious unwilling victim. My hands remained tethered behind my back, but it didn't stop me from doing my damnedest to hurt him. "Don't! Don't touch me!"

"Shush." He placed a harsh kiss on my shoulder blade. "Obey me. Do what I say, Nila. I'll make it feel good, I promise."

"I'll never obey you. Never!" I fumbled with the sheets, wishing I could see. I wanted to bite him, knee him in the balls.

"Goddammit." Grabbing my hip, he flipped me over with a burst of power.

I cried out as he jerked the pillow away from my mouth, pressing my cheek against the mattress. My breasts flattened and tears spurted from my eyes. "How can you do this to me?" My mind filled with his kindness teaching me how to tend to Moth. How could he be two totally different people?

"No more questions. Alright?" His voice was short with frustration. "Just—for once—let a man fucking control you."

That was the last straw.

"*What* did you just say?" I arched off the bed. "Let a man *control* me?" Hysteria took hold. "I've been controlled all my life by every man I've ever met! How *dare* you say that? How dare you!" I couldn't stop tears cascading down my face, drenching the bed below.

Kes grunted as I squirmed harder.

I couldn't move beneath his weight. His heat warmed me like an unwanted sun. I *hated* him.

Fisting my hair, he pressed my face into the bed. "Listen to me and pay attention. *Behave.* Don't fight me. Don't make Cut believe I can't control you or it'll encourage him to fucking participate. Don't make this worse for yourself." Letting me breathe, he hissed, "Don't believe in the evil of everyone you meet. You'd be surprised just how wrong you'd be."

I froze.

Silence reigned while we both breathed hard.

Slowly, his grip on my hair loosened. "Now...will you be more reasonable?"

I laughed coldly, sucking in cotton from the sheets. "*Reasonable?* You're asking the trussed-up girl if she'll be more reasonable? You're as insane as your damn brother."

Turned out madness ran in the entire family tree. They all had to die.

"I'll let that slide." His fingers dug into my side. "But I need you to listen to me. Okay?"

Every instinct boycotted the idea but what he said before echoed in my ears. *Don't believe in the evil of everyone.*

Could the man who taught me to ride still save me? Could I trust him enough to wait and see? Did I have the strength to hope?

*Do I have a choice?*

Haltingly, I relaxed.

The instant he felt me give in, he let me go. "Good girl."

I hated that phrase.

All I could do was take whatever he gave and hope I survived.

*I have no other option.*

This wasn't a physical debt—although parts of it would hurt and no doubt destroy me for life—it was more mental. The stripping of everything that made me female—of any right over my own body.

Rustling sounded as Kestrel grabbed the bedding and placed it over me. The warm comfort of cotton covered my nakedness.

*He's drawn the covers.*

*Why?*

Kes's naked body moulded along my side, his hand resting on the swell of my arse. My skin smarted with revolting dislike.

"I've covered us. No one will see what we do. It will be our little secret."

I frowned. Secret? Why would it be a secret? He was doing what he'd been told. The bed dipped a bit as he wrapped his arm around my waist, rolling me from my stomach to side.

I flinched as his warmth nestled behind mine in a loving embrace. His hand stayed on my belly. I was achingly aware of how close his fingers were to my pubic bone.

Questions formed: *What will you do to me? How long am I yours before you hand me over?* But I couldn't voice them. I couldn't ask, because I couldn't stomach the replies.

Kes kissed my cheek, nuzzling his nose into my hair. "You're so beautiful, Nila. So goddamn beautiful." Dragging his fingers along my collar and down my spine, he whispered, "I've wanted you since the moment you arrived. I'd never wished to be firstborn before. I'm happy with my allotment within this family, but seeing you that night and knowing Jethro had full rights to you—well, it was the first time I was jealous of my brother."

I gasped as his touch landed on my arse again. Every muscle clenched. My eyes squeezed and I panted faster, terrified of him invading my body—especially in a place I'd never been touched before.

"Just because you have me now, doesn't mean this is right." I kept my eyes closed behind my blindfold—a double layer of blackness.

"I know." His fingers suddenly latched around my jaw, angling my neck.

His lips landed on mine.

All sensation ceased to exist.

The switch inside me flipped. I shut down completely. I didn't feel the heat of his lips or taste the flavour of his mouth.

Everything was chalk and beige and nothingness.

His lips coaxed mine, but I clamped them closed—remaining forbidding and not softening in any way.

Pulling back, he ran gentle fingertips over my chin. "I'm

not going to make this worse for you by dragging it on." Kes shifted his weight, rolling me closer. Gathering me against his naked form, I tried to ignore the heat of his erection against the crack of my arse.

"Kes, please…" I begged as his hand disappeared down my front and found my clit. His fingers didn't venture lower—just stayed on the outside of my pussy. I flinched but had nowhere to run.

His hips rocked, pressing himself into me. "My father expects me to hurt you. That sex isn't sex unless you're screaming and bruised." He imprisoned my face again, sealing his lips over mine.

I tried to angle away, but his mouth locked against me with swift finality.

He didn't force me to kiss him back, just kept his mouth on mine and his fingers rubbing my clit. His hips rocked harder and a moan swelled despite my horror.

Tearing himself from my mouth, he nibbled on my earlobe. "I'm supposed to rape you, Nila. Take from you what you don't want to give and break apart your mind piece by piece."

My unwilling moan turned into a sob. "You don't have to. You could just let me go."

He chuckled. "No, I can't. That's the thing. No one can leave. Not you, Jet, myself. We're all locked in this game until the very end." He trailed kisses along my cheek. "There can be no victors if there are no players."

Fury prickled my skin. I snarled, "If that's the case, just do it then! Destroy me—seeing as *Daddy* told you to." My mind wouldn't shut up; my lips wouldn't censor. "What is it with you and Jethro? You are *men*. You know right and wrong. You could end this by stopping him. Why don't you grow some balls and do it!"

Kes stiffened. His cock twitched against my lower back. Instead of anger, he laughed quietly. "So black and white to you." Cupping my throat, he thrust once. "Nothing is ever black and white, Nila. You should know that by now. It's all how you survive the grey."

His fingers fluttered over my clit—reminding me he had me at my most vulnerable. His touch wasn't cruel or hurtful—not the way Cut had commanded. My heart scampered in hope.

"What happens next has to be authentic. Do you understand?" His fingers moved faster, teasing my body, forcing nerve endings to respond despite my mind screaming with loathing.

His breathing turned harsh. "You need to relax and let me do what needs to be done."

"What—" My mouth parted as he strummed my clit harder. "What do you mean?"

With a soft grunt, he buried his face in my hair. "I'm going to make you come—to ensure you play your part. But I won't violate you, and I won't take advantage of you any more than I am right now." He angled my face and kissed me again. "You have my word."

My eyes flew open behind my blindfold. I didn't understand.

*What does he mean?*

He pressed his cock against my arse, rocking seductively. He whispered, "Pretend I'm hurting you. Cry out. Scream."

*What?*

"Do it," he hissed.

What the *hell* is going on? My body wound tight, growing wet against my wishes. My eyes were blinded, wrists tied, and my mind a mess with confusion.

"Cry, Nila. Otherwise, I'll have to make you cry for real." He pinched my clit, throbbing the bundle of nerves.

I jerked in his arms. More tears escaped. It wasn't hard to cry. It was a relief to complain—to verbalize how much I wanted this to end.

"*Stop!*"

If he wanted me to beg like a rape victim, I would. He'd given me permission to fight back, even if it was only vocal.

*I'll make your eardrums bleed.*

I thrashed, rubbing our bodies together and drawing a ragged groan from him. "Fuck you!"

He grunted as I tried to kick his kneecaps. "Get off me, you asshole."

"Not anger, goddammit. Pain!" He fisted my hair, yanking my head back. "Be in pain, begging. Forget about fighting."

That was asking the impossible. I could hate and curse and scream. But *plead?* It was blasphemy.

"If you want to get through tonight without being fucked in every hole you own, then do it!"

Images of Cut pounding into me, of Daniel strangling me, and the horrific violation of being a Hawk plaything gave me enough obedience to give up my courage and beseech. "*Please!* No, you're hurting me!"

"Good." He bit my ear, pinning me harder against him. "Again, louder this time."

"Noooo!" I gave into the sobs waiting just beneath my ribcage. "Don't. I'll do whatever you want. Just, don't—*no!*"

He groaned, rocking harder against me. "Shit, that's too good. Now I'm hard as fuck."

He rolled his hips, rubbing his erection, making the bed rock.

"Again." He thrust, groaning theatrically. "More. Pretend I've entered you and it hurts."

I couldn't speak through my tears.

His fingers stroked me faster, making my body twitch and tense. His hips worked harder, bruising my back. His voice licked my ear. "I'm not going to fuck you, Nila. But it needs to look like I am."

Suddenly—it all made sense.

*That's why he put the cover over us. That's* why he wanted me to move and squirm and scream, so our movements would *look* like he fucked me.

*Oh, my God.*

The sheer relief made me cry harder. And with relief came

the performance of a lifetime. My fingers stretched behind me, rubbing his chiselled belly in acknowledgement. The trust that'd tried to grow in the past sprouted into a beautiful flower. I gave myself over to this second-born Hawk, who was a true ally and friend.

"No!" I bellowed. "God, no!"

I arched my back, deliberately pressing into his cock.

He growled, his hands latching around my hips, half to hold me in place and half to drag me back to meet him thrust for thrust.

We lost ourselves as we became what others would see.

"Fuck, you feel good, little bitch!" he yelled, his volume way louder than required.

Cameras. Microphones. Recording devices that would capture this degrading act. It was all for the people watching.

My heart burned. *Is Jethro watching?*

The anger I felt toward him only spurred me on.

Kes wrapped his hand around my nape, holding me away from him while his other hand found my clit again. "Fuck, yes. Take it. Fuck, you're tight."

He paused, waiting like any good actor for his fellow screen star to read her script.

"Ahh! No more. Please, no more!"

"You'll take it until I say fucking otherwise, bitch."

We both groaned as he thrust so hard the boundary between faking and reality became blurred.

My legs scissored as he rolled me from my side to halfway on my belly. His next thrust slipped, sliding between my legs and pressing against my clit.

We both jolted.

"Fuck me," he hissed. His muscles trembled.

I froze.

We were so close to breaking every rule between loyalty and decency.

He bit my ear. "Don't stop. Pretend, I'm ripping you in two. Scream harder. Just—don't stop making them believe."

My body hummed, growing wetter and heavier. I didn't know if it was the pantomime or relief, but my nipples tingled and sensation came back with full force. "Stop! No. It's too much. Nooooo!"

He pressed his forehead against my skull. "You're driving me insane, Nila." Louder, he growled, "Little bitch. I'll teach you a lesson about your place. I'll show you what tonight is all about."

I let go of dignity and bawled. My cheeks rivered with tears; the blindfold was drenched. I stopped trying to talk in sentences and settled for monosyllables instead. "No!"

Thrust.

"Stop."

Rock.

"I'm begging—"

He groaned, bending my body until I slotted perfectly in his strong embrace.

I couldn't ignore his hardness or the way his muscles vibrated with need. In that moment, he was a saint. A man with a tied-up woman rubbing against his body and not using her. My trust layered with respect. He was good. He was kind. He was true.

We both panted as we turned frantic. There was no rhythm anymore—only debasing fake-fucking, rustling sheets, and creaking springs. As much as I despised what tonight represented, I couldn't help the tiny flutter of desire unfurling thanks to his never-ending coaxing fingers.

Unfounded hurt crept over me.

Jethro hadn't tried to stop this. He'd run.

But Kestrel had stepped up to protect me. He put his own life on the line.

*That's more than Jethro's ever done.*

My heart twisted in a resentful agonising braid. I didn't want to sleep with Kes. But in a way…I was almost offended that he had the self-restraint to keep me safe even from him.

I was baffled.

I was endlessly grateful.

He was turned on. He'd admitted he'd wanted me since setting eyes on me...yet he made no move to dip his fingers inside me or try to work his cock anywhere but between my thighs.

The bed rocked with every thrust. My back arched as his fingers turned harder and demanding. For non-sex, it gave the ultimate impression of being ridden and used.

Sickness rolled inside to think of Jethro watching this.

But then anger slapped the nausea away.

*He* should've been the one to stop this. If only he'd given up trying to fit in and realised that he would never be the man his father wanted. If only he could see the *truth*.

*Now, it's too late.*

"Scream," Kes whispered.

"Fucking, ride my dick, bitch," he yelled.

"Stop. Oh, my God. Stop!"

My body rocked backward, seeking a release against all rationality. Kes panted in my ear, his cock throbbing and hot between my thighs. I pressed my legs together, giving him friction to rub against.

"Goddammit, don't do that." He pulled away, pressing himself against the small of my back. "You're fucking beautiful." His fingers worked me harder. "Shit, I wish I could climb inside you for real."

His words clenched my core. An orgasm I *never* expected brewed into being.

I moaned as my wrists hurt, being squashed every time Kes thrust.

"I'm losing it," he muttered. "I need this to end before we both get into trouble."

His gruff voice attacked my nervous system, sending me into quakes. My body took over; my toes curled with building pleasure.

Kes grasped my wrists, tugging on the sash, arching my back.

He nipped at my throat, running his warm tongue down the top of my spine. His fingers quickened, along with his hips. My thoughts disintegrated as his touch slipped on my clit and found wetness.

"Fuuuuck." His thrusts turned erratic and savage. His fingers lost uniformity.

I moaned.

I couldn't help it.

It felt *good*.

I wanted to cry.

I wanted to embrace it.

I wanted to die for who I'd become.

The covers shifted and clung, no doubt making it seem as if Kes took me with nothing barred. My mouth opened to breathe faster. Kes surprised me by sealing his lips completely over mine.

I stiffened.

I didn't know what to do.

A kiss was somehow even more intimate than the fake-fucking we indulged in. Then his fingers tickled from my clit to entrance. I moaned. I couldn't decide if it was a beg to stop or permission to keep going.

The fear that any minute he might stop being a gentleman trying to save me and fuck me against my will added the element of danger.

He shuddered as he slipped a fingertip barely inside me.

The taboo. The forbiddenness. The wrongness of what we were doing consumed me.

I couldn't stop the detonating bliss just like I couldn't stop my blood from flowing.

I came.

The second my body exploded around his finger, his tongue entered my mouth and I didn't fight it.

I welcomed it.

For one delicious spiralling moment, I let go of right and wrong. I forgot about Jethro and ignored the messy aftermath.

I gave into pleasure.

Kes pulled me back against him, pleasure and need rumbling in his chest.

My fear completely subsided.

I *trusted* him.

All this time he'd been there guiding me. Looking after me.

His hand clutched my hip, forcing me to rock against his fingers. His cock branded my back as my core contracted again and again, heaven shooting through my system.

He spooned me harder, his legs entwining with mine. "Shit."

I let out a cry of ecstasy as my orgasm took me high, high, *higher* before snipping me free and hurtling me back to earth.

My ears rang. My heartbeat was a noisy jackhammer.

His lips sought mine again and I kissed him back. Our tongues tangled and I catalogued the difference between brothers. Jethro was fierce and controlling. A dominant, mysterious man through and through. Kestrel was eager and ferocious, taking everything with boyish charm. "Fuck, I don't want to come. I promised myself I. Would. Not. Come."

I believed him. I understood his decency and I couldn't thank him enough.

But there was one thing I could do to show him my gratitude.

It was a gift I could give on my own accord.

I forced my hips back, crushing his cock against his stomach. His mouth opened wide; his body jerked as he poured curses down my throat. "Fuck, don't do that. I'm going—"

"It's okay," I breathed. "It's okay."

A guttural grunt tore from his lungs as he lost all reason and rode my back.

His body bucked, his arm wrapped tight around me. The sheets glued to our mutual sweat as heat enveloped us. Remembering the performance, I cried loudly, "Stop. Please stop!"

He grabbed my wrists, locking them at the base of my spine.

For a split second, pain blared in my back.

"Shit, I can't. I can't fucking stop." The bed creaked and his hand rose to cup my breast. He tweaked my nipple, gasping as my body bowed into him. "Fuck, he's gonna *kill* me for this." Then a hot wet spurt stuck us together as his legs twitched around mine.

Every tiny tremor vibrated his body.

His orgasm went on for a while, each jerk of his hips gluing me further to him. Our heartbeats raced, and the outside world ceased to exist. In that second, we cemented a deeper bond. Not of lust or love or even erotic connection—but a trust that would be forever lifelong.

We hadn't had sex, but *something* had happened between us.

Something no one could take away.

He'd gone against his family. He'd saved me in the only way he could.

I owed him.

A lot.

And I would never *ever* forget it.

# Kestrel

I LOVED MY oldest brother.

A fuck ton.

I'd always believed I'd been brought into the world in order to save him from himself.

I'd never begrudged him or wished our roles were reversed. I knew the tightrope he walked every damn day and was happy to be scot-free and living my own easy life.

But when I'd removed Nila's clothing and she'd stood there bound and blindfolded, I fucking *hated* him.

I hated him for being too much of a pussy.

I hated his fucking condition.

I just wished he wasn't so *damaged*. That I didn't love him as much as I did. That I didn't know every single trial he'd been through and just how deep and strong he was—beneath the bullshit layered on him by Cut.

When I'd grabbed her and put her on the bed, I'd been so hard I could've killed someone with my cock. When I'd removed my clothes and slid in beside her, I could've come from the gentle friction alone. And when I'd slipped and felt her wet heat when I had no right to touch that part of her, I couldn't stop it anymore.

I *had* to come.

I would disintegrate if I didn't.

He'd asked me to do this.

This was *his* plan. Not mine.

When he'd come to me with his scheme, I'd told him. Full disclosure. I hadn't held back. He knew that I found her fucking gorgeous. He knew I found her spirit, sharp tongue, and stubbornness a huge turn-on. His temper had flared. His condition reacted. And he'd looked like he wanted to sucker-punch me then tear my dick off. But he'd come to the same conclusion I had.

There was no other way.

His heart had made the decision, and there was no other alternative.

So, we'd agreed. Against my better judgement, I'd promised. And against his instincts, he'd *trusted* me.

Unfortunately, tonight I'd betrayed that trust.

I wanted to fuck her so badly. I wanted her writhing with pleasure and calling out my name. *My* name. Not his.

Seeing her bare dragged desires from me that I'd kept buried out of respect for Jet. He was my fucking brother. We'd grown up together. There was no other loyalty stronger than that.

But Nila...

*Shit.*

When I'd undone my belt and stepped from my boxers, I'd wanted to tear off her blindfold and show her who would be taking her. I wanted her to look at *me*. Truly *see* me. I wanted her eyes on my cock and her breath on my skin. I wanted her to look at me the way she looked at my brother.

My dick was harder than it'd been since I'd had a foursome with some club bunnies. I craved Nila with every cell, but I didn't want her for my own.

I wanted to 'borrow' her. Taste her—just once live in my brother's shoes and have what he had. Was that so wrong? Was it so scandalous to want a piece of his inheritance?

I could answer my own question.

Yes, it was wrong. Yes, it was scandalous. And no, I would never go behind my brother's back.

He'd given me permission to do this. He'd *begged* me to do this.

I hadn't asked for payment or demanded anything in return.

Nila was gift enough.

When her tongue had tentatively touched mine, I'd wanted to grab her hair and kiss her with abandon.

Fuck the debts.

Fuck the family.

For once, I wanted what I wanted for *me*—not for any other reason.

But I was too damn honourable. Too well trained in hierarchy and fidelity.

I couldn't do it.

She was so pretty. So tiny. Her stomach so flat and her small breasts the perfect handful. She truly was a doll. A woman I could easily fall for if I wasn't a loyal Hawk.

Discipline and primogeniture—it'd all taught me my place from day one. But my love for Jethro...that was the padlock on coveting anything I might want.

Touching her pussy had been the hardest part of all. I'd almost fucked up and lost myself. It would've been so easy to open her arse cheeks and slip inside her—like Cut expected me to.

There was nothing worse than having a naked woman, with expectations to fuck her, when I couldn't. But no matter how hard it was for me, it killed me to think of him watching.

I was doing this for him—but every thrust and moan from Nila would've torn his fucking heart out. Pills or no, he wouldn't get through tonight without some serious problems.

Nila didn't know it—but she'd broken him completely.

And I'd been the conductor for his destruction.

Every sweep of my hands up her sides and every press of my fingers on her clit, I forced myself to remember who I was ultimately doing this for.

It was the only way I could continue.

However, then she'd given me permission. She'd understood my intentions and gave into me.

She let me come.

And I'd never been more fucking grateful.

Ever since she'd arrived, I'd been hypnotised by her dark eyes and the simplistic honesty of her truth.

I'd never seen a more perfect woman.

And when I said perfect woman. I meant for *him*, not for me.

He needed someone pure. Someone transparent and honest. He needed unconditional-no-bullshit-love. No lies. No tricks. Clarity and understanding.

Nila was all those things. Against all odds, he'd found his perfect other. What sort of brother would I be if I didn't support him and ensure both our futures were safe?

Our time was over too quick.

If it were real, I would've spread her legs and licked her. I would've pushed her gently down my body and requested she repay the favour with her tongue.

I would've stolen every ounce of her pleasure. I would've worshipped her tits and wrung every whimper from her soul. She would've hovered in erotic pain and drowned in bliss.

I wanted her on top of me, riding my cock and her kissing me, not *me* kissing *her*.

Ah, fuck.

I would've drained her of everything.

But that wasn't allowed.

It took every willpower I had left, but I was able to rein in my needs and focus.

I'd bucked my hips, driving my aching flesh against her lower spine.

Everything I wanted didn't matter. What did matter was the camera footage and what was to come. Jethro and I would win tonight.

We'd broken every rule and hadn't finished yet.

The Third Debt was ours to control—not Cut's.

But now, as I wiped my cum from Nila's back and grabbed the syringe that I'd hidden beneath the pillow in preparation, I knew I'd done the right thing.

By everyone.

Rubbing her arm, I uncapped the needle and slid it into her flesh without warning.

Nila winced, her head tilting to see, even though the blindfold meant it was an impossibility.

"What did you do?" she breathed, fear lacing her tone.

I kissed her forehead, untangling my body from hers.

I'd borrowed her. I'd tasted her. Now, it was time to give her back to her rightful owner.

"I did the only thing I could. I don't want you to be awake for the next part."

"Wait...please, don't...let...them..." Her body twitched as the anaesthetic quickly stole her.

My heart calmed its erratic rhythm and my cock deflated as she fell into the unnatural sleep of medicine. Once her breath regulated, I undid her blindfold and untied her wrists.

Climbing from the bed, I tucked a sheet over her nakedness.

Standing over her, I murmured, "I want you to think I'm the hero in this, Nila Weaver. I want you to believe I'm the saint and that all of this was my concoction." My eyes rose to the blinking red camera in the top of the room. I saluted it. "But I'm not the one who loves you. And I'm not the one who's playing the game better than I ever thought possible."

Bending over her, I kissed her parted lips and gathered my clothing from the floor. "It was all his idea. The only way he could keep protecting you. The only way he could stay alive to save you another day."

Looking at the camera one last time, I hoped my brother would forgive me. With a heavy sigh, I gathered Nila's unconscious form and carried her away.

# Jethro

I WAS DRUNK.
Motherfucking obliterated. Off-my-tree intoxicated.
There. I admitted it.
Drunk as a fucking alcoholic.
I'd been clearheaded all night. But the moment Kestrel took my woman into the bedroom and stripped her, I couldn't do it anymore.
I wanted to delete all knowledge any way possible.
It didn't work.
I winced, opening my eyes.
*Where am I?*
Instead of darkness and flickering flames from the fireplace, the windows welcomed pink, tentative dawn.
The room swirled, balancing on a stomach full of liquor.
Dawn.
The blank slate of a new day.
*Dawn.*
The eraser of yesterday's mistakes and the pencil of today's new ones.
I groaned, blocking out the pink light with smarting eyelids. I wished the awakening sun could eliminate the past couple of months. I wished everything could be washed away, granting a fresh start.

What happened last night?

The moment I probed my pounding brain, I wished I hadn't.

Thanks to Kestrel, I'd done what I didn't think I would ever be strong enough to do.

Plans I never thought I could put in place. A future I never thought I could earn.

My mind slipped a few hours into the past.

*When I left the billiards room, I followed strict orders on where to go and what to prepare.*

*And I did—just like the fucking pussy I was.*

*As the Third Debt depicted, one man would rape, the others would wait their turn. An orgy with witnesses. A night of entertainment for devils and a night of horrors for angels.*

*I stormed into the security room, turned on the feed between the three cameras dotted around the room where the Third Debt would take place and waited for Cut and Daniel.*

*Only, I added something else to that to-do list.*

*Opening the liquor cabinet that the Black Diamonds stocked when on security detail, I poured copious amounts of second-rate bourbon down my throat.*

*The pills were fucking useless. They blocked emotions from tainting me, but they didn't do anything about taming my own.*

*When Kestrel appeared with Nila in his arms on screen, I almost smashed the bottle and sliced my wrists open with jagged glass. And when he'd stripped her and climbed into bed, I buckled under heartbreak—my insides cascading with broken blood.*

*Cut and Daniel arrived.*

*I drank more disgusting alcohol. Their thoughts and enjoyment splashed around my burning body, cocooning us in a cesspit of nastiness inside the small, windowless room.*

*The sounds of Kestrel grunting tore at my eardrums. The sights of sheets bunching and bed moving dug daggers into my eyes. Nila's begs echoed like a never-ending reflection in my soul.*

*It was all…too…fucking…much.*

*Cut and Daniel laughed. They peered closer for a better view. They*

whispered and high-fived and muttered what horrific things they would do during their turns.
I kept drinking.
And drinking.
And motherfucking drinking.
Each swallow only stoked my pain, and if it wasn't for my trust in my brother, I would've slaughtered everyone in the bloody room.
It felt like it went on for decades—who knew how long it truly was. But slowly, my attention turned from the fiasco on the TV screen to my brother and father.
Their evil plans became slurred and unfinished. Their eyes hazy and glazed. Cut saw me watching him and stole the bourbon to swig a healthy dose.
He could have the damn bottle—it didn't matter. I was past legal levels of blood intoxication. I saw double. I heard triple. I felt quadruple pain.
Keep it together.
Kes assured me, they'd be out cold in approximately ten minutes.
Not long…
I grimaced when Cut slapped me on the back. I hid my murderous intentions when Daniel sneered as Nila screamed.
Inch by inch, I died inside.
All my life, I'd been in pain. Emotional pain. Physical pain. Psychological pain.
But this…
This pain—especially the moment when Nila realised what Kes intended and gave in to him—was like nothing I'd ever felt before.
It was physical, emotional, and psychological all at once.
A ransacking of my very marrow. An acid on my soul.
I couldn't break. I couldn't cry or scream or yell.
All I could do was crowd around the camera with my condemned family and witness the rape of the woman who held my fucking heart. If Kes and I pulled this off, we stood a chance of ending this. I was done trying to win on my own. Nila was my team. Kes was my team. Together, we would win against wrathful corruption.
Kestrel picked up his pace; the sheets tangled harder around two

*thrusting bodies.*
*And that was my limit.*
*I completely lost my shit.*
*Daniel cackled. "I'm going to fuck that cunt's mouth."*
*Cut laughed. "Her arse is all mine." He turned to me. "You haven't ploughed that yet, have you, Jet?"*
*Yep.*
*I lost it.*
*I fucking punched Cut in the jaw.*
*He fell.*
*Hard.*
*Cut smashed against the door, folding to the floor.*
*"Hey!" Daniel launched himself on me, but he was too slow. I slammed my fist into his face. With a grunt, he crashed against the keyboard, bouncing off the desk.*
*Two throws. Two men down.*
*My knuckles throbbed. I waited to deliver more.*
*But they never woke up.*
*I liked to think it was my powerful punch, but…it was all thanks to Kes.*
*Everything was all thanks to fucking Kes.*

I groaned, grabbing my head, willing the memories to stop.

The hardness of the floor and coolness of sleeping with no blankets forced me to haul myself to my knees. My lips pressed together against the backwash of stale bourbon. The pills I'd taken at the start of the night had worn off, but the liquor was well and truly still controlling my blood.

I should've headed to bed once it was all over, but I couldn't.

How could I?

Inching higher on my knees, I peered over the edge of the bed. The remaining shadows painted her in a ghostly collage.

My hands fisted on the bedspread as her eyelids twitched and fingers strummed a nonsense beat on her sheets.

The drugs Kes had given her would wear off in another

hour—it never lasted long. Already, her body fought it off—legs jiggling and feet battling imaginary beasts.

I wanted to step into her dreams and slay the figments for her.

I wanted to reassure her that nothing had happened.

"Nila, I'm so fucking sorry." I stayed vigil, stroking her arm as she whimpered. Silent tears tracked down her cheeks. She would wake soon to a different kind of nightmare. She would be told a lie. It would tear her apart, but in order for this deception to work, she had to *believe*. She had to believe, because my father and Daniel had to believe.

My mind skipped backward again.

*I looked up as the door to the security room opened.*

*My brother stood there fully dressed with a grim line for lips.*

*The moment I saw him, hatred billowed, and I wanted to kill him with my bare hands. "Did you fuck her?"*

*His eyes flashed. "What do you think?"*

*"I think you went above and beyond what we'd discussed."*

*He shook his head. "I did exactly what you said."*

*"You did more than what I said, Kes." Rubbing my eyes to stop the fucking tears from prickling, I growled, "You touched her. You made her come. You touched what's fucking mine!"*

*Kes swallowed, dropping his eyes. "I told you everything. I told you how I felt about her—how hard that would be for me. Yet you made me do it anyway. I didn't fuck her." Holding up his finger and thumb, he pinched air. "I was this close, Jet. This fucking close to taking what I wanted. But... I didn't. I didn't because I'm on your side and have your back."*

*My hatred turned inward, battering and pouring yet more acid on my already flayed wounds. I asked more of him than any brother should. I ought to thank him and never speak of it again. But my lips formed another question, spewing it forth. "Did you come?"*

*He looked away.*

*Gratefulness or not, I couldn't stop my possessive rage.*

"Motherfucker."

*I lunged.*

*I caught him off guard, landing a right hook and a left before he wizened up and punched me in the gut.*

"Shit, Kite. Calm the fuck down. I didn't do anything we didn't agree."

"We agreed you wouldn't come!"

"We agreed on other things, too." *His eyes narrowed.* "Or are you forgetting about those?"

*I froze.*

*He's right.*

*I hadn't honoured past promises, no matter how hard I'd tried.*

*Looking past me, his attention switched.* "Shit, that was fast. How long did it take to kick in?"

*Shaking out the pain in my knuckles from punching three of my family members, I glanced at Daniel and Cut on the floor.* "It didn't. I helped them along."

*Kes dragged a hand through his silvering hair.* "What the fuck did you do? You know they can't wake up in the morning and think it didn't happen. Shit—what was the point in all of this if you couldn't even let it run its course!"

*The room tilted and weaved.*

*I heaved as my stomach tried to revolt against the booze.* "Had no choice. Couldn't do it anymore."

*Suddenly, I couldn't look at Kes without reliving what he'd done to my woman. It shredded my skin, turned my muscles into quivering agony.* "I can't—I can't stay in here with you."

*Kes stomped forward and gripped my shoulders.* "You have no choice. It's not over yet."

*I tensed against his thoughts, preparing myself to flounder in his coital bliss from Nila, but like most times, Kestrel protected me. I picked up on faint frequencies, but he kept the majority hidden behind a calm curtain of nothingness.*

*I sighed, pushing him away.* "Sorry."

*He nodded.* "I get it." *Pointing at comatose Cut and Daniel, he added,* "Let's finish up. Then we can call it a night, yeah?"

*Swaying on my feet, I moved to lock the door.* "You're right."

*Together, we faced the archives of previous debts and extractions. I*

*pulled up old footage of Emma Weaver. "It's time to get creative."*
*With a solidified bond, we each took a keyboard and began.*
Goddammit, I was a monster.
Covering my face, I folded over her bed.
I was so tired.
So fucking drained.
*It's all so fucking hard.*
All I wanted was to give in. To tell her the truth and end the lies I'd always lived.
Pulling the tiny bottle from my pocket, I deliberated taking another. The drugs helped me stay sane—they were the only thing that had a power over me—but as much as I appreciated the silence, the numbness from overwhelming intensity, I hated the severance between Nila and me.
She deserved so much more than what I'd given her.
And now she would hate me for eternity.
Clutching the bottle, I cursed the swirling room.
Nila was safe and untouched.
She would *remain* safe and untouched.
I was done being unhappy and selfish. My sacrifice would keep her safe.
I would trade a lifetime in a straitjacket to give her a long, happy existence.
Those were our futures. And her hating me would only make that separation easier on her.
Sighing, I slid back to the floor and curled up beside her bed.
I would guard her for the rest of my days.
It would be the one good thing I'd done before I died.
Falling to my side, the room spun quicker and quicker.
I closed my eyes and succumbed.

# Nila

THE WORLD SOLIDIFIED.

I traded treacle-unconsciousness for cumbersome reality. One moment I was off in make-believe land with deformed unicorns and black rainbows, the next, I was awake.

*Where am I?*

Groggy, heartbroken, stupefied.

I clutched my head, warding off the gentle headache and fuzzy taste on my tongue. I smacked my lips, trying to get rid of the taste. The metallic residue was...familiar.

*But where from?*

It reminded me of the one and only operation I'd had when I was seventeen to remove my tonsils. I'd been sick for a year with tonsillitis until I'd begged to have them out.

Waking up from the operation had been terrifying. Surrounded by piercing beeps and turned into a pincushion with needles.

Massaging my temples, I forced my brain to work.

*What happened last night?*

I blinked.

The Weaver quarters pieced together like a storybook—bolts of fabric hanging from the walls, messy table with scissors and chalk, and the grey centrepiece for my collection draped otherworldly on the mannequin.

My eyes flew to the towel discarded on the emerald W embroidered carpet.
*Did I get dressed in a hurry?*
I followed the trail of fuchsia pink dress draped over the wingback by the fireplace. I frowned at the unwanted lingerie on the foot of the bed.
Then I saw the zipped garment bag.
And *everything* propelled into me with razor blades.
Poker. Cognac. Blindfolds. Daniel. Cut. *Kestrel.*
My hands flew to cover my mouth.
*Oh, my God. What have I done?*
I cringed, reliving the way I've softened toward Kes, the way I'd found unwanted pleasure in his arms, then I buckled under my hate for Jethro at leaving me there. He just left!
And Kes stayed and helped and—
*He drugged you!*
My heart catapulted into a thousand beats.
*Oh, God. What did they do?*
Panic and horror shook my hands as I shoved the duvet away and looked at my body. I didn't know what I expected to find—bruises and cuts and obvious marks of rape—but the stark whiteness of a nightdress hid answers.
*I have to know.*
I had to see, had to come to terms with what foul, disgusting things might've been done while I was unconscious.
*I need a mirror.*
Swinging my legs over the edge of the thick mattress, I leapt.
My feet touched something cool and hard, rather than warm and soft. My balance tripped, my ankle twisted, and I tumbled forward to land on all fours.
A masculine curse filled the space. Something shoved me, turning my fall into a somersault. I cried out, coming to a halt on my back.
Jethro.
The instant my eyes landed on him, the betrayal over the

past few days choked my lungs. Those damn drugs. His twisted family. A lifetime of conditioning and a soul thoroughly broken from circumstances I could never understand.

My heart bled for him. But at the same time, I no longer cared.

He'd thrown me to the wolves and left.

He didn't deserve my compassion or affection or tenderness.

He deserved *nothing*.

Jethro groaned, but his eyes remained closed. The fumes of alcohol soaked the air around him. His arm flung out, seeking something.

I scrambled out of reach.

He mumbled, his face screwed up and sunken.

*What the hell is he doing in here?*

I couldn't stop the crashing waves of dislike, distrust, and utter resentment taking hold.

He flinched, grunting as if in pain.

Climbing to my feet, I darted around the bed and snuggled back into warm sheets. I wanted him gone!

Curling my legs up beneath me, I wrapped the covers tight like a fortress. "Get. *Out*." My voice was full of contempt.

Shuffling sounded below, but no reply. A few tense minutes ratcheted my heart rate, before he slowly inclined from lying to sitting. His back rested against my bed as he groaned, grabbing his head. "Fuck."

He didn't look up. His long legs bent, the rest of his body wrung out and weary.

The love I'd had for him wanted to comfort, but the repulsion of him leaving me last night made me hunker deeper into my quilt and glower.

Rubbing both hands over his face, he yawned. Every motion was lethargic and reeking of drunkenness.

So he'd left me at the fate of his family to drink last night?

Asshole. Complete and utter *asshole*.

Looking over his shoulder, he froze.

My breathing ceased. My blood curdled. "Leave."
The single syllable hung between us like a deflating balloon falling to the carpet.
Jethro swallowed. Pain and intoxication swam in his eyes. Finally, he nodded. Gone was the refined gentleman who hid so much. Gone were the chiselled cheekbones and radiant golden eyes.
The man before me...the man who'd hurt me, crushed me, and still held my heart in his traitorous hands was a mere shadow of himself—not even a shadow—an extinguished, extinct, broken thing.
We stared for a millennium.
Slowly, his lips tilted into a grimace; he bestowed the saddest, sweetest smile and staggered to his feet. "I'm sorry." With an unsteady wave, he swayed to the door. "Didn't want you to wake...alone. Wanted to keep you...safe."
His voice roped around my heart, forcing it to beat and flurry. His steps were terminally empty, staggering toward the exit.
That was it?
No heartfelt plea or fervent explanation?
Just *I'm sorry?*
"No, you know what?" I threw the duvet away and hurled myself out of bed. Storming after him, I grabbed his forearm and dug my nails into his flesh. "Sorry isn't good enough." Tears exploded into being—a salty river flowing unheeded down my cheeks. "*Sorry* doesn't cover what you've done to me. *Sorry* will never be good enough!"
He stood there like a township sacked by pillaging enemies. He didn't move to shrug me off or argue or explain. He just curled into himself, squeezing his eyes as tight as possible.
I hit him.
"Tell me what they did to me!"
I hit him again.
"Look me in the fucking eye and tell me why you let them

do this!"

I hit him again and again and *again*.

"Explain to me why you didn't save me. That you left me to suffer when I know you care for me!"

He jerked away from my barrage, backing toward the door. "I'll leave. I won't put you through any more—"

"No!" I screamed. I'd never been so loud. My voice bounced off the chandelier, disappearing into luxury fabrics waiting to be turned into garments. "You leave now and you will *never* be welcome in my life. You hear me? I hate you for what you made me go through last night." My voice cracked. "Kestrel—he proved to be twice the man you are and I *liked* him touching me. At least he deserved a reward for doing whatever he could to save me."

Jethro stumbled backward, rubbing his forehead. "I don't want to hear about—"

"Tough shit!" I stalked him as he lurched away.

My stomach coiled and spat with pain. What Kestrel did last night stained my entire outlook. Yes, I was grateful to him for trying. Yes, I'd come under his touch. But it made me feel dirty and whorish to speak about Kes to Jethro.

I didn't have feelings toward him other than friendship. And even then, I still didn't trust him. He'd drugged me for heaven's sake!

But I wanted to hurt Jethro so much. I wanted him in pieces like I was. I wanted him fucking bleeding at my feet and begging for forgiveness.

I turned feral. Vibrating with the need to hurt. I'd never been so callous to crave their pain. But this...I'd never experienced anything like this.

Shoving his chest, I snarled, "Where did you go, huh? Where were you while your brother put his finger inside me and came all over my back?"

He grunted, shaking his head. "Nila—don't—"

"No. *You* don't." I pushed him again. My hands curled into fists, raining on his chest. "Talk to me! Tell me what the fuck you were thinking! I'm done existing this way. I won't let you use my emotions against me anymore."

He swallowed hard, running a shaking hand through his hair. "I get it. You hate me and want me to leave." He stumbled forward, pushing past to reach for the doorknob as if it was centimetres away not metres. "I'm leaving…I'll g—go."

The slurs and hesitation spoke of a tongue still tangled with booze.

"You're drunk." I laughed, letting my pain frolic in the brittle sound. "I can't believe you left me last night and got drunk!"

He shook his head. "Not anymore." His eyes watered. "I wish I was. Fuck, I wish I was drunk. Then this wouldn't hurt so damn much."

"What wouldn't hurt so much?!" I plucked the strange nightgown I wore. Who dressed me after they'd finished raping my unconscious form? Who put me to bed to wake alone and discarded?

*But you weren't alone. He slept beside you.*

"What wouldn't hurt, Jethro? The fact you're a monster? That you're a horrible human being? That you're a pussy? Oh perhaps, none of the above?" My eyes narrowed. Anger boiled over, stripping body from bone. My temper was corrosive—an acid eating its way like a worm inside my mind. I couldn't go on living like this. I couldn't go on loving a man who refused to love me in return. I couldn't exist in this *hell*. "Maybe you hurt, because you finally see how fucking wrong all of this is!"

"Stop." He covered his mouth, shaking his head. "Just stop—"

"No! I won't stop. Not until you tell me. Tell me what they did to me last night. I need to know. Don't you get it? Not knowing is worse!" I balled my hands, wanting to kick him. "I want you to keep your bloody promise. Tell me what you were going to tell me the day the police came for me."

He froze. "I—I can't. Not now."

"Yes. Now. This instant." I pointed at the door. "You

leave, you never come back. I'll never again acknowledge you, look at you...kiss you. Do you understand? *Never*, Jethro. This is your last chance."

I ran hands through my hair, pulling the stands. "I don't even know why I'm giving you that. After what you did last night, you don't *deserve* a chance to explain. You deserve to die a miserable death and leave me the hell alone."

A tortured groan echoed in his chest. "Just let me go, Nila. I can't—"

"No!" I stomped my foot. "You don't get off easily this time. Not again. Spit it out. Tell. Me!"

The air around him withered and wilted. He shrunk, closing himself off from everything.

I stood there like an island as his regret and confusion waked around my ankles. His utter devastation undermined my anger, but I refused to break.

It was his turn to grovel. His turn to show me light in this never-ending blackness.

I'd tried to help him so many times. I'd made excuses for him. Trusted in the stolen touches and bone-deep knowledge that he loved me. I'd begged him to let me in. To love him. To cherish everything he was—even his secrets.

But he'd pushed and shoved and hurt me so damn much. And no matter how badly he treated me, I couldn't tear out the love I had for him. He was a confused, cruel, crippled human being who wasn't good for me.

My anger switched to sadness. If he couldn't even give me this—when I was at my most violent and open—he couldn't give me anything.

*Just let him go. End this charade.*

I sighed, taking a step backward. "Go. Just leave."

His spine stiffened as he glared at the wall.

Tears ran down my face as I stared at the cold animal I'd given my heart to. The icy fear that I'd been abused by Daniel and Cut filled my mind. Was that why Kestrel had drugged me? So I wouldn't have to live through something so heinous? Had he done it out of concern for my wellbeing?

Would Jethro ever do something so heroic?

He gritted his teeth, finally looking at me. "I'm supposed to tell you that my father raped you and my youngest brother degraded you to the point of ruin. I'm supposed to stand here and fill your vacant memories with pain and evil abuse."

He took a step toward me.

My skin crawled at the thought of him coming closer.

"But, no matter how this will backfire, no matter if my plan fails and everything I've tried to avoid comes into play, I can't—I can't do that to you." His eyes were wild and dilated, thanks to drugs and liquor. "Nila, I swear on my fucking life, no one touched you. Kestrel knocked you out, so we could do what we needed behind the scenes." He punched his chest. "But I give you my word as a Hawk that the only person who touched you was me." His eyes fell on my nightgown. "I dressed you, kissed you, put you to bed. And then I curled up on the floor to ward off any more assholes. Even though I've proven I'm not worthy, even though you hate me—as you should—I couldn't live with myself if I told you a lie on top of all the others."

A sob wrenched through my chest.

*Oh, thank God.*

Thank, thank *God.*

They hadn't touched me.

I almost puddled to the floor in relief. But the complications in those sentences—the truth, the distress—forced me to keep pushing, keep talking. How could he take my anger and twist it so inexplicably? How could he warm my hate so it boomeranged back on me and made me crumble?

Wrapping my arms around myself, I took a step closer. My need to hurt him hadn't receded but beneath my violent rage, there was the incessant urge to hug him, touch him—fix both of us.

He shied away. "Don't." His voice was strangled—a sharp warning to keep my distance.

We stood apart. Two figurines in an emerald sea of carpeting. The air was cool, coaxing my temper to simmer. Not being allowed to touch was torture. I couldn't deny myself the need to connect—either to strike him or stroke him, it didn't matter.

Ignoring his beg for space, I closed the gap and touched the back of his arm. My eyes flared at how hot he was—how unnaturally warm for his normal frigid form. "Thank you for finally being honest."

I swallowed. "You can't keep fighting. Whatever it is you're going through. Whatever reason that's making you take drugs and obey the vilest man in history, you have to stop." My voice lowered. "You'll end up killing yourself if you don't get help."

He tumbled backward, his voice raspy and low. "You can't help me. Nobody can."

"Don't be a cliché, Jethro. *Everyone* can be helped."

He snorted, pain layering upon pain.

I hugged myself again, trembling and quaking, struggling with the thick tension in the room. "Tell me and I give you my word I'll listen."

*What are you doing?*

"If you tell me the truth, I won't judge. I'll stay quiet and withhold judgement until everything makes sense."

*You're truly giving him another chance?*

I gritted my teeth.

Everybody deserved a second chance if they were willing to admit a lifetime of troubles. My father handed me over, even though he knew what my mother went through—I forgave him. My brother made me a laughing stock of the gossip columns—I forgave him. And Jethro? He made me fall in love with the bad guy and trade innocence for corruption. I fell for him when he was closed off and arctic. If he thawed and let me in, there would be no greater gift. No symbol deeper than two souls screaming to connect.

"I'll be able to forgive you if you tell me," I whispered.

"I'm here for you. How many times do I need to tell you that?"

Fury twisted his face, dissolving his disbelief at my confession. "You say you won't judge, yet I feel your hatred toward me, Nila. You say you're there for me, but how far will that willingness go?" He stepped back again, moving to the door.

*He can't leave.*

"You know nothing. And it's best if you continue knowing—"

"Shut up." I stalked toward him, my toes sinking into carpet. "Shut up and tell me. Tell me what you're hiding." My voice remained level, not rising to anger once again budding inside.

This wasn't a fight. This wasn't an ultimatum.

This was the end.

The breaking point of everything that'd been crushing us deeper and deeper into untruths. The sooner he let himself snap, the better we would be.

Sighing heavily, his shoulders rolled. "I wish I'd never met you. I wish all of this would disappear."

His words sliced a wound deep and true. His voice was a horrible blade; cutting my arteries and making me bleed a river.

"Listen to me, Jethro Kite Hawk," I said through fresh tears. "I'm only going to say this one more time. If you listen and see what I'm offering, all of this could be different. But if you don't; if you choose your family over me again, if you push me away and pretend that what exists between us isn't worth fighting for, then I'm done. Do you get it?"

My voice gathered momentum. "You've hurt me. Everything inside wants to switch off and cut you from my soul. I'm close. So damn close to that—to slicing you free and never talking to you again."

He hunched into himself with every word.

I swallowed back a sob. I kept going. "There's a place inside me that's fading. What I feel for you is dying, and once it's gone, I won't have the strength to get it back. Do you think

I enjoyed paying the Third Debt? Do you think I enjoyed having Kes do what he did?" Tears spilled with no authority. "It was absolute torture, Jethro. The worst one I've had to pay because *you* weren't there for me. You weren't there to feel my pain or help me get through it. You *left* me! Do you have any idea how much that killed me? To think we had something, only for you to walk out and deliver me to that horror?"

His teeth locked together, backing away from me, moving toward the door.

I advanced all the while talking, hoping he listened. "But despite all that—the Debt Inheritance, the unforgivable handing me over, the lies and horrible behaviour—none of that matters if you make me understand."

I lowered my gaze, looking at his bare feet. If I wanted ultimate honesty for him, I had to be prepared to do the same. It hurt to look deep inside—to give myself no room to hide and to come face to face with a girl I no longer recognised. But I did it. Because I was strong and brave and ready to give in order to receive. "No matter how screwed up and wrong the past few months have been, they've been the best thing that's ever happened to me."

Jethro sucked in a breath.

"If a guardian angel had told me this would happen. If they'd come to me the night before you stole me and explained the atrocities I would live through, I would *still* have come with you."

A groan cut short as Jethro froze in place.

"I would've waited for you with open arms. I would've gladly said goodbye to my life and let you torment me because it made me a better person—a stronger person—a person worthy of what I feel for you." I stiffened. "So *don't* tell me you wish you'd never met me, Jethro Hawk, because I would live a thousand debts just for the gift of having you love me."

Goosebumps covered my naked arms. "I was wrong when I said you were weak. You're not. You're strong. Loyal. So twisted inside, no one can save you but *you*."

Our breathing laced together as we let the impact of truth tear us apart.

If what he said was true and no one had touched me but Kestrel, then I had both brothers to thank. Somehow, they'd conspired together; I owed them my sanity.

Jethro didn't move—he seemed atrophied with guilt and shame.

I breathed hard, forcing myself to expose the last exquisitely vulnerable honesty. "I can't help you if you don't want me. But this...this is me asking you to love me. I'm begging you to trust me. I'm telling you that you're strong enough to survive whatever it is you struggle. I'm asking you to choose *me*, Jethro. Before it's too late."

*Choose me. Love me. Save me.*

His fists clenched. His head bowed and the most heart-clenching gasp fell from his lips. "I'm sorry," he whispered. "I'm so fucking sorry."

I choked back a sob, caught between needing to hide and going to hold him. "I know. But I'm not looking for an apology for what's happened. I would've paid a million times over to deserve you."

My tummy fluttered with an aviary of birds. *Please, listen. Please, see me.* "I'm looking for a promise, Jethro." I drifted toward him.

He didn't move as the distance diminished. Hesitantly, with the gentlest touch, I placed a hand over his heart. The same irregular beat hammered back. The same uncertainty and lostness from the springs.

"I'm asking you to make me yours," I murmured. "Take me into your heart. Let me enter your soul. Give in to what we have."

He swallowed a moan and everything crested inside him. His eyes snapped to mine. With savage strength, he grabbed my collar and swung me around to press against the door. His lips landed on my ear, his breath fast and erratic. "That's what I've been doing. Letting you inside me—permitting you to ruin me every fucking day. You already know how I feel about you. You already know that I'm worthless because of it."

My heart raced. "You're not worthless. If you show me the goodness inside you, I can prove you're priceless."

He laughed harshly. He looked dangerously unhinged. "Try telling that to my father." His fingers twitched around my collar. "I've made myself clear. I've been nothing but transparent about what happened. I've done everything that I could."

My eyes popped wide, even as more tears fell. "You think you've been transparent!" Shoving him backward, I slapped him. "You're not transparent! You're so damn obtuse—so tied up in your lies—that you have no idea what you're saying anymore!"

His entire body tensed. "The Debt Inheritance is my cross to bear—not yours. This isn't about what your family did to mine—it's about if I'm worthy enough! Don't you get it? This was never about you! It's always been about me, and I'm fucking everything up. I'm killing myself!"

A half-sob half-laugh erupted from my mouth. "The moment you took my hand in Milan, this ceased to be about you. This isn't about Hawks or Weavers or any other bullshit you can come up with." Shoving him again, I screamed, "It's about us! About what we've found. *Together*!"

"There *is* nothing between us but debts!"

I shook my head, my palm itching to slap him again. "How do you explain what happens when you're inside me then? How do you explain the link we feel when we let ourselves be honest?"

"What happened in the springs was a mistake. It was just fucking—"

I punched his chest, making him stumble. "*Liar*. Such a damned awful liar! You love me—you just can't admit it. You want me over wealth and inheritances and family—you're just too fucking terrified to man up and see the truth!"

I advanced on him. Everything I'd been dying to say

spewed forth in a torrent of accusations. "I see the way you look at me. I feel the way you touch me. I hear the hidden messages in your voice. Unlike you, I've been blessed knowing the warmth that comes with love. The way a person's eyes glow and body softens. You love me! And if you can stand there and deny it—when it's so blatantly obvious—then there really is no hope for us. You might as well march me outside and complete the Final Debt, because I'd rather you kill me quickly than live through this endless death!"

I sucked in a breath. My lungs gasped for oxygen as if I hadn't breathed since entering Hawksridge. There was clarity and blazing freedom in chopping up our lies, letting them fall around our feet like confetti.

Looking at the carpet, I rubbed the ache in my chest. "I'm done," I whispered. "If you can't say anything after I just revealed everything, then there truly is no hope and I refuse to waste—"

Jethro's breathing turned heavy. He backed away until his spine slammed against the wall. His chin dropped; his hands clutched at the smoothness behind him.

Our eyes met.

A terrible storm howled inside, twisting him into knots. His hands flew to grip his skull, his chest rising and falling with sporadic agony. "What do you want from me, Nila? You want to know that I fucking love you more than I can stand? That I'm breaking because I know I'm not good enough for you? *What?*"

My world stood still.

"*...I fucking love you...*"

He admitted it.

A tortured groan echoed around the room as his eyes squeezed.

Fighting to keep it together, he sucked in huge gusts of oxygen.

He fought the truth.

He fought the tears.

He fought himself.
But...
Slowly...
Gradually...
He.
Lost.
The.
Battle.
He cracked.

The dam, the barrier he'd always hid behind, came smashing down. He crumpled like a paper building until he was stripped bare.

My heart hollowed as he shattered into pieces.

"Christ," he breathed, his voice completely undone. "What have I become?"

He fell.

His knees gave out.

He slid down the wall like a melting glacier.

The moment he hit the floor, his knees came up caging his body, barricading him from the pain he couldn't handle. His arms wrapped around them, curling into himself, pressing his forehead onto his legs. *Hiding.*

I stood there unable to move.

"...*I fucking love you...*"

Then my world turned inside out as Jethro Hawk—the most confusing, complex, and confounding man I'd ever met—started to cry.

His shoulders bunched.

His chest heaved.

He gave up the fight.

The man I feared, adored, and wanted to steal away from a life of emotional blackmail plummeted from lies, and I could *see* him for the very first time.

His anguished groan ripped out my soul, leaving it bleeding in hell.

His legs moved higher, his arms wrapped tighter, but

nothing could hold together what was happening.
   Blistering agony clutched me as I witnessed him coming apart. It was if every stitch holding him together ripped open, leaving him gasping and dying.
   I wanted to be the needle to sew him back together.
   But I couldn't.
   Not yet.
   He needed to do this.
   He needed to get it out.
   This was his unthreading.
   This was him becoming more than just a Hawk.
   "It's okay," I whispered.
   I pooled to the floor in a nightgown I didn't remember him dressing me in, and wrapped myself around his quaking body. "It's alright." I rested my forehead on his temple, running my fingers through his hair.
   He tried to pull away; he tried to stop his tears, but nothing could stop this.
   He was utterly ruined.
   Hanging his head, his shoulders quaked as silent tears erupted from his beautiful golden eyes. My stomach twisted as the man I loved came completely undone.
   I didn't let him grieve on his own. I willed him to feel how much I cared, how much I was there for him, regardless of how damaged he was.
   He stopped fighting my hold and let loose.
   He cried.
   As his tears fell, my own dried up. We changed roles. His arctic shell finally thawed—shards of ice broke into smithereens, blizzards became snowflakes, and permafrost became liquid. There was no space inside him anymore; it had nowhere else to go but out.
   Out his eyes, his soul, his heart.
   I hugged the man who'd done so much wrong and let him purge until his body wracked and shook.
   He didn't make a sound. Not a single gasp or moan.

Utterly silent.

"What did they do to you," I whispered. "You have to tell me. You have to let it go."

My hands skated down his back, touching every inch: his face, his throat, his knees. I needed him to know that I brought him to this point, but I wouldn't abandon him.

I would be there. Through thick and thin.

He didn't stop crying.

Every quiver and silent sob exhausted me. I wanted to take back every cruel thing I'd said. I wanted to apologise for hurting him and for saying I would stop loving him.

I could never stop loving him.

*Never.*

He was inside my every cell.

I would never be able to carve him out—even in death.

"Give me your pain. Share it with me." I wanted to do whatever I could to heal him, to fix him, and make him become the man buried inside.

Jethro suddenly turned in my embrace. Gathering me close, he pushed upward to his feet. I didn't move as his arms clutched me painfully, stumbling across the bedroom.

The moment the mattress was within tumbling distance, we fell together.

Facing each other, Jethro never let me go. He buried his face in my neck, hiding his wet eyes but unable to disguise the steady trickle of moisture down my throat.

*God, I'm sorry. So sorry I broke you.*

I squeezed him so damn hard.

His breathing hitched. His body shook.

No amount of armour or courage could've prepared me for Jethro coming apart.

*Tell me what you're dealing with.*

*Show me how to save you.*

"It's okay, Kite. It's okay." My voice was a steady metronome, granting acceptance in repetition. "I'm not leaving. It's okay, Kite. It's okay."

His arms banded until my bones ached in his embrace. Without a word, Jethro raised his head. One arm unwrapped, and his hand captured my chin, tilting my mouth to his.

Before I could breathe, his lips crashed over mine. His touch was violent, harsh—all-consuming.

Need sprang sharp and fragrant. Desire hijacked my mind with such weight and demand, I buckled with it.

We spiralled together.

His fingers bruised and his tongue dived into my mouth, stealing my gasp and conjuring lust so brutal, I came alive and died all at the same time.

Together, we merged tighter. Jethro cushioned my head with his arm as he rolled me onto my back, covering my body with his. His hand drifted down my ribcage, branding me with every inch. His lips continued to dance with mine—our breathing harsh, tongues violent.

I cried out as his fingers captured my breast, pinching my nipple. My back bowed, forcing more of me into his hold.

He groaned, his breath losing its brokenness, becoming rapid with lust.

Desire swirled and demanded, giving us nowhere to hide.

I became instantly wet as he tugged the hem of my nightdress, shoving it over my hips. I wriggled as he fumbled between us, undoing his button and zipper. He grunted as he yanked his jeans and boxer-briefs down, only making it to midthigh.

His teeth pinched my bottom lip as he forced my knees to spread. His elbows dug into the covers, positioning himself higher.

We both cried out as his hard cock settled between my legs.

There was no foreplay, no preparation. We didn't need it. We were too far gone—too terrifyingly open and desperate for connection. He angled the head of his cock and thrust.

I groaned into his mouth as his size blazed with tender

agony.

He kissed me, slinking his tongue with mine, rocking his hips, using my wetness to spread me wider. He forced my body to yield and melt.

His tears continued to fall, trickling into my mouth and lacing his taste with salty pain. I imprisoned his cheeks, rubbing my thumbs in the dampness, hoping he understood how much I loved him.

That I was there for him.

Forever.

His breathing turned ragged, each exhale releasing soul-burning agony he'd carried all his life. With an arm around my shoulders, he reached down and clutched my hip, holding me firm.

He thrust harder, slipping past the final barrier and filling me completely. We sighed as that heavenly link slotted perfectly into place.

My body quivered around his. There was no warning. No anticipation. The moment he'd filled me, his rocking turned from questing to vicious.

Without his arm around my shoulders, I would've shifted upward with every brutal thrust. But he held me for his pleasure.

He used me.

We used each other.

We used passion to defeat pain. Wielded need to combat despair.

It would either heal us or break us, but there was no stopping the tsunami we rode.

"I'm sorry. So fucking sorry," he mumbled into my hair. His tears had stopped, but his voice remained shaky.

His hips never stopped thrusting, driving us higher.

"I'm sorry," I whispered. "Sorry for making life so hard for you."

He groaned, rocking faster.

Our minds switched from words to releases. We gave

ourselves over to pleasure. Somewhere deep inside me, I let go. I floated upward, acknowledging that fate stole me from a life I thought I wanted, but that was never my true destiny.

*He was.*

Something slotted into place—bigger than a puzzle piece, more poignant than scripture or knowing.

It was the accumulation of fighting for something and finally earning it.

It was *home*.

Jethro pulled back, his jaw locked. His eyes burned as he rocked headfirst into a devouring tempo. I couldn't look away. His body inside my body. His soul inside my soul.

I couldn't contain the magic we sparked. "I need to tell you—how I feel...what this means."

He shook his head, his lips grazing mine. "I know. I feel it, too."

Tears leaked from my eyes as his mouth sealed tight. The wet heat of him and the scorching power of his cock splintered me in two.

There was no break or reprieve. Jethro fucked me, made love to me, and consumed me with no thought to us being watched or catalogued. Long, deep, dominating strokes dragged echoing moans.

Arching my hips, I rubbed my clit on the base of his cock. "More," I begged. "Harder."

He obeyed.

I couldn't breathe, straining for an orgasm that would shatter me.

"Faster, deeper."

He grunted, following my every command.

I'd never lived through something so intense.

It broke me.

It fixed me.

It stole. It gifted.

Devastating.

Rewarding.

Destroying.

Renewing.

"I'm going to fill you. I need to fill you," Jethro groaned.

His voice whispered through my blood, setting fire to the gunpowder between my legs.

I came.

Spindles and shooting stars and spectacular bliss.

He swallowed my pleasure, his tongue diving in time with his erection.

"God, Nila." Every emotion he'd kept hidden lashed around my name like a vow. "I love you."

Wetness spurted inside me as he let go.

He let go of everything.

For a split second, my heart hardened remembering what he'd done. How he'd stolen my right to carry his baby for the foreseeable future, but then I gathered him closer. There was time for that. Time for us to grow together with no more games or traps.

This was us.

This was freedom.

He'd conquered whatever demons had ridden him. He'd given them to me to share the weight.

When his body relaxed and the last wave of his orgasm filled me, he pulled away.

His eyes locked on mine; he traced his thumb over my mouth. "No more winners or losers. No more hiding or pretending or lies.

"I'm ready to tell you. I'm ready to face something new."

I settled back into bed, never taking my eyes off Jethro.

He placed the tray he'd brought from the kitchen between us, tucking his long legs under the sheets, giving me a fearful smile.

For the past hour, he'd prepared himself.

We'd showered silently.

We'd dressed wordlessly.

Then he'd disappeared to the kitchen to grab some freshly made baguettes, pâté, cheese, and grapes. He'd also fetched some painkillers for his hangover but didn't make a move to swallow any of the drugs he'd popped like candy.

All he wore was a pair of black-boxer briefs and a dark grey t-shirt. I'd slipped into an oversized jumper and a pair of white knickers. Together we'd made camp in my bedroom. I never wanted to leave.

His tinsel hair was still damp from the shower and his eyes kept flickering away from mine. He focused on preparing a cracker with smoked cheddar and mushroom pâté before passing it to me.

I took it, brushing my fingers with his.

He winced but smiled softly.

I didn't rush him.

I couldn't. Not after seeing him crack so deeply.

We ate in silence for a time.

Jethro was the one to start—as I'd planned—as he needed to be.

"Remember that text I sent you?" His head tilted, watching me closely.

I swallowed a grape and sat back, ready to talk with no distractions. I knew the one he meant. The one he sent after I saw the graves of my ancestors. "Yes. You said you felt what I felt. That my emotions were your affliction."

He nodded. "Exactly. I told you the truth right there. I'd hoped you'd guess, but I suppose it's hard to understand. There was no trick in those words. No lies. It was God's honest truth."

I waited for him to continue. I had so many questions, but I needed patience. I believed Jethro would answer them when he could.

Jethro sighed. "The reason why I don't like anyone calling me insane or crazy is because I've been told I was throughout my entire childhood. My father never understood me. Kes didn't. Jaz didn't. Shit, even I didn't know what was wrong with me." His eyes glazed over, thinking of the past. "Some days I was fine. Hyper like a boy should be. Happy to play with my siblings. Confident in my place within my family. But other days, I'd cry for hours. I'd claw at myself, trying to rid the overwhelming intensity from my blood. My mind would seize with darkness and sadness and anger—such, such anger.

"I wanted to kill. I craved violence." He smiled wryly. "That doesn't sound so unique, but it was when I was barely eight years old. I had fantasies of tearing men apart. I stressed over money and business—things I had no right to worry about as a kid. It got so bad, I was admitted to a local hospital. I'd stopped eating or drinking; I attacked Jasmine whenever she got too close. I couldn't handle the thoughts inside my head. I fully believed what people said—that I was crazy."

I shifted closer, looping my fingers through his. He didn't pause, almost as if now he'd started, he had to finish as fast as possible.

"The hospital was even worse. There, I worried about dying. I fretted over a child down the hall dying of terminal cancer. I cried all the fucking time, devoured by grief and feeling the keen absence of someone I loved dearly—only thing was, I didn't *know* any of the other patients.

"A nurse found me one night trying to hang myself after watching a movie of a man who couldn't survive life anymore."

His lips twisted into a smile that held both annoyance and appreciation. "If she hadn't have found me, I would've been free. Free from living a life no one could understand. But she did…and she both condemned and saved me."

"How?" I breathed.

"She was a psych major. After a few days of me screaming and self-harming due to a busload of students slowly dying in the ward next to me, she gained permission to check me out and take me to a psychiatric facility instead."

He laughed. "I know this isn't helping my case when I said I wasn't insane."

I shook my head, willing him to continue.

Jethro looked off into the distance, seeing things I wasn't privy to. "Once there, I was even worse. I started having seizures and developed heart arrhythmia. I screamed for no reason, spoke in tongues no one could understand. I self-harmed to the point of disfigurement—all to get the fucking intensity out."

With every glimpse into his past, his present made so much more sense.

"Did—did they diagnose you?"

Jethro nodded. "It took a year of being shuttled between my home and that mental hospital. A year of working with the young nurse who took it upon herself to rescue me from myself."

I held my breath, waiting for a final answer.

But Jethro stayed silent.

I squeezed his fingers. "What was wrong with you?"

He snorted. "Wrong?" Shaking his head, he said condescendingly, "Everything. Everything was wrong."

Untangling his fingers from mine, he traced the blue veins visible beneath my tanned skin. "One day, my father flew in a child psychology specialist. The doctor made me do a lot of tests. After a week of assessment, he was as clueless as the rest of them.

"But there'd been one saving grace. The entire time I'd spent with the doctor, having no contact with others, locked in a cool white room with only puzzles for company, my thoughts became calm, diligent, focused on facts and data. I wasn't emotional or crazed. I found happiness and silence once again. And that's what gave the answer away."

"What answer?"

Jethro huffed. "The one that ensured Cut would never accept me, because there was no cure for what I am. Back then, it seemed like I was making this shit up. That I was rebelling and putting on a show. Nowadays, it's one of the first things a doctor checks for."

I needed a name—something to call what Jethro was. I leaned closer, waiting.

"I'm a VEP, Nila."

I blinked. He'd announced it as if it were a foul, common disease that would make me hate him. I had no idea what it was.

He half-smiled. "Also known as an HSP."

I frowned, racking my brain for any remembrance of such a thing. "What—what is that?"

He smirked. "Exactly. No one knows, even though approximately twenty percent of the population has it. Most people don't understand when I say a touch is a curse or a noise is a fucking bomb. People's misfortune is a damn tragedy to me. Joy is utopia. Love is divine. Failure is ruin. Unhappiness is absolute death."

I shook my head. "I—I still don't understand."

Jethro laughed sadly. "You will. Basically...my senses are heightened. I feel what others do. I *live* their pain. I go insane living too close to people who exist in hate or revenge. It consumes me to the point where I can't breathe without being influenced."

"What does VEP stand for?"

Jethro sighed, pinching the bridge of his nose. "It stands for Very Empathetic Person."

My heart ran faster. "And HSP?"

"Highly Sensitive Person."

"And that means..."

His eyes tore to mine. "Weren't you listening? It means I'm screwed up. It means I'm more attuned to others' personalities and emotions than most. Their moods overshadow mine. Their goals steal mine. Their hate corrupts my happiness. Their fear and rage eclipses everything. I can't control it. Cut's tried. Jasmine's tried. Hell, I've tried. But every time we think we've found something that works...it fails. Not only am I doomed to always feel what others do, but I'm oversensitive to smell, noise, touch. My brain is too damn perceptive, and I suffer every fucking second of every day."

We sat in silence.

I digested everything he said, slowly piecing together what I knew about him: how he reacted in situations. How cold he was when he first came for me. He was the perfect image of Cut when he collected me—because that was all the influence he had.

Then I came along and made him *feel*. Made him live my fear, my lust, my never-ending fight.

*It's true. I did break him.*

Jethro muttered, "Whenever I told you to be quiet. Whenever I couldn't handle it and snapped—it wasn't your voice I was trying to hush but your emotions. You're the worst of them, Nila. You project everything you feel. You're like a damn kaleidoscope with the range of emotions you go through. Falling for you, sleeping with you... Fuck, it was all I could do to stay standing and not cripple beneath the weight of it."

Tears shot to my eyes. I hated that I'd hurt him. Unintentional or deliberate. How did I miss the warning signs? How did I not see the changes in him—the anger hiding pain and the commands cloaking calls for help?

I pictured Jethro as a young boy going through so much trauma. Of being poked and prodded and called insane. It physically hurt to think about what he'd gone through—surviving a family such as his.

I touched his hand. "Are you sure the doctors got it right? That they diagnosed it correctly and there's nothing they can do?"

*Surely, there must be a cure?*

Jethro snorted. "Do you want the hallmark characteristics? Okay, here we go: One, Empaths feel more deeply. Two, we're emotionally reactive and less able to intellectualize feelings. Three, we need down-time away from everyone if we're to survive living with others. Four, it takes us longer to make a decision because we're bombarded with so many scenarios every time we try to decide. Five, I'm more prone to anxiety or depression. Six, I can't for the life of me watch a horror movie. I relate too much to the character about to die. Kes made me watch one when I was ten. I had to be drugged for two nights just to calm me down."

He looked away, laughing darkly. "Seven, we cry more easily—it's the only way we can purge. Eight, we have better manners when we're in control of ourselves. More cordial to fight the chaos we're feeling inside. Nine, every criticism slices through my heart until I feel as if I'll fucking die. Needing my father's approval is more than a stupid boyhood wish but a goal that rides me into an early grave. Ten, we look for ways to hide. We become chameleons by adopting the habits of those strongest emotionally. And finally eleven, we're highly intuitive."

He dwindled off, twisting the sheets. "Does any of that sound familiar?"

Pieces slotted into place, all making perfect sense now I knew.

Jethro was explosive because he felt everything so much more. He rode Wings a lot to outrun the emotional upheaval forced on him by living with men like Cut and Daniel. He kept switching alliances between his father and me, unable to make a decision when faced with two personalities. He turned inward and festered when everything became too much. He shut down when he'd reached his limit and was so damn cold when we first met as it was the only way he could survive.

"The tablets, they were to—"

"Block the over-sensory perception. To numb me." He fisted the duvet. "They worked while you weren't here. In fact, they were the first thing in my life that actually gave me silence." He smirked. "But then you came back with your screaming feelings and battering ram of ideals and tore that apart."

My heart beat faster. "So when we slept together at the polo match...when I asked if you knew what I was feeling..."

He sighed. "I told you the truth. I knew. I felt your need,

your sadness, your confusion. You'd fallen for me, but you weren't happy about it. I bore your worry as if it were my own, but I also basked in the love you had."

Leaning forward, he cupped my cheek. "I'd never felt so much emotion from anyone. You selflessly gave me something warm and safe and so fucking delicious to hide in. There were no conditions or commands—you were fully open, letting me inside."

His eyes darkened. "It killed me to think you were still unsure. That you could feel such a way but not want it."

I leaned into his palm. "I'm sorry."

He shook his head. "Don't be. I've had this curse all my life." He gathered me close, nuzzling into me. "I've never let myself give in. But before, when I slid inside you, I stopped fighting. I did what Jasmine told me to do. I let myself drown in what you feel for me. And fuck, it was the best thing I've ever felt."

My heart cast into a never-ceasing knot. "And Jasmine told you to do that?"

He dropped his gaze. "Jaz has been researching my condition ever since I was diagnosed. She read somewhere that Empaths who remain single and cloistered from society don't have long life expectancies. Others slowly chip us away, until one day, it's too much. I swore to her that I would never find love. That the agony I had from loving her as my sister was enough to swear me off ever marrying. But she showed me another article about Empaths who *do* find their perfect others. They live longer than most because they no longer have to fight on their own."

His hand never stopped stroking, his body tense but happy.

I asked, "What does that mean?"

His eyes became hazy, dreamy. "It means we rely on the person we love to love us so much in return that we can forever hide in their adoration and acceptance. Knowing there's a well of immeasurable affection helps heal us if we encounter a

mourning mother or psychotic serial killer. We can stay level—
or at least better than we would if we're alone."

"So when Jasmine yelled at me for hurting you and cursed herself for destroying you—that's what she meant?"

His forehead furrowed. "When did you see Jasmine?"

*Whoops.*

"Doesn't matter. Is that what she meant?"

Jethro scowled but nodded. "Exactly. She pushed me into making you fall for me. In fact, just before the polo match, she told me to stop fighting and make you love me. To forget about the debts and inheritances and find something far more precious."

I couldn't speak.

"She told me to find my cure in you, Nila. She saw what I couldn't. She hoped for something I never dared dream of. She taught me that love can be the cruellest force imaginable, but it also heals."

He pressed a kiss reverently on my lips. "I'm done fighting. You're mine and I'm yours, and now you know everything there is to know about me. Now you know I'm broken and can never be cured. Now you know why I am the way I am."

# Jethro

IT WAS DONE.

Out in the open.

My disease verbalized and acknowledged.

And she hadn't run.

She hadn't looked at me with pity or disgust. She'd accepted it and loved me even more.

Her emotions came in crashes, echoing in my soul. By being honest, I'd given her answers. And with answers came freedom to give in and trip from new love into forever love.

I wanted to crush her to me and never let go. I wanted to get on my fucking knees and thank her for the rest of my days for being brave enough to accept me.

Life together hadn't been smooth. Our past was full of debts and degradation. Our future—if we even had a future—would be full of miscommunication and misunderstanding.

*I'm not an easy person to love.*

I knew that. Kestrel knew that. Jasmine knew that. There were times when I was too much. When their good intentions just weren't enough and I'd have to leave to regroup on my own.

I could never hate them for that—for needing timeout from dealing with a fucked-up brother. But Nila…she would be drained of everything. I would take and take and take until that blistering, joyous love would turn to putrid ash.

*Can I do that to her?*

Could I suck her dry and hope to God she was strong enough to save us both?

*Do I have any right to expect her to?*

No. I had no right at all.

I should ship her overseas and kill my father to end this entire fucking mess. But now that I had her...how could I ever let her go?

Nila hadn't moved or spoken, her eyes full of thoughts.

I murmured, "The day Kestrel gave you Moth, I very nearly broke. I came to your room that night. I sat outside for hours, trying to get myself together so you wouldn't see how much it fucking hurt that he'd given her to you."

Nila sucked in a gasp. "He told me it was your idea. That you wanted to give her to me the day after the Second Debt."

I flinched. It sounded like I'd hoped to buy her forgiveness for the ducking stool by gifting her a horse. "It wasn't like that. I only wanted you to have something you'd never had before." I would've stopped normally, censored my thoughts and deleted things that would show the truth, but now...I had more to say. There was so much more, and for the first time, I was able to speak openly.

Pushing the food tray further down the bed, I reclined against the pillows and pulled Nila beside me. We lay down, legs entwined, arms around each other.

For an extraordinary second, I held her and drank in her thoughts. To have no barriers between us—no lies or deceptions—*it's more than words can say.*

"That moment in the horse float, heading to polo, I knew how you felt about her. The softening in your soul, the desire to own another's life, to have something reliant on you—all flowed in a wash of desire." Inhaling the floral scents of her hair, I whispered, "You fell in love with her a lot faster than you fell for me."

Nila snuggled closer, squeezing me tight. "All this time

you knew how I was feeling?"

*Does that hurt you? To know I felt what you did, heard your panic, lived through your agony?* Did that make me a terrible person to be able to withstand, not only doing awful things to her, but receiving the consequences of my actions through her, too?

I nodded. "Every debt. Every argument. I felt you."

She stayed silent; a wave of unfairness flowed from her. I didn't want her feeling as if I used her—that I'd eavesdropped on her emotions.

I said quietly, "That's why Cut hates you. He can see the power you have over me—a power that I've been taught to hide my entire life."

Nila went still. "It's not only Cut who has a power over you. Jasmine does…and Kestrel."

My muscles locked, but I forced myself to relax. I'd committed to being open. I would continue to keep my promise. "Yes, Jasmine has the same condition as me but not nearly as bad. There are different levels of HSP. I'm on the unusual end of the scale where I'm borderline sixth sense—if the doctors believed in that phenomenon, of course. I'm highly empathetic, to the point where I'll grow sick when others are ill. My heart rhythm becomes irregular if the stress of the person I'm with goes past my realm of capabilities."

Nila twisted in my arms. "Oh, my God. The springs." Her mouth popped wide. "Your heart was irregular then. I thought you were ill…" She dropped her eyes. "Actually, I didn't think that. I thought you were…"

"What? Tell me."

Her black gaze swooped upward, capturing me completely. "Lost. I thought your rhythm was lost."

I swallowed hard. "Perhaps you're an HSP yourself. Not many people notice my moods or complexities—unless I get terribly bad. Over the years, I've been able to hide it better. From the ages of nineteen to twenty-six, I was pretty perfect. Apart from a few episodes from my father's temper on a deal gone south or my little brother's arrogant lunacy, I managed to keep their thoughts from creeping too much into mine."

Nila smiled almost smugly. "But not me."

I kissed her, slinking my tongue into her mouth. Taking my time, I tasted her as if this was the first time I'd kissed her. And it was in a way. The first time I'd let myself be so open and honest.

I was a changed man.

A totally different person.

"I couldn't withstand you." I licked her softly.

I couldn't stop touching her. Couldn't stop the need to be close.

*Perhaps, I can show her exactly what this means? What I truly need from her?*

She broke the kiss. "How does Kes have a power over you?"

My gut churned to think of Kes with Nila last night. But I also couldn't deny it was my idea—my choice. He'd only obeyed and done the best he could. I'd forgive him...in time.

I sighed, thinking how selfless my brother truly was. How helpful and kind he'd been ever since he'd come to bust me out of the mental hospital. It'd been the third I'd visited all before I hit fifteen. He'd only been twelve, but he'd packed a bag and run away from Hawksridge. He hitchhiked across town and sneaked through the compound to get me.

Needless to say, we never managed to get free. The doctors found us and sent him home, but our bond was forged that night and nothing—no anvil, blade, or threat—could sever it.

"Kes is special." I shrugged. "While I was going off the rails crying over things I couldn't control and wanting to murder people for no apparent reason, he learned how to control his inner thoughts around me. He mastered the art of blocking his every whim, desire, and impression until I could hang around him and have my own thoughts for once. I became addicted to his emptiness and silence. The doctors said he acted like a shield for me. That as long as we stayed close, he helped me cope."

Nila never took her gaze from mine, her body taut with understanding. "I always wondered why Kes was able to touch you when you were about to lose it. I expected you to hit him, but you never shrugged him off. You always seemed to...relax."

I nodded. "That's because I *did* relax. Kes manipulates me in a way, but I let him because it's the only reprieve I get."

"And Jasmine?" Her voice lowered. Her eyes dropped from mine, filling with nerves. I knew then what she wanted to ask. It was a question I wasn't ready for. I would never be prepared to speak of what happened to my sister that night.

Pressing a finger over her mouth, I shook my head. "I don't want to talk about Jaz. Not yet."

She frowned. "I can accept that." Clouds formed over our idyllic oasis; I tensed against the next question forming in her thoughts.

I groaned, wishing I didn't have to answer but knowing I had to. "You want to know why I put you through what I did last night, don't you?"

She stiffened. "I don't think I'll ever get used to you knowing what I'm about to say. But yes...I would."

Every second that ticked past, she rebuffed me a little more, remembering the way I'd shut off and abandoned her last night. But I'd never abandoned her. I left her to play a part in an orchestra that hadn't finished playing yet.

"It's complicated."

"Try me."

I stared at the ceiling, holding her tight. "You knew you were being recorded last night." It wasn't a question.

She shifted in my embrace. "Yes. I know Kes wanted me to act hurt and terrified."

My fists curled, recalling what Kes had done against my wishes. I couldn't begrudge either Nila or my brother for finding a small measure of pleasure, but it didn't mean I would ever get over it. It would take time to live with it but forever to forget it.

"There are other recordings, Nila."

She bit her lip, sadness coming thick and heavy. "I know. I guessed you'd have videos of my mother and her payments of the debts."

"I asked Kestrel to do what he did to give the drugs long enough to knock Cut and Daniel out."

"What?"

"You and Kes were the performance, while I created a bigger show." My heart bucked, knowing she'd hate me for what I'd done. She'd have to come to terms with it, because it'd been the only way I could think of to keep Cut's suspicions down, prevent her from being raped, and live to see another day to find another solution.

"Do you trust me?" I murmured.

She tensed. For a moment, her emotions screamed *'no.'* Then she relaxed, letting love replace her resentment. "Yes."

My heart swelled; I ached to kiss her again—to prove her trust would never be squandered or broken. "I know what I'm doing. Just leave it with me."

It took a minute, but she finally melted against me, pressing her mouth against my chest. "Okay..."

*Okay...*

Such sweet permission. Such ardent concession.

I'd never been so weightless and free. It was a damn novelty to let down my bomb-battered walls and truly give myself over to her. I didn't tense or hide in ice—I permitted myself to feel everything she did. To sense how much she wanted to save me. How much she wanted to keep me. How much she needed to understand me.

I even acknowledged the parts she tried to keep secret—the things she would never say aloud but I knew anyway.

She wanted me to choose her over everyone.

Over Jasmine.

My inheritance.

My world.

She wanted it so fiercely, it throbbed with every beat of her heart.

She was afraid I would cut her out again. Afraid I would ask more heinous things of her. Terrified that I'd once again put up my walls, sink back into snow, and fall under my father's command.

Once upon a time, I would've. I would've reverted to what I knew because I'd been too chicken shit to believe I could be better.

But not this time.

Coming apart before her had changed me irrevocably. I hadn't wanted to break. I'd tried to keep it together. But the moment she told me to leave; the second she said the part of her that loved me was dying—I'd *felt* it.

I'd felt the ember of affection flickering its last breath. She told the truth. I tasted the end. And I shattered to have something so pure taken from me.

I knew what it was like to live alone. I knew what it was like to live with her loving me.

There was no comparison, no choice.

Not now.

And the honest to God truth was, she didn't need to worry. I would *never* hurt her again. I would spend the rest of my life ensuring I protected her like the fucking goddess she was. I would dedicate my days building a fortress, a shrine, an entire world for her, and it would all pale in relation to what she'd given me.

She was my number one.

Over everyone.

Even myself.

There was no turning back from this.

*She is my salvation, my reason for existence, my queen.*

# Nila

"YOU'RE SURE YOU have to go?"

I looked down at my fingers, twisting, turning—never resting. We'd spent a blissful few hours together, but now the sun was at its zenith, and Jethro tensed with anxiety. I hadn't asked why he slipped from sated to stressed, but I could guess.

If Daniel and Cut didn't touch me last night, something had been done to protect me. And it was precarious.

"I don't want to, but I have to." His golden eyes glimmered with openness. After talking, we'd dozed in each other's arms—perfectly content to let silence heal the wounds left behind by honesty.

I shuffled, digging my toes into the carpet. We stood by my door. I'd gone to escort him out, but in reality, I couldn't stomach the thought of being away from him longer than a second. The connection we'd built throbbed with intensity.

I knew he had to leave to fabricate whatever tale Cut had to believe. I knew our very safety was at stake. But it was inconsequential when faced with saying goodbye.

"I'll miss you." My voice was sex-laden and a blatant invitation. *Come back to bed, so I won't have to miss you.*

He sucked in a breath. His eyes flickered down the empty corridor behind him. He'd slipped back into his clothes from last night and the faint scents of cigar smoke and cognac clung to him. "Don't tempt me, Nila..."

My nipples tingled. He was as reluctant to end this as I was. "I don't want you to go."

His lips parted as he leaned into me, planting his hand on the doorframe beside my head. "I don't want to go, either."

Sadness pinched. "Then don't."

He shook his head, looking weary and tired. "I have to. I can't be here when they wake up. And I have to delete the camera footage of what just happened in your room."

My shoulders slumped. "Okay, I understand."

Whatever he'd done to rig the Third Debt was reliant on Cut and Daniel believing a lie. If they saw evidence against that lie, everything that'd been done last night would be for nothing.

*It would be a waste.*

Jethro groaned. His hand dropped from the doorframe, capturing mine.

The instant he touched me, I sparked from head to toe. I shivered as he stroked my knuckles with his thumb. "Goddammit, I never want you out of my sight again."

I swayed toward him. "Surely, we have a little more time?"

*You're playing with fire, Nila.*

That was true. My core burned for him. My body blazed for his. I couldn't think of anything but sex. I was reckless, drunk on him.

His forehead scrunched.

I couldn't help myself. I stood on tiptoes and kissed the faint lines around his mouth.

He froze.

"Nila..."

I kissed him again. A butterfly kiss. A goodbye kiss.

Suddenly, he grabbed my chin, slamming his lips on mine.

His touch was delicate but fierce. His tongue teasing but demanding.

With a soft moan, I opened for him and the kiss waltzed straight into forbidden.

Breathing hard, he pulled away. "Come with me."

Wrapping his fingers around my wrist, he dragged me from my room and down the corridor. His eyes were nothing but lust and urgency.

I trotted beside him in knickers and a t-shirt. "Where are we going?"

"I can't say goodbye. But I can't do what I want in there."

My stomach somersaulted. "What do you want to do?"

He lowered his head, watching me from beneath his brow. "Do you trust me?"

I no longer had to think or doubt or lie. "Yes."

His lips twitched in love and gratefulness, moving quicker through the Hall. "I want to do what I've needed ever since I knew you cared for me. I want to show you what it's like for me." We careened around a corner like two eloping lovers. "Will you let me do that, Nila?" The devoted need in his voice circumnavigated any excuse or negation I might've had.

"I'll let you do whatever you need."

Yanking me to a stop, he kissed me fiercely. His fingers held the back of my skull as if he was afraid I'd float away and leave him. "Thank you. A thousand times thank you."

Dropping his hand, he looped his fingers with mine and together we ducked around corners, scurried beneath paintings, and entered the secret door to his bachelor wing.

*He's no longer a bachelor. He's taken. He's mine.*

My eyes drank in the maroon painted walls as Jethro prowled the halls of his own quarters. He seemed more at ease here, safe. Ever since finding his chambers, I'd wanted to return. I wanted to explore and see how many secrets his personal space would divulge.

Jethro guided me past gaming rooms, studies, and elaborate dayrooms until he opened the last door and pushed me through.

The moment we were inside, he locked it.

My eyes darted, taking in plasterwork of swooping birds of prey, the deep red carpet, leather-gilded walls, and priceless furniture that out-shadowed any antique my family had back in

London. His room was masculine, almost medieval, yet there was a tranquillity about it, too.

I trembled as Jethro came up behind me, wrapping his arms around my front. His lips kissed the diamonds around my throat, drifting to my collarbone. How did he feel about my collar now? Did he have a strange love-hate relationship with the beautiful jewellery like I did?

I swayed backward, pressing myself into him.

His hot breath cascaded over my shoulder. "There aren't any cameras in here."

"Oh..." My heart rate skyrocketed.

Jethro's hand cupped my breast, rolling my nipple between his fingers. "I can do whatever I want to you."

Once upon a time, that would've been a terrifying threat. Now, I knew him. Now, I trusted him.

I moaned as he palmed my other breast. "You can?"

"I can do whatever I need."

"And what do you need?"

His teeth sunk into the flesh between my neck and shoulder, his tongue stealing the sting. "I can be completely myself. I can take everything you have to give."

Words deserted me as he spun me around and captured my lips.

His taste slipped down my throat. His eagerness wrapped around my heart.

We only kissed for a moment.

But it felt as if we kissed forever.

Sliding, licking, tasting.

He swept me away from this dimension, guiding me to a different one—a more spiritual one where our hearts beat to the same rhythm and our desire thickened with every breath.

Walking me backward, his arms swooped down and hoisted me off my feet. I gasped at his power, kissing him harder. Instinctually, I wrapped my legs around his hips. He groaned as my pussy pressed against his straining erection.

Still kissing, he headed forward. Arms bunched, lips

slippery, he marched me to the bed.

Then I was falling.

And he was falling with me.

The soft mattress cushioned me, while the hard demand of Jethro landed on top, squashing me with fervent need.

My lungs deflated; a small vertigo wave tried to steal the magic of the moment.

He chuckled. "I've gone dizzy from switching from vertical to horizontal."

In that second, I loved him so much I might burst. "Now you know how I feel most days."

He pulled back, brushing hair from my face. "Is it terrible? To have your brain work against you all the time?"

His question was so much deeper than just enquiring about my imbalance deficiency. It was a probe into how I coped—a mutual understanding of what it was like to have a condition rule your life. "I manage."

"You manage better than me."

I cupped his cheek. "Everyone has complications. Some harder than others."

He smiled softly, pressing another kiss on my mouth. "Yes, but some of us are stronger than others." His lips trailed to my ear. "And you're the strongest person I've ever met."

His hand disappeared down my side, tugging at my t-shirt. I wriggled, helping him slip it over my head. I lay in just my knickers in the arms of the man who'd been given a task that would never come to pass.

Jethro would never kill me.

I knew that with utmost certainty.

He couldn't because it would kill him, too.

His jaw locked, eyes devouring my naked chest. "You're so fucking beautiful."

A prickle of sensitivity darted over my skin, centring in my core.

He ran his fingertip around my nipple, causing it to pebble. "I've never felt this way about anyone. Ever. Never let myself open to the pain it can cause." His finger drifted down my sternum, moving toward my bellybutton. "I need you to know." His finger coasted lower, dipping into the manicured curls between my legs. "I need you to know that I adore you. I worship you. I don't just love you, Nila Weaver. I treasure you. I've never had anything so goddamn precious as you."

My mouth fell open as he pressed a single finger inside me. Words flew from my mind as every part of me focused on his touch.

"I'm going to show you what it's like in my world. Will you let me?" His finger slipped deeper, pressing against my inner walls.

I bit my lip, nodding. My eyes were heavy, body begging.

I was warm, content, and truly happy for the first time in my life.

I didn't want to move or talk or do anything to burst this magical bubble.

Another finger entered me, stretching, coaxing, dragging me from needful to insane with desire.

"I'll never be able to repay you for last night. I'll never be worthy of what you've given me. But I'll make it my life to repent and prove how fucking sorry I am for what I put you through."

I opened my eyes. My heart clenched at the sublime beauty of the *true* Jethro. He blazed brightly in the softly lit room. His every thought and desire, his every fear and insecurity—it was all there for me to witness and wonder.

Never looking away, he withdrew his fingers and used the glistening digits to pull his t-shirt over his head. Shadows danced over his muscles, highlighting ropes of power in his forearms, chiselled planes of his stomach, and faint bruises on his ribcage.

His injuries from whatever fight he'd been in the night I found his room had healed and faded.

Sliding off the bed, he unbuckled his belt and eased the denim down his legs. Stepping free of the material, he didn't hesitate pulling his boxer-briefs to the floor.

My mouth dried up at his naked perfection.

His cock hung heavy and hard between his legs. His hands opened and closed by his side self-consciously.

I couldn't tear my eyes away from his incredible body. He was mine now. This insane specimen of a man was *mine*.

Lifting my hips, I shimmied free from my knickers, tossing them over the edge of the mattress. His eyes zeroed in on my exposed core. The smell of sex and musk filled my nose.

He smirked, slipping from intense to playful. "What we did before was the entrée to what I truly need. Taking you so quickly didn't satisfy either of us. And I mean to satisfy you *extremely* well."

I quirked an eyebrow. "Oh? What does 'extremely satisfied' entail?" I dropped my voice as a delicious thrill ran through my belly. "What are you going to do to me?"

He bent over and grabbed my ankles. "You'll see." His signature scent of woods and leather seemed stronger, more intoxicating as he pulled me down the bed. "Stay there."

Moving toward his private bathroom, he returned with several long sashes from a bathrobe. Without a word, he tied it around the post at the bottom of the bed. Never looking away, he imprisoned my ankle and ever so gently wrapped the terry-cloth sash around me.

My heart splattered with a mix of erotic excitement and spellbinding fear.

Jethro paused, his eyes tight. "I feel what you're thinking, Nila." He stroked my calf, calming me. "You're intrigued what I'm about to do to you, but afraid of being tied up again. Am I right?"

I blinked. *I will never get used to that.* "Yes."

Every time he'd tied me up, he'd done something awful.

His jaw clenched. "It's understandable. Every time I've tied you up, I've done something unforgivable."

I jolted at how eerily close his conclusions were to my own. I nodded slowly. "You're right—"

Jethro scowled. "And why wouldn't you despise me for what I've done? The First Debt I tied and whipped you. The Second Debt I bound and drowned you. The Third Debt—"

"I know what happened, Jethro. You don't have to torture me or yourself by reminding us."

There was no telling how I would react to being tied while he pleasured me. It could cancel out the bad he'd caused but also ruin whatever good he attempted. If I was honest, I didn't want to be trussed up. I didn't want to be helpless to his whims. But at the same time...wasn't that what trust was? To have faith in someone that they wouldn't go too far?

His fingers stroked my ankle. "I promise on my soul I will never hurt you again."

My body screamed yes. My mind screamed no. I struggled to choose.

"This is pleasure," Jethro murmured. "I give you my word; I'll release you the second you ask." His eyes glowed with need, begging me to grant one more sacrifice.

Slowly, I nodded.

He exhaled heavily, moving his attention to my other ankle. "Thank you."

He wrapped a similar sash around me, spreading my legs apart. The vulnerability and almost degrading way my legs were held open made me squirm with nervousness and need.

Jethro ran a hand over his face, drinking in my body. "Fuck, you're stunning." He grabbed his cock, working himself. "I've never been so attracted to anyone as I am to you. Never wanted to worship anyone. Never been so fucking besotted."

My nervousness popped like champagne bubbles, leaving me tipsy on lust.

"What I want to do to you isn't degrading or demanding, Nila. It's so much more than that."

Breathing shallowly, I didn't move as Jethro climbed onto the bed, crawling over me to place my hands above my head. "It's not about control; it's about showing you my world." Climbing higher, he fastened my wrists above my head with another sash.

His cock nudged my chin as he bent forward, reaching over me.

Without thinking, I opened my mouth and sucked him. The tang of his desire coated my tongue as I swirled around his crown.

He froze.

A groan wrenched from his lungs. "Christ, Nila."

His hips twitched, feeding a little more of his length into my mouth. He trembled as my head bobbed, sucking him as much as I was able to while imprisoned below him. I looked up.

His eyes scorched mine, melting with love. "You're so perfect."

With a grimace, he withdrew. "I'm too fucking close as it is. This is for you. My pleasure can wait."

I licked my lips, missing the small burst of power I'd had over him. I wriggled, completely constrained but not helpless.

"This isn't about dominant or submissive, Nila. This is about showing you how I feel. How earning your ultimate trust is better than any drug, better than any promise. This is about making you understand."

"I don't need to understand. All I know is my heart belongs to you."

Jethro placed his fingertips over my mouth, shaking his head softly. "That isn't enough—I owe you so much more than that. I want to show you the level of intensity I live with. I want you to know first-hand the sensory overload I suffer now that I've fallen in love with you."

*Fallen in love with you.*

No words would ever compare.

I trembled as he stood up, gazing at my spread body. He stepped back; the bedside lights illuminated his spattering of chest hair and gleaming cock. His eyes hooded, filling with salaciously carnal intentions.

Even though I was the one tied up, he was the one

bound—locked in a life that demanded so much from him. The longing on his face clenched my core, making me wet.

"You look incredible like that," Jethro whispered. "Knowing you can't run. Can't hide. That you're all mine." He prowled to the side of the bed, dragging his fingertip over my knee, my thigh, between my legs, my belly, my breast, my chin, my mouth.

With a gentle press, he pushed his tattooed index past my lips. The thought of my initials stamping ownership on him reminded me we hadn't done the tally for the Third Debt. I shouldn't want something so ridiculous on my flesh, but I wanted him to sign and approve every inch of me. I wanted to be his completely and forever.

My tongue swirled around his finger.

He pulled his digit free. "Wait here. I have to get a few supplies from next door."

*Supplies? What supplies?*

Ignoring my racing heartbeat, I laughed. "Where exactly can I go?"

He grinned—such a light-hearted sight. "Precisely. And that's what makes this such fun." He kissed the tip of my nose. "Wait for me."

Then he was gone.

The moment he disappeared, doubt filled my mind. Did I want this to happen? What would he do?

Testing the bindings, I squirmed. Fear lurked on the outskirts of my brain, but my body only grew wetter. No matter what rational thinking told me I should want, I couldn't deny I'd never been so turned on.

Jethro appeared again, locking the door behind him. He kept his hands behind his back, obscuring what he'd collected. "Remember you said you trusted me."

Stopping at the base of the bed, he slowly brought forth the hunting whip he'd used the day he chased me through the forest. I recognised the diamond glinting on the handle. I'd seen it while hiding naked in the tree, begging for a chance to escape.

I flinched. "Hell, no..."

*He can't be serious.*

He shook his head, his eyes flashing with pain. "It's not what you think." He stalked around the mattress, trailing the tip of the crop along my skin. Every touch sent my nipples pebbling, core dampening. I didn't want this—yet my body only grew more sensitive.

A stroke was no longer a stroke but a tease.

A smile was no longer a smile but a promise. A deliciously dark, *dangerous* promise.

"You trust me?"

I breathed faster. How could I say I trusted him then doubt him the moment that trust was tested?

Locking eyes, I nodded.

Jethro relaxed a little, then his wrist flicked and he brought the whip down across the top of my thigh. Not hard, but hard enough that heat flared.

I jerked, panting at the scrambled messages my nervous system gave. Was it hot or cold? Did it feel good or bad? Did I want to run or stay?

*I don't know!*

Jethro swallowed hard.

*Can he sense my confusion?*

His voice was thick as he demanded, "Tell me how it feels."

I shook my head, drowning under another influx of sensation. There was no way to describe it.

"Try, Nila. I want to know."

I scrunched up my face. "Um...it's warm...tingling."

Jethro chuckled. "No, I don't want to know physically. I don't care about physically." He sat on the edge of the bed, stroking my cheek with tenderness. "I know how it feels on your body." His stroking dropped to my breast, not touching flesh but something so much deeper. "I care about what you feel in *here*." His fingers pressed firmer as if he could carve out my heart and protect it forever. "I want to know how your heart feels, your mind, your thoughts, your soul. I want everything. I want the truth."

I gasped as his hand drifted from breast to pussy.

His mouth tightened as he pressed a finger inside me. "Tell me how this makes you feel."

My hips arched, wanting him to push deeper, give me more. "I'm wet…"

He withdrew his fingers. "No." Drawing my wetness up my belly and back to my heart, he murmured, "In here. Tell me. Go deeper than physical. Ignore mental. Tell me your deepest, darkest sensation."

I trembled as his hand returned between my legs; his long, delicious finger pressed inside me.

I moaned. My head fell back as I clenched around his touch. He made me feel idolized and wanted, dropping all his barriers, driving me upward to a familiar goal.

My mind was a mess. I couldn't understand the threads of racing thoughts. But he needed this from me, I would do my best.

Jethro crooked his finger, rocking. "Tell me or I'll stop."

*Don't stop!*

"I—I feel heavy. As if I'm too full and filling more and more the longer you touch me."

"Good. Go on."

"Um…I feel weightless as if I'm exactly where I need to be. I'm confused and crazy and needy and hazy. But through it all, I'm excited."

He grunted. "Fuck, that's a turn-on." Bending over, he kissed me hard. "Having access to your body isn't what I crave. It's access to your mind. Your feelings I can sense, but your thoughts I can't. It's the one part of you I need to own—in order to give in completely."

I quivered as he removed his finger and raised the whip again, torturing me slowly with it licking over my skin. "Do you understand what I need?"

"Yes, I think so." I bit my lip as he circled the bed, never stopping his incessant stroking with the supple whip. With every stroke, I forced myself to focus on how I felt *inside* rather than how I reacted outside.

The physical was so much easier. My pulse thundered. My skin prickled. My blood raced. My core clenched. My body needed him desperately. And my libido scaled a mountain that terrified me.

But emotionally...I wasn't prepared to go so deep. It was foreign territory to look so far inside. How could I truly understand who I was—not just as a woman or Weaver but as a human—a creature of breath and bone...of animalistic desires?

Were my thoughts normal? Were they acceptable? Was I weak or strong or broken? I didn't know.

*And Jethro wants to know...*

On his second circuit, Jethro flicked the whip, striking my clit with a short, sharp burst.

"Oh, my God!" The intensity swooped hard, jerking my shoulders as a blistering wave of need spread from my core. The sweetest strangest buzz travelled through me. I became weightless all while heavy with colliding thoughts.

"Tell me how you feel," Jethro purred.

I had no clear-cut answer, but I'd promised. *I have to try.* Closing my eyes, I focused inward. "There are too many thoughts to articulate. They're all racing too fast." Pulling on the restraints, I begged, "Jethro..."

"Quiet." He dragged the whip up the centre of my body.

Every muscle bunched, preparing for the next strike.

He didn't disappoint.

He struck me short and sharp on my bellybutton.

I convulsed, soaking up the decadent bite. One moment, my thoughts were tamed, untangling themselves from the twisting mass of nonsensical nonsense, the next, they were a jumble of madness.

"And now," Jethro said. "Now, how do you feel?"

"Now...I'm quiet. I'm tense. I can feel something inside me unlocking, opening."

*That's the truth. I don't know what's unlocking but keep going—I want to find out.*

Jethro sucked in a breath. Our eyes connected.

The unlocking inside flung wide open like a rusted gate. It was the weirdest thing. To feel your own soul unfurling. I'd never taken the time to truly *feel* myself. To know who I was. To rifle through my history, experiences, and fears.

"I'm—I'm letting you in."

Jethro flicked the whip again. "More." The leather kissed my ribcage.

I cried out at the sweet, burning sting.

"That's what I want. That's what I need." He circled the bed again, flicking me in different spots: my hip, my bellybutton, my nipple.

*Oh, my God, my nipple!*

Fire flamed through my blood. A trickle of wetness slipped between spread thighs.

My body sang. My soul rejoiced. I'd never been so free...so unencumbered even while bound in place.

The crop licked my throat, slapping quickly on my diamond collar. The sound of chastisement and the swift burn of intoxicating pain throbbed my nipples. Jethro rained gentle punishment down my sternum toward my pussy.

My head tossed back as I writhed, wanting him to strike faster. To fuck me. Love me. Claim me.

"Does it feel good?"

"Yes," I whimpered. "Better than good. It feels..." My eyes closed as I threw myself into a maze of complexities. My body had brought me to this place, but my thoughts took over. They made this more than sex. More than love. They made this *transcendent*.

Jethro struck me quicker—like tiny breaths—working his way all over my body.

"Please." I thrashed. "Take me. I need you inside me."

"Why? Why do you need me inside you?"

*Why?*

There were so many reasons why. One fell from my lips before I could think. "Because I can't handle the intensity anymore!"

Jethro sighed heavily, wrenching my eyes open. "Now you know...now you know how it feels to live with my curse." He struck me particularly hard. "There is no stopping for me. No reprieve. It's one piercing thing after another."

The agony in his voice sent me higher; I strained for a release. "That's awful. So awful." I couldn't handle the poignant need to explode another second. "But please, Jethro. I need you."

"Quiet." He struck my clit again. "I love feeling what you feel. I love having no barrier between us."

*Shit!*

I almost came. My core clenched; sparks detonated in my blood. I never expected something like this could unravel me so quickly.

I was lost.

Drifting on an ocean of everything.

"God, you're wet." Jethro dragged the tip of the whip through my folds.

I moaned.

He consumed me. His body was supple and noble—every muscle proudly ridged. Something had melted inside him. He was no longer ice but magma. No longer snow but sunshine.

I wanted to grab him. Hug him. Fuck him.

My thoughts became a froth of temper. "Take me, Jethro. Fuck me, Kite. I can't do this any longer."

I didn't think he'd obey, but without a word, he threw the whip across the room and climbed on the bed. Straddling me, he fisted his cock and bent to kiss me. "You want me to end your misery. If I do, can you end mine?"

He didn't give me a chance to reply. His mouth crashed on mine, and we turned savage. Biting, licking, tasting. His hand clutched my hair, pulling hard, forcing my mouth to open and take whatever he gave.

His hot thighs imprisoned my hips, twitching as he worked his cock.

The kiss ended. He collapsed on top of me.

I moaned at the comfort of having him touch me after so many teasing strikes.

"God, Nila, you're incredible." His lips covered mine again, feeding me his voice. "I want to make you come. I want to come inside you over and fucking over again."

His hips slotted between mine. His fingers dove inside me, testing my wetness. Then I screamed as he filled me with one wicked impale.

There was no pain. No bruising. Only the most majestic completion imaginable.

I couldn't hold on. I wanted to grip his strong shoulders for balance. I wanted to wrap my legs around him for connection.

He thrust deeper, slipping through my wet heat. In some mystical way, this felt like an ending to everything he'd been and the beginning of everything we'd become.

A beginning he was finally strong enough to face.

*It's exquisite.*
*It's raw.*
*It's debasing*
*and*
*mind-blowing*
*and*
*real.*

I gritted my teeth, riding the tsunami of pleasure. Jethro took hostage of every thought and dream I'd ever had, making it his.

My body hummed with possession. Every part of me was ravaged, disconnected, unable to concentrate on anything but the way he thrust and took.

I cried out, biting his shoulder as every cell tightened,

quickened.

"Come. I need you to come," Jethro panted in my ear.

I'd never been commanded to do something outside of my control. I never believed I could do something as miraculous as come with only a few words. But his cock stretched and filled. His lower belly rubbed and stroked my clit and every part of me combusted.

My body obeyed him utterly. I let go, spindling into the sharpest, quickest orgasm I'd ever had.

"Fuck, Nila." Jethro pinned me to the mattress, taking me faster. His guttural groan wrapped around my body, replacing it with unlimited pleasure. "Goddammit, you feel good." His face buried in my hair; his heart beat a war drum against mine.

I wanted to cradle him—give him safe harbour to come undone and find himself in this new world we'd conjured.

Thrust after thrust. We were stripped totally bare.

Jethro never stopped. His arms curled around the top of my head, keeping me in place. The ropes around my ankles jerked with every rock, bruising me.

I dissolved into his embrace. I was exhausted and spent. Aftershocks of my orgasm continued to squeeze my pussy.

Jethro suddenly reached toward his bedside and pulled a knife from the drawer. I tensed as he sliced the binds around my wrists and pulled my torso up with him. He sat on his knees, still inside me. Twisting around, he sawed the sash around my ankles, freeing me.

Throwing the blade to the carpet, he cushioned me in his lap. "Wrap your legs around me. I've got you." His arms cradled my spine, creating a basket of muscle. I melted into him, bouncing with every thrust.

His large hand captured my nape, pressing me firmly, keeping my body pinned close and his cock deep inside.

With a savage rock, he groaned, "I'm going to ride you. And then I'm going to come."

I nodded, every part of me drained. I'd never been so used, so abused, so *sleepy*.

His lips found mine, pouring energy down my throat as he drove deeper and deeper. Straddling his lap gave him complete control. His cock hit the top of me again and again.

His kiss turned demanding. His hands roved up my back and around my sides to palm my breasts. His dextrous fingers tweaked my nipples, tugging in time with his thrusts.

I moaned, biting his throat as I fell into him.

"You have the most incredible body." His hands swooped to my back again, moulding me tight against him. "You're so damn wet. I fit inside you. You take me completely." Wonder dripped in his voice, sheer joy at finding me and me finding him.

"Hold onto me. I need to take you hard and fast." He grabbed my hips, hoisting me higher on his lap. He looked at me.

I gasped at the molten love evident in his gaze. Tears prickled my eyes.

*He loves me.*

He'd said it. Whispered it. Cursed it. But now he'd shown me: he unequivocally loved me.

He smiled softly. "You sense what I'm feeling, don't you?"

I shook my head. "I don't sense, I know. It's not a feeling but the truth in your eyes."

His fingers dug into my hips, pressing me down, giving me nowhere to hide. "You should know you're it for me, Nila. There's no turning back from this. I'm on your side until the end." He surged upright, filling me endlessly deep. His hand disappeared into my hair, wrapping the long black strands around his wrist, holding me firm. "I love you."

The burn in my scalp scorched my body.

To be so adored but controlled.

To be so loved but dominated.

The combination was the best aphrodisiac in the world.

He slammed into me, bouncing me in his embrace. My arms wrapped around him as we glued ourselves together, holding on and riding each other fast.

My muscles burned, my legs wobbled, and my scalp yelped in pain, and through it all, another orgasm brewed.
*Shit, I can't come again.*
I'd collapse.
I'd never come twice so quickly. I wouldn't survive—I knew it as surely as I knew my heart was one beat away from exploding.
Jethro kept riding, kept fucking. And my body kept responding, gathering tighter and stronger, wanting to release and snap me into paradise.
"I'm yours, Nila. All fucking yours." Jethro's lips skated over my jaw.
I became nothing but lust and spirals and mindless passion. The ache in my womb increased, throbbing with the familiar agonising urge to let go.
His harsh breathing filled my ears.
My body detonated again.
I cried out as I clenched with delirium.
I didn't think I had the power to combust so spectacularly. I feared I'd splinter into teeny, tiny pieces and flutter away in the breeze.
"Christ, yes. Take me." He thrust hard and deep, following me. His teeth latched onto my shoulder as we rode waves of bliss. Spurt after spurt, he filled me, coming apart in my arms.
Minutes passed where all I could think about was liquid. Liquid and wetness and heat. We clung to each other until my muscles started to seize and cramp, and a chill turned my sweat into goosebumps.
I never wanted to let him go.
Jethro slowly pulled out, laying me gently on the bed. Our ragged breathing matched as he pulled me into him, spooning me, protecting me.
If I could move, I'd cuddle him back but I had nothing left. I was drained beyond all comprehension.
"Thank you." Jethro kissed my hair. "Thank you for letting me in." His arms squeezed tighter, giving me gratitude in

both actions and words.

I yawned, snuggling into him.

"Was it hard?" he asked quietly. "Was it painful to look inside yourself?"

I shook my head, unable to keep my eyes from closing. "No. To be honest, it was scarily easy."

"It's not hard to let go when you trust the person you're with."

I nodded. "You made it right, Jethro. You made it perfect."

A few minutes passed. Sleep settled heavier on the outskirts of my thoughts.

Jethro sighed. "I want to do more with you. Fall deeper into you. Would you let me do that?"

The moment hovered. I could pretend to be asleep. I didn't have to answer. The thought of stripping myself even further scared but also excited.

"Yes," I whispered. "Yes, I would." My voice was soft and full of love.

He hugged me hard. "I love you, Nila." Pressing a kiss on my cheek, he said, "I've only just started. I have so many ways to show you the depth of my feelings."

My eyes flared. Did he want more *today*? There was no way I had the stamina or strength. I was utterly spent.

"You can do whatever you want with me. But first, I have to sleep." With his body heat and legs tangled in mine, I'd never felt so safe.

Jethro chuckled. "I want more—so much more. More than you can possibly imagine. But I'm patient. I've waited this long for you. I can wait another hour or two." Kissing me again, he murmured, "Sleep, Ms. Weaver. Dream of me. And then I'll steal you away."

He gathered me closer.

Together, we drifted from this world into dreams.

# Jethro

LIFE WAS PERFECT.

The most perfect it'd ever been.

I couldn't remember the last time I'd been this happy or this uncaring about my fate.

Nila was mine. I'd found my one true place.

I should've known a man like me would never be worthy of such a gift. I should've known that death was around the corner. I should've seen the devil rubbing his hands together, waiting.

I didn't deserve peace or togetherness or a future I wanted more than fucking anything.

There was nothing good left for me.

Only death.

No matter that I'd lived my entire life beneath death's shadow, no matter that I'd expected it around every trial, and feared it every time I closed my eyes to sleep, I still wasn't prepared for when it finally came for me.

It was quick.

It was painful.

It was over.

# Nila

I'M SO LUCKY.

I *looked over the balcony. Below me, bright lights and camera flashes immortalized my newest collection. The grey dress I'd made before paying the Third Debt caused a standing ovation among critics and fashionistas alike.*

*"You did so well, wife."*

*I swayed into my husband's arms. Jethro's hair caught the lights, making him seem like some fantasy knight come to life. We'd eloped two weeks ago. We'd barely left the bedroom since.*

*My pussy clenched just thinking about what we would do when we returned home after the show.*

*Something cold and sticky splashed against my silver ball gown. Time turned to slow motion as I looked down in horror.*

*Blood.*

*Gallons upon gallons of blood.*

*It stained my bodice, train, hands...everything.*

*The audience below no longer watched the show but looked up at us. At me specifically. "What?" I screeched. "What did I ever do to you?"*

*Then, I heard the most dreadful sound in the world. The symphony of dying. The excruciating noise of ending life.*

"Get up, you filthy fucking whore!"

My eyes wrenched open. My heart lurched into my mouth. Warmth and cocooned-safety was traded for biting fingers and hard floor as Cut wrenched me out of bed and threw me across the room.

"Wh—no!" I landed on my wrist, screaming in agony.

"What the—" Jethro's sleepy voice rang out but was sliced short by a punch to his face.

"You motherfucking backstabbing son of a fucking bitch." Cut rammed his fist into Jethro's jaw again, drawing blood, crunching cheekbones. "Get up." He tore off the sheets, jerking him from his bed.

Jethro groaned, falling into a pile of limbs at his father's feet.

"No, wait!" I crawled forward, flinching at my wrist.

Daniel appeared, blocking me with his hands on his hips. "Ah, ah, ah, little Weaver. You can no longer interfere with family matters."

Through the barricade of his legs, I watched Cut kick Jethro repeatedly in the stomach, screaming obscenities, puce with fury. "Did I not give you every fucking chance? Did I not respect you and trust in you as my fucking son!" He kicked him again. "Goddammit, you leave me no choice!"

*This can't be real.*

It had to be a dream…a nightmare.

*Please, don't let this be real.*

Cut turned his back on Jethro, storming toward me with throbbing anger. "And you! You're done meddling with my fucking family, girl. You're through. *Both* of you!"

Grabbing my hair, he jerked me to my feet.

He strength was insane—no residue of the drugs Jethro had used. No hint that he'd been unnaturally asleep for hours. He was a demon.

I screamed, dangling in his enraged hold. My bare legs showed the faint whip marks from Jethro's attentions, and his t-shirt I'd slipped on when I went to the bathroom barely covered my black knickers. "Let me go!"

"You and him—you've fucked me over for the last time." Cut breathed hard, his face gleaming with sweat. "Did he think

I wouldn't notice? That I would let you get away with this shit!"

I fought his hold, willing tears to hide. "I don't know what you're talking about! Stop hurting me. Let me go!"

Daniel cackled. "You know *exactly* what we're talking about, bitch." He marched over to his brother, scooping the bloody body of Jethro into his arms. Jethro moaned, his eyes squeezed and blood rivering from his mouth. He tried to fight Daniel off, but the vicious attack before left him half dead.

"I don't! Leave him alone."

"Yes, you fucking do," Cut snarled. "I just witnessed the so-called video of you paying the Third Debt. Kestrel thought I'd buy his bullshit doctored video?!" His eyes turned deathly cold. "Two of my sons. Both of them betraying me. But it's the last time. The last fucking time they make a mockery out of me."

Dragging me from Jethro's room, he didn't stop or care that I crawled and stumbled beside him. His fingers noosed in my hair, leaving me no choice but to fumble in agony.

I couldn't see Jethro, but Daniel's footfalls vibrated the carpet behind me.

"Please!" I scratched Cut's hands over and over, but he didn't flinch. Too amped on fury to feel a thing. "Please, let us go!"

"Oh, I'll let you go alright. I'll fucking let you go to Hades."

Hawksridge Hall covered acres of land with twining halls and cavernous rooms, but it seemed like a postage stamp with how fast we left the bachelor wing and burst into the day parlour with its swan-silk loveseats and ornamental music boxes.

The moment we exploded through the doors, Cut threw me forward. I fell with vertigo and inertia, slamming to the floor. I crawled away as fast as I could. Daniel mimicked his father, tossing Jethro to his knees, kicking him violently in the gut.

Jethro coughed loudly, air refusing to filter into his lungs.

He fell to his side, gasping, bleeding.

I scrambled toward him, but Daniel stepped in front of me. "Look behind you, whore."

I glowered. I wanted heaven to smite him into stone. "Leave him alone!"

He chuckled. "You sure about that?" Leaning over me, he yanked me to my feet, twisting my head to look behind me. "You sure you choose him?"

I fought in his hold. I worked up saliva to spit in his face. But then I set eyes upon my undoing.

The past twenty-four hours, disappeared.

The love I'd found, vanished.

The promises I'd made, disintegrated.

Gone.

Dust.

Ash.

No. *No, no, no.*

I keened in awful horror.

*This can't be true!*

"Threads," Vaughn mumbled through bleeding lips. His eyes were puffy and half-shut, his body as mangled and bruised as Jethro's. He sat on the floor between two Black Diamond brothers who I didn't recognise. His entire demeanour weary and beaten. He was no longer Robin Hood sent to rescue me but a thief about to be killed.

Terror fed my heart—it raced out of my chest straight toward my twin.

"No!" I tore myself from Daniel's grip and crawled toward V. Tears waterfalled down my cheeks. Guilt and self-hatred layered. I'd done this. *I'd* cause this. V was hurt all because I made a Hawk choose me over everyone.

"V!"

Vaughn shook off his handler's hold, throwing himself toward me. We crashed together, hands clutching, arms hugging, hearts thundering. "What happened? Are you okay?"

V hugged me hard. "I'm okay, Threads. I'm so sorry."

Daniel stood over us, arms crossed; his lips twisted in a sadistic laugh. "Fucking cocksucker deserved it."

Jethro let out an agonising cry. My attention split from my twin to my soul-mate. Cut kicked him, his fists clenched and ready to rain. "I saw the fucking video, Kite." Cut's voice was death and eyes evil incarnate. "Kes might know computers, but did you honestly think I wouldn't notice!"

Everything happened too fast. Way, way too fast.

*What is going on?!*

"Stop!" Jethro shouted, bracing himself for another kick. "Let me explain."

"Explain?" Cut laughed coldly. "Explain the fact that you drugged Daniel and me, then proceeded to splice a fucking video of Emma Weaver. You had the fucking nerve to trick me into believing we'd had a turn with Nila?"

Vaughn choked, his face turning ghostly. "What—what are they talking about, Threads?"

As much as I feared for my brother, my loyalties were to Jethro first. He was my family as much as V was. I staggered to my feet, balling my hands. "Don't take it out on him. It was my idea."

Cut paused, his eyes spinning with hatred. "Your idea?" He stalked forward. "*Your* idea. So you were the stupid one to believe I didn't imprint every moment of that night. I remember everything about Emma. I have fucking dreams of using her. Do you think I wouldn't fucking notice!"

My heart split with a thousand swords, thinking of my mother being hurt by Cut. But that was the past. She was gone. I couldn't save her anymore. But I could save Jethro and V. They were mine to protect—mine to rescue.

"I'm sorry! Just forget it. Leave my brother alone and don't hurt Jethro anymore."

Cut dragged hands through his hair, shaking his head with abhorrent disbelief. "You think I'll listen to you? Why should I, bitch? What will you give me in return?"

Jethro stumbled to his knees, wrapping an arm around his

side. Every breath rattled in his lungs like broken china. "Don't, Nila. It was my idea. My mistake." Speaking to Cut, he glared. "Do whatever you want with me, but leave her the fuck out of it. Kill me. End the Debt Inheritance. Let this all be over!"

Cut whirled on his firstborn. "This isn't over until *I* say it's over." Pointing a livid finger at me, Cut snarled, "She didn't pay. The Third Debt was never completed."

Daniel stepped in front of me, slapping me hard on the cheek. My head whipped, and a vertigo wave made me trip sideways. "You fucking drugged us. That's against the rules."

"Leave her alone, you bastard!" V shouted, trying unsuccessfully to climb to his feet.

Vertigo attacked harder. I swallowed, doing my best not to vomit. My cheek ached but it was nothing compared to the pressuring terror building inside.

I cried, "Just let him go!"

*Please, end this. Someone save this disaster, before it's too late.*

"Don't touch him!" I shouted again. "Please, leave him alone."

Daniel snickered. "Leave who alone, princess? Your pussy brother or my brother who you're fucking and no one else?"

Vaughn threw himself at Daniel's legs. With a yelp, Daniel punched him but fell sideways, landing on the carpet. The fight didn't last long. Vaughn was strong and stayed fit with regular gym visits, but it was nothing compared to Daniel's manic insanity.

Rolling away, Daniel kicked him right in the jaw.

V crumpled.

My heart shattered. "No!"

"What on *earth* is the kerfuffle in here?" a prim, papery voice said.

All eyes turned on the recent addition to the parlour.

Bonnie Hawk.

Her attention surveyed her son, grandsons, and me before smiling coldly. Leaning heavily on a brand new walking stick, she snapped her fingers. "Jasmine. Kestrel. Would you come and join us, please?"

The sudden madness seemed to cease—her appearance granted a strange kind of peace to the battleground. She acted as if we'd all popped by for tea and cakes, completely ignoring or not caring that blood stained the pristine carpet and my brother was unconscious at her feet.

My heart stuck in tar as Jasmine rolled sedately into the room. Her bronze eyes hid her terror, but her face couldn't hide her dislike. She didn't look away from Jethro.

Jethro looked back at his sister, hanging his head in shame.

Kestrel came into the room, his hands tied behind his back, his face a mismatch of purple, black, and blue.

He gave me a sad smile, flicking his attention between Jethro, V, and his father.

"Glad you could join us," Cut snarled, glaring at his offspring.

Jasmine sat taller in her chair, her pink angora jumper matching the deep rose of the blanket thrown over her legs. "Father, don't do this. Think about what this will—"

"He knows the consequences, child," Bonnie interrupted. "And he's accepted the payment as a necessary sacrifice." Her matching skirt and blazer were black, as if she were already in mourning. A string of pearls graced her throat, bobbing with every swallow. Her eyes landed on Cut. "It's your decision, son."

Cut nodded, getting his temper under control, slipping back into a ruthless, terrifying man with far too much power.

I trembled, trying to work out the dynamics in the room. *What is going on?*

No answers came, and in a seamless move, Cut reached behind him and pulled free a pistol.

My heart stopped.

I stood transfixed in the centre, stuck between Jethro and Vaughn. I couldn't move. Couldn't decide who was the most at risk of a madman waving a gun.

"Help him up, will you, Daniel?" Cut pointed the muzzle

at Jethro.

I blinked back another vertigo spell as I darted forward. "No!"

Cut trained the gun on me. "Do not move, Ms. Weaver."

Daniel obeyed, grabbing Jethro under his arms, yanking him upright. The moment he was on his feet, Jethro bent forward, looking like he would throw up or pass out. Sweat darkened his hair, his naked thighs bunched with effort to remain standing. He looked so defenceless in a t-shirt and boxer-briefs—clear evidence that we'd broken every rule and slept together.

Cut cocked the weapon, glaring at his son. "I'm going to give you one last choice, Jethro."

Jethro shook his head, smacking his lips. "No more choices. Just kill me and let the Weavers go." His eyes flickered to my unconscious brother. "*Both* of them."

Daniel snickered—completely in his element. Bonnie just watched while Jasmine and Kes remained mute with nerves.

No one spoke. No one wanted to bring attention to themselves while Cut wielded a gun.

"One more choice," Cut repeated. "You better choose wisely." Planting his stance in the thick carpet, he raised the weapon.

Jasmine whimpered as the muzzle pointed at Kes. "Father, please...don't do this. We love you. We're your children!"

"Silence," Bonnie commanded. "You will do as I say, child. No more talking without permission."

Jasmine seemed to wilt, but her shoulders remained defiant.

Kestrel puffed out his chest, facing death with the decorum of any worthy fighter. "You'll never live with yourself if you do this," he muttered. "I'm your son."

Cut bared his teeth. "You ceased being my son the moment you uploaded the atrocity of a video and thought I was so fucking stupid to buy it." His head whipped to Jethro. "Choose, Jet!"

"I don't know what you want me to do!" Jethro yelled. "You expect me to name a sibling for you to murder? Why would I when it was all my fault? They had nothing to do with this. Nothing!"

Cut stiffened, closing his eye to aim.

I ran forward—to do what? Who knew. But I was too late.

"Wrong choice." His finger squeezed the trigger.

The gunpowder ignited.

The room ricocheted with noise.

A bullet leapt from the gun, tearing faster than sight to lodge into a Hawk offspring.

"No!" Jethro bellowed, charging forward.

A flare of red appeared on Kestrel's chest the second before he collapsed to his knees. His face went blank with shock, lips round with disbelief.

"You never had a choice," Cut murmured, aiming at his daughter.

Jethro moved the second Cut pulled the trigger.

I saw it all.

I felt it all.

One moment, Jethro was alive. His heart beating. His soul linked with mine.

The next, he threw himself in front of his wheelchair-bound sister, accepting the bullet into his own body.

I didn't react for the longest moment.

I couldn't believe the story before me.

He couldn't be dead.

*He can't be dead.*

*He's not dead!*

I staggered forward, my hands clamping over my mouth.

*He cannot be dead!*

Jasmine screamed as her brother fell over her, his torso slamming against her atrophied legs, his knees crashing to the carpet.

And then he rolled.

He rolled off his beloved sister, lying face down on the

carpet.

"*Nooooooooo!*" I threw myself beside him, shaking him, begging him. "Jethro. Please, open your eyes!"

Daniel laughed. Bonnie stared. Jasmine screamed.

And through it all, Cut said nothing.

I could barely stay in one piece. My body wanted to dissolve into a billion fractals and float away in despair. I trembled so badly, it took two attempts to roll Jethro onto his back.

His eyes were closed, lips slack, blood blooming from his chest like a morbid rose—petals upon petals spreading with glowing crimson.

"Jethro…" Tears gushed down my face. Breaths were non-existent as I gagged and choked on sobs. "Please, don't leave me. Not now."

Then I was plucked up and away, dragged further and further from my lover.

I lost awareness of my body.

I shut down.

In my mind, I still kneeled beside Jethro feeling him grow colder by the second—leaving me.

Cut appeared in my vision, his face tight and strained. I hung lifeless in Daniel's arms, unable to comprehend what just happened.

I was numb.

I was lifeless.

I was gone.

"Listen to me, Ms. Weaver. I'm only going to say this once." Turning me in Daniel's arms, Cut pointed at Vaughn. My brother lay splayed on the carpet just like Jethro and Kestrel, but unlike them, he was still with me. Still alive. Still in danger.

"Your brother is a recent addition to our family. He's what you'd call collateral." He stroked the sulphur-smoking muzzle of his gun. "I'm sick of you not obeying and I'm sick to fucking death of pinning hopes on a son who isn't trustworthy. There's been a change of plans."

Daniel held me closer. "A *good* change of plans."

Cut pointed at V. "If you're good, he lives. If you're bad, he dies." He shrugged. "It couldn't be any simpler than that."

V moaned, rousing.

I wanted to feel something, but I'd switched off. Unable to cope.

I was a brittle leaf about to turn to dust in the wind.

Cut whispered, "Jethro and Kestrel are no longer your concern. They've paid for their lies and stupidity. I only hope you're smarter than they were."

Daniel sneered. "Only the worms will be interested in them now."

*No...it can't be true.*

Bending over me, Cut cast both Daniel and me in his monstrous shadow. "You should keep that in mind. I won't hesitate to hurt you, Ms. Weaver. Think how easily I dispatched my sinning sons." His face shadowed. "I would be afraid if I were you. Afraid and *highly* obedient."

Cupping my chin, he pressed a dry kiss on my mouth.

My innards shrunk and died.

Jasmine's sobs were background noise. V's curses nothing more than a hum.

I'd just lost everything in a few short minutes.

*He's just lying there.*

*Get up, Jethro. Please, get up.*

Cut ran his gun over my jaw. "Say hello to my new heir, Nila."

*No, he can't mean...*

Daniel jiggled me in his arms, never letting me go. He cupped my breasts with harsh fingers. "Be polite, whore. Say hello."

I clamped my lips together.

I kept staring at Jethro, begging for this to be some terrible mistake.

"Along with inheriting my power, my fortune, and my

title, Daniel has acquired the Debt Inheritance's responsibility." Cut placed himself in front of me, blocking Jethro's bleeding body.

Every word made me crave a bullet. I wanted to end it. I wanted to chase Jethro to the underworld and leave everything behind.

*There's nothing left. Not anymore.*

Bonnie shuffled forward, her cane sinking into the carpet. "We've all agreed to nominate a new master. If Daniel carries out the remainder of the tasks, he will take over my son's position before his thirtieth."

She came closer, bringing the stench of death with her. Her hazel eyes flashed, red lips spread in a victory grin. "When you left two months ago, I knew something special would have to be done upon your return. No one makes a mockery of my house like your family has done without paying a serious price. Consider this the beginning of a bigger debt. You owe us for the inconvenience your brother caused."

Cut laughed, pressing cold fingers beneath my chin, angling my face to his. "Understand, Ms. Weaver, Daniel will carry out the Final Debt. And if he does, as I trust he will, everything goes to him. And unlike my previous sons, he will *not* disappoint me." Placing another dry kiss on my lips, he murmured, "Congratulations Ms. Weaver. You now belong to Daniel 'Buzzard' Hawk…

…

And he's going to make your life a living fucking hell."

## Fourth Debt
## Releasing 11th August
Updates, teasers, and exclusive news will be released on

www.pepperwinters.com

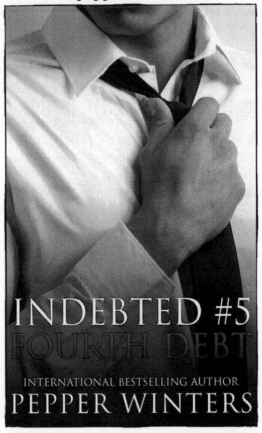

*"We'd won. We'd cut through the lies and treachery and promised an alliance that would free us both. But even as we won, we lost. We didn't see what was coming. We didn't know we had to plan a resurrection."*

Nila Weaver fell in love. She gifted her entire soul to a man she believed was worthy. And in the process, she destroyed herself. Three debts paid, the fourth only days away. The Debt Inheritance has almost claimed another victim.

Jethro Hawk fell in love. He let down his walls to a woman he believed was his cure. For a moment, he was free. But then he paid the ultimate price.

There is no more love. Only war. Hope is dead. Now, there is only death all around them.

\*\*\*Information on HSP & VEP taken from
http://healing.about.com/od/empathic/a/HSP_hallowes.htm.\*\*\*

\*\*\*Jethro's comment about his condition was taken from:
Pearl S. Buck, (1892-1973), recipient of the Pulitzer Prize in 1932 and of the Nobel Prize in Literature in 1938, said the following about Highly Sensitive People:

"The truly creative mind in any field is no more than this:

A human creature born abnormally, inhumanly sensitive.

To him... a touch is a blow,
a sound is a noise,
a misfortune is a tragedy,
a joy is an ecstasy,
a friend is a lover,
a lover is a god,
and failure is death.

# About the Author

Pepper Winters is a New York Times and USA Today International Bestseller. She loves dark romance, star-crossed lovers, and the forbidden taboo. She strives to write a story that makes the reader crave what they shouldn't, and delivers tales with complex plots and unforgettable characters.

After chasing her dreams to become a full-time writer, Pepper has earned recognition with awards for best Dark Romance, best BDSM Series, and best Dark Hero. She's an #1 iBooks bestseller, along with #1 in Erotic Romance, Romantic Suspense, Contemporary, and Erotica Thriller. She's also honoured to wear the IndieReader Badge for being a Top 10 Indie Bestseller, and recently signed a two book deal with Hachette. Represented by Trident Media, her books have garnered foreign and audio interest and are currently being translated into numerous languages. They will be in available in bookstores worldwide.

Her Dark Romance books include:
**Tears of Tess (Monsters in the Dark #1)**
**Quintessentially Q (Monsters in the Dark #2)**
**Twisted Together (Monsters in the Dark #3)**
**Debt Inheritance (Indebted #1)**

First Debt (Indebted Series #2)
Second Debt (Indebted Series #3)
Third Debt (Indebted Series #4)

Her Grey Romance books include:
**Destroyed**

Upcoming releases are
**Fourth Debt (Indebted #5)**
**Ruin & Rule (Motorcycle romance)**
**Final Debt (Indebted #6)**
**Je Suis a Toi (Monsters in the Dark Novella)**
**Forbidden Flaws (Contemporary Romance)**

To be the first to know of upcoming releases, please follow her on her website
**Pepper Winters**

You can stalk her here:

**Pinterest**
**Facebook Pepper Winters**
**Twitter**
**Instagram**
**Website**
**Facebook Group**
**Goodreads**

She loves mail of any kind: **pepperwinters@gmail.com**
All other titles and updates can be found on her **Goodreads Page.**

**Bet my life** by Imagine Dragons
**Shots** by Imagine Dragons
**Gold** by Imagine Dragons
**I Know You** by Skylar Grey
**The Fall** by Imagine Dragons
**Coming Back** by Dean Ray
**Let it Go Tonight** by Foxes
**Yours** by Ella Henderson
**Echo** by Foxes
**Battlefield** by Jordin Sparks
**Hurts** by Only You
**Bleeding Out** by Imagine Dragons
**Tainted Love** by Marilyn Manson

# Sneak Peek into Ruin & Rule

Coming 7th July 2015

**Ruin & Rule (Pure Corruption MC #1)
Coming 7<sup>th</sup> July 2015 from Forever Romance
(Grand Central)
In Bookshops & Online**

**Learn about Arthur Killian who you just met in Third Debt.**

I love reading MC books but this has to be the best one I've read! I couldn't put it down —***Nikki Mccrae, Amazon Review***

One of the best stories I've ever read. Period. —***Tamicka Birch, Amazon Reviewer***

Ruin & Rule is another dark masterpiece from Pepper Winters. Buckle yourself in for a wild ride that is pure page-turning bliss! —***Rachel, Goodreads***

\*

*"We met in a nightmare. The in-between world where time had no power over reason. We fell in love. We fell hard. But then we woke up. And it was over..."*

She is a woman divided. Her past, present, and future are as twisted as the lies she's lived for the past eight years. Desperate to get the truth, she must turn to the one man who may also be her greatest enemy...

He is the president of Pure Corruption MC. A heartless biker and retribution-deliverer. He accepts no rules, obeys no one, and lives only to reap revenge on those who wronged him. And now he has stolen her, body and soul.

Can a woman plagued by mystery fall in love with the man who refuses to face the truth? And can a man drenched in darkness forgo his quest for vengeance-and finally find redemption?

**Pre-order Links to Buy on All Major Online Stores**

# Prologue

WE MET IN a nightmare.

The in-between world where time had no power over rhyme, reason, or connection. We met. We stared. We knew.

There was no distortion from the outside world. No right or wrong. No confusion or battles from hearts and minds.

Just us. In our silent dream-world.

That nightmare became our home. Planting ghosts, raising fantasies. Entwined together in our happily skewed reality.

We fell in love. We fell hard.

In those fleeting seconds of our nightmare, we lived an eternity.

But then we woke up.

And it was over.

# Chapter One

I ALWAYS BELIEVED life would grant rewards to those most worthy. I was fucking naïve. Life doesn't reward—it ruins. It ruins those most deserving and takes everything. It takes everything all while watching any remaining goodness rot to hate. *–Kill.*

\* \* \*

Darkness.

That was my world now. Literally and physically.

The back of my skull hurt from being knocked unconscious. My wrists and shoulders ached from lying on my back with them tied behind me.

Nothing was broken—at least it didn't feel that way—but everything was bruised. The fuzziness receded wisp by wisp, parting the clouds of sleep, trying to shed light on what'd happened. But there *was* no light. My eyes blinked at the endless darkness from the mask tied around my head. Anxiety twisted my stomach at having such a fundamental gift taken away.

I didn't move, but mentally catalogued my body from the tips of my toes to the last strand of hair on my head. My jaw and tongue ached from the foul rag stuffed in my mouth and my nose permitted a shallow stream of oxygen to enter—just enough to keep me alive.

Fear tried to claw its way through my mind, but I shoved it away. I deliberately suppressed panic in order to assess my predicament rather than lose myself to terror.

*Fear never helps, only hinders.*

My senses came back, creeping tentatively, as if afraid whoever had stolen me would notice their return.

Sound: the squeak of brakes, the creak of a vehicle settling from motion to stopping.

Touch: The skin on my right forearm stung, throbbing with a mixture of soreness and sharpness. A burn perhaps?

Smell: Dank rotting vegetables and the astringent, pungent scent of fear—but it wasn't mine. It was theirs.

It wasn't just me being kidnapped.

My heart flurried, drinking in their terror. It made my breath quicken and legs itch to run. Forcing myself to ignore the outside world, I focused inward. Clutching my inner strength where calmness was a need rather than a luxury.

I refused to lose myself in a fog of tears. Desperation was a curse and I wouldn't succumb, because I had every intention of being prepared for what might happen next.

I hated the sniffles and stifled sobs of others around me. Their bleak sadness tugged at my heartstrings, making me fight with my own preservation, replacing it with concern for theirs.

*Get through this, then worry about them.*

I didn't think this was a simple opportunistic snatch. Whoever had stolen me planned it. The hunch grew stronger as I searched inside for any liquor remnants or the smell of cigarettes.

Had I been at a party? Nightclub?

Nothing.

I hadn't been stupid or reckless. *I think...*

No hint or clue as to where I'd been or what I'd been doing when they'd come for me.

I wriggled, trying to move away from the stench. My bound wrists protested, stinging as the rope around them gnawed into my flesh like twine-beasts. My ribs bellowed, along with my head. There was no give in my restraints. I stopped trying to move, preserving my energy.

I tried to swallow.

No saliva.

I tried to speak.

No voice.

I tried to remember what happened.

I tried to remember....

Panic.

Nothing.

*I can't remember.*

"Get up, bitch," a man said. Something jabbed me in the ribs. "Won't tell you again. *Get.*"

I froze as my mind hurtled me from present to past.

*I'll miss you so much," she wailed, hugging me tighter.*

*"I'm not dying, you know." I tried to untangle myself, looking over my shoulder at the 'final call' flashing for my flight. I hated being late for anything. Let alone my one chance at escaping and finding out the truth once and for all.*

*"Call me the moment you get there."*

*"Promise." I drew a cross over my heart—*

The memory shattered as my horizontal body suddenly went vertical in one swoop.

Who was that girl? Why did I have no memory of it ever happening?

"I said get up, bitch." The man breathed hard in my ear, sending a waft of reeking breath over me. The blindfold stole my sight, but it left my nose woefully unprotected.

Unfortunately.

My captor shoved me forward. The ground was steady beneath my feet. The sickness plaiting with my confusion faded, leaving me cold.

My legs stumbled in the direction he wanted me to go. I hated shuffling in the darkness, not knowing where I came from or where I was being herded. There were no sounds of comfort or smothered snickers. This wasn't a masquerade.

This was real.

*This is real.*

My heart thudded harder, fear slipping through my defenses. But full-blown terror remained elusive. Slippery like a silver fish, darting on the outskirts of my mind. It was there but fleeting, keeping me clear-headed and strong.

I was grateful for that. Grateful that I maintained what dignity I had left—remaining strong even in the face of the unknown terrors lurking on the other side of my blindfold.

Moans and whimpers of other women grew in decibels as men ordered them to follow the same path I walked. Either death row or salvation, I had no choice but to inch my way forward, leaving my forgotten past behind.

I willed snippets to come back. I begged the puzzlement of my past to slot into place, so I could make sense of this horrible world I'd awoken in.

But my mind was locked to me. A fortress withholding everything I wished to know.

The pushing stopped. So did I.

Big mistake.

"Move." A cuff to the back of my head sent me wheeling forward. I didn't stop again. My bare feet traversed…wood?

Bare feet?

*Where are my shoes?*

The missing knowledge twisted my stomach.

*Where did I come from?*

*How did I end up here?*

*What's my name?*

It wasn't the terror of the unknown future that stole my false calmness. It was the fear of losing my very self. They'd stolen everything. My triumphs, my trespasses, my accomplishments, and failures.

How could I deal with this new world if I didn't know what skills I had to stay alive? How could I hope to defeat my enemy when my mind revolted and locked me out?

*Who am I?*

To have who I was deleted….it was unthinkable.

"Faster, bitch." Something cold wedged against my spine, pushing me onward. With my hands behind my back, I shuffled faster, negotiating the ground as best I could for dips or trips.

"Step down." The man grabbed my bound wrists, giving me something to lean against as my toes navigated the small steps before me.

"Again."

I obeyed.

"Last one."

I managed the small staircase without falling flat on my face.

My face.

*What do I look like?*

A loud scraping noise sounded before me. I shied back, bumping against a feminine form. The woman behind me cried out—the first verbal sound of another.

"Move." The pressure on my lower back came again, and I obeyed. Inching forward until the stuffy air of old vegetables and must was replaced by...copper and metallic...*blood?*

*Why...why is that so familiar?*

I gasped as my mind free-fell into another memory.

*"I don't think I can do this." I darted away, throwing up in the rubbish bin in the classroom. The unique stench of blood curdled my stomach.*

*"Don't over think it. It's not what you're doing to the animal to make it bleed. It's what you're doing to make it live." My professor shook his head, waiting for me to swill out my mouth and return white-faced and queasy to the operation in progress.*

*My heart splintered like a broken piece of glass, reflecting the compassion and responsibility I felt for such an innocent creature. This little puppy that'd been dumped in a plastic bag to die after being shot with BB gun pellets. He'd survive only if I mastered the skills to stem his internal bleeding and embrace the vocation I was called to do.*

*Inhaling the scent of blood, I let it invade my nostrils, scald my throat, and impregnate my soul. I drank its coppery essence. I drenched myself in the smell of the creatures' life-force until it no longer affected me.*

*Picking up a scalpel, I said, "I'm ready—"*

"Holy fuck!" The man guiding me forward suddenly whacked the base of my spine. The hard pain shoved me forward and I tripped.

"Wire—get me fucking reinforcements. He's started a motherfucking war!"

Wind and body-buffets swarmed me as men charged from behind. The darkness I lived in suddenly came alive with sound.

Bullets flew, impaling themselves into the metal sides of the vehicle I'd just stepped from. Pings and ricochets echoed in my ear. Curses bellowed; moans of pain threaded like a breeze.

Someone grabbed my arm, swinging me to the side. "Get down!" The inertia of his throw knocked me off balance. With my wrists bound together, I had nothing to grab with, no way to protect myself from falling.

I fell.

My stomach swooped as tumbled off a small platform and smashed against the ground.

Dirt, damp grass, and moldy leaves replaced the stench of blood, cutting through the cloying sharpness of spilled metallic. My mouth opened, gasping in pain. Blades of grass tickled my lips as my cheek stuck to wet mud.

My shoulder screamed with agony, but I ignored the new injury. My mind clung to the unlocked memory. The fleeting recollection of my profession.

*I'm a vet.*

The sense of homecoming and security that one little snippet brought was priceless. My soul snarled for more, suddenly ravenous for missing information.

I skipped straight from fumbling uncertainty into starvation for *more*.

*Tell me! Show me. Who am I?*

I searched inside for more clues. But it was like trying to grab onto an elusive dream, fading faster and faster the harder I chased.

I couldn't remember anything about medicine or how to heal. All I knew was I'd been trained to embrace the scent of blood. I wasn't afraid of it. I didn't faint or suffer sickness at the sight of it pouring from an open wound.

That tiniest knowledge was enough to settle my prickling nerves and focus on the outside world again.

Battle cries. Men screaming. Men growling. The dense thuds of fists on flesh and the horrible deflection of gunshots.

I couldn't understand. Had I fallen through time and entered an alternate dimension?

Another body landed on top of mine.

I cried out, winded from a sharp poke of an elbow to my ribs.

The figure rolled away, crying softly. Feminine.

*Why aren't I crying?*

I once again searched for fear. It wasn't natural not to be afraid. I'd woken up alone, stolen, and thrown into the middle of a war, yet I wasn't hyperventilating or panicked.

My calmness was like a drug, oozing over me, muting the sharp starkness of my situation. It was bearable if I embraced courage and the knowledge that I was strong.

My hands balled, grateful for the thought. I didn't know who I was, but it didn't matter, because the person who I was in this moment mattered the most.

I had to remain segmented, so I could get through whatever was about to happen. All I had was gut instinct, quiet strength, and rationality. Everything else had been taken.

"Stop fighting, you fucking idiots!"

The loud growl rumbled like an earthquake, hushing the battle in one fell swoop. Whoever had spoken had power.

Immense power. Colossal power.

A shiver darted over my skin.

"What the fuck happened? Have you lost your goddamn lovin' mind?" a man yelled.

A sound of a short scuffle, then the fresh whiff of tilled dirt graced my nose.

"It's done. Throw down your weapons and bend a fucking knee." The same earthquake rumbled. The weight of his command pushed me harder against the damp ground.

"I'm not bending nothing, you asshole. You aren't my

Prez!"

"I am. Have been for the past four years."

"You're not. You're his *bitch*. Don't think his power is yours."

Another fight—muffled fists and kicks. It ended swiftly with a painful groan.

The earthquake voice came again. "Open your eyes and follow the red fucking river. Your chosen—the one you hand-picked to slaughter me and take over the Club—he's dead. Did you ever stop to think Wallstreet made me Prez for a fucking reason?"

Another moan.

"*I'm* the chosen one. I'm the one who knows the family secrets, absorbed the legacy, and earned his way into power. You don't know shit. *Nobody* does. So bend a fucking knee and respect."

Another tremor ran down my back.

Silence for a time, apart from the squelch of boots and heavy breathing. Then a barely muttered curse, "You'll die. One way or another, we won't put up with a Dagger as a Prez. We're the Corrupts, goddammit. Having a traitor rule us is a fucking joke."

"*I'm* the traitor? The man who obeys your leader? Who guides in his stead? *I'm* the traitor when you try and rally my brothers in a war?" A heavy thud of a fist connected with flesh. "No...I'm not. You are."

My mind raced, sucking up noises and forming wild conclusions of what happened before me. Was this World War Three? Was this the apocalypse of the life I couldn't remember? No matter how I pieced it together, I couldn't make sense of anything.

The air was thick with anticipation. I didn't know how many men stood before me. I didn't know how many corpses littered the ground, or how such violence could be permitted in the world I used to know. But I did know the ceasefire was fragile and any moment it would explode.

A single threat slithered through the grass like a snake. "I'll kill you, motherfucker. Mark my words. The true Corrupts are just waiting to take you out."

The gentle foot-thuds of someone large vibrated through the ground. "The Corrupts haven't existed for four fucking years. The moment I took the seat, it's been Pure Corruption all the way. And you're not fucking pure enough for this Club. You're done."

I flinched as a sulpheric *boom* of a gun ripped through the stagnant air.

A crash as a body fell lifeless to the grass. A soft puff of a soul escaping.

Murder.

Murder was committed right before me.

The inherent need to nurture and heal—the part of me that was as steadfast as the beat of my heart—wept with regret.

Death was something I'd fought against on a daily basis, but now I was weaponless.

I hated that a life had been stolen right before me. That I hadn't been able to stop it.

*I'm a witness.*

Any yet, I witnessed nothing.

I'd been privy to a battle but seen nothing. Knew no one. I would never be able to tell whom shot whom, or who was right and who was wrong.

My hands shook, even though I managed to stay eerily calm. *Am I in shock?* And if I was, how did I cure myself?

The woman beside me curled into a ball, her knees digging into my side. My first reaction was to repel away from the touch. I didn't know who was friend or foe. But a second reaction came quickly; the urge to share my calmness—to let her know that no matter what happened, she wasn't alone. We faced the same future—no matter how grim.

Voices cascaded over us, whispers mainly, quickly spoken orders. Every sound was heightened. Being robbed of sight made my body seek other ways in which to find clues.

"Get rid of the bodies before daybreak."

"We'll go back and make sure we're still covered."

"Send out the word. It's over. The Prez won—no anarchy today."

Each voice was distinct but my ears twitched only for one: the earthquake rumble that set my skin quivering like quicksand.

He hadn't spoken since he'd condemned someone to death and pulled the trigger. Every second of not hearing him made my heart trip faster. I wasn't afraid. I should be. I should be immobile with fear. But he invoked something in me—something primal. Just like I knew I was female and a vet—I knew his voice meant something. Every inch of me tensed, waiting for him to speak. It was wrong to crave the voice of a killer, but it was the only thing I wanted.

Needed.

*I need to know who he is.*

Wet mud sucked loudly against boots as they came closer.

The woman whimpered, but I angled my chin toward the sound, wishing my eyes were uncovered.

I wanted to see. I wanted to witness the carnage before me. Because it was a carnage. The stench of death confirmed it. It was morbid to want to see such destruction. but without my sight all of this seemed like a terrible nightmare. Nothing was grounded—completely nonsensical and far too strange.

I needed proof that this was real.

I needed concrete evidence that I wasn't mad. That my body was intact, even if my mind was not.

I sucked in a breath as warm fingers touched my cheek, angling my face upward and out of the mud. Strong hands caressed the back of my skull, fumbling with my blindfold.

The anticipation of finally getting my wish to see made me stay still and cooperative in his hold.

I didn't say a word or move. I just waited. And breathed. And listened.

The man's breath was heavy and low, interspersed with a

quick catch of pain. His fingers were swift and sure, but unable to hide the small fumble of agony.

*He's hurt.*

The pressure of the blindfold suddenly released, trading opaque darkness for a new kind of gloom.

Night-sky. Moon shine. Stars above.

Anchors of a world I knew, but no recognition of the dark-shrouded industrial estate where blood gleamed silver-black and corpses dotted the field.

*I'm alive.*

*I can see.*

The joy at having my eyes freed came and went as blazing as a comet.

Then my life ended as our gazes connected.

Green to green.

*I have green eyes.*

Down and down I spiraled, deeper and deeper into his clutches.

My life—past, present, and future—lost all purpose the second I stared into his soul.

The fear I'd been missing slammed into my heart.

I quivered. I quaked.

Something howled deep inside with age-old knowledge.

Every part of me arched toward him, then shied away in terror.

*Him.*

A nightmare come to life.

A nightmare I wanted to *live*.

If life was a tapestry, already threaded and steadfast, then he was the scissors that cut me free. He tore me out, stole me away, changed the whole prophecy of who I was meant to be.

Jaw length dark hair, tangled and sweaty, framed a square jaw, straight nose, and full lips. His five o' clock stubble held remnants of war, streaked with dirt and blood. But it was his eyes that shot a quivering arrow into my heart, spreading his emerald anger.

He froze, his body curving toward mine. Blistering hope flickered across his features. His mouth fell open and love so achingly deep glowed in his gaze. "What—" A leg gave out, making him kneel beside me. His hands shook as he cupped my face, his fingers digging painfully into my cheekbones. "It's not—"

My heart raced. *Yes.*

"You know me," I breathed.

The moment my voice webbed around us, storm clouds rolled over the sunshine in his face, blackening the hope and replacing it with pure hatred.

He changed from watching me like I was his angel to glowering as if I were a despicable devil.

I shivered at the change—at the iciness and hardness. He breathed hard, his chest rising and falling. His lips parted, a rumbling command falling from his mouth to my ears. "Stand up. You're mine now."

When I didn't move, his hand landed on my side. His touch was blocked by clothing but I felt it *everywhere*. He stroked my soul, tickled my heart, and caressed every cell with fingers that despised me.

I couldn't suck in a proper breath.

With a vicious push, he rolled me over, and with a sharp blade sliced my bindings. With effortless power, so thrilling and terrifying, he hauled me to my feet.

I didn't sway. I didn't cry. Only pulled the disgusting gag from my mouth and stared in silence.

I stared up, up, up into his bright green eyes, understanding something I shouldn't understand.

This was him.

My nightmare.

Printed in Great Britain
by Amazon.co.uk, Ltd.,
Marston Gate.